Lynne Graham was born in Northern Ireland and has been a keen romance reader since her teens. She is very happily married, to an understanding husband who has learned to cook since she started to write! Her five children keep her on her toes. She has a very large dog, which knocks everything over, a very small terrier, which barks a lot, and two cats. When time allows, Lynne is a keen gardener.

Michelle Smart's love affair with books started when she was a baby and would cuddle them in her cot. A voracious reader of all genres, she found her love of romance established when she stumbled across her first Mills & Boon book at the age of twelve. She's been reading them—and writing them—ever since. Michelle lives in Northamptonshire, England, with her husband and two young Smarties.

THE BABY
THE DESERT KING
MUST CLAIM

LYNNE GRAHAM

BOUND BY THE
ITALIAN'S 'I DO'

MICHELLE SMART

MILLS & BOON

First published in Great Britain 2023
by Mills & Boon, an imprint of HarperCollins*Publishers* Ltd,
1 London Bridge Street, London, SE1 9GF

www.harpercollins.co.uk

HarperCollins*Publishers* Macken House, 39/40 Mayor Street Upper,
Dublin 1, D01 C9W8, Ireland

The Baby the Desert King Must Claim © 2023 Lynne Graham

Bound by the Italian's 'I Do' © 2023 Michelle Smart

ISBN: 978-0-263-30668-2

03/23

THE BABY
THE DESERT KING
MUST CLAIM

LYNNE GRAHAM

MILLS & BOON

CHAPTER ONE

EVEN ANCHORED OUT in the bay, the mega yacht, *Mahnoor*, towered above every other craft moored at the marina of the Greek island of Kanos, including the local ferry. For all its size and the looming tiers of deck, however, the slick lines of the pristine vessel had been designed for speed and elegance.

From the shelter of the top-deck office, the owner, Prince Raif Sultan bin Al-Rashid, better known in the business world as the billionaire resort and property developer, Raif Sultan, was receiving a prearranged call from his royal father, King Jafri of Quristan. What on earth could the father who had virtually ignored him since his birth want from him? Only seconds into the awkward opening dialogue, Raif found out and it wasn't pleasant.

'You have signed a contract to build a town *and* a resort on Quristani land,' his father hissed. 'You will tear it up and forget about the idea!'

Raif bristled. 'It has the government's support.'

'It does not have mine!' the older man exclaimed. 'I do not want tourists in my country.'

'I can only be sorry for that,' Raif countered stiffly.

'The new port and luxury resort would bring a lot of employment to a poor area. All conservation advice will be respected in the development and the resort will have the minimum possible impact on the natural habitat.'

'I have told you how I feel. That should be sufficient to change your mind,' the older man interrupted in another burst of outrage.

'I cannot pull out of a contract that has already been signed and approved by the government,' Raif responded wryly.

'I will not call you my son again if you disobey me,' King Jafri cut in fiercely. 'Obeying me is your primary duty as my son and I will not tolerate your disobedience!'

The phone went crashing down in Quristan. Raif breathed in slowly and carefully and then swore long and low in English. His duty? *His duty?* Was he a child to be told what to do and how to do it? And by a man whom he barely knew? A man who had never once acted like a father to him? A man who had never made a personal call to him in his life before? Nor granted him a single one-to-one meeting?

Unlike his two much older brothers, Hashir and Waleed, Raif had grown up in the UK. His brothers were the heir and spare to the monarchy of Quristan and had grown up there, separated from Raif and his mother. The King's third son had become an irrelevant extra after his father had said goodbye to him and his ex-wife when Raif was still a baby. Possibly guilt over the divorce and the damage that that divorce had inflicted on the former Queen's mental health had ensured that his father had turned his back on both ex-wife and third son, because the older man had taken little further interest in Raif's development. Aside of the royal summons Raif would receive to attend occasional ceremonial events in his birth country, it seemed that Raif was surplus to his father's requirements.

Pure rage now roared through Raif as he recovered from the shock of his domineering royal parent's demands and his lean hands knotted into fists. He recognised the pain of rejection laced through that rage and that only made him angrier. He was twenty-seven years old, no longer a child desperate for his father's attention. He should be long past such weak feelings. He had survived without his father's regard and had learned to value his own achievements.

He had realised that he had to stand on his own feet at twenty-one, when, after his obligatory year's national service in the Quristani army, he had opted to leave soldiering behind him and return to the business world. His father hadn't approved of that move either. He would have preferred a career soldier for a third son. Raif had merely reminded himself that neither of his older brothers had even managed to complete that single year's service. Hashir had dropped out with a minor ankle injury and Waleed had used a weak stomach as an excuse to evade the army altogether.

In a volatile mood, he left his office to stride down the companionway and leave the yacht. He needed fresh air and activity. He stepped into the waiting speedboat, only to frown when a surge of security staff rushed in after him. He wanted to be alone. He wanted the freedom to scream to the skies if he wanted to. What did he need with a protection team on a sleepy Greek island he barely remembered the name of? There were no tourists around, no paparazzi, nobody to arouse concern.

'But, Your Highness, we must keep you safe,' At the Quristani government's insistence, the crack Special Forces guard imposed on him protested while his private security team stood back.

'I only want to go for a walk,' Raif breathed tautly.

'Danger lurks in unexpected places,' Mohsin told him worriedly.

'Watch me from a distance,' Raif urged wearily, worn down by that intensity focussed on his safety.

Aware that he was poorly dressed for such an outing because he was wearing a business suit, Raif stepped out onto the quay, the warmth of the sun beating down on him, but it was no challenge for a man accustomed to the scorching heat of the desert.

He had spent every summer in Quristan, wandering the sands with his uncle's nomadic tribe in Rabalissa. His mother had been the Queen of Rabalissa before she married his father and united the two countries. It had been a very popular alliance. Rabalissa was small and backward and Quristan was large and oil rich. Sadly, in spite of his late mother's hopes, Rabalissa had profited very little from that marriage and the current government was keen to redress that inequality.

Unfortunately, his father was too rigid in his views to acknowledge the poverty and dissatisfaction creating unrest in the area.

Striding away from the harbour, Raif chose to follow a worn track out of the village that followed the coastline. Only briefly did he consider contacting his brothers for advice and he quickly discarded the idea. From what he had witnessed from afar over the years, his older brothers managed their father by never ever disagreeing with him, no matter how unreasonable he was. But surely even the King had to recognise that a legal contract could not be set aside once it was signed? Raif breathed out in exasperation, his pace picking up as he strode below the trees. Frustration currented through him because he realised that the vast development project would now be beset by every stumbling block his father could find to throw in its path.

As the path dipped into a small, secluded cove, Raif crossed the sand. He wrenched his tie loose, tugging it off to put it in the pocket of his jacket. The blue-green water looked so inviting and he was getting warm. It was peaceful being alone and he didn't get to be alone often enough, he conceded ruefully. Well, he no longer felt like screaming to the skies, but he did feel like getting into the water to cool off.

From below the shade of the tree sheltering her from the sun, Claire was taking a video of the gorgeous view for the benefit of Lottie, her friend back in London. When a man in a suit appeared in the lens, she frowned in bemusement because he was such an incongruous sight. Nobody got dressed up on the island unless there was a wedding or a funeral but, come to think of it, she reflected, she had seen flowers being carried into the village church, so he could well be a guest. He peeled off his jacket and set it down on a rock and then removed his shirt. So, he was going in for a swim, she assumed, watching him haul off the shirt to reveal a muscular golden torso straight out of a superhero movie.

At that point, Claire was transfixed, peering into her phone, intent on the sight. He was very tall and black-haired, and he was indisputably incredibly well built. It had been longer than she liked to admit since she had seen such a very attractive man because most of the islanders were middle-aged or elderly. He tossed off shoes and socks and peeled off the narrow-cut trousers to reveal what she assumed to be boxers, rather than swim shorts. However, at that point, she got a little uncomfortable and decided that if the boxers came off as well, she should stop filming and look away. But without hesitation he turned and walked into the sea, long, powerful, hair-roughened legs ploughing through the surf.

He was a strong swimmer as well, bowling through the currents near the rocks that made her nervous. With a sigh, Claire stopped filming and sent the clip off for Lottie's enjoyment. At least it would give her friend a wicked giggle.

'You're the only person I know who's spent over six

months in Greece and hasn't even picked up a boy-friend,' Lottie had lamented during their most recent chat. 'I'm a mum, a wife and an employee in a very boring job. I need some titillation.'

A boyfriend was the last thing she needed, Claire thought ruefully, although since her mother's demise, she had felt agonisingly lonely and isolated. The past tumultuous ten months had been a time of confusion and emotional turmoil but ultimately a kind of renewal even though she had been left sad and alone. She had learned so much about herself, yet everything she had once believed she knew about her parentage had been thrown up in the air and the pattern of the truth had proved startlingly different once all the pieces had set-tled back into place. It had all begun when she had been clearing her father's desk out after his death...

'I'm sorry, I didn't realise that there was anyone here,' a rather correct English masculine drawl imparted.

Claire emerged from her reverie and went rather hot in the face as she looked up and saw the man who had strayed into her video of the bay, standing only a few feet away. He was holding his clothes in a bundle in front of him. And close up he was the best-looking guy she had seen in her entire life, so excitingly, wick-edly hot he was literally off-the-scale perfection. Fine ebony brows slashed over dark golden eyes that were deep set, rimmed with dense black lashes and frankly stunning. Add in a refined bone structure, cheekbones like blades, a classic nose and a wide full mouth and he just about took her breath away.

'I hope I didn't disturb you,' he completed, studying her with an intent gaze, because she was an outrageously pretty woman with long, silky corn-gold hair sliding round her shoulders, big blue eyes and a scattering of freckles.

'No, but you gave me a great video clip,' she told him with a radiant smile. 'I was filming the cove and I wasn't expecting a man to walk into view and do a strip for me.'

'You filmed me...*undressed*?' Raif breathed in shock, because that was not the kind of thing he could afford to have floating about the Internet. Although he had grown up in a very different world, he tried to honour the very conservative mores of his Quristani family as best he could.

'It's not as though you were naked!' Claire declared, picking up on his discomfiture and colouring over the suspicion that he believed that she had done something that she shouldn't have done. 'It's a public beach. People take off their clothes to go swimming. It's no big deal.'

'I must ask you out of courtesy to delete it from your camera.'

Claire froze and noted the grim hold he had on his clothes. In a sudden move she pulled out the towel she had used as a pad at her back and extended it to him. 'Here. You might as well get dressed while we argue.'

'Thank you. I have no intention of having an argument with you,' Raif told her smoothly, accepting the towel and walking away to turn his back on her to towel himself dry and dress. He was kind of cautious and almost shy for a guy who looked as though he would be a complete extrovert. His rock-solid confidence and sophistication had been dazzlingly obvious until she'd made the mistake of mentioning the video clip.

Disconcerted by that jarring contrast, Claire shook her head slightly as though to clear it and watched the long golden muscles of his back flex, her face warming again. He was somehow like chocolate when she was on a diet. He had an irresistible allure she had never seen in a man before. One look didn't cut it. She would keep on looking as long as she could. Instant attraction, she supposed. That was a new experience for her.

He walked back towards her, all lean and long and golden with still damp black hair. He looked amazing. 'Look, let me buy your phone from you and replace it because I am inconveniencing you,' he suggested levelly.

'Let's not get silly about something so trivial,' Claire urged in dismay as voices sounded on the path above them.

'Are you on holiday here?' he enquired.

'No. I've been living here for a while but I'm planning to return to the UK.' Her voice trailed off because she wouldn't be doing that until she had saved up enough for the flight home and had sufficient cash to put towards accommodation. Her decision to stay in Greece with her late mother had left her pretty much penniless but she had no regrets about the sacrifices she had made.

A bunch of local children with a lone adult in tow

flooded the beach with whoops and cries and a football. As her companion returned the towel to her with an air of reluctance, Claire gave him an uneasy smile. She stood up, gathering her book, and hesitated before deciding to be honest. 'There would be no point in deleting that clip from my phone. I've already sent it on to a friend. I will, naturally, ask her to ensure that she doesn't share it with anyone else and I doubt if she will. I'm afraid that's the best I can offer...*oomph*!' She gasped as the football struck her squarely in the solar plexus and knocked her off balance.

She almost contrived to right herself and then she fell, glancing off the rocks below her into the sand, striking one leg painfully on the rough surface.

She was instantly the centre of attention and it was the sort of fuss Claire hated. The adult rushed over to apologise and to ask if she was all right. Her male companion lifted her out of the sand in silence and expressively eyed the blood running from the abrasion on her knee. He addressed the little footballer in a censorious tone as the boy bleated out fervent apologies. He was the son of Claire's landlord, a nice child, and she was quick to assure him that accidents happened and that she was fine.

'But you're *not*...fine,' the man beside her pronounced.

'I'll survive!' Claire hissed up at him, intimidated by the sheer height of him now that they were standing level. She was exactly five feet tall and he topped her by more than a foot.

'You have been *hurt*,' he continued with concern.

And in truth she had been. She had bashed her leg and her hip, and both were aching, while her knee was stinging like mad, but she had no intention of parading either her bruises or her wound. She flung him an upward glance that heavily suggested he stay silent. 'I'm on my way home anyway,' she announced brightly in the hope that the crowd of interested onlookers around her would lose interest.

'Where do you live?'

'Only a few yards up the hill. You can't see the house because of the trees. This cove is almost my front garden,' she joked, wincing as she moved up the beach.

'I'll see you back to your home,' he insisted.

'It's not necessary.'

He gave her a look of unapologetic disagreement. Heavens, those tortoiseshell eyes practically talked, she thought in a daze as they both moved up the steep path to the small house behind the trees where her mother had lived for years.

'Are you in the habit of taking pictures of random strangers taking off their clothes?'

'Why are you making me sound like some pervert?' Claire gasped in horror. 'It's a public beach. If you're so precious about your privacy, why did you undress there?'

'I was thoughtless. I believed I was alone. I was enjoying that sensation. I wasn't trying to make you feel like a pervert. I was simply trying to understand what made you do such a peculiar thing.'

'Well, you wandered into the viewing lens, and I saw you, and I sort of stared without thinking about what I was doing...' Claire snatched in a ragged breath because the hill had a stiff gradient and she was embarrassed. 'And I thought... I thought—'

'You thought what?' he sliced in impatiently, his tension palpable in his wary appraisal. 'That you recognised me from somewhere?'

Claire stopped dead outside the low-built house. 'No, why would I have? I thought you were beautiful. No harm in that, is there?'

Raif eyed her burning face. 'Beautiful?' he repeated incredulously. 'Men aren't *beautiful*.'

'Don't be sexist.' Claire stiffened her shoulders, wondering why she had mortified herself with that admission, but he was as relentless as a train roaring down a track at speed. When he had a goal in view, he couldn't be headed off.

'So, you're saying it was lust,' Raif gathered with a sudden flashing wicked grin.

'No, I wasn't saying that at all. I just admired you for a few seconds.'

'While I took my clothes off. If you were a man, you would surely be arrested for such an invasion of privacy,' Raif quipped, starting to enjoy himself in a way he rarely did in female company. He could not credit that she was a member of the paparazzi tribe or that she had the smallest clue who he was. Her lack of tact and inability to dissemble were phenomenal.

'It wasn't *lust*,' Claire repeated with dignity. 'I can

admire a painting without needing to own it, but I will agree it was thoughtless of me not to consider your feelings…although most of the men I've met aren't quite so modest and would be quite flattered by admiration. You're in a class of your own, it seems.'

'Very much so,' he confirmed with another slanting grin as he paused by the outside table and chairs. 'Now, sit down. Have you a first-aid kit? Your knee needs attention.'

'What's your name?' she demanded abruptly, quite dizzy in the radius of that charming smile of amusement.

'Raif…' he told her. 'Although it sounds the same as the English name Rafe, it is spelt differently.'

'I'm Claire. It was my mother's favourite name and she's gone now,' she told him, pushing open the back door and disappearing inside. 'Would you like a cold drink? I have a jug of lemonade in the fridge. It's very refreshing.'

'Bring out the first-aid kit first.'

'No, the first thing I'm going to do,' she said, walking back to the door to look out at him with sparkling blue eyes in which mischief danced as bright as stardust, 'is warn my friend that she must on *no* account show that clip to anyone else. I will also ask her to delete it.'

'At the same time as you delete your own version,' Raif incised.

'Oh, must I?' Claire teased him, helpless to resist that temptation. 'If you're my object of lust, won't I be wanting to keep it and savour it on dark lonely nights?'

Raif laughed out loud. Her ready tongue and her liveliness were extraordinarily appealing. He had never been a womaniser; in fact, he saw himself as being of a sombre, serious disposition and he definitely didn't know how to flirt. Growing up with a depressed and suicidal mother, while striving to tolerate the promiscuous lifestyle that had eventually become her sole consolation, had matured Raif much faster than his peers. After divorce had destroyed Mahnoor's life by depriving her of the husband she loved, her two elder sons and the royal role she had cherished, his mother had only had Raif to sustain her. Her chaotic private life had put him off casual sex and everything that went with it.

Yet he was no longer so sure of the rigid decisions he had reached when he was younger because, for literally the first time, Raif was very much tempted by a woman. Claire was small and curvy and full of personality, the complete opposite of the polished, socially repressed young women he usually met, who calculated every expression and every word in his radius. Claire didn't know he was wealthy and, what was more, he suspected that even if she did she wouldn't be impressed by the superficial show of his material possessions.

'First-aid kit,' he reminded her, having already noticed in some exasperation that she drifted and darted from topic to topic like a colourful hummingbird sipping from flowers, finding each as alluring as the previous one.

'And lemonade?'

'Why not?' Raif said easily, following her indoors to a tiny galley kitchen, suspecting that he would have to find the first-aid kit for himself while she poured lemonade and chattered.

'I suppose I should have offered you a beer.'

'I don't drink.'

'Neither do I,' she confided cheerfully. 'But I keep some beer for a friend who calls in occasionally.'

'A man?' For some reason, Raif found himself tensing at that idea.

Claire pulled a face. 'Good heavens, no. It's a small island and it wouldn't do to get the neighbours talking. My friend, Sofia. I work with her sometimes down at the harbour bar.'

Relieved by the explanation, Raif found the first-aid kit shoved in a corner and clicked it open to find it empty, which didn't surprise him. Claire opened a drawer and rustled madly through the cluttered interior to produce plasters and medicated ointment, passing him kitchen towelling on demand and dampening a piece for him. 'I'll do it,' she told him as she poured the lemonade and lifted the glasses to pass him one. 'But I warn you, I'll probably scream if it hurts. I'm not that brave.'

'Sit down,' he told her as he set aside the glass.

'There's no seats in here.'

'If you will allow me...' Raif extended his arms. 'I will set you on the counter.'

Claire laughed. 'If you like, but I'm no Skinny Minnie… Mind you, you do have all those muscles I was insensitive enough to admire.'

Laughing, Raif scooped her up and found her even lighter than he had expected. Blonde hair that had a lemony scent brushed his jaw and flared his nostrils, unleashing a vibrant awareness of her femininity. A heaviness settled in his groin. He settled her down gently and turned his attention to her knee, cleaning the cut with tiny careful movements, frowning over the sand he had to remove, impossibly conscious of her every wince but, apart from the occasional flinch, she didn't make a sound. 'It's bruising and it will scar,' he warned her.

'I'll survive,' she told him buoyantly as he used the ointment and fixed on an adhesive plaster. 'To be honest, I'm going to have more than a few bruises from that fall.'

'You insisted that you were fine.'

'I didn't want to upset Dimitris. He's a good kid. Accidents happen.'

'Not if due care is exercised.'

'You sound like you swallowed a health and safety manual,' Claire reproved.

After a disconcerted pause, Raif straightened and laughed with genuine appreciation of that criticism. That kind of impertinence rarely came his way. 'Boring, you mean?' he chided.

'A little set in your ways. I bet you were raised as a child to be seen and not heard. I know I was. My father believed an outspoken child was the devil's work,' she confided ruefully. 'He was very strict.'

The rules of the royal nursery even under his adoring mother's sway had been hard and harsh, not least because his father had insisted on a strict nanny for his youngest son. 'So, you rebelled,' he assumed, lifting his hands to her waist to lift her down again.

'Not when I was a kid. I was too hooked on wanting my father's approval,' Claire admitted ruefully, one flimsy flip-flop falling off as he set her down. She lurched against him to steady herself, her hands flying out to clutch at his jacket.

She looked up into smouldering dark golden eyes, her heart beating so fast it felt as though it were in her throat. It was one of those out-of-time moments, freezing her there as this great wave of yearning surged through her. She couldn't look away from his eyes and as his head came down she stretched up, her breath parting her lips. She had never wanted a kiss so badly.

'Kiss me,' she urged, helpless in the grip of that powerful craving.

And Raif unfroze at the invitation, insanely aware of his arousal and the sheer temptation of those soft luscious lips. He shook off the discipline of years with an unfamiliar feeling of daring, of resentment for all the times he had stepped back from women, always telling himself that he was living up to his ideals. For what reason? For what ultimate purpose? he questioned now.

He drew her up to him with slow, careful hands, brushed his mouth very softly across hers and then doubled back to steal a fierce, hungry kiss. His tongue eased in, plundered, tasted, taking everything and more that she offered, his lean, powerful body thrumming with all the raw, flaring excitement he had always restrained. But there was something about her, something about Claire that made that restraint impossible.

Claire emerged trembling and perspiring from that passionate kiss. She had been waiting a long time to feel that passion with a guy and she was shaken by suddenly finding it. So great was the shock that she stepped back from him, immediately denying that unexpected bond. And she thought of letting him go, indeed showing him to the door for daring to tempt her to that extent. But just as quickly came the need to explore that sense of connection and discover if it was only an illusion.

'Stay for supper,' she told him instead, backing away, flushed and bemused by what he had made her feel and yet unable to send him away.

Raif hovered, unbearably aroused, fighting for control—for the cool that was usually his with a woman. Supper? *Food?* The suggestion that he stay longer? He was fully on board with that idea when he didn't want to leave her.

'Why not?' he responded, grateful for the jacket that concealed his arousal, striving to remain cool in spite of the embarrassing truth that he was deeply out of his depth. His phone thrummed silently in his pocket and he clenched his teeth. His security team?

'Excuse me,' he murmured softly. 'I must take this call.'

Claire watched him step outside and pull out a

phone, but she was infinitely more interested in that moment about what she planned to feed him.

Raif stepped out onto the terrace, which was paved but full of weeds, and studied the clutch of bodyguards stationed at the bottom corner of the small front garden under the trees with raised brows and irritation.

'Sir?' Mohsin queried. 'You are in a strange house.'

Raif grinned. He wanted to laugh. His security team were not accustomed to him deviating from the norm. He was breaking out of his expected routine and they were nervous, concerned by his behaviour.

'I am fine. I am staying here and… I may be late back.' He framed that prospect stiffly. 'I will return to the harbour when I am ready. There is no need to remain here on guard.'

And that was the instant that Raif appreciated that he had reached a decision. He was done with control and restraint, ready to run a risk for the first time ever.

CHAPTER TWO

'GO AND RELAX in the sitting room,' Claire advised when he reappeared. 'I'll be busy in the kitchen.'

Resisting the ridiculous temptation to admit that he only wanted her to be busy with him, Raif strode into a tiny room ornamented with plants, books tumbled on the floor and a window seat on which a very elegant black cat posed. Claire followed him in. 'This is Circe,' she told him. 'Don't worry if she ignores you. She's very fussy about who she likes. I really had to work at impressing her when I first arrived.'

'And when was that? When did you first come to Greece?'

Claire froze on the way back into the kitchen. 'Ten months ago. I came to the island to meet my mother... and I ended up staying here,' she confided reluctantly.

'Sounds like a story. Meet her...for the *first* time?' Raif stressed in surprise.

Claire nodded. 'She left my father and me when I was still a baby.'

Raif frowned.

'It's not as bad as it sounds,' Claire proclaimed defensively on her mother's behalf. 'I grew up being told what a wicked woman she was. I was about four when my stepmother told me that my mother was a bad person and that I had to be careful not to grow up to be like her.'

'That must have been challenging,' Raif remarked, utterly enchanted by her honesty and the less than perfect background that she was revealing. People literally *never* made him the recipient of such revelations. He was as hooked on her outspokenness as someone exposed for the first time to fresh air. He had often felt that he was the only person he knew who had grown up with a dysfunctional background. His brothers had been teenagers when he was a baby and had grown into adults as pampered, indulged princes in a royal household, barely missing the mother forced to leave them behind with their father. None of their experiences had mirrored Raif's and their pity for him when they had later learned of the former Queen's alcoholism and fondness for young men had only lashed his pride, accentuated the differences between them and ensured that the brothers remained politely distant with each other.

'I have to make supper,' Claire told him.

Raif observed the standoffish cat and ignored it. He knew that, unlike dogs, cats didn't like to be courted. He took a seat and within a few minutes the cat made its approach. It paraded in front of him, showing off its sleek black elegance, big measuring green eyes locked to him. It folded into a relaxed repose at his feet. He let a careful fingertip drift down to stroke along its spine in a fleeting caress until it arched. A moment later, it had leapt onto his lap, the better to receive his admiration, and he smiled.

'Circe!' Claire called in reproof from the doorway.

'It's okay. I'm used to felines. My mother kept Siamese cats.' Interrupted, the cat sprang down from him and leapt back up onto the window seat.

'My mother took her in as a kitten and I want to take her with me when I leave the island. It's a link, well, she's really the *only* link I have,' she admitted ruefully.

Raif rose lazily upright, every movement fluid, attracting her gaze. 'When did you lose your mother?'

'Last week. But it wasn't a surprise. She was terminally ill when I got here,' Claire explained in a troubled rush. 'Every day we had together was incredibly precious.'

'That's a very recent loss,' Raif murmured from the doorway as she returned to the vegetables she appeared to be chopping. He watched in some astonishment as she wielded a very sharp knife with the speed and efficiency of a professional.

'But just think, I mightn't have met her and got to know her at all,' Claire pointed out with a grimace at that concept. 'I was lucky. I'm so grateful I grabbed the chance to get to know her and didn't listen to everyone trying to stop me coming out here.'

'Who's everyone?'

'My boss, my stepmother, my boyfriend. Nobody wanted me to come here. But it was my one and only chance,' she admitted, big blue eyes wide. 'I had to take the chance...didn't I?'

'I agree. But what did it cost you?'

'The boyfriend and the job,' she confided wryly. 'But I would make the same choice again. It was worth it... *she* was worth it.'

Raif smiled slowly, his attention fully locked to the animation so vividly etched in her heart-shaped face. 'I'm glad of that for your sake. But how on earth did you forgive her for leaving you in the first place?'

Claire stiffened and paused to heap the diced vegetables into a bowl. 'If you had asked me that question a few years back, I would've said I *couldn't* forgive her,' she confided. 'But then my father passed away and my stepmother asked me to clear out my father's desk. She and my half-brother had to move, because it was a clergy house and it was needed for my father's replacement.'

'You didn't live with them?'

'No. I moved out as soon as I could afford a flatshare,' Claire admitted ruefully. 'My stepmother and I never jelled.'

Raif watched her move about the kitchen with surprising competence. She whipped out plates and reached for the bowl to carry them into the sitting room and lay the small table by the window. 'Take a seat,' she told him.

She trekked back into the kitchen and returned with a basket of bread, a bottle of water and two glasses. 'This is a very casual meal,' she warned him.

'You didn't have to feed me,' he told her gently.

'*I* was starving,' she replied.

'You mentioned clearing out your father's desk,' he reminded her. 'What did that have to do with anything?'

'I found all these letters my mother had sent over the years pleading for permission to see me,' Claire confided in a pained undertone. 'I was stunned. I was only told that she had met another man and run off with him. Nobody ever admitted that she had tried really hard to see me again. When my father agreed to the divorce, she let him have full custody because she felt guilty. She didn't appreciate that that meant that he could refuse to let her see me again and...she didn't have the money to take him to court.'

Raif helped himself to a portion of the salad and some bread. 'Your father must've been very bitter.'

'Yes. He never forgave her for leaving him even though he remarried very soon after the divorce.' She leant forward, her face troubled. 'My mother, though, was only eighteen when she married him, and she gave birth to me within the year. Way too young to be married to a man fifteen years older and a mother,' she opined.

'Obviously she won your sympathy, but I feel some sympathy for your father,' Raif admitted. 'Fidelity in marriage is an expectation for most people. She was his wife and she betrayed his trust.'

Claire grimaced. 'She did. She went on holiday with her sister against his wishes and fell madly in love with a Greek fisherman. Eventually she married Kostas and they lived together in this house for almost fifteen years. He died at sea in a storm a few years ago and she stayed on here alone.'

Raif shrugged a broad shoulder and said gently, 'She was still an unfaithful wife.'

Claire sighed. 'Life isn't that black and white.'

'Sometimes it is,' Raif incised in disagreement. 'My father divorced my mother because he was bored. She did nothing wrong. She had given him three sons, and had been a good wife in every way, but he still ended their marriage. It destroyed her life. She lost almost everything that she valued and sank into depression.'

'That must have been really tough for her and you.' Claire looked thoughtful. 'What about your brothers?'

'They were almost grown at the time of the divorce and they remained with my father.'

'So, really you had no family support with the parent you were living with,' Claire registered in dismay on his behalf.

'This bread is incredibly good,' Raif remarked, reluctant to discuss his mother any further, some topics being too private. He had already shared much more than he usually did but now his reserve had kicked in.

Claire smiled. 'It should be. I trained as a pastry chef.'

Raif tucked into the seasonal salad with appreciation. He hadn't been that hungry but fresh, tasty food had a draw all of its own.

'Is your mother still alive?' she asked quietly.

'No, she's been gone for a few years now,' Raif confided. 'I can't imagine how you must feel meeting *your* mother after so long and discovering that you liked her…even though you weren't supposed to.'

'My father and stepmother raised me to be ashamed of her. They were very religious. That's why it was such a shock to read those letters. My father hung onto them even though he had no intention of letting us meet,' Claire said with distaste. 'I pictured him gloating over those letters, enjoying his power to deny her and me. That was his revenge. He was that kind of man.'

'You weren't close to him.'

'No, how could I have been? He could never see me as being a different person from my mother,' she pointed out ruefully. 'He had a son with my stepmother and he treated him very differently. He probably would have been happier had my mother taken me away with her. I was just the reminder of a marriage that had gone wrong and humiliated him.'

'I'm sorry you lost your mother so soon after finding her,' Raif murmured, pushing his empty plate away.

Claire's eyes prickled with moisture and she blinked rapidly. 'That's life,' she said with forced lightness of tone. 'What are you doing here on Kanos?'

As she began clearing the table, Raif stood up. 'I've been travelling for the last few weeks.'

'In a suit?'

'I had a business meeting this morning.'

Claire nodded slowly. 'It's been nice having company here for a change. The house feels so empty without my mother.'

'You have to give yourself time to grieve.'

'But I knew she was on borrowed time,' Claire protested chokily. 'I *should've* adjusted better.'

Watching a tear drip down her cheek, Raif closed a hand awkwardly to her shoulder and squeezed it. 'Preparing for a likelihood is not the same as dealing with the actual event.'

'Don't I know it?' she agreed wryly.

'I don't want to leave you here alone,' Raif admitted flatly.

Claire parted dry lips. 'Then *stay*… I'm not pushing you out.'

Raif sighed. 'You want company…and I want to kiss you.'

'Did I say kissing was off the table?' Claire reddened, fingernails biting into her palms as she voiced that uncharacteristically bold invitation while wondering what had come over her and why it seemed so important not to let him walk away.

'I won't take advantage of the fact that you feel lonely and sad,' Raif declared tautly. 'I'm not that kind of man.'

'But sometimes you have to go with the flow,' Claire muttered tautly.

Raif had never gone with the flow in his life. He worked to schedules based on a routine from which he rarely deviated, yet the concept of simply relaxing and following his own inclinations for even as long as an evening had immense appeal. 'Yes,' he conceded with a slow-burning smile of agreement.

'Nobody's waiting for you to return?' Claire prompted, her mouth drying at that possibility.

'Nobody.' A faint flush lined Raif's sculpted cheek-bones, because the yacht had a crew of over sixty, not to mention his security team and admin staff. He knew very well what it was to be alone in a crowd of people, but he really didn't know what it was to be physically alone because from childhood there had always been domestic and security staff surrounding him.

Embarrassed by the tears she had let momentarily overpower her, Claire stacked the dishes busily and moved out to the kitchen with them.

Raif set the glasses uncertainly on the sink drainer. 'Leave them for now.'

'Tidy house, tidy mind,' Claire quipped. 'That was how I was brought up.'

'Does it make a difference?'

'No, it just keeps you constantly busy.'

Claire settled the dishes into the sink and began washing them and setting them on the drainer.

Raif hovered and then swept up the tea towel some-what uneasily, vaguely recalling a woman drying dishes in one of the homes he had visited for the week-end while he was at boarding school.

'You don't have to help.'

'I can't stand here doing nothing.' Raif felt that he already spent far too much time doing nothing. He took care of Quristan's investments while running his devel-

opment empire on the side. He had often been called a
workaholic and saw no reason to disdain the label. He
took pride in working to advance his country's interests and wealth. Or at least he had done so when he'd
still believed that he could do a good job without infuriating his father. The recollection of his predicament
made him bite back a groan. Well, he had never been
a favoured son and now he never would be.

He reached for a plate and began to dry it with care,
determined not to plunge himself into pointless self-re-
criminations. The Quristani government was pleased,
the locals were ecstatic, and his father was outraged.
There was nothing he could do about that. Many, many
things in the modern world outraged King Jafri, who
wished to remain a feudal ruler like his ancestors in
a country with a democratically elected government.
His father had been raised to be domineering, what he
saw as 'strong'. But such methods only worked for an
absolute monarch with unfettered power, such as his
own father had been. And shorn of that power, forced to
accept government interference and advice, King Jafri
had seethed with frustration and the belief that he was
not being awarded the royal respect he saw as his due.

Raif set down the plate, just as Claire twitched the
drying cloth from his fingers and took over. He lounged
back against the fridge while she finished and stacked
the china back in a cabinet. As she passed by him
again, he propelled her gently backwards into his arms
and pressed his mouth to the slope of her shoulder,
drinking in the warm, lemony scent of her, and was

almost lost to the steady pulse of arousal at his groin. No woman had ever had such an effect on him, but then he rarely allowed himself to get close enough to be tempted. Claire, however, had an indefinable quality that both relaxed and enticed him. She was so honest, so natural, so much what he needed in a woman to be attracted.

With a compulsive shiver, Claire leant back into the heat and strength of him. She had never been so intensely drawn to a guy in her life and while in one sense it was scary, in another it was wildly exciting. She knew what she was inviting but she had no doubts. It was her decision if she chose to go to bed with someone, nobody else's. Her last boyfriend had tried to guilt her into sex and she had dug her heels in hard, needing more of a connection than she had found with him. It had never felt right with him. How was it that a stranger could connect with her so easily? How was it that she found Raif absolutely irresistible?

Squirming round in his light hold, Claire stretched up to find his mouth again and hunger ignited like a flame low in her tummy as his lips engulfed hers. It was what she had always sought and never found with a man: that crazy, uncontrollable surge of need to continue, to explore, to *experience*. It warmed the chill of loss inside her, gave her hope that her usual zest for life was within reach again.

Raif drew her back into the sitting room. 'Don't stop,' she told him, pausing the kiss only to refill her lungs.

'Where's your room?'

Claire laced her fingers into his and walked him into the first room off the sitting room, a freshly painted space her mother had had decorated for her in bright Mediterranean colours and fluttering, fringed arty drapes in advance of her arrival. It was the perfect backdrop for the unconventional, artistic daughter Jo had imagined Claire would be because Jo had liked to paint and make jewellery and pottery. Sadly, Claire was a girlie girl, who liked flowers and pastels, and she didn't think she had a single crafty, creative bone in her body. She liked to garden and she loved to cook, but she had never wanted to make stuff or wear anything bohemian that might make people raise a brow.

Sadness pulled at her and she pushed it away to the back of her mind. She wanted to celebrate life, seize it by the throat and go for it instead of following every careful cautious rule she had been raised with because that merely made her feel *scared*. Only in rebelling against those restrictions had she found her mother and begun to find out who she really was...

'I could do with a shower,' Raif confessed abruptly. 'I'm covered with salt from my swim.'

'I never thought of that,' Claire muttered, showing him into the bathroom next door and pulling out a clean towel for his use.

She returned to her room and hovered. She wondered if she should tell him that he would be her first while also wondering whether he was deliberately giving her a chance to change her mind. No, why would he do that? Men didn't do that when a woman seemed confident, did they? Determined to commit to her decision, she stripped and dropped her clothing in the laundry hamper before scrambling into the bed. For the very first time, she felt she was with the right man. There was a connection, an understanding she couldn't explain but it was a great deal more than she had ever felt before.

Raif stood under the slow flow of lukewarm water in a daze. He was nervous. He knew that he wasn't supposed to be, but he was. He was about to ditch a lifetime of celibacy and he was about to do it in the heat of a reckless moment. But Claire made him *feel* reckless, and that was an indulgence he had never tasted before, and he wanted more of that feeling. She gave him a sense of pure freedom and joy, a feeling that was equally rare in his world. She wanted him and he wanted her. It was straightforward and simple. There was no need to make it into something more challenging or meaningful than it was. Once he had thought that he would save the experience for his bride and now he questioned that he had ever been that naïve.

Raif strode into the bedroom, the damp towel wrapped round his waist. 'Still think I'm beautiful?' he teased.

Just looking at him, Claire ran out of breath all at once. He was like a lean, mean fighting machine out of an action movie, his abdomen laced and indented with hard muscle, biceps flexing below smooth brown skin as he tossed the towel aside. 'Yes,' she said without hesitation.

Laughing, Raif swung into the bed beside her and closed her into his arms. His mouth caressed hers and his tongue pried between her lips, darting and delving and sending a rush of splintering energy through her. Hunger was a hot pool of liquidity at the centre of her, a pulse point of growing desire. Her hips squirmed into the mattress as his hands came up to cup her full breasts, thumbs brushing her swollen nipples.

'You're the beautiful one,' he murmured, pressing her back into the pillows, staring appreciatively down at her as her honey-blonde hair tumbled across the dark linen, her cornflower-blue eyes wide with disconcertion against her flushed cheeks, her lips swollen from his kisses. He drank in the warmth in that scrutiny like a starving man.

He lowered his mouth to a rosy peak and sucked strongly, every fantasy fulfilled because she was the most glorious mix of soft and firm, silky and luscious. Her hands ran up over his corrugated abdomen to his shoulders in exploration and he shifted with sensual pleasure thrumming through him like an intoxicating drug, his spine bowing as she trailed her hands down over his back.

His skin was smooth, and he was so warm that she revelled in every path she took across his body, so different from her own and yet equally responsive. Every tug of his lips on her nipple sent an arrow of electric heat straight down into her pelvis. His hands roamed deftly over her curves and then he pulled her back into his arms to ravish her mouth again with a wild intensity that thrilled her. He was exploring now, tracing her inner thighs, locating the most tender spot of all and circling there gently before dipping a finger between her slick folds.

'Oh…' she moaned, the hollow ache between her thighs now joined by an inner clenching sensation as excitement and anticipation built.

'Are you on contraception?' he asked her without warning.

'No…' Claire stilled to stare up at him. All of a sudden, he sounded very serious and yet anxious too.

Raif groaned and began to pull back from her. 'I don't have a condom. We should've talked about this sooner.'

Claire's brow had furrowed. 'You don't carry anything?' she said in surprise.

'I don't have any reason to…well, I didn't until now.'

Claire sat up, her cheeks burning. 'Well, I have a condom.'

'That's a relief.' Raif watched as she scrambled out of bed and dug into the battered wardrobe to extract a handbag from which she took a small foil packet. 'My mother insisted I carried one round…just in case,' she explained uncomfortably. 'She thought I was weird because I'm still a virgin and she didn't want me to—'

Raif froze in shock. 'You're a virgin?'

Claire wrinkled her nose in embarrassment. 'You think it's weird too, don't you? But in the household I grew up in, where premarital sex was a hanging offence, I didn't dare experiment. I couldn't face being accused of being promiscuous like my mother. I was too scared of my father…and then as I got older, it got harder to cross that bridge. Gosh, I'm gabbling!'

'You don't need to be embarrassed.' Raif caught the tiny packet she tossed at him and sat up to reach for her hand and pull her back to him. 'I'm not very experienced either…for reasons I prefer not to go into right now.'

It was Claire's turn to still, gazing up into those stunning golden caramel eyes of his, accentuated by spiky black lashes. He was gorgeous. How could he possibly be inexperienced?

'So, you'll have to make allowances for me,' Raif told her gruffly.

Claire smiled. 'As long as you do the same for me,' she whispered shyly.

He curved her back into his arms, tumbling her back into the pillows with renewed confidence. 'I don't need to make allowances. All I need to do is fully appreciate you,' he declared with a roughened sound low in his throat as he ran his big hands over her.

He kissed her and her heart started beating insanely fast. Her hands crept up the back of his neck to tangle in his luxuriant silky hair and smooth over his skull. A curl of heat snaked through her, swiftly followed by another, the same hunger tugging at her again. He traced the hot liquid centre of her again and it was almost unbearable, her body ramping up tension and need faster than she could control it. She squirmed, a gasp parting her lips, wanting more, not even quite knowing what more was but knowing that the way she felt she wanted it yesterday.

'I know,' he groaned, running his mouth down the valley between her breasts. 'But you're not ready yet.'

'I feel ready,' Claire said unevenly.

'I don't want to hurt you,' Raif muttered thickly, sliding down her restless body, pressing his mouth gently to her writhing length, pausing and lingering at the most sensitive place of all.

Shocked by that sensual assault though she was, she was instantly plunged into a world of intense sensation. Halfway through demanding that he stop, she realised that if he stopped she would probably kill him because exquisite sensation had destroyed all resistance. Now she was twisting and jerking and moaning, the hollow ache between her thighs merely strengthening in intensity. And then the tension pushing up through her tightened every muscle in her body and the surge of her climax blew her away. She literally saw stars, cried out as the sweet convulsions of pleasure engulfed her and the aftermath of peace flooded her.

'Now you're ready,' Raif told her raggedly.

And she couldn't have spoken at that moment to save her life. He tipped her back and slid into her, slow and sure; her body seemed to accept the fullness of him. She stayed very still, wildly conscious of his every movement, tilting back her knees, feeling the push of his lean strong hips as he gathered power and sank deeper into her resisting flesh. And resist her body did.

He paused, melting dark eyes holding hers levelly. 'I'm worried about hurting you.'

'I always expected it to hurt the first time,' Claire confided fatalistically.

Raif was incredibly tense.

'Don't stop,' she urged.

And that galvanised him into action. He drew back and surged into her once more and a sharp, tearing pain made her cry out.

'I guess this isn't quite a fantasy experience for you,' Claire quipped, gathering her breath again, hoping he hadn't noticed the inadvertent tears that had filled her eyes. Raising her hips to his and angling back, she locked her legs round him in encouragement.

With a ragged groan, he succumbed, pushing deeper. 'You feel so good,' he bit out rawly. 'Like hot liquid silk enclosing me.'

The friction of his invasion made every nerve ending sit up and take notice. His rhythm vanquished her discomfiture, persuaded her to move in concert, no longer a bystander but a full participant. The wave of excitement gripped her afresh as his pace quickened and then he was groaning over her, her body jerking from the fierce onslaught of his orgasm.

'It'll be easier the next time,' she told him soothingly as he gazed down at her in a fierce combination of satisfaction, guilt and apology.

'There'll be a next time?' he muttered in a daze. 'A second chance?'

The most extraordinary wave of tenderness flooded

her. She had never felt as close to another person as she felt to him at that moment. 'If you want one,' she whispered, wrapping her arms round him, smoothing the tension from his broad shoulders, watching the stress ebb from him again.

'I want one,' he confessed with a brilliant smile that filled her with warmth. 'I want you.'

'But we don't have any protection, so you'll have to pull out…or something,' she warned in a rush.

Raif continued to hold her close, stroking her hair back from her flushed face, revelling in her generosity and warmth. 'It was special,' he murmured softly. 'Very special because it was with you.'

With reluctance, he eased back from her and his ebony brows flared up in consternation as he muttered something in his own language. 'The condom split…'

'Oh, dear…' Claire could think of nothing else to say while she wondered how long that little foil packet had been lying around before her mother embarrassed her by forcing it on her.

His lean darkly handsome face shadowed. 'I was rough with you. That's probably why.'

'You weren't rough,' she scolded quietly. 'Don't say that.'

'Why do I feel like I've known you for ever?' Raif studied her with a frown of bewilderment before he left to go into the bathroom and clean up.

'Are you leaving?' Claire called in his wake.

'Are you joking? After you offered me a second chance?' Raif teased.

And Claire laughed and relaxed, relieved that he was staying and that any awkwardness had dissipated. He returned to the bed, switched off the light and gathered her into his arms as if he had been doing it all his life.

Claire woke up with a start and found herself alone. Naked, she got out of bed, yanked her wrap off the back of the door and went to check the rest of the house. Raif had gone. But on the table by the window there was a note printed with a phone number.

'In case of consequences or if you simply want to keep in touch.'

But he was *gone*, and a terrible hollowness spread through Claire. What had she expected? A one-night stand with a stranger would rarely lead to the start of anything more lasting. It was done and dusted and she would never see him again.

Her heart ached as if it had been squeezed dry. It hurt. At the time she had told herself that parting wouldn't hurt but she had lied to herself because she wasn't that tough, wasn't that unfeeling. In an incredibly short space of time, Raif had come to mean something to her. He had been kind, caring, warm, affectionate, everything she craved in a man and had never found, but how hard was it to be any of those things when he was only planning to be around for a few hours?

And now it was back to real life. Work at twelve down in the harbour bar where she cooked and wait-ressed at weekends, the only employment currently available to her and with tips and pay just enough to cover the rent. Yannis, who owned the bar, was hoping to give her more work over the summer when the marina got busier and tourists arrived. But there was no dependable flow of trade on an island as small as Kanos. Sometimes the boats called in, sometimes, they didn't bother. That was why she needed to return to the UK. There was no reliable winter employment for someone like her.

She stepped into the shower. How weak was it that she wanted to make use of that phone number already? How sad was that? As she got dressed, she could not help reliving the night that had passed. The second time had been amazing. He had taught her what pleasure was all about, but they had discovered it together, which had somehow made it more intense and meaningful, only how meaningful could it be when they had been a couple for just a single night? And he had left in the early hours before she even awakened? Why was she being sad and immature? Why wasn't she accepting the reality of what had happened between them? A flashfire attraction that flared and passed? He had said he was travelling. Of course, she wasn't likely to see him again. At least he hadn't made her any empty promises.

Dressed in frayed denim shorts and a tee shirt, she opened the door to head out for work and froze. A giant basket of roses adorned with glittery balloons sat outside. She laughed out loud and reached for the card envelope. The card simply read, 'Raif'. No words. After all, what was there to say? But a huge smile had wiped away her frown as she rushed indoors and began to drag out vases and carefully settle her beautiful flowers in water. What a wonderful, thoughtful gesture! He hadn't stayed until she wakened and maybe that had been for the best, she conceded reluctantly. What had there been left to say but goodbye?

CHAPTER THREE

RAIF STOOD ON the sun deck staring out to sea.

He had done what he had to do, so why did he feel so bad about it? Claire was wonderful but there could be no future for them. There was nowhere for a relationship to go. He was in love with another woman and had been for years. He couldn't offer Claire the whole heart that she deserved. He didn't want some sleazy occasional affair, did he?

Even so, he had never wanted any woman the way he wanted her and that acknowledgement shook him. He had never thought of Nahla that way. She was another man's wife, the mother of children. Hell...she was his third cousin's wife! He had always appreciated the barriers between them and remained respectful in thought and deed. Claire, however, had the most amazing luminous sex appeal, he conceded abstractedly, registering that he had barely recalled his father's fury since he first saw Claire on that beach.

Yannis, the bar owner was already rearranging chairs round a large table outside when Claire walked into the village. 'We've got a big party coming in around eight from one of the yachts,' he warned her. 'I asked Sofia to come in and serve to leave you free in the kitchen.'

'How big is "big"?' Claire asked.

'Ten, no children. Someone's birthday bash,' he told her cheerfully. 'They're bringing their own cake.'

'Well, that will save some time.' Claire laughed because the place was empty aside of a couple of elderly regulars propping up the bar. She would have had plenty of time to knock up a cake, had she so desired.

'I told Sofia to tell her sister to bring us in a load of fresh veg,' Yannis told her with pride. 'You see, I do think ahead.'

'You do,' Claire conceded, walking out back to the kitchen to check on the other supplies, which the older man often overlooked when unexpected customers arrived.

She had studied for three years to become a pastry chef and copious working experience had been included in her degree course. In fact, only the year before she had got a position as a pastry chef at a top restaurant. Unhappily, that was the job she had had to give up when she'd decided to fly out to Greece to be with her mother. Claire, however, was pragmatic about that sacrifice. Chefs were always in demand, and when she got back to the UK she would soon find a job, even if it didn't have quite the prestigious status of the one she had quit. Eventually she would climb back up the ladder and start paying off her student loans again.

Her father had thoroughly disapproved of her chosen career. In truth the only version of her future that would have pleased her father would have been her marrying some approved man in his congregation and settling down to raise children. Her half-brother, Tom, had just entered theological college and, last she had heard, already had a church placement waiting for him. Claire was willing to admit that the long and often late hours in the catering trade were a drawback but, aside of that, she enjoyed cooking and loved the frantically busy pace of a working kitchen.

She spent the afternoon baking bread and a selection of desserts and pastries. It was a busy evening. Yannis dropped in to tell her that her food, the desserts in particular, had received many compliments. Around finishing time, she was invited out to meet the customers. 'I think I may have found you a cheap way of getting home,' Yannis told her.

A personable middle-aged man introduced himself as Captain Hastings of the *Mahnoor*. Her brows rose when she realised that he was referring to the giant yacht that resembled a cruise liner anchored out in the bay.

'Are you interested in temporary employment?' he asked. 'We'll be docking in Southampton in just over two months. Our assistant chef broke a leg mountaineering and he's out of commission. We need a replacement for the rest of the trip.'

'I'm Gregoire, the head chef,' a bald older man with a thick French accent interposed. 'Tell me about your training and experience.'

Someone pulled up a chair for her and there was a

flurry of introductions to the crew seated round the table. About a quarter were women.

Gregoire asked exacting questions but hope and anticipation were already bubbling up inside Claire. Working onboard a yacht sailing back to the UK would solve all her problems. She wouldn't have travel expenses and she would be able to save her salary, which would give her a cushion of cash towards affording accommodation on arrival.

'I think you'll do, and you'll pick up useful experience on the yacht,' Gregoire pronounced.

Claire breathed in deep. 'Can I bring my cat? She's well trained.'

The captain frowned and rubbed his chin. 'I don't see why not as long as you keep her under control.'

'She hasn't got pet travel papers yet.'

'You can get that taken care of at one of our ports of call.'

The yacht was moving on the next morning and naturally that was when they wanted her to start. It didn't suit. She would have liked longer to pack up, but she knew that Sofia would happily donate her mother's possessions to the local charity she supported and she herself would only be a retaining a few small keepsakes because nothing else made sense in her situation. After staying for a drink with the younger crew members and getting to know Liz, the onboard beauty consultant, and a couple of cabin stewards, Claire began to look forward to her new job.

'Oh, I forgot to ask. Who owns the yacht or is it on a private charter?' she asked.

'His Royal Highness, the Prince—'

'Royalty?' She gasped.

'Foreign royalty. So rich I'm surprised he doesn't shed diamonds or drip oil as he walks. You don't need to worry though. You almost never see him. He works on board. He's some gobsmackingly important big business whizz. He has a large party of guests joining us, though, so we'll all be run off our feet this trip,' she forecast.

Raif wakened at dawn and headed straight into the gym as was his wont. An elegant black cat awaited him there, a cat called Circe, which belonged to someone on the crew. Raif had tried to ignore the cat because it plunged him into memories he preferred not to recall. But the cat was persistent and refused to be ignored, following him back to his private quarters and graciously allowing him a brief caress before he stepped into the shower.

How many black cats like Circe lived around the Mediterranean ports? Probably thousands, he reasoned, and at least fifty with the name of a Greek goddess. In any case, he had only noticed the cat since they had docked in Trieste, where presumably the new crew member had boarded. Since then, the sleek black cat had become a ship mascot. As far as he knew he was the cat's first port of call on its wanderings. It visited the captain on the bridge every morning and, apparently, the unsentimental older man had shopped for fresh fish for the cat's benefit and Raif's famous head chef had created some special dish for it.

The cat visited the entire crew at different times of day. It had its own bed in the beauty parlour and toys in the office of Raif's admin staff. In the afternoon, it slumbered in Raif's office. So self-possessed and fearless was the cat that Raif would not have been surprised to find it kicking back on a sun lounger with a fat cigar and a tumbler of the most expensive whisky on board. It took adoration as its due.

But worst of all, it reminded Raif of Claire and he didn't need the reminders when he was peculiarly conscious of every mile that took him further from her. She had texted him once to thank him for the flowers but had not contacted him again. Why would she have when he had neither responded to that text nor contacted her? No doubt he would have heard from her had she been pregnant but, since he had not heard from her, he told himself that he should be grateful that that unforgettable night had not ended in a conception. Only, at heart, he knew he wasn't grateful when he still couldn't get either Claire or that extraordinary night out of his head.

Several decks below the owner's suite, Claire was contemplating the pregnancy test she had finally purchased at their last port. It had taken her two missed periods to accept that there could be genuine cause for alarm. The first month she had assumed it was stress from losing her mother, but the second month panic had begun to build inside her. It truly hadn't occurred to her that she might fall pregnant the very first time she had sex or that the repercussions from one night with a guy could be that massive. As she groaned out loud at her stupidity, her foolish naïve confidence in her sound judgement, she looked around her comfortable cabin for the comfort of her pet...her *roving* pet. Of course, as usual, Circe was absent.

Penning up Circe for a large part of the day hadn't worked and eventually the cat had slid out of a porthole and discovered that there was very large and interesting boat filled with people to explore. There had been no caging Circe after that and as Claire's pet had ranged far and wide and she'd realised that the cat wasn't annoying anyone, she had relaxed and stopped worrying. Now she only locked up Circe when she went ashore and that had been only a handful of times because there was no room in her budget for shopping trips when she had to save up.

In truth, she acknowledged, she loved working on the yacht. The pay was terrific and the accommodation top of the line. There were enough other women onboard to ensure she had company when she wanted it and there were all sorts of extras on the *Mahnoor*. When there were no guests, they were allowed to use the beauty salon where Liz, the resident beauty consultant and massage therapist, was going mad with boredom. They also had access to a pool and a gym and the latest movies.

But she still worked long hours and, although she had enjoyed the sheer frantic pace of the galley while catering to a large demanding party of well-heeled guests, she was glad that the last event of their stay was due that morning, a barbecue on the top deck. It would be the first time she had been allowed near the upper decks to which only senior crew members enjoyed access. Once the guests disembarked, there would be perfect peace and nothing taxing for the remainder of her trip back to London.

She did the test for which she had prepared and sat down again to await the result. Would Raif help as he had implied in his note? She had been tempted so often to phone or text him, but he had pretty much ghosted her, had certainly not started up a conversation when she'd thanked him for the flowers. Where did he even live? She knew nothing about him. Would he offer her financial help? Or had he just offered support without ever meaning to do anything concrete?

Claire peered at the result and felt sick, indeed as nauseous as she had felt on several occasions in recent days. She had sore breasts and couldn't stand the taste of coffee any longer. The nausea came and went at different times of the day but the extreme tiredness and the sleeping like the dead at night was there all the time. It was positive, pretty much what she had expected, and shock and fright vibrated through her and she had to dash into the bathroom to lose her early lunch in the most undignified way possible.

The extravagant furnishings on the busy top deck blew Claire away as she assembled plates at the built-in barbecue service counter for the lunch. Wonderfully attractive, shapely women strolled around in minimal bikinis. One in particular caught her eye because she was a famous supermodel and so gorgeous that she looked as unreal as a beautiful doll. Long black hair like silk streamed down her narrow spine, a big hat sheltering her perfect photogenic face from the sun's rays. Her beautiful body was close to naked in a thong bikini that revealed her bottom and all of her long, long legs, her feet clad in very high heels. A special carpet had been put down to protect the floor of the deck.

Glancing away from the beauty, Claire was craning her neck to catch a glimpse of the prince. As the crowd round the top table moved, she saw a middle-aged man with a trio of what might have been bodyguards stationed behind him. That had to be him, she thought, although she didn't know why the other females on board had insisted that she was in for a treat when she saw His Royal Highness.

A sudden shriek erupted from the gorgeous brunette and Claire turned back in disbelief to see something black hit the hard wall with a crunch and fall. It was Circe. She looked on, refusing to believe what she was seeing.

At her elbow, Gregoire said something unrepeatable in French.

The brunette was having hysterics. 'It touched my leg. Everybody knows I can't stand animals anywhere near me!' she screeched accusingly.

'You didn't need to kick it and hurt it!' someone else commented.

Claire crept out from behind the counter to approach her cat's still body. Gregoire reappeared at her elbow with a large serving salver. Before Claire did anything, he eased his hands very gently below Circe and lifted the animal onto it. 'We'll get a vet,' he told her. 'We'll get a vet immediately.'

'See that is done directly,' another voice continued, a very familiar English drawl, unusually clipped and curt and unmistakeably commanding.

Claire glanced up, her eyes rounding with pure incredulity. Raif was standing over both of them. He angled his head at one of the other men standing nearby and he hurried off. 'Raif...?' she whispered weakly.

'Please continue serving,' he urged Gregoire as he held out his hands to take charge of Circe. 'Let my guests enjoy their last party.'

After a disconcerted pause, the chef passed the injured animal over to Raif.

'I will ensure that the cat receives the very best attention,' he declared.

'Not without me,' Claire chipped in helplessly, taken aback by his sudden appearance. 'Are you one of the guests?'

And Raif looked at her properly for the first time and froze in consternation, his tortoiseshell eyes widening before he dipped his black lashes to conceal his reaction. It occurred to her then that he hadn't recognised her, not with a chef's cap and net hiding her hair, not in her shapeless kitchen scrubs. 'I'm so sorry about this.

I shouldn't have brought her onboard,' she muttered. 'I can't bear to see her hurt.'

'Claire, we will go inside and allow you to recover from the shock of this…incident.' Raif selected the word with care and rested a light hand at her spine to direct her towards the nearest door. She preceded him into a very spacious living area decorated with the utmost luxury and elegance.

One of the bodyguards she had seen in the crew canteen appeared and addressed Raif in another language.

'A car is already waiting at the quay to take you to the vet. The cat will have to be scanned for injuries and we can't offer that facility onboard. Mohsin will accompany you.'

Claire watched Mohsin bow low and her mouth ran dry. An awful, impossible suspicion was occurring to her. It should have been impossible. Raif could not be *the* royal prince, who owned the vast yacht, could he? 'Let *my* guests enjoy their last party,' he had said, indicating that he was the host and, truly, he had taken charge to the manner born, hurrying her indoors to ensure that she said and did nothing that could offend.

She was shaken and horrified and furious all at one and the same time. He had pretended to be someone ordinary…*hadn't he*? He had concealed his identity, misled her. Understanding and realisation set in hard. Dear heaven, she was working for him and he hadn't known…hadn't known she was on his wretched yacht until he'd recognised her! Whichever way she looked at the situation, it was an embarrassing mess for both of them and when she added in the reality that he had got her pregnant, the mess turned into a complete disaster!

The bodyguard removed the salver holding Circe from her frozen hands and angled his chin at another door. 'You come this way?' he said in guttural English.

Raif was staring at her, full-on staring as if he had never seen a woman before. Claire turned scarlet, suddenly aware of how unflattering her working garb was and hurriedly turning away to follow the older man holding open a door on the other side of the room for her.

Raif watched her depart. She was so small. How had he forgotten how small she was? He could not credit that she was working on the yacht. Circe was hers but naturally it had not crossed his mind that Claire could be on the *Mahnoor*. She had said she was a chef, and he had seen her at the counter, but until she'd looked up at him with those very blue eyes, he had not recognised her.

How long had she been on board? All these weeks when he had been thinking about her, wondering about her, she had been within reach and only a few decks below him. He did not participate in the hiring of crew members because that was the captain's job. How could he have guessed that she was no longer on the island? Had he phoned her as he had been tempted to do, he would have found out, he conceded ruefully. But then what could he have done with the knowledge that she was on his yacht? He did not and would not harass anyone who worked for him and anything of a personal nature would be inappropriate and indiscreet.

Claire followed the bodyguard down a long companionway and then downstairs to a gangway and on to the quay where a long white gleaming limousine awaited them. He set the salver carefully into the back seat and stood until she had slid in beside her immobile pet and then he climbed into the front passenger seat beside the driver.

She stroked a fingertip along the cat's spine. Her eyes were wet and scratchy with unshed tears. She wouldn't be able to bear it if Circe died. Had she noticed the cat mingling with the guests she would have removed her. After all, she understood that not everyone liked animals...but had that awful woman had to kick Circe with such violence? Circe must have brushed against her legs, had possibly given the beauty a fright. The nausea in Claire's tummy increased. It was shock, shock at everything that had happened.

In her mind's eye, she saw Raif poised in the saloon again, sheathed in a lightweight summer suit that only a man as formal as he was would have worn to such an event. But linking that version of Raif to the Raif she had met and liked and laughed with two months earlier was impossible for her. His reaction to the attack on Circe had been so polished, so smooth, so reserved.

Mohsin ushered her into a smart surgery where they were immediately attended by a veterinary nurse, who, clearly expecting their arrival, took charge of Circe and bore her off. Claire sat down shakily in the waiting area, trying not to wonder what such attention and treatment would cost, and all the time she was blaming herself for not restricting her cat's freedom once the guests came onboard. She had been thoughtless, *stupid* and in the same way she had been reckless and stupid with Raif. It was a bitter truth that continuing to follow her father's rigid rules of behaviour would have kept her safe. Asserting her independence and taking advantage of her freedom to do as she liked had steered her down a dangerous path. What could she possibly offer her baby as a single parent without even a decent income?

Mohsin approached her with a cardboard cup of cold water. 'The Prince will make everything all right again,' he assured her confidently.

No, he wouldn't. The Prince would be severely challenged to make anything right in her life again, although it was perfectly possible that he would hope that she was willing to terminate her pregnancy. But she wasn't prepared to even consider that option. She pulled off her hairnet, cap and apron and folded them together neatly.

The door opened and she glanced up. More than an hour had passed since their arrival. She tensed when she saw Raif speaking to the receptionist. He addressed her in fluent French and a few moments later, an older man appeared and began to speak to Raif at length. That conversation concluded, Raif approached her.

'What's happening?' she whispered apprehensively.

'Circe requires careful surgery but that will not take place until later when the requisite surgeon arrives. Her leg is fractured and she has concussion. It is safest for her to remain here under supervision for the present,' he advised.

Claire nodded very slowly. 'Is she likely to survive this?'

'Assuming there are no further complications with the head injury.'

Claire swallowed thickly.

'We will leave now,' Raif decreed.

She wanted to ask if she could see Circe again, but didn't want to make demands, and all the time she was frantically worrying about what all this veterinary attention and treatment would cost. Surgery here in Monte Carlo for an animal would not be cheap. 'I don't know how I'm going to pay for this,' she mumbled shakily.

Raif reached for her hand. 'That is not a concern you need consider. *My* guest caused the injuries at my party. I cannot abide cruelty to animals,' he bit out in a curt undertone. 'I am responsible for ensuring that this situation is put right...as far as it can be.'

Claire tugged her chilled fingers free and whispered, 'I can't let you pay the bill. It wouldn't be right.'

Raif sighed as he accompanied her outside where it seemed a whole fleet of vehicles awaited them. There were men standing about with earpieces, his security guards. She wondered absently where they had been hidden while he'd spent half the night with her. Bitter resentment and anger bubbled up through her again.

She was shown into another limousine and he slid in beside her, prompting her to move to the far end of the seat. Her hands twisted the folded kitchen apparel on her lap as the silence thickened.

'Claire.'

Her head whipped round, blue eyes bright as sapphires with temper. 'I'm not speaking to you. I don't know you. I want nothing to do with you. I will do the job I was hired to do and hopefully our paths won't cross again. Thankfully, we'll be back in the UK in ten days.'

Even as she spoke, she was wondering how she could possibly adhere to her statement. She was pregnant with his child. She had to tell him, didn't she? It wouldn't be fair not to tell him, would it? It would be wrong to remain silent and her unborn baby deserved more consideration from her. Her teeth gritted.

Raif said nothing. She was entitled to her feelings even if they conflicted with his own. Unfortunately, life was not quite so simple and straightforward as she would like it to be, and he owed her an explanation for his behaviour.

CHAPTER FOUR

'WHERE ARE WE?' Claire demanded abruptly as the limousine drove down a lane with a high concealing hedge and drew up outside a large white villa. She immediately blamed herself for getting so lost in her own thoughts that she had not even noticed where they were going. Of course, she hadn't known they were travelling to anywhere other than back to the busy harbour and the yacht, so she had not paid attention.

'This is my home in Monte Carlo. I want to speak to you, and it would be indiscreet to seek a private interview with you on the *Mahnoor*,' he pointed out. 'Here we may talk in private without fear of awakening speculation.'

'So, you're kidnapping me to protect my reputation and yours,' Claire deduced.

'Don't be ridiculous. Clearly, you are angry with me.'

'Gosh, you can really read the room, can't you?' she mocked with a toss of her head.

Raif forestalled further argument by getting out of the car. She thought about sitting on in the car alone like a truculent schoolgirl. Her cheeks reddened and as the door beside her opened, she climbed straight out.

'Tea or coffee?' Raif enquired politely as an older woman greeted him in the hall.

'Tea…and a cloakroom?' Claire asked stiltedly.

At the vanity unit of the very fancy cloakroom, she splashed her face, washed her hands and finger-combed her tousled hair. She leant on the sink and said a prayer for her pet's well-being. The tears threatened to over-flow again. She didn't know what was wrong with her because she had never been someone who cried easily and yet recently the most foolish things could make her eyes water. It could be her surging hormones. She re-called her friend, Lottie's tears while she was pregnant. Lottie had sworn that pregnancy had turned her into a watering pot. Claire sighed heavily and turned away from the unflattering mirror, knowing that she looked pale and drawn because she didn't bother with make-up when she was in the galley preparing food as the heat only melted it off again and left her face streaky.

She walked back out to the hall and espied Raif standing in a plush drawing room furnished in opulent shades of cream and sage green. It looked as new as though nobody had ever set foot in it, sat on one of the sofas or so much as dared to crease a single cushion.

The older woman appeared with a tray and set it down on the coffee table. Claire looked at Raif and then wished she hadn't because for a split second be-fore he saw her, his expression was unguarded and his tension, his discomfiture showed. As the refreshments arrived, he unfroze and smiled at the woman, thanking her. It was his habit to make an effort to fit into any situation, she conceded heavily, remembering him inexpertly trying to wield a drying cloth at the cottage, trying to be as ordinary as he was not ordinary.

And yet the perfectly tailored lines of his casual light blue suit, trousers taut against his long muscular thighs, his jacket merely accentuating his wide, hard torso, narrow waist and broad shoulders, spoke of his high income. There was nothing ordinary about a guy so gorgeous that she had a compulsive need to stare at him. His lean features were flawless. Why hadn't she smelt a rat in the sudden appearance of such masculine perfection on a public beach? There he had stood stripping in the bay, burnished male beauty and strength in every honed line of him. Nothing ordinary about that or those amazing dark golden eyes below his ridiculously long, lush black lashes. She should have been suspicious and cautious, and she had been neither.

Aware her breathing had shortened and her body heated while she scrutinised him, Claire looked away fast, but he was still freshly imprinted back in her brain. Even now, she stuck by her original belief that he was the epitome of male beauty and it had blinded her.

'You should have told me that you were a blasted prince!' Claire condemned as she leant forward, desperate to occupy her restless hands, and poured the tea into the china cups.

'What difference would it have made?'

'Well, for a start if I'd known that yacht was yours, I'd never have taken a job on it!' she fired back unanswerably.

Raif compressed his lips. 'There is little point in exchanging what ifs or might-have-beens. You cannot blame me for an accident of birth.'

'You're a *royal*, for goodness' sake!' she reminded him sharply.

'A minor one. I'm third in the line of succession after my father but I have two older brothers, both married and likely to produce male heirs and the birth of each child will push me further down the inheritance line,' he explained. 'I grew up in the UK. I'm not an important person in Quristan.'

'And you're very rich,' Claire remarked. 'I would never have got involved with you had I known how unequal we were in status.'

'Attraction trumps all such differences. At the time such thoughts weren't important to either of us. I did not set out to mislead you in any way,' he countered gently.

'But you were happy to *avoid* telling me about your real status.'

'Was that so wrong? To enjoy being accepted simply as a man? I had had an altercation with my father that morning. I found freedom and peace in that cove for a few minutes of relaxation.'

'And then I entered the picture and everything went to hell,' Claire inserted doggedly.

'I have not a single regret about what happened between us,' Raif told her with conviction. 'It was the most real connection I have ever enjoyed with a woman. Why would I wish that we had never met at all?'

'You'll regret it deeply once I tell you what I have to tell you,' Claire warned him tautly.

Raif frowned as he lifted his tea from the tray. 'So, talk…'

'I've done a test and I'm pregnant,' Claire informed him quietly.

He set down the tea with a jarring rattle of china. 'Are you sure of this?'

'The test was positive.'

He was pale now, his bone structure starkly outlined by his tension. 'I didn't think—'

'No, neither did I,' Claire cut in. 'But we took a lot of risks that night. We had the accident with the contraception and then we went ahead twice more without protection.'

His high cheekbones were edged with slight colour now. He had taken to sex with all the enthusiasm of a sex-starved healthy man. He had run an insane risk with very little encouragement. Keeping his hands off Claire had proved impossible and the withdrawal method he had sought to embrace had been more challenging than he had envisaged. He had had no restraint, no control with her and that was one very good reason why he had left her before he could succumb to the temptation of waking her up *again*. And still he wakened every morning, remembering the hot, tight glory of her curvaceous body writhing against his own and the high of every single climax they had shared. She had blown his every expectation out of the water and he had gloried in every indulgent moment of their intimacy.

And now she was carrying his child. That knowledge stunned Raif. He could barely credit it when he had assumed that he would never have a family of his own. 'When did you find out?'

'Today. I didn't do the test until I had to. I was avoiding it, burying my head in the sand. I'm at least two months along already,' she admitted uncomfortably.

He pulled out his phone and rang a number, spoke in French to whoever was answering and at length. 'We will see a doctor together this evening if it can be arranged. We need official confirmation of that test of yours before we go any further.'

'There isn't a possibility of a mistake,' she protested. 'And I need to get back to work. The excuse of needing a few hours off to take care of Circe has lasted long enough.'

'You can't work in a kitchen when you're pregnant,' Raif said with a straight face that told her he was being completely serious in voicing that belief. 'You could have an accident. You could hurt yourself or the baby.'

'Raif,' Claire murmured gently. 'Pregnant women have been cooking on everything from campfires to stoves for thousands of years.'

His ebony brows drew together. '*You* will not. I do not want anything to happen to either of you. I am sure any doctor would agree with me.'

'So, you're presumably not hoping that I will consider a termination or an adoption?' Claire gathered with relief at that reasonable assumption.

'Of course not. A child is precious and I could not

bear to part with my own flesh and blood,' he responded, frowning again. 'How could you think that I would want or dare to suggest such remedies?'

'We don't know each other well enough for me to assume how you are likely to respond to this situation. But I do assure you that no doctor is likely to tell you that it's dangerous for me to cook,' Claire stated wryly.

His phone buzzed and he answered it with a frown, which slowly cleared. A couple of minutes later, he shoved the phone back into his pocket. 'We have an appointment with an obstetrician in an hour,' he informed her.

Money talks, she thought in wry acceptance, grateful that she hadn't blurted that provocative belief out loud. But Circe had received instant access to treatment and now Claire would not have to await a medical appointment in the normal way. That was the privileged world that Raif lived in, a world that operated, it seemed, on the power of wealth and influence. But his attitude was not what she had expected in any way. She had thought he might be angry, even denying any knowledge of her or implying that perhaps the child could not be his. She had been prepared for the worst reactions and the unkindest suggestions, yet she had been absolutely wrong. The discovery shook her.

'We will have a late lunch now,' Raif continued smoothly.

'I thought you'd be angry, that…er…somehow you'd blame me for this development,' Claire heard herself admit in a strained undertone.

'What use would anger be to us now?' Raif quipped

as he held the door open for her to pass by him. 'One man's adversity is another man's opportunity.'

'That's a truly mature outlook you have,' she remarked, walking into a dining room with a smartly set table. 'You know… I could have made us lunch.'

'Eileen would have been offended. She owned her own restaurant before she came to work here. She's more of a caretaker than a housekeeper as I only occasionally use the house. She found full-time retirement boring,' he explained.

'You employ a lot of people.'

'Yes. And I'm always surrounded and rarely alone,' he agreed comfortably. 'I have learned to adapt to that. When I was a boy, though, I hated it.'

Claire sighed as a colourful salad was set in front of her. 'And I ruined your moment of escape on the beach.'

'In return you gave me an exceptional experience.'

Claire went pink and studied him anxiously. 'You don't have to put on a front about how you really feel about this. I can take the truth. I thought you'd blame me.'

'Why would I blame you? We took the risk together and it was a risk too far,' Raif conceded. 'But neither one of us was in the mood to be sensible and weigh the potential consequences.'

The light meal was exactly what her too sensitive tummy needed. Raif received a call, which he stepped out of the room to take. He reappeared with a smile.

'Circe has come around from the surgery and is doing well. I can take you back to spend a few minutes with her before we go for our appointment.'

Claire stood, wreathed in smiles, her relief written across her face.

Raif's own mood had lightened considerably with that news. Her suspicion, however, that he was putting on a front had been perfectly correct. While he preferred honesty, diplomacy had taught him that honesty was not always wise in sensitive circumstances. He did not blame her, he blamed himself much more. He was older, more sophisticated and he had known that she was vulnerable in her grief.

If he had not been able to walk away, he should have simply acted like a friend and given her the company she needed. He should have withstood her appeal, stood firm against that outrageously seductive sense of intimacy that he had never felt with a woman before. Now they were both trapped in a bind that would inevitably force them into marriage. He saw no other possible way to extricate them both with the credit that would also give their child what he or she deserved.

They left the villa in the same limousine and returned to the veterinary surgery. Raif stood by while Claire gently stroked her bleary-eyed pet, who now had a cast enclosing one leg. A sleepy tail moved lethargically in acknowledgement.

'The vet said that she's a young cat and should heal well but that there is still a risk of seizures from the head injury, so it would be best if she remains here until she is stronger.'

'There's going to be the most ginormous bill for her

treatment—' Claire began, stricken, back in the limousine.

'Claire…we have more important matters to worry about than that,' Raif pointed out drily. 'I wish it had been possible to punish the woman who hurt her, but I do believe it was an unfortunate accident. She didn't mean to hurt the animal, only to get it away from her. And in any case, the gossip will cause her a good deal of embarrassment.'

Her brow furrowed. 'Gossip?'

'Too many people witnessed the incident for it to remain unreported. She's a celebrity and someone will talk about it and rumours travel. Many people like animals and many will judge her for the injury she caused to your pet.'

Claire said nothing because she felt responsible for what had happened, feeling that she should have known better than to let the confident, independent Circe roam as she pleased on the luxury boat.

They were ushered into a private waiting room at the obstetrician's surgery. She was taken off first for a blood test and a preliminary examination with Mr Laurent. They waited for a little while before both being invited back in to see the older man again. He confirmed her pregnancy and offered her an ultrasound.

'Is there anything that can actually be seen this early?' Raif asked with a frown.

'You'll be surprised. Do you want to know the gender?'

'Yes.' Claire got up on the examination couch and

the ultrasound technician helped her bare her stomach, which was relatively easy with the stretchy waistband of the trousers she wore.

'I'll be able to forward the blood-test results to you within a couple of days and that will tell you whether you're having a girl or a boy,' Mr Laurent informed them.

Raif refused a seat and hovered tautly beside her as the wand was moved over her tummy.

Her mouth running dry, Claire stilled as the three-dimensional image formed on the big screen and she quite clearly saw a baby shape, a little face, little hands, little feet. Her heart sounded very loud in her ears.

'There's your child,' she was told.

'My child…' Raif whispered in such an impressed tone that he actually stole her attention, which had been locked to the picture on the screen of the baby.

'Congratulations,' the older man told them cheerfully.

She was told that tiredness and nausea were normal in the first trimester.

'I will be very careful with Claire and our child,' Raif asserted squarely, trying to be disciplined about the image he had been shown but, in truth, he was utterly entranced by what he had seen. 'I only wish we didn't have to wait so many months until we can meet him or her.'

Claire stared at him in even greater surprise, but he was still staring at the first copy of the ultrasound, which he had intercepted on its way to her hand. 'Come on, *share*!' she urged him, reaching for it.

Having gazed in smiling fascination at the image, he handed it over with reluctance. 'I think I must like babies,' he commented.

'Don't you know?'

'No, I've only seen my brother's little girls once or twice and they were older, not infants,' he told her. 'And few of my friends have either married or started a family.'

'We're in the wrong age bracket for this,' she muttered uneasily then as they climbed back into the limousine. 'I have only one friend with children…she got married straight out of school.'

Claire pondered her distant relationship with her own surviving family members, her half-brother and her stepmother. She remained in touch with both but her relationship with her stepmother would never be anything other than strained. It struck her as very sad that she would not be able to give her child loving parents. It seemed to her then that history could sometimes repeat itself in the worst ways. She hadn't enjoyed loving parents, and neither would her baby, although at least her baby would have a loving mother, she reasoned.

'We will cope,' Raif intoned with assurance.

She wanted to query his use of that word, 'we', but decided to say nothing until he had outlined his intentions towards her and their unborn child. His unhidden interest in the baby and her welfare had, however, impressed her. Not that he was going to have much opportunity to enquire into her welfare until the yacht returned to the UK, she reflected wryly. She did hope that she wasn't going to be forced to argue with him about her ability to continue her work as an assistant chef. She wanted a good reference from Gregoire to add to her CV because it was now all the more important that she find a decent job on her return.

'I asked for your possessions to be brought here from the *Mahnoor*,' Raif informed her, surprising her, as they walked back into the white villa. 'Eileen will take you upstairs to your room.'

Thrown to the heights of disbelief by that startling information, Claire blinked and whirled round. 'You did...*what*?' she asked dangerously.

Raif straightened his broad shoulders and gave her a stoic appraisal. 'When you have had the chance to change, we will discuss the future on the terrace at the side of the house. Is that acceptable to you?'

Claire sucked in a calming breath, her hands clenched into angry fists by her side as she struggled to keep her temper. 'As long as discuss isn't another word for a command.'

'It is not,' Raif murmured softly. 'But understand now that I will not invite a scandal that would damage our child's future prospects in life. It is my duty to protect you *both* from that threat.'

And it was as though Raif had decided to suddenly drop the Mr Nice Guy façade. That cool, strong dark gaze locked to her was unexpectedly intimidating, as was the harder set of his lean, darkly handsome features. Claire paled and, turning on her heel, she joined the older woman waiting to show her upstairs. She could hardly have a fight with him in the hall in front of a witness, she reasoned unhappily. Everything they had to discuss was far too private for that.

Eileen showed her into a large and opulent bedroom. Her case was sitting ready to unpack on the bed, the bag of her pet's belongings set by a wall. Claire practised deep breathing for a minute to get a grip on her heaving emotions. How had she been naïve enough to assume that she could return to work on his yacht as an employee when she was pregnant with his child? Of course, he would not take the smallest risk of *that* news leaking into the public domain. She supposed he had to be a person of interest to the media, a VIP, the type of rich, titled single man who featured in gossip columns. She reminded herself that he had been genuinely concerned about that video clip she had taken of him undressing on the beach. He actively avoided any kind of public exposure. Did he think she might talk to someone and let the secret out? she wondered worriedly.

She pulled a dress out of her case and her toiletries and went into the en suite bathroom, helplessly awestruck by her luxury surroundings and feeling slightly guilty about the fact because only the greatest fluke had brought her into Raif's life. Had she not been in that cove at that time that one particular day, they would never even have met. The acknowledgement was oddly chilling and she wasn't quite sure why.

After a quick shower, she felt calmer and was counting her blessings, no longer fuming about the future that was being reorganised without recourse to her wishes. She had been foolish to think that she could go back to the yacht as though nothing had changed. Everything had changed and it had changed without warning. But the father of her child *was* being supportive and that was a big positive in such a situation. She simply needed to respect his sensitivities as well.

Raif watched as Claire walked out hesitantly onto the terrace. A simple cotton dress in a daisy pattern floated round her slender thighs. It occurred to him that his father would have choked at the sight of a woman's bare legs and that his brothers' wives dressed as though time had stopped fifty years ago to satisfy his father's outdated notions. Raif smiled, thoroughly entranced by Claire's sheer natural loveliness, sunlight gleaming off her fair hair.

Eileen brought out the drinks he had requested. Claire accepted a glass with an uncertain look.

'Mocktails, no alcohol,' Raif explained.

'Oh.' Claire grinned and sipped, scrutinising him below the veil of her lashes, heartbeat quickening.

He had changed as well, but only into another suit.

'Do you ever wear jeans?' she asked. 'Or shorts?'

'Occasionally. But I'm usually working and meeting people and formal apparel is expected.'

'So…' Claire compressed her lips. 'You don't want me to return to my work on the yacht to finish the trip. Is that because you think I might talk and tell people about us? I wouldn't. I may have been a chatterbox when we were together on the island, but I do know when to hold my tongue.'

'I believe that,' Raif replied soothingly. 'But where my family and my country are concerned, I am careful not to cause any scandal and now that we have a baby to consider, I have even stronger reasons for ensuring that no questionable rumours about either of us can circulate.'

'I won't tell anyone who the father of my baby is,' Claire promised him abruptly.

'That won't work, Claire. For my family to accept my son or daughter, he or she must be born within marriage. My child will never be accepted otherwise,' Raif murmured grimly. 'Nobody is more old-school than my father and what he decrees rules the whole family.'

'Because he's King,' Claire gathered, saddened to learn that her child would be denied acceptance by Raif's family on the basis of illegitimate birth.

'And because he has the power to make life very difficult for anyone who challenges him or his convictions. Quristan, however, is not an old-fashioned country,' Raif told her with perceptible pride. 'But within the palace walls, life goes on in much the same way as it did when my father was born seventy odd years ago.'

'I'm sorry that circumstances will make it impossible for our child to know your family because I really don't have any family on my side to offer,' Claire confided ruefully. 'I have a friendly enough relationship with my younger half-brother, Tom, but we're not close.'

Raif rested stunning dark golden eyes on her troubled face. 'I want you to marry me, Claire.'

Claire's eyes widened. 'You can't mean that!'

'I want you to become my wife and give our child the best possible start in life and a future that he or she is free to choose,' Raif intoned, ignoring that exclamation. 'We must not allow our impetuosity to deprive our child of the many advantages that our marriage would bring.'

Claire swallowed hard. 'You're serious,' she finally registered. 'But it would be insane.'

'We need that marriage certificate for our *baby's* sake, not for our own,' Raif pointed out. 'The ceremony would take place at the Quristani embassy in Spain. I hold diplomatic status, which makes it easier to override the usual formalities. We can be married within days…if you are willing to agree?'

Her knees were wobbling, shock winging through her, and she backed down into a seat. 'It would be insane,' she repeated weakly.

CHAPTER FIVE

'THEN I MUST be insane,' Raif countered with calm, measured diction. 'Because at this moment marriage is what I want most. It will right the wrong that we would otherwise be inflicting on our child.'

'But marriage,' Claire almost whispered. 'That's a drastic measure.'

'It need not be. If you want nothing more to do with me on a personal basis that is acceptable too,' Raif informed her tautly. 'I will ask nothing more from you than that you go through a ceremony of marriage with me.'

'You mean…we sort of fake it?' Claire looked even more dismayed by that suggestion.

'If you wish to walk away from me after the birth of our child, I will do nothing to prevent you from reclaiming your freedom,' he extended, appreciating that she still didn't grasp what he was suggesting. 'It does not have to be a for ever and ever marriage. We do not have to share a bed if you do not wish to do so. I am trying to pitch the marriage idea in terms that you will find satisfactory, but I don't know your terms.'

It crossed Claire's troubled mind that really the only thing she wanted in marriage was *him*. Not his money, not the security he offered, not some fake deal to legitimise their child. But he wasn't offering her himself on any terms. She noticed that. She noticed that the *one* thing he wasn't offering her was the chance to see if their marriage could turn into a real relationship. Clearly that wasn't on the table and why would it be? she scolded herself.

She was a chef and he was a royal prince. His background was pedigreed and rich and privileged while she was from an ordinary home with a dash of scandal in her family tree. Of course, Raif saw no prospect of his ever feeling anything more for her than he had felt the day they had first met. He had walked away from her. He hadn't texted, hadn't done anything and he was in a blasted big yacht and in charge of everywhere it went. He *could* have seen her again had he so desired. And the lowering, hurtful truth was that he *hadn't* so desired.

'You have to tell me what *you* want,' Raif prompted gently.

'I want to give my child the best I can and if that means marriage, naturally I'll consider the idea. But I don't want to fake anything. I don't think I'd be very good at that.'

'So, what *do* you want?'

Claire winced and sipped her mocktail to occupy her trembling hands because she was all worked up. 'Obviously you want a temporary marriage that will only last as long as you need it to last,' she dared to state. 'But it just seems wrong…to use holy matrimony like that, but I understand that you see it as a marriage certificate and nothing else.'

'And that makes you uncomfortable,' Raif slotted in. 'It could be as real a marriage as you want to make it and last as long as it needs to for our child's benefit.'

'How can you go from one idea to something so totally different?' Claire pressed in sincere bewilderment.

'This is a negotiation in which both of us must compromise to some extent,' Raif pointed out. 'Basically, I will give you whatever you want if you agree to make me your legally wedded husband.'

'Then it could be a proper marriage,' Claire assumed, showing the very first tiniest, wariest hint of enthusiasm.

'And in a proper marriage, I would be able to have regular and easy access to my child, which is why I would agree to it,' Raif told her truthfully. 'I definitely don't want to be only an occasional visitor in my child's life. I would also have no objection at all to acquiring a very beautiful, sexy wife on a less temporary basis.'

Claire had turned pink. 'Sometimes you use an awful lot of words to say simple things.'

'I still want you,' Raif admitted more frankly.

'I'm not sure I can believe that when you walked away and never got in touch again,' Claire said baldly.

'There was a reason for that…' Raif compressed his lips.

'One night was enough?' Claire suggested flatly, shrugging her slim shoulders in an effort to deny her sensitivity on that score. She was embarrassed for herself because she had taken the dialogue in a direction that was too personal and revealing.

'I was very tempted to see you again, but it wouldn't have been fair to you.' Raif breathed in deep and slow, hesitating because he was not an insensitive guy. 'I'm not convinced that you truly want to hear me being *this* honest.'

'If we can't be honest even now, what kind of marriage could we have?'

'I'm in love with another woman. I fell for her many years ago,' he confessed with grim reluctance. 'But she is not someone I have ever been with or ever could be with because she is married to another man and seems perfectly happy with him.'

'There's been no affair?' Claire checked with a horrid hollow sensation spreading in her tummy.

'That was never an option…it would not be my style, nor would it be hers.'

'If it's someone you can never be with and you recognise that, you *should* have got over her by now,' Claire opined with strong conviction.

'Do you think I haven't tried?'

'Try harder,' Claire instructed with a brittle smile of encouragement, because the little hopes and dreams she had been on the brink of nourishing about his marriage proposition had just been snuffed out and stamped into dust. In love for years with an unobtainable woman? How was she supposed to fight that? *Live* with that? But then he was suggesting marriage for their child's sake and she was getting far too involved in much more personal feelings, feelings she shouldn't have and could hardly share with him. 'But thanks for telling me the truth.'

'But where does it leave us?' Raif enquired a shade drily.

'With a better understanding of each other, I hope. I assume we're staying here tonight?'

Raif nodded, trying and for once failing to read her shuttered face.

Claire was already engaged in burying his confession deep at the back of her mind. Reassured that there had been no affair and that he believed he could never be with the woman of his dreams, she told herself that she shouldn't be hurt by the unavailability of his heart. What was more, she did respect him for telling her an ugly truth, which no woman would welcome. 'I was going to ask you to let me sleep on my decision, but I don't think that's necessary now. I'll marry you.'

'I won't give you cause to regret it.'

'You have to be faithful and honest,' she told him ruefully. 'That is all I ask from you. I also don't *ever* want to know the identity of the woman you told me about. Let's be clear about that point.'

Raif released his breath in a slow hiss. 'I can meet those terms. Then we have a deal.'

'No, *not* a deal, a marriage. You're too much of a businessman sometimes,' she reproved.

Raif grinned with appreciation of that criticism, enjoying the way she treated him: hiding nothing, pretending nothing, indeed disdaining pretence. There was much he admired about Claire that went way beyond her physical appearance and her effect on his libido. Looking at her, he was aroused, fiercely aroused, at the awareness that soon they would be married and she would be his again. When she married him, together they would be able to give their child a stable, loving home. He did not want anything fake either, any more than he wanted to contemplate a future divorce. Divorce, after all, had ripped his life and his mother's asunder, as well as separating him from his brothers and his father. He would not allow their child to suffer such cruel losses and mercifully the answer to preventing that risk was in his own hands. If he made Claire happy, she would not seek a divorce.

They had a late supper on the terrace, and it was magical, fairy lights twinkling over the trees, apparently left over from some fancy business dinner he had once held at the villa. His reserve was back squarely in the control of him by then. Personal questions still made him tense. He did admit barely knowing his father in any other guise than as the King at ceremonial events. She made him laugh when she told him about being forced to join the church choir as a child even though she had the harsh singing voice of a corncrake. He frowned, though, when she mentioned being loudly rebuked by her father from the pulpit when she whispered or squirmed in her pew as a little girl at Sunday service.

She went up to bed with a little knot of sadness locked up inside her heart. If he hadn't told her about his love for another woman, she knew she would have crept out of her own bed to find his, but such boldness no longer felt possible. Yes, he still might want her in the most basic way of all, but pride warned her that he should also learn to appreciate her for other things. What exactly those other things might be, well, she had no very clear idea, but somehow slipping covertly into bed with Raif in a way that once would have felt utterly natural and normal to her no longer felt so straightforward.

Claire wasn't someone accustomed to hiding her emotions and she was used to acting on them, but intelligence told her that in the future she would have to be more guarded, even if it was just in an attempt to match Raif. A princess wouldn't have an unruly tongue, a silly giggle or think of fluffy, flirty stuff like putting on fancy underwear with which to shock him. And he would be shocked because he had finally admitted that that night he had been a virgin as well. She cherished that fact. At least that other woman couldn't steal *that* from her as well.

Raif went for a cold shower, but it didn't solve his problem and he decided that cold showers were very overrated. He marvelled at all the years he had remained impervious to such cravings. Now he craved Claire as much as though she were some illicit drug already in his bloodstream, but after the casual way their relationship had started out he was convinced that he ought to treat her with the greatest possible respect to ensure that she did not think he would ever take her beautiful body for granted.

In the morning, Claire asked what she should wear for the wedding ceremony and Raif frowned. 'I'll consult my staff and organise something here at the house.

You will require a complete wardrobe, but we can't shop together here in Monaco where I am well known.'

He didn't want to hurt Claire by telling her the truth that if his father found out that he was marrying a woman without his approval he would move heaven and earth to stop him because Claire was neither royal nor connected to some important Quristani family. At the same time, however, his father had never once indicated any interest in when or even if Raif would ever get married, although he had exerted himself to personally select his older sons' wives. Having consulted his lawyer, Raif knew there was nothing in the constitution that even implied that he needed anyone's permission to marry and once the deed was done, it was done. He would not risk his child being born out of wedlock.

Claire went to visit Circe again, but this time with Mohsin as her escort. Her cat was more responsive than she had been the day before and Claire was glad, because it looked unlikely now that her pet would suffer any further problems from her injuries. She regretted her inability to take Circe back to the villa with her, but that wasn't possible when they were about to fly to Spain, and she could hardly saddle Eileen with a convalescent cat.

'So, what do I wear?' Claire asked Raif again when on her return he informed her the 'fashion people' had arrived and awaited her in the main salon. 'A wedding dress or something less bridal?'

'That is immaterial. We will not be visible once we arrive at the embassy. You will like our ambassador and

his wife there. I went to school with Kashif, and Stella
is English, like you,' he told her cheerfully.

'I would like a wedding dress,' Claire admitted.

'Claire…' Raif traced a long finger across her anxious and downcurved lips, troubled by her uncertainty.
'*Smile.* I don't care if you dress up like a pirate. I only
care that we take this important step together.'

Claire quivered and smiled so brightly that he smiled
as well. And, heavens, he was so beautiful to her in
that moment that she almost stretched up to kiss him.
The smouldering glow in his tortoiseshell eyes lit her
up like a firework inside herself where it didn't show,
and her thighs pressed tight together to contain the lingering hollow ache of longing. She wanted him as she
had never wanted him before, even more than she had
wanted him the first time, because now she knew what
he could do to her with his mouth, his hands and his
body. Blinking rapidly, she forced herself to turn away.

The 'fashion people' were a stylist and representa-
tives of several designer salons, each vying with the
other to fulfil her requirements. She was measured,
shown pictures to establish her likes and dislikes and,
in a whirl of activity and useful advice, was promised
a dream wardrobe that would suit both hot and cool cli-
mates. She knew that within months most of the apparel
wouldn't fit her but, mindful of the need for discretion,
she didn't mention the fact that she was pregnant. And
she was downright excited at having picked her dream
wedding gown, grateful that her tummy was still flat
for the occasion while inwardly apologising to the baby
she carried for her ridiculous vanity.

The next day, Raif handed her his phone and explained that it was the obstetrician on the line with her test results. Tensing, Claire wandered across the terrace and listened as the sex of her child was shared. She handed back the phone.

'We're having a boy!' she proclaimed with a smile.

Raif grinned. 'I truly didn't mind which,' he confessed. 'But perhaps because I'm a boy, having a boy as a first child seems an easier prospect.'

Forty-eight hours later, they moved separately through the airport and ignored each other in the VIP lounge. 'It was like being a spy!' Claire told Raif in delight when he finally boarded his private jet to join her. 'And Mohsin is like a shadow when he moves around. I loved it. I was careful not to even *look* in your direction!'

'You are a very good sport, Claire,' he countered with a helpless grin. 'Most women would kill me for forcing them to hide on their wedding day!'

'I'm not most women.'

'I know that very well.'

It was true that the fabulous clothes that had begun arriving the day after her consultation with the fashionistas had given Claire more confidence than she had ever had before. There was a newly discovered pleasure in knowing that she looked her very best in an elegant dress the colour of cinnamon, teamed with toning shoes and a stylish bag.

They landed in Barcelona and travelled separately to the embassy where she would put on her wedding gown. The embassy was a big, tall, classical stone building behind secure walls, and she climbed out of the limo to be shown indoors, where she was greeted by a young brunette with a bubbly personality.

'I'm Kashif's wife, Stella,' she announced. 'This is so exciting!'

'Yes, isn't it?' Claire agreed, relaxed by that greeting from someone she reckoned was only a few years older and happy to follow Stella up an imposing staircase into an elegant bedroom where her luggage already awaited her.

'I can't wait to see the dress!' Stella confided. 'I think it's awful, though, that Raif feels like he has to get married in secret just because of that old dictator of a father!'

Alerted to the fact that her hostess had no idea she was pregnant, Claire resisted a smile at the full extent of her future husband's reserve even with a personal friend and his wife. Only as the rest of that speech sank in did the urge to smile die altogether. So, that was the *real* reason for the secrecy, she registered in dismay. Obviously, understandably, Raif was taking a wife of whom his father would not approve. Resolving not to feel wounded by that reality, she whisked her dress out of the cloaking garment bag that had enclosed it and dug out the rest of her bridal outfit.

'No man deserves to be loved more than Raif,' Stella told her, seating herself on the edge of the bed. 'He had an awful childhood and he'll never tell you about it.'

Claire wrinkled her nose. 'He's very reserved but we're all different, aren't we?'

'Do you want to know the facts?'

'I could know already,' she pointed out. 'I know the basics…his parents' divorce, his mother's depression. But I don't think I'm entitled to know anything he hasn't chosen to tell me.'

'Sorry, removing foot that I had inserted in mouth!' Stella commented with a guilty giggle. 'You're loyal. He's never had that either, someone loyal to *him*. He's too busy being loyal and respectful to a family that act like he barely exists, except when it suits them to recognise him. They only invite him to official events. He got left out of all the weddings, new births and family celebrations.'

'He's a very special guy,' Claire muttered helplessly, hurt that Raif had to endure such poor treatment from the family who should have been closest to him.

Of course, was she really one to talk? Her own childhood had been no walk in the park. Her father and her stepmother had raised her without affection or praise of any kind. Even so, nobody had beat her, nobody had starved her and, for those reasons, she didn't feel that she had that much ground for complaint when others went through much worse experiences. It had been rather distressing to appreciate as a teenager that her father didn't even appear to like her and only seemed to look at her to find fault. Of course, she had reminded him of her mother, having the same hair colour and eyes, but that didn't excuse him, in her opinion, for punishing her for his ex-wife's choices. Perhaps Raif was paying the same price as she had for *his* resemblance to *his* mother!

'You *care* about him,' Stella murmured with warm approval. 'That's all I really wanted to know.'

Claire reddened as she undressed. She could have asked for privacy, but she would never manage to get into her romantic confection of satin organza without female assistance. It was a designer gown with tight lace sleeves and a sweetheart neckline, the bodice neat and fitted and the skirt narrow and long. It was the colour of pale sepia, the shade that most suited her skin tone, and the shape flattered her curves without showing too much skin. The fabric was scattered with seed pearls.

'Raif had his mother's jewellery brought here from London for your use,' Stella informed her. 'There's enough in that chest to sink the *Titanic.*'

'He didn't mention it.' Claire climbed into her gown and eased her hands into the sleeves while Stella helped to untangle the skirt. Righting the shoulders, Claire straightened.

'It's really beautiful.' Stella sighed as she proceeded to close the back of the gown. 'We had a civil wedding. I wore a suit. If I'd my time over again, I'd wear a wedding dress.'

Claire dug her feet into her ridiculously fancy wedding shoes with pleasure and approached the giant chest by the wall. 'The jewellery is in here?'

The chest was filled with boxes. Claire flipped a lid on the largest box on top and gasped at the rainbow reflections of the diamonds.

'That necklace is perfect for your neckline,' her companion declared.

The diamond necklace and the earrings that matched were donned.

'There must be a tiara in here, more than one, I would assume. She *was* a queen.'

'A tiara would be over the top for me,' Claire demurred.

'But not for a princess and Raif has organised a photographer,' Stella warned her, surprising her in turn.

A tiara was indeed located with ease and Claire allowed her companion to anchor it above the short veil at the back of her head. Nerves clogged her throat as she surveyed her reflection because, with all those diamonds and clad in her dream gown, she barely recognised herself. That disturbing title 'Princess' struck her as more threatening than something to which she might have aspired because she knew herself to be absolutely ordinary in every way.

They went downstairs into a large room where Raif and two other men awaited them. As she was introduced to Stella's husband, Kashif, and the minister present to perform their ceremony, Claire only had eyes for Raif, resplendent in a morning suit, a pearl-grey cravat at his throat to match the cummerbund round his narrow waist, a custom-made jacket with a tail outlining his splendid physique. He looked amazing, she thought. Well, he always looked amazing, but he contrived to look especially amazing in that garb, his black hair gleaming above his stunning eyes, his strong jawline freshly shaven, framing his wide, sensual mouth. For an instant, she really couldn't credit that he was about to marry *her*. He reached for her hand with his easy smile and led her over to the table that had been topped with a giant floral arrangement. He looked down at her as though she were the only woman in the world.

It was a short and sweet ceremony, but Claire listened to every word and exchanged rings with Raif in breathless wonder that they were actually becoming man and wife.

Raif studied her with mesmerising dark golden eyes. In that highly feminine dress, she was every dream woman he had ever had and Kashif had done everything he had asked him and more in preparation for their wedding. Sadly for Claire's sake, there were only two guests, he acknowledged, but there had to be some drawbacks to a secret event.

'That was wonderful,' she told him brightly as their hosts led them to the rear garden with its ornamental box-hedged flowerbeds for the photographer to take advantage of the setting.

'You look fantastic,' Raif whispered only loud enough for her to hear.

More colour warmed her already flushed cheeks and her blue eyes sparkled with pleasure. 'I wasn't expecting a Christian minister and ceremony,' she whispered back.

'I wanted you to be comfortable,' Raif responded.

And she ate sparingly of the delicious dinner that followed because she was lost in a reverie. There had never been a man in her life, including her late father, who had worried so much about what would make *her* happy. She had never enjoyed such thoughtful consideration. Yet Raif had had her injured cat treated and had had Claire ferried back and forth on pet visits, which others might reasonably have deemed unnecessary. He had ensured she had new clothes for her future role, and he had even had his late mother's jewellery collection offered to her for use. Yet he made no demands on her whatsoever.

She decided that he was the most unselfish person she had ever met and that melted her heart, because there could be few men as rich and in possession of a superyacht who, in his position, would have made so much silent, kind effort on her behalf. And he always brushed away any attempt to thank him.

'You've made it a wonderful day,' she murmured.

'That was the goal,' he confided with satisfaction.

Below the table, she rested a hand on a lean thigh and petted him as though he were a cat, unable to express her gratitude in any other way. His hand came down briefly over hers and then shifted again and she took the hint and retrieved her own. No, Raif was never ever going to be demonstrative in front of others, she reflected fondly. No PDAs from him!

Claire knew that she was already halfway in love with the man she had married. She had never met a man like him, never dreamt he could even exist, and now here she was with his wedding ring on her finger, and she could not believe that fortune had smiled on her to such an extent. Mentally she was listing his every plus and those pluses just kept on mounting in number.

Raif was thinking that even the touch of her tiny hand on his thigh was too much for him to bear. He was already as hard as a rock. He wanted to defy every civil, social tenet to snatch her away somewhere private where he could *touch* her. He had genuinely not appreciated that one foray into the world of sex would leave him so agonisingly needy because in every other field he was very controlled, very cool and unfailingly practical. Claire, however, punched buttons he hadn't known he had. Just a smile, a bright glance from those eyes of hers, the peachy pout of her lips when she laughed, and she laughed frequently, unlike most of the people he knew. Being with Claire felt vaguely to him like being in the sunshine all the time, where all the usual things that worried him miraculously vanished.

It was after ten that evening when Raif smoothly extracted them from their hosts' convivial company. He explained that they would be spending the night in the suite of rooms created for his father at the embassy when he first became King. As a young man King Jafri had happily travelled abroad.

'And then there was apparently some kind of scandal with a young woman that had to be hushed up and he never left Quristan again,' Raif informed her wryly, opening a door into a large formal drawing room. 'It soured him on travel, foreigners and tourists as well.'

'Not a forgiving person,' Claire gathered as he opened the door into the most grandiose bedroom she had ever seen.

A gilded four-poster bed, garnished with scarlet and gold drapes, sat on a polished dais at the far end of the room, rather resembling something that she thought might have featured in a big-budget royal film. 'Oh, my goodness…are *we* going to spend the night in that monstrosity?' She gasped.

'Yes, it is a monstrosity, isn't it?' Raif agreed with humour, relieved it wasn't only him who found his father's taste for medieval splendour weird in modern times. 'But this is where I have to sleep when I stay here. Kashif tells me that it's an exact replica of my father's bed in the palace. I've never been in his wing of the palace, so I wouldn't know.'

Claire was reminded by that remark that he had been denied a close relationship with his surviving parent. That he had never seen his father's private quarters said it all.

'Do you want anything to drink?' Raif enquired, hovering beside the drinks cabinet.

'No, thanks. After that elaborate meal, I'm full,' she quipped, moving over to the ornate gilded dresser to begin removing her diamond jewellery.

'We're leaving first thing in the morning to spend a few days alone in the Alpujarra.'

'I wasn't expecting a honeymoon,' she told him. 'And I never thanked you for offering me these beautiful pieces to wear today.'

'I inherited my mother's jewellery and, as my bride, you're entitled to wear the pieces,' Raif countered. 'Do you need some help?'

'I'm afraid you're likely to have to unwrap me like a parcel tonight,' Claire muttered shyly as she struggled to undo the necklace.

'Let me…' Cool fingers brushed her nape as he

opened the clasp and laid the necklace down on the dresser.

Claire removed the earrings and turned back to him, colour in her cheeks at the silence spreading round them.

Raif extended a wrapped gift box to her. 'It's a wedding present from me.'

'I didn't get you anything!' Claire wailed in immediate dismay.

'Claire,' Raif murmured with a smouldering smile. 'My gift today was *you*!'

Claire was busy reddening and ripping open the packaging to discover the diamond-studded watch within. 'Wow, triple wow!' She gasped, suddenly short of breath as she had not been at the loan of his mother's jewellery because the watch was a personal gift for her alone. Without hesitation, she undid the serviceable chrome watch she wore to attach the new one. 'It's beautiful, Raif. Thank you very much.'

Gazing down into her smiling face, he bent down and captured her lips hungrily with his own. 'It was nothing,' he started to say, intending to say more but too drawn by the taste of her to linger on speech.

A little quiver of vibrant response ran through Claire, and she leant into that kiss like a drowning swimmer reaching for a life ring, hands closing over his shoulders, slender body sealing to the hard muscular contours of his.

CHAPTER SIX

'I NEED YOUR help to get out of this dress,' Claire mumbled against the allure of his mouth.

With effort, Raif took a step back from her, one hand already engaged in wrenching loose his cravat and cummerbund. 'We're both wearing far too many clothes.'

'Like you on the beach,' she reminded him with a smile, no lingering hurt now in the memory of him walking away the next morning. She understood him better even if she wished things weren't the way they were with him being in love with another woman. Only the conception of their child had given Raif the framework to fit her into his life as well and just at that moment she didn't resent that prosaic truth, even though she suspected that there might come a time in the future when she would be more sensitive and might well long for more.

As he doffed his jacket, she turned round to present him with the hooks and ties at the back of her gown.

'I like the subtle little opening...*here*,' he confided huskily as he traced the keyhole shape with a fingertip. 'In fact, I love the dress. It's sexy without showing anything much.'

He unhooked the bodice, unlaced the ties and she began to pull her arms out of the sleeves. 'The lingerie isn't quite so subtle,' she warned him carefully.

'What *only* I see can be as daring as you like,' Raif told her with a slashing grin. 'I may have chosen not to engage in casual flings, but I am not a prude.'

Face colouring and fully aware of his intense interest, Claire let the gown drop to her ankles to expose her thigh-high stockings and garter, matched to a white filmy silk bra and knickers adorned with blue ribbons.

'That word you use…*wow*, just about covers my appreciation,' Raif confided, colour flaring along his high cheekbones as he looked his fill at his bride, her luscious curves cupped in fine silk and lace. He embarked on his shirt buttons with alacrity.

'No, I open those,' Claire announced, stepping forward, empowered by his appreciation and still wearing her heels, to undo those buttons for him because she wasn't about to mention it *again*, but she loved the look and shape of him as well. The shirt parted on a sliver of bronzed chest and his taut, indented abdomen. He was on gym equipment every day and it showed.

As Claire tipped his shirt off his shoulders and let her hands drop to slide up over his muscular torso, Raif was mesmerised by her touch and the hunger for him in her bright blue eyes. Being desired to that extent struck him as a blessing to be savoured. The shirt dropped, he toed off his shoes and peeled off his socks without removing his attention from her for even a second.

Claire reached round to unclip her bra and his hands came up to hold hers. 'I want to do that,' he admitted. 'I want to strip you naked and live out every fantasy I've had about you over the past two months.'

Her eyes widened, she swallowed and stilled. His husky words made her even more aware of the pool of urgent heat forming in her pelvis and the tightness of her nipples. He undid her bra and let it fall, pulling her back against him, letting his hands glide up to cup the firm curves and his thumbs catch her swollen nipples. 'I have dreamt of this,' he groaned, tugging her back against him, making her awesomely conscious of his erection.

'Can't deny having the odd recollection of that night myself,' she admitted.

'It was amazing,' Raif told her. 'But tonight will be even better.'

She spun round and unzipped his trousers, fingers delving beneath the fine weave to stroke his hard length. He shuddered against her and kissed her with unleashed hunger before dropping down on his knees in front of her and gently tugging down her knickers.

'We will take this slow tonight,' he asserted.

Naked, Claire squirmed in front of him, horribly conscious of her unclad self and every defect she had ever believed her body had. 'I'm quite happy with fast…'

'Think of yourself as a gourmet meal,' Raif advised.

'Right…' Claire gasped as he pried her thighs apart and pressed his mouth to the heart of her because she hadn't been expecting that. All the lamps were lit and she felt floodlit and embarrassed. 'We could get into the bed—'

'It looks like Count Dracula's bed.'

'He slept in a coffin,' she incised.

Raif ceased his attentions and looked up at her. 'What's wrong?'

Claire winced. 'I just feel a bit shy about standing here… I *know* it's stupid—'

Raif sprang up and lifted her up into his arms to carry her over to the bed. 'Nothing you feel is stupid. I'm afraid you're dealing with a bridegroom set on living out every sexual fantasy he ever had…and almost all of those were about you and very recent.'

Her awkwardness melted away at that admission while her spine met the cool crisp white linen beneath her. Not a scrap of shyness in his bearing, Raif peeled off his trousers and his boxers and joined her on the bed. Hot, golden, muscular flesh met hers.

He stared down at his bride in fascination, thinking that he *finally* had a family, someone who would look to him first and a child whom he would cherish. He had never really had anyone of his own. Claire and their son, however, would be wholly and absolutely *his* and that meant a lot to a man who had pretty much felt alone all his life.

He had loved his mother, but she had had too many other interests with her travel, her endless parties and affairs with unsuitable men to spend much time with the little boy in the nursery. And when he got older, she had tried to make him a friend rather than a son, which had often been very uncomfortable for him. Yet he had long understood why his mother had only found comfort in her life of excess: his father's rejection had decimated her pride and when his father had swiftly chosen a much younger beauty as a second wife, Mahnoor had been absolutely gutted. Her wounded ego had driven her into the arms of other men.

'You're beautiful, Claire,' he murmured softly, gorgeous black-lashed eyes locked to her smile. 'And I'm incredibly happy about our son. I'll be with you every step of the way.'

She drew him down to her, fingers sliding up into his luxuriant black hair, and his mouth crushed hers in a remarkably sensual and urgent claiming that made the blood chase through her veins faster. She arched up to him, her whole body craving his, the nagging ache pulsing at the heart of her almost unbearable to endure. As her legs wrapped round him Raif shifted against her with a roughened sound deep in his chest and sank deep into her, her body stretching to enclose him while a delicious friction burn rippled through her.

'Slow!' Raif reminded her in reproof.

And Claire laughed because he was so serious about the concept, as if they had to proceed from point A to point B to win the points and skipping a possible stage could be a hanging offence. 'No, it's win-win all the way for us the way I'm feeling.'

'I wanted it to be perfect this time,' Raif confided, his big strong body trembling over her as she shifted up to him in a quite deliberately inviting way.

Claire gazed up to his lean, dark, wonderfully handsome face and ran a thumb along the lower edge of his compressed lips. 'I think it's always perfect with you,' she murmured softly. 'I don't want to go slow *this* time. If you start treating me like an invalid here in bed as well, I'll kill you.'

An unwilling edge of amusement tugged at the corners of his unsmiling mouth. 'Is that so?'

Claire gave him another hip-tilting motion to urge him on. 'Yes, because there is no such thing as perfect when we're together. Being happy is a much better goal.'

Raif nodded and moved in a remarkably enervating way that sent the pleasure she craved winging through every sensitive nerve ending. Her head fell back because he had got the message and that was really all that mattered. Only later would she wonder if that was what Raif did to himself, held himself to some impossible, unsustainable high standard in every field of his life because someone somewhere at some stage of his growing years had made him feel as though he would never be good enough. And she understood that, because she had been made to feel the same way.

She strained up to him, her serious thoughts flying away as a new urgency gripped her. Raif was moving and every lithe thrust of his body into hers gave her so much sensation she felt as though she were drowning in the sensual waves building at the centre of her, tightening inner muscles she had not known she had, her tension rising fast. He shifted them over onto their side and slid a hand between them to find that tiny nub that controlled her and as he drove into her one last forceful time, the whole world splintered round her and she was flying high on such excitement that something uncommonly like a shriek was wrenched from her.

'Oh, my goodness, did I—?'

'Yes, and loudly, but there's nobody else to hear in this wing of the embassy because below us are the offices,' Raif told her, holding her gripped to him as if she were likely to make a sudden break for freedom. 'I'm not sure I deserve you.'

'That'll teach you not to get naked in a public place again and use your beautiful body to tempt an innocent woman into what my father would have called improper behaviour!' Claire teased, tickling his ribs because once again he looked quite ridiculously serious.

Raif started laughing. 'My father would also have found our behaviour improper but without it I wouldn't have you...and I can't bring myself to feel a single atom of regret,' he confessed ruefully. 'Even though I plunged us both into a storm of trouble.'

'It takes two to tango,' Claire reminded him, throwing off the sheet, because Raif burned much hotter than she did, and she was roasting. 'Is there any air conditioning in here?'

Raif let her go and sprang out of bed to stride back

naked to the door and hit a switch. 'I always leave it off...sorry.'

'The heat doesn't usually bother me this much. It may be because I'm pregnant...or because I have a very hot guy walking naked across my bedroom floor...a very hot *aroused* guy!' she tossed at him irrepressibly, giggling at his arrested expression.

'Well, since this wedding night doesn't appear to be under my control,' Raif intoned lazily as he flung himself back on the bed, 'maybe *you* would like to tell *me* what we do next.'

'I'm not about to tell you, I'm much more likely to *show* you,' Claire declared, rolling closer to investigate every fascinating part of his body that she could see and touch.

'I like that,' he groaned at one point. 'Oh, I really, *really* like that...'

Sooner than either of them would have ideally liked, it was morning and time for a quick breakfast in their palatial suite and then departure.

'On your way back to the yacht, spend one last night here and join us for dinner,' Stella pleaded.

They flew to Almeria and completed the journey to the mountain villa by car. From the moment they stepped down onto the first paved terrace of a series, Claire was enchanted by the view of the wooded hillsides and that was even before Raif pointed out the Rock of Gibraltar and Morocco in the misty distance. A forest of pine and oak trees surrounded the wonderfully colourful lush tropical garden. High on a nearby hill and surrounded by a rambling village stood an old, ruined castle, its jagged roofline piercing the bright blue sky.

With wide eyes, Claire stared at the spectacular infinity pool complete with steps, wet bar and a miniature island, before turning on her heel to walk inside the house.

'What's wrong?' Raif followed her. 'Don't you like it?'

Claire tugged her appreciative attention from the beautiful tiled living area, patio doors open on all sides to make the most of the fabulous views, and swallowed hard in her dazed state. 'It's fantastic,' she whispered. 'How could I *not* like it? Do you own this place?'

'It's a rental but I own the company. I developed the villas in this area, a handful from scratch and others from derelict homesteads,' he explained calmly. 'I suppose I do own it, only I don't regard it as one of my private homes.'

She peered into the kitchen with its pretty blue shutters, catering-sized stove and smooth surfaces. *I suppose I do own it. One* of my private homes. She blinked and almost laughed. He had brought her into a disconcerting new world of wealth and opulence, and she could still barely credit that such a lifestyle was now hers to share with him. Her exploration continued into a stunning bedroom with a mosaic of richly coloured traditional tiles on the wall and a superb marble bathroom.

'Someone will come in every day to look after us,'

Raif revealed, stilling behind her to tug her back into his arms. 'I know you would cook but you're not supposed to on your honeymoon.'

'Is that so, Your Royal Highness?' she teased, wriggling back into much-needed contact with his long, lean, powerful body, her own nerve endings flaring at that necessary physical connection. The sudden pinching of her nipples and the stirring pulse of need between her thighs were already becoming familiar to her.

'Yes, that is so,' he breathed raggedly as he backed down on the bed and flipped her to face him, large hands framing her cheeks as he tasted her lush mouth with raw, driving urgency.

'I can't wait to be inside you again,' he groaned, dazzling dark golden eyes locked to her pink face. 'I want you all the time. Every time I look at you, I end up wanting you again.'

Her reddened lips curved into a playful grin. 'So, we didn't burn ourselves out last night, after all...'

'I can't believe I'll ever burn out on you,' Raif forecast.

'You're not allowed to wear a suit the whole time we're here,' Claire warned him bossily. 'You're here to *relax*.'

'I'm not good at relaxing.'

'But I am,' she told him brightly, unknotting his tie, embarking on his shirt buttons.

Raif took the hint with alacrity, standing up to peel off his clothing at speed.

Claire kicked off her shoes and removed her jacket to sit on the bed as if she were overseeing a strip show. 'Yes…yes…*yes*!' she told him irrepressibly, delighted by the slivers of bronzed muscular torso and hair-roughened thighs being bared.

Raif rolled his eyes. 'You're objectifying me,' he complained.

Claire tossed her head, rumpled blonde tresses flying back to expose her smile. 'But I think you *like* being appreciated by me.'

Faint colour accentuated the sculpted slant of his high cheekbones. 'You are right,' he conceded, sliding down the zip on her dress, burying his mouth in the sensitive skin between her neck and her shoulder and laughing as she gasped at the sensation.

His hands cupped her breasts as her bra fell away, catching each nipple between finger and thumb to tug at the sensitive buds. And then he was turning her over again, addressing his attention to the rest of her with glorious attention to every responsive part of her. She was wet and ready for him, arching as he drove into her with a helpless cry of delight. And the tension buzzing through her entire body reached a swift and breathless height in a hail of sensual excitement and the sweet convulsions sent her straight to sleep afterwards.

Raif shook her gently awake in the dusk light filtering through the light drapes at the window. 'Dinner will be ready for us in thirty minutes.'

'My goodness, how long have I been asleep?' Claire exclaimed, sitting up in a rush.

'Obviously you needed the rest and perhaps I should be a little more careful about overtiring you,' he murmured worriedly.

'No, I'm not listening to talk of that kind on our honeymoon!' Claire covered her ears with expressive hands in emphasis. 'Were you not in the same meeting we had with the obstetrician? It's *normal* for me to be more tired. It's all right for me to sleep more.'

'Got it,' Raif groaned, vaulting upright.

'I'm sorry. I'm just a little…touchy about being pregnant…sometimes,' she mumbled, sliding out of the bed double quick to head for the bathroom because she knew that she was only sensitive about that subject because he had married her purely because she had conceived.

That little awkward moment was forgotten over dinner on one of the terraces. Since Raif had visited the Alpujarra before, he knew the prettiest villages to visit, and plans were made for the next day. He was wearing jeans, and she was convinced that they were entirely for her benefit because they were decidedly new, and she smiled and smiled at the reflection. She listened to him talk with an abstracted expression, admiring the sound of his voice, his lean, strong face, his truly stunning eyes and the length of his lashes, even his gestures once he relaxed and began to use his hands to express himself more.

Yes, she was falling for the guy she'd married, falling head over heels over common sense but there didn't seem to be much she could do about it. And why would she want to change her feelings anyway? After all, they had married for the long haul, not merely to legitimise the birth of their baby son, she reminded herself soothingly. All the same, had she had better control over her emotions she would have chosen to slow down the development of those feelings because that would have been more sensible. Falling madly in love so fast with a guy who loved someone else was kind of scary, because she knew she was leaving herself wide open to being hurt. What if he got bored with her? What if he decided he wasn't happy with her? How would she feel then, when she had already given him her all?

Over the following week, they slowly became inseparable. Raif kept on warning her that he would need to do some work, but he never got to grips with leaving her alone for long enough to accomplish much and Claire had no objections to make. They explored the Moorish ruined castle on the hill, wandered through the picturesque village full of whitewashed houses, a charming little church, and she began to browse handicraft shops obsessively. By the time they had finished touring the local villages, she had become the proud owner of three colourful hand-woven Alpujarra rugs, a couple of baskets and several ceramic items. There was a trip to an artisan chocolatier, a picnic within view of a glorious waterfall, which they had walked to, Raif thankfully keeping any misgivings about the effect of too much exercise on her fecund condition to himself.

And she cooked because he couldn't keep her out of the kitchen, no matter how hard he tried. She made all the dishes she loved, with the added extra of local almonds, figs, honey and cheese.

For their last evening at the villa, Raif had made special plans. He had organised private access to the Alhambra complex. At sunset the ancient Moorish buildings glowed pink. As one of the best surviving historic palaces in the Islamic world, it was of particular interest to Raif, who had visited several times before. There was no need for a tour guide as he showed her around. He explained the irrigation system to her and told her that there was a similar arrangement of aqueducts and water channels in the Old Palace in Quristan. He translated the poetry on the walls for her and then urged her outside again where a table and two chairs awaited them beside a tranquil pool that reflected them like a still mirror.

'We're actually going to dine here?' she exclaimed in sheer wonder, her head turning as a small flamenco group sat down several yards away and began to play evocative Spanish guitar music, the singer's atmospheric voice soaring soulfully into the night air. 'This is amazing, Raif. When did you arrange all this?'

'At the start of the week. I wanted you to have a special memory for our last day,' Raif proffered, shrugging off her astonishment as a meal was served to them by uniformed waiters while their security team fanned round the edges of open space.

'It will be a beautiful memory for ever,' Claire declared, with over-hormonal tears prickling the backs of her eyes, but she was resisting an urge to stand up and hug him, which she knew he would dislike with an audience.

The following day they packed for the return to Barcelona and arrived early evening to a chirpy welcome from Stella and a quieter greeting from Kashif. They dined with the other couple, sat up late over coffee and went to bed in the grand four-poster that still made them laugh.

Someone was banging on the door and a phone was buzzing incessantly somewhere. Claire opened her eyes on complete darkness and knew it was the middle of the night and she experienced that intense sense of something being wrong. It made her fumble to light a bedside lamp and shake Raif awake.

He came awake and was alert much faster than she was. He vaulted straight out of bed to head for the door stark naked.

'Clothes, Raif!' she called, scrambling out of bed to race into the bathroom and yank a towelling robe off the hook and throw it to him. He put it on in haste, knotted the sash and went straight to the door.

She heard Kashif's voice, but he was speaking in their language, not in English. She slid hurriedly out of bed and began rooting for a robe. Then as Raif came back inside, pale, his features oddly tight and expressionless, she decided just by looking at his face to put on clothes instead.

'Something's happened…a car accident in Quristan, family involved. I need to get dressed and go downstairs,' he framed flatly. 'Kashif is breaking the bad news in little nuggets to keep me calm. I know him of old.'

'I'm so sorry, Raif,' Claire whispered. 'What can I do to help?'

'Nothing if what I suspect is true.' He sighed and by that she registered that, apparently, he was already convinced that someone had died. His father? An accident though? From what she understood his father was more likely to pass away from ill health and old age. Her brow furrowing in a frown, she went into her suitcase to find her clothes, choosing trousers and a light top.

She felt as though the world had stopped turning without warning and flung her off into frightening freefall. They had had a wonderful wedding day and an even more incredible week together at the mountain villa. She was happier than she had ever thought to be in her entire life and now she had one of those sixth-sense creeping suspicions that that was all about to fall apart before she could even get to enjoy it. A sense of doom, she registered unhappily. Why wrap it up?

Raif went for a quick shower and emerged to dress, choosing, she noticed, a business suit and a plain white shirt, stuffing a dark tie into one pocket as if he didn't yet have the heart to put it on.

'Shall I come downstairs with you?' Claire asked hesitantly. 'I should.'

'No, this is for me to deal with. I don't want you getting upset about anything,' Raif informed her levelly, his seeming confidence in that necessity overruling every personal feeling.

'I was thinking of you…maybe wanting company,' Claire almost whispered, not knowing how to sensitively say that she was unlikely to get upset on anyone's account but *his* when his family were all strangers to her.

Raif shook his handsome dark head, already walking towards the door, spine rigid, shoulders squared as though he were already preparing himself for the worst possible news.

And tears stung Claire's eyes as the door closed in his wake because she now felt that she had somehow failed in the first duty of being a wife. In such a situation, he needed support as well, but she could hardly force her company on him. Sadly, their marriage was too new for that, and she couldn't afford to make assumptions and push the point because undoubtedly there *were* people who preferred to deal with such matters alone. And it was perfectly possible that her presence would be more of an added stress factor than a comfort because he could never forget for long that she was in a delicate condition, even though she didn't feel the slightest bit delicate.

Ten minutes later, Stella arrived in the sitting room beyond the bedroom with a laden tray, containing tea and snacks, her bubbly personality muted in contrast to her liveliness over dinner the night before. 'I guessed you'd be up and pacing. I would be too,' she said, pursing her lips.

Claire took charge of the tea and poured. 'Do you know—?'

Stella lifted both hands in a negative motion. 'No. No, I don't know who's involved. What I do know is that it's very confidential information, which came direct from the Quristani government, and when it comes to work issues, Kashif is a professional to his fingertips, even with me.'

'I wanted to be with Raif,' Claire admitted then.

Stella leant over and patted her knee consolingly. 'Of course you did, but men are stubborn and proud. Most of them don't do vulnerable if they can avoid it.'

Even though her companion talked good sense, Claire's nerves were leaping up and down inside her like jumping beans. Only good manners kept her seated beside Stella when she wanted to pace the floor and go frantic because she couldn't bear to think of Raif getting bad news without her. Not that she could *change* bad news, she reasoned ruefully, but she did think she could offer relief just by being there for him.

In less than thirty minutes, a knock sounded on the door and Stella departed. A maid entered with a tray of coffee and sandwiches. The food was clearly being delivered in expectation of Raif's reappearance and Claire stood up and finally allowed herself to pace.

There was no fanfare to Raif's return. The door opened quietly and he walked in equally quietly, his lean, strong face as stiff and furiously composed as it had been when he'd left her.

'Was it bad news?' she whispered, still crazily hoping that there had been some kind of melodrama that had got everybody hot and bothered by something that was in reality not as important as it initially seemed.

Raif glanced in her direction, but it was almost as if he didn't really see her well enough to focus on her. She realised then that he was suffering from shock.

'The very worst,' he told her flatly.

'Come and sit down,' Claire urged, tugging his sleeve.

'I can't. The jet's on standby at the airport. I have to fly out to Quristan immediately for…f-for,' he stammered, 'the funerals.'

'You can still have a hot drink and a sandwich before you leave,' she told him firmly.

Like a robot, he dropped down into the armchair closest to him. 'My brothers were travelling through the mountains. As my father's heirs, they are not supposed to travel in the same vehicle, but Kashif tells me that they routinely ignored his edict. There was an avalanche. The car and the security car behind it went off the road into a ravine. Hashir and Waleed, their driver and bodyguards are all dead,' he told her in the same measured tone.

Claire dropped onto her knees by his side and reached for his hand. 'I'm so very sorry,' she muttered, fighting back tears, for even she had not imagined such a terrible tragedy.

Raif squeezed her hand and instantly withdrew his own. His dark eyes shone with tears. 'I never really knew them. Over the years when I visited, I always told myself that there was time to get to know them, but now that future possibility has gone with them.' Swallowing convulsively, Claire bowed her brow against his knee because she knew what those feelings could do to a person. All the years that she was growing up she had made herself believe that once she was an adult, she would manage to build a better relationship with her father, that he would like her more and understand her better once she was mature and settled into her career. Only she hadn't got the chance either when her father had passed away quite suddenly. Disappointed hopes, things done and said or not done and said, all of it piled high on top of grief. Yes, she knew exactly what Raif was feeling and struggling to contain. And the worst fact of all in such situations was that there were rarely good memories to revisit as a consolation.

'I must leave,' Raif breathed abruptly, pushing himself upright again with force. 'My father is in Intensive Care. He had a heart attack when he was told about the death of my brothers. I need to see him.'

'Of course,' she murmured, shaken by that final, additional blow.

She wanted to ask questions, loads of questions about wives and nieces and his father's condition, but she swallowed all those enquiries back because Raif had quite enough on his plate to cope with. 'Can I come with you?'

Raif froze, stunning dark golden eyes unreadable. 'Best not. You can join me when all the formalities are complete but there would be little point in you accompanying me now.'

Two maids arrived to pack for him. His bodyguards hovered in the background. Claire approached Mohsin. 'He hasn't eaten anything. Please make sure he eats.'

'Of course, Your Royal Highness.'

It was the first time she had been addressed by that title and it hugely disconcerted her. Paling, she blinked and stepped away, returning to the bedroom to supervise the packing. In truth, her assistance was not required but it made her feel a little less surplus to requirements.

In too brief a time, Raif was gone, momentarily clasping her to him stiffly, all too aware of their audience in the embassy foyer. 'I'll phone,' he said prosaically.

'We might as well have breakfast,' Stella said brightly as Raif climbed into the waiting limo and it wended its way out of sight, demolishing, it felt like then, all Claire's hopes and dreams. The guy she had married and begun to love was gone and she had never felt more alone or abandoned in her life. 'It's almost dawn. We should eat and then go to bed for a nap.'

All of a sudden, Claire was appreciating that Raif had somehow become all the brightness in her world and that was a frightening truth for a young woman who had once cherished her independence and her strength to manage her life alone.

Stella guided her into the dining room. 'You're in shock as well,' she said gently. 'Eat and then go back to bed.'

'I'm fine. I just didn't like Raif leaving alone to deal with this,' Claire admitted stiffly.

'He wouldn't have a minute to spare you over the next few days. He'll be much too busy,' Stella explained. 'I would imagine that's why he chose not to take you with him.'

'I thought he might want to let me meet his father,' Claire whispered. 'I appreciate it wouldn't be ideal with him in a sick bed *but*—'

Stella was staring at her with a frown. 'Claire... King Jafri is unlikely to be alive this time tomorrow. It was a serious heart attack. The medics don't think he'll make it through—'

'Does Raif know that?'

Stella nodded uncomfortably. 'He should have told you.'

Claire dropped her head, the food on her plate untouched as she sipped doggedly at her tea. 'That's tragic news too,' she whispered shakily. 'He's losing everyone.'

'But not you. Try to eat. I appreciate that it's difficult in your new position, but you need to keep up your strength for the days ahead.'

What new position? Claire blinked and studied her plate, her thoughts on her baby, and she lifted the knife and fork and managed to eat a morsel of egg and toast. Her tummy felt hollow and her brain was all at sea.

'The government is afraid of instability and unrest. King Jafri was a figurehead and, although he wasn't popular, he was an institution,' Stella explained. 'Raif, however, is very popular.'

'He told me that as a third son he was very unimportant in Quristan,' Claire muttered uncomfortably.

Kashif's voice entered the conversation as he dropped down into the seat at the head of the table. 'Even at school when he was acing every exam, Raif was very modest in his attitude towards his own achievements. He's raised millions for Quristan charities. He has worked tirelessly to help the poor and disadvantaged in our country and there is no one who cares more for the place of his birth. He is very highly regarded in Quristan and he will be asked to accept the crown tomorrow.'

'The *crown*?' Claire exclaimed loudly, dragged with a vengeance from her quiet reverie of pride while she was being told that Raif was simply humble and not the wisest judge of his own status.

'Surely you were aware of that?' Stella questioned in surprise. 'It's not as if there is anyone else to take the throne.'

'Didn't his brothers have children, who come first?' Claire almost whispered in her shock at what she was being told.

'Hashir had girls and Waleed had no kids. The line of succession to the throne is determined by the male collateral line,' Kashif informed her.

'I had no idea,' she admitted.

'There is no one else now,' Stella informed her quietly. 'Raif will be King and you will be Queen. Neither of you has a choice.'

'Raif would never turn his back on his duty,' Kashif interposed gently, scanning Claire's ghostly pale face and arrested expression. 'He will need you ten times more tomorrow than he needed you today.'

'Excuse me…' Claire could feel that single morsel of toast rising back as nausea threatened to overcome her and she scrambled in haste from the chair and fled back upstairs to the privacy of the bathroom.

Afterwards, she looked at her wan, perspiring face in the mirror. No potential queen could ever have looked rougher, she reflected sickly. A king and a queen? It was as if the world around her had gone insane. Claire was overwhelmed with panic and the sheer impossibility of her ever being able to live up to such a role…or Raif even thinking for one moment that she was good enough for the challenge. My goodness, had ever a guy had *greater* cause to regret his hasty marriage?

CHAPTER SEVEN

CLAIRE ENDEAVOURED TO relax on the sundeck of the *Mahnoor*, only that was impossible with her audience.

It was no longer possible for her to be alone, it seemed. Government-appointed bodyguards had arrived to team up with the security squad Raif had already cursed her with. Her apparent rise in status, announced only by the sound of the crew referring copiously to her as 'Your Majesty', had been unaccompanied by any warning or, indeed, explanation from her married-in-haste husband, the new *King* of Quristan.

It had been announced on the television news, as well as the speculation that the new Queen was of British extraction, so on that basis she assumed it was true and she had been miraculously promoted to being royal even though she knew that she was manifestly unsuitable for such a role. She was an assistant chef, for goodness' sake, only accidentally lifted to the lofty heights of royalty by the conception of their son!

When Claire had left the embassy in Barcelona, having been informed that the *Mahnoor* was in port awaiting her arrival, the quay had been packed with paparazzi, shouting questions and waving cameras but she had been swept on board by her team with all the smooth inaccessibility required by a celebrity accustomed to such limelight and avoiding it. Unfortunately, that level of public attention was so great a shock to Claire's system that it utterly unnerved her.

The first morning, Gregoire had arrived to personally give her a breakfast of eggs Benedict in her bed because he knew it was her favourite treat. That had been a sufficient surprise, particularly when he'd beamed at her and offered his congratulations on her marriage. Captain Hastings had followed later that day, proffering the good wishes of the whole crew for her future happiness. In fact, onboard the yacht, everyone seemed totally happy for her and Raif, not even hinting that she was as unbefitting as she knew herself to be, and that had amazed her.

Raif, however, had neglected to surprise her, finally getting in touch two long days after the event to inform her that his father had died, having only briefly regained consciousness during his vigil by the older man's bedside.

'And now you're a king!' she had pointed out almost aggressively.

And Raif had hummed and hahed, as if that small fact weren't of any real importance in the current state of chaos, and he had dared to ask her instead and repeatedly how *she* was! He had buried three of his estranged family members in succession and gained a crown and, incredibly, he was acting as though it were just another day at the office!

'I *can't* be a queen!' she had warned him straight away. 'I'm just not cut out for that sort of thing.'

'Neither am I,' Raif had countered levelly. 'But sometimes we have to do what we have to do and take the rough with the smooth.'

He was good at platitudes, not so good at dealing with the crux of an issue, she acknowledged unhappily. He hadn't taken her response seriously because, typically hugging his personal feelings to himself, he was busy acting as if everything were absolutely normal. How was she supposed to deal with that? How was any ordinary woman supposed to respond to being raised without warning to such elevated status in a country she had never even visited? And how could she baldly admit that she didn't want any of it?

Was he even considering those facts? That she didn't speak the language or know the culture or the history or even the smallest thing useful for such a position? She had tried to get those points across but he hadn't been listening. Indeed, in Claire's opinion, he had stubbornly *refused* to listen to her perfectly valid points. And he had completed that piece of male idiocy by simply telling her that she would be picked up by helicopter the next morning before the yacht sailed into British waters.

It was not that Raif was dense about everything like other men she had met, Claire conceded, feeling guilty over her critical thoughts. When she had returned to the yacht to occupy the giant stateroom that was Raif's she had found it complete with the biggest cat tree and most luxurious cubby cat bed in existence.

Circe, now restored to her mistress, was living life to the manner born. She was back to roaming the boat with her cast, restrictive head collar and a forlorn look of cat martyrdom that ensured she received loads of sympathetic attention and every treat available. And at night, her pet curled up in a cosy bed lined with fur. So, Raif had thought about her cat's needs in spite of his family losses and sudden gaining of a throne and it was just a shame that he preferred not to address his wife's feelings or needs about those same developments.

Raif sprang out of the helicopter and strode for his bride's hiding place, apparently the rarely used private sun deck attached to their stateroom. He knew that courtesy of Mohsin, who at his instigation had remained in Spain to watch over Claire. He reckoned that even the bodyguard had registered that Claire was freaking out at the prospect of what lay ahead of her because she had not left the owner's suite since she had boarded.

Raif had been surrounded on all sides by people advising him that he shouldn't leave the country again so soon after arriving and certainly not while still in official mourning. He had defied all that unwelcome advice. He was too well aware of what he had to do to even listen to their strictures. He was not his father, chary of foreign travel and change of all kinds. He was not afraid to be different and he could not afford to be. He was willing to sacrifice a lot to be the monarch Quristan required but he was *not* willing to risk losing his wife.

Claire was in the stateroom staring at all the suitcases that had been packed for her while she was out on deck with her book. What a coward she was, she thought painfully. She had not flat out told Raif that she *wasn't* planning to fly out to Quristan. She had texted him and merely said that she wasn't ready to travel…*yet* being the optimum word included because she didn't have the guts to tell him that their imprudent marriage was surely over and that he should get a divorce in the pipeline as soon as possible. After all, in such circumstances, what else could they do? Neither one of them had even considered that such tragedies could occur and radically change the whole landscape of their lives.

She moved out to the sun deck to return to the book she was reading. It had been a relief to discover that most of Raif's books were in English. She had been reading about the history of Quristan, which seemed to her to relate to constant fierce fights between varying tribes right up until his father had assumed the throne. Since those long-ago days, however, democracy had arrived and peace and prosperity had settled in for most of the kingdom.

'Claire…?'

She spun round in disbelief when she heard Raif's familiar drawl. And there he stood, sheathed in a tailored suit as was his wont and indisputably looking totally, utterly breathtaking in his gorgeousness. Olive skin, cropped black hair, stunning bone structure…not to mention his lithe and muscular physique. Dazzling dark golden eyes held hers fast for several seconds and she was literally pinned to the spot. Her heartbeat sped up, her nipples tightening into taut buds, her complexion flushed as she approached the patio doors where he stood. 'We need to talk,' she semi-whispered, woefully aware of all the listening ears around them.

'Yes,' Raif agreed in the mildest of tones as he guided her indoors again where at least they would have privacy.

He rammed the sliding door back into place and turned. Lean, strong face bland, he reacted to the knock on the stateroom door by crossing the room to answer it. A crewman entered with a luggage trolley and began to pile on her cases. Claire froze, bit her lower lip and waited until the trolley had exited again before murmuring flatly, 'I wasn't expecting you to make a personal visit.'

'I would guess not,' Raif conceded with the shadowy edge of an unexpectedly sardonic smile that tugged at the corners of his compressed lips.

'But it won't change anything,' she declared baldly, mustering her arguments while refusing to look at him any longer. 'I'm not returning to Quristan with you. I'm planning to return to London and let you get on with a divorce. As short-lived as our marriage has been, I shouldn't think it would take long to wipe it out again. We could even lie and say the marriage wasn't consummated and have it dissolved.'

Raif marvelled at her naivety, considering that she was pregnant with *his* child. But he was simultaneously appalled by how much her outlook had changed in the space of a handful of days. In little more than a week and a half, he had been condemned and found wanting by a woman who didn't think enough of herself to even contemplate that she could be his queen. That in itself was the bigger sin, but, as he recognised the same weakness in himself, he was unwilling to allow it to destroy their future. He could only see his future as being with her, the two of them *together*. They were a couple, stronger with each other than without, and as a family they would face and handle any and all difficulties that might threaten them.

'You're full of inventive ideas,' he remarked.

Claire stiffened, braced her hands on her hips in what she hoped was a pose guaranteed to emphasise her strength of purpose. 'Let's face it… I'm not queen material.'

'It's a personal opinion, of course,' Raif breathed, studying the picture she made in a flowing turquoise sundress that highlighted her anxious blue eyes, guiltily conscious of the all too ready quickening at his groin and the incipient throb of arousal. 'But I believe you'll make an amazing queen. You're down to earth, practical and normally steady under stress. Everything that makes you efficient in catering will make you perfect to stand by my side.'

Her troubled eyes opened very wide. 'That's ridiculous, Raif,' she told him with deep conviction. 'Queens are all about women who wear silk and fabulous tiaras! Have you looked at your late mother's jewellery?'

Hearing the edge of panic in her voice, Raif merely laughed with genuine appreciation. 'Claire, my mother was Queen in another era, for a generation long buried. Luckily, the world has changed and moved on. You are a working woman with a career and that is much more relatable to our people. A social butterfly like my mother, only seen on ceremonial occasions wearing that fabulous jewellery, would be much less admired and desirable these days.'

'I disagree,' Claire declared firmly as he strode past her to let Circe enter through the sun-deck glass door and join them. *Her* pet that proceeded to fawn at *his* feet in the most embarrassing way.

'Circe was born to be a royal cat,' Raif pointed out cheerfully. 'She just knows she's a queen and dares us all to treat her any other way. Our leading newspaper has asked permission to develop a cartoon around her. I suspect that Circe has the chops to become much more famous than either of us.'

'A *cartoon*?' Claire gasped incredulously. 'But how does anyone even *know* that I own a cat?'

'You can blame me for that. I have provided certain facts about you, that you're an English chef and you have a cat,' he admitted levelly. 'I'm very proud of my wife. She's strong and beautiful and she has her feet on the ground like a contemporary queen should have.'

Losing colour at those disconcerting assurances, Claire became very tense, the weight of his expectations bearing down on her and feeling like a judgement rather than a vote of confidence. 'Look, we're not going to agree about this. You think I can do it. I know I *can't*. There's no room for a compromise there.'

Another knock sounded on the door. On the way to answer it, Raif scooped up Circe and went out into the corridor with her. A dim exchange of voices was heard. Claire frowned but stayed where she was until he reappeared. 'What have you done with my cat?'

'Oh, she's all set for the palace. Has no doubts whatsoever regarding her future,' Raif told her airily. 'So, this is as close as I will ever come to blackmail. The cat's coming to Quristan. Will you come too?'

'For goodness' sake!' Claire spluttered, torn between anger and amusement at that move. 'Raif…'

'Are you really prepared to give up what we have together?'

Claire got flustered. 'It's not fair to ask me that. These are very, very unusual circumstances. We got married and it was ordinary—'

'And now we have the opportunity to make our marriage *extraordinary*,' Raif sliced in with fierce determination. 'You're prepared to give up without even trying to make it work with me?'

'Stop making it all sound like it's simple!' Claire wailed accusingly. 'You were like that on the phone when you called…acting like everything was still the same.'

'Between you and me, it *should* be the same,' Raif stated with uncompromising confidence. 'Nothing else should matter but you and me and our son. Nothing should come between us.'

'I *can't* do it!' she exclaimed in a pained rush.

'But giving up without even giving it a go is cowardice.'

'That's a low blow.'

'But it's the truth. If I let you go, will you look back on this decision as something you're proud of...or will you always wonder what might have been?'

Tears stung her eyes like mad. She was furious with him. He had confronted her with so many unanswerable questions. He had warned her that fear of the unknown shouldn't be allowed to influence such a major decision. Unmistakeably, he was telling her the truth and how could she fault a man for telling her the truth, no matter how little she wished to hear it?

'Claire, be reasonable,' he murmured levelly. 'You're my wife. You're carrying my son. I value what we have. I want you to remain a part of my life.'

'Shut up!' she condemned on the back of a sob, no longer convinced that she could take the path she had planned. When push came to shove, actually walking away from Raif felt comparable to sticking a knife in her own chest and she had never been of a self-destructive bent.

'I need you to keep me level,' Raif breathed in a raw undertone. 'Absolutely nobody will tell me to shut up now.'

'I just can't do it!' she exclaimed, stricken, tears choking her. 'I'm not good enough or clever enough to be a queen...even for you!'

'I understand,' Raif murmured flatly, walking back

to the door, propping it open with the holder. 'I *do* understand but I can't let you make this decision for us both.'

'What does that mean?' Claire whispered tearfully.

'That sometimes fate needs a bloody good push!' Raif intoned as he swung her up into his arms and locked her in place over one powerful shoulder.

'What on earth are you doing?'

'I believe I'm abducting you. I'd be grateful if you didn't scream, but even if you scream blue murder I'm *still* abducting you.'

Two small fists struck his back in concert. 'You have to be joking!' she launched back as he strode out into the corridor and straight up the steps to the top deck and the helipad.

'I never joke about serious stuff…and this *is* serious,' Raif pointed out almost conversationally.

'Raif…put me down! You *can't* do this!'

'International waters? King? I think I'll get away with it,' Raif quipped as he strode to the helipad and very carefully lifted her again to stow her into the helicopter as if she were made of impossibly delicate glass that might shatter.

Since there was absolutely no point in trying to argue above the noise of the helicopter, Claire donned her protective headphones, gritted her teeth and stared into the distance until it was time to get out at the airport. On arrival, they immediately crossed the tarmac to board the private jet awaiting them and she didn't fancy throwing a scene in front of the assembled air crew stationed at the foot of the boarding steps. Flanked by bodyguards, they boarded the jet.

Facial muscles tight as highly strung wires, Claire dropped straight down into an opulently upholstered tan leather seat and buckled in, her temper like a sharpened razor because Raif had no right, no right whatsoever, to force her into doing what she did not want to do. And she didn't care whether or not that was craven, *did she*? Her husband had kidnapped her to make her do his bidding and that was unpardonable. She simmered like a pot of oil over a fire as the bodyguards left the main cabin to settle into the rear one and the jet prepared for take-off.

'Claire...?'

'I'm not speaking to you,' she told him, even though she knew that she was too mad to keep her feelings locked up tight and would inevitably speak to him.

'This way, we get a chance to see if we can still work,' Raif breathed tautly. 'Your way? We would have no chance at all. I couldn't accept that.'

'*My* way had advantages. I could have slipped off the stage of your new life as if I'd never been there in the first place,' Claire protested vehemently. 'If you have not been seen in public with me it could have been done *quietly* and the divorce could surely have been achieved discreetly as well.'

'How quiet and discreet do you expect me to be while you steal my son from me?'

Claire's mouth fell open in shock at that response. '*Steal*?'

'What else do you call it? You leave and my son goes with you?'

'For goodness' sake, he's not even born yet!' Claire proclaimed, ramming loose her seat belt to stand up now that the jet was airborne.

Raif subjected her to a fulminating appraisal. 'Yes, I would in all probability miss out on his birth as well, as divorced couples are unlikely to share such an event. I would also miss out on a great deal more. I will not be free to travel whenever I like and, since I assume you would plan to base yourself in the UK, I could at best hope to be only an occasional caller in my son's life. That is unacceptable to me.'

Claire was outraged by his raising of perfectly valid points that she had not considered. Maybe it was a sign of her lack of future vision, she thought furiously, but her infant son was only a passenger in her life at present and she was not already thinking of his birth and his life beyond that. 'You're not being reasonable!' she condemned, already terribly afraid that *she* was the one being unreasonable.

'You're only just realising that after I abducted you?' Raif came back at her drily as he too rose to his feet. 'I will not be reasonable, as you call it, when you're threatening to deprive our son of a father. I *had* no father! He was a man in the distance in a crowd and we never got any closer than that. That was the result of a divorce. Divorce can only be a bad word in my vocabulary!'

Claire was thoroughly disconcerted by the anger

Raif was no longer striving to hide. His caramel-gold eyes were bright with annoyance, his lean, strong face set into hard lines. Suddenly she was being bombarded by undeniable facts.

'I felt it was too soon to be thinking of our child,' she muttered unevenly. 'I'm sorry about that. I should have considered the effect of a divorce on your access to him.'

'You should also keep in your mind,' Raif murmured dulcetly, 'that that little boy will be Crown Prince of Quristan from the moment he is born. That is his birth-right, his heritage, and his path now.'

Claire lost colour and sank back heavily into her seat because once again that was a reality that had not entered her head and she was deeply embarrassed by her failure to identify that fact.

Raif sat back down again as well. 'Being in the palace now is a *very* steep learning curve for me, Claire, because I didn't grow up there and I wasn't trained for my role. There are strange traditions to be respected, ceremonies that I am unversed in. Growing up in the UK deprived me of more than I appreciated at the time. My summers with my great-uncle in the desert were not quite as educational as I once naively assumed,' he concluded grimly.

As the awful silence fell, smouldering with unhappy, dissatisfied undertones, Claire was cut to the bone with mortification. She swallowed hard. How could she not have thought of their child's needs or their child's future in Quristan? And yet she hadn't, probably because all that seemed too distant while also being utterly unfamiliar to her. She was someone who took a broad view of events, not a detached, detailed view. But she was very much shaken by Raif's bitter admission that even as the King he was struggling to find his path at the palace because he had not been raised with that background. He was working to fit in. She recognised that trait in him: if he failed at something, he would probably just work harder and he would blame himself for any mistakes or omissions.

And where did such a sterling character trait leave her in comparison? She had been ready to run in fear and panic, ready to turn her back on the new and unfamiliar without even taking account of her son's needs or giving their new life a chance. She hadn't thought that far ahead, she excused herself unhappily. But the lowering truth was that Raif *was* thinking that far ahead and already foreseeing the pitfalls of a divorce because he had grown up with separated parents and a father he had never got to know.

Raif glanced at her, his amazing black-lashed tortoiseshell eyes calm again. 'I haven't been fair to you, but I couldn't let you and our child leave me like that.'

Moisture was prickling at the backs of her eyes and she nodded stiffly. 'I hadn't thought everything through. I was panicking.'

'I know. I too am still finding my way in this role, and I will be for some time,' he admitted in a harsh undertone. 'But people are depending on me to succeed, and I will do the best I can.'

All of a sudden, she wanted to grab his hand, do something physical to show him that she truly understood, but she couldn't reach him where he sat on the other side of the aisle and clasped her hands together tightly instead. 'I'll give it a go,' she promised abruptly. 'But my best… I warn you…may not be good enough.'

'I only ask that you *try*. Give us some time in which to adapt to these changes,' he urged.

'I'm sorry you had to abduct me,' she told him in all seriousness. 'But in a way, I sort of enjoyed it too…'

Raif gazed back at her in wonderment and then he threw back his head and laughed with huge appreciation. 'This is why I wanted you back, Claire. I haven't laughed once since I last saw you.'

'You haven't had anything to laugh about.' She sighed.

Raif studied her from below drowsy lashes. He was so tired. Indeed, he had never been more tired in his life. The funerals, his father's passing as well as certain painful facts he had learned in recent days, not to mention the demands on his time and understanding, had all combined to plunge him into exhaustion. The prospect of Claire leaving his life, however, had galvanised him into a level of aggressive action he could barely credit in the aftermath. But now she was here with him. Claire *and* his child. Relief was slowly filtering through him, pushing out the tension that had filled him with stolen energy. His sensible queen…his sensible, sexy queen… A dim smile formed on his expressive lips before he fell asleep.

The door at the far end of the cabin opened a crack and Circe prowled into view, set free from her carrier. Claire lifted her pet onto her lap and stroked her. Tea was brought and sandwiches and a bunch of fashion magazines she had not the faintest interest in when she was about to start searching out maternity wear. She watched Raif sleep, his bronzed features smoothed out by rest, making him look younger. But he would rise to the challenges ahead of him…and now she was committed to rising to those same challenges because she loved him to bits. How could she ever have convinced herself that she would be able to walk away from him?

CHAPTER EIGHT

THEY ARRIVED IN Quristan without fanfare.

Kazan, the capital city, also had the main airport. Within minutes they were tucked into an SUV with dark windows and, with a cavalcade of security in attendance, driven through the city. It was a much more urban contemporary landscape than Claire had naively expected, for the skies were full of towering skyscrapers, including several obvious city landmarks, which were of architectural significance.

'My father hated all this development but there wasn't anything he could do about it,' Raif told her wryly. 'We were not greeted by journalists when we landed because early in his reign my father imposed draconian rules on the media.'

'Why?'

Raif grimaced. 'When he was a young man in Spain, there was that scandal with the young woman, and he blamed the media for it. He was very shaken up and determined to ensure that such a thing never happened to him or the family again. It made him very controlling in his behaviour. Now, of course, the government wants the media restraints loosened. In fact, the government pretty much wants to roll back everything my father supported to prevent Quristan from joining the rest of the modern world. But they will have to do it slowly to keep the traditionalists happy.'

'And where do you stand?' Claire asked, turning back from an appreciative scrutiny of a gleaming shopping mall and the cleanliness of the street.

'In the middle ground. I'm fresh to all this and I have to learn and listen more than direct, which is hard. I've been my own boss for too long,' he reflected. 'But I can utilise my experience in business and development, which is good.'

The palace was a vast hotchpotch of stone buildings set in the desert beyond the city. Surrounded by tall stone walls, it resembled a fortress more than a palace until the SUV pulled through the gates and she glimpsed the greenery, fountains and shaded pathways within the enclosure.

'It looks medieval.'

'It is at its core but since the onslaught of my father's second wife it rejoices in every modern comfort on the market. It's more like a hotel than a home. The staff quarters, however, are shockingly poor and the kitchens are hundreds of years behind the times. You are free to make improvements.'

'Me?' she exclaimed in surprise.

'You must certainly know how to modernise a kitchen and utilise health and safety rules to make improvements. As for our future home, you may consult with the builders I've brought in.'

'I thought this was our future home?'

'My father's private quarters belong in a museum.'

'With the Count Dracula bed?' she asked with a wince of dismay.

Raif nodded confirmation. 'Every room in his wing is like that. Very ornate, grand and dark. He didn't allow my mother's replacement wife to change anything there. It's not where I want to spend my down time, and eventually I would like to open that part of the palace to the public, so it must be left as it is.'

'Then where do we live?'

'In the old section of the palace. It's a massive building. Every generation extended it,' he explained, handing her out of the vehicle with care. 'Our staff are waiting inside to welcome us.'

A huge throng of people awaited them indoors. And indoors was totally unexpected. The foyer rejoiced in all the opulence of an exclusive hotel, which Raif had mentioned, and he had hit that luxurious but soulless note right on target in his description. There was no character, nothing to ground the reality that it was the royal palace of Quristan. Claire moved forward to accept introductions but there so many faces and so many job titles, she knew she would have to learn them at a slower pace. Shahbaz, the head of household, she would remember for his carefully coiffed grey hair and moustache, but other faces were not so easy to commit to memory.

'Now come and meet my uncle, Prince Umar. He's my mother's little brother,' Raif informed her fondly.

He was a small, rotund man with white hair and a white beard and, with a twinkle in his kind dark eyes as he greeted her, he bore a striking resemblance to Santa Claus. He turned his head to call someone and a slender brunette in a black dress stepped forward with a rather anxious smile as though she were intimidated either by her surroundings or the company.

'Your Majesty,' she said breathlessly, bowing her head to Raif.

For a split second, Raif seemed frozen in place by surprise and then a stiff smile slowly crossed his face. 'Nahla, how are you?' he said, before turning to Claire to say, 'This is Nahla, my uncle's ward.'

'Nahla needs occupation,' his uncle announced cheerfully. 'And I thought work at the palace would be perfect for her now that she and the girls are living with me.'

'You're living with my uncle again?' Raif queried with a frown.

'Since my husband died, yes,' Nahla said uncomfortably. 'I'm sorry, I thought you would have heard but then how would you have? It's been some time since your last real visit.'

'Nahla, go and chat to my wife,' Umar instructed. 'I'll explain in private, Raif.'

Raif moved on to greet someone else, a light hand at Claire's spine carrying her along. 'What's the secrecy about?' she whispered.

'I don't know,' he said in a curiously flat voice. 'I've known Nahla since I was a teenager. My uncle and aunt had only one child, a daughter. She died tragically young and when Nahla was orphaned, they took her in because she was their daughter's best friend. She married straight out of school to a much older man. I didn't realise he'd died.'

'And she has children?'

'Two or three. I'm not quite sure how many,' Raif admitted wryly. 'They'd be at school by now, I would think.'

As Raif was cornered by an older man with an air of importance, his uncle appeared at Claire's elbow. 'I was hoping that Nahla might find favour with *you*,' he stressed in a hopeful undertone. 'She could be a big help to you here. She speaks your language and would be a good guide.'

'Of course,' Claire agreed, not really knowing what else to say, but it scarcely needed to be said that Claire was an uninformed complete beginner in the royal family. She would need advice on who was who and how to behave and all sorts of things. In fact, her head just spun at the prospect of all that she had still to learn about Quristan, the Quristani people and her new role.

'Thank you,' he said, as though she had given him a promise when she had not.

Raif returned to her side to usher her into a lift concealed by fancy panelling. 'Let me show you where we will be living for the present.'

'You mean, there's going to be more than one move?'

Raif dealt her an apologetic appraisal. 'Possibly. It depends how much you like the building that I've chosen and if you can tolerate living in the middle of a construction site.'

Claire laughed. 'Will it be that bad?'

They emerged from the lift into a huge airy space. 'This is the entrance hall, and we will have three floors of rooms,' he explained with enthusiasm. 'You will be relieved to hear that the bathrooms have already been installed.'

Claire nodded slowly and almost laughed again. Yes, she would have been loud in her complaints without those facilities. It occurred to her that engaging in the renovation of their living quarters had inspired Raif with a lighter mood than she had seen him show since the combined tragedy that had deprived him of his brothers and his father. Of course, design and development were crucial elements of his property empire, she reminded herself, so it was hardly surprising that he should relax within a familiar field.

She remained mostly silent while he showed her round incredibly grand large rooms being stripped down to their antique bones to preserve the character. In every room, workmen downed tools and bowed with extreme formality. Raif, evidently, had a vision, but when he stopped in the most massive space she had ever seen in a property and told her that it would be their bedroom her eyes widened. 'Why so big?'

'Because we're sharing it.'

'Well, of course, we're going to share,' she muttered.

'But that's not the norm in the palace,' Raif explained with his sudden flashing smile. 'According to

Shahbaz, no previous ruler has shared a bedroom with his spouse. Partly because you will need a maid to look after your wardrobe and I will need a valet and that entails separate dressing areas, therefore we shall need a very big space to cover those necessities.'

Claire couldn't imagine having a maid merely to preside over her clothes and she simply nodded as though she understood, because she could not even imagine Raif sleeping in another bedroom, or, at least, she didn't want to even picture such an arrangement and the loss of intimacy that would result. She suspected that their bedroom would be the only place where they got to be genuinely alone, which was rather an intimidating acknowledgement. He showed her into the bedroom that he was currently occupying and her heart, which had been sinking on that last thought, lifted at a glimpse of familiar items.

As she paused to absently stroke the back of a carved wooden brush on a dresser, Raif's phone buzzed and he checked it with a frown.

'I must return to the ground floor,' he said simply. 'There are people awaiting my reappearance. I should make the effort to speak to them.'

Claire connected with his brilliant dark golden eyes and a tingle ran over her entire skin surface. That was the effect Raif always had on her. Sometimes it felt like touching a live wire, an electric surge of energy that flared through her whole body, awakening every intimate nerve cell. Her breasts felt full, the core of her pulsing, sending colour to flare over her cheekbones.

Raif studied her with flaring intensity and paced forward. 'I do not want to leave you here alone.'

'I will be fine,' Claire told him more calmly than she felt, reckoning that their future would be full of such moments. He would always be carrying the burden of large expectations. She was an adjunct as his queen, not a leading light. She couldn't step in for him, she could only offer the support of understanding.

'I'll order tea for you,' he told her. 'The room next door is a sitting room and furnished…' A groan escaped him and he drove his fingers through his thick black hair in a gesture of frustration and embarrassment. 'That I should tell you that it is *furnished* as though that were some kind of consolation.'

'Raif…' Claire lifted her hand and stretched up to tidy his hair again. 'Stop worrying about me. I'm good at managing and at being independent.'

'Yes, *but*—'

'No buts,' she declared cheerfully. 'You didn't marry a woman who needs you hovering over her every minute of the day. I'm not helpless.'

And then he was gone, and she swallowed back the thickness in her throat and walked to the room next door. A few minutes later an older woman arrived with a tray, and she was in the act of pouring a cup of tea when a knock sounded on the ajar door.

'Yes?' she called.

Nahla appeared on the threshold. 'I'm so sorry to disturb you, Your Majesty,' she murmured tautly. 'But I wanted to apologise for my uncle's behaviour.'

'Please come in and sit down,' Claire suggested, seeing the brightness of tears in the delicate brunette's eyes and marvelling that she could look so sad without losing an atom of her soulful beauty. 'Prince Umar didn't say anything which could have caused offence,' she declared calmly.

Nahla sat down awkwardly opposite. 'But he is downstairs now cornering your husband. He will list my recent…er misfortunes and attempt to push Raif into hiring me onto the household staff. It is very trying, and I can assure you that I am *not* expecting you to employ me. I have no special skills to offer. I have only been a wife and a mother since I left school. I know little about the world beyond our borders. But now I'm a widow, even worse, the widow of a bankrupt, and those facts are a social embarrassment to my uncle and aunt.'

'And you and your children live with them,' Claire recalled quietly. 'That must be awkward.'

Nahla flushed. 'They have been very good to me. Please believe that I am not complaining. But my uncle can be too insistent in his requests without meaning to be and once he gets an idea in his head, he is very stubborn.'

Claire offered her tea and let her talk, recognising that she was distressed. Nahla had gone through depression and a nervous breakdown after losing the husband she described as her soulmate and the loss of the business that had supported her family had been an additional blow.

'You speak terrific English,' Claire remarked.

Nahla smiled. 'I attended an English school up until my parents died.'

'And you speak the language here and know the culture and presumably many of Quristan's VIPs,' Claire commented as Nahla nodded in understated confirmation. 'Well, then, I would like to offer you a job. I need someone to interpret Quristani life for me. Raif will be too busy to help me much.'

It took quite a bit of convincing for Nahla to be persuaded that she could be of help. The other woman had a low estimate of her own abilities and clearly felt both uneducated and insufficiently well-travelled to suit such a role. But Claire had taken a liking to her and knew that she would much prefer someone sincere and unassuming like Nahla to some polished court official who might well make *her* feel inadequate.

An hour later as Raif returned to his private wing of the palace he was inwardly celebrating the fact that he had successfully and with great tact derailed his uncle's hope of palming Nahla off on the royal household. The very last thing he needed was daily exposure to the woman he had fallen in love with as a teenager, and it would be horribly inappropriate for her to work for his wife. His loyalties had changed, he recognised with wry acceptance. Once he would have done anything to aid Nahla, and, indeed, she had his full sympathies in her current plight. However, Claire was his wife and the future mother of his son and his strongest loyalty now belonged to her…

CHAPTER NINE

CLAIRE WAS FEELING mightily pleased with herself by the time evening fell. She had been very busy, and she loved being busy.

She had got on with Nahla like a house on fire. Only Nahla would have stepped straight into the job of acting as Claire's guide and interpreter the same day that she accepted the position. Claire had fully explored the section of the palace that was to be their home and decided where she wanted certain things and, there being no shortage of either rooms or space, it had been a most enjoyable enterprise. Of course, over dinner she would have to run her ideas past Raif first and gauge his reaction.

After reaching those decisions, she had asked Nahla to escort her down to the palace kitchen and conditions down there in the string of basement rooms that acted as the palace kitchens had horrified her. Shahbaz, the head of household, had joined them and waxed lyrical in his agreement that something had to be done to renovate those dark medieval caves.

Nahla had contrived to find them a table and chairs for a room that could act as a dining room for her and

Raif in the short term. Thanks to Nahla's presence, she had even been able to tell the chef in the basement what sort of food Raif liked to eat. Who knew better than his former assistant chef on board his yacht?

Raif was emerging from the shower, wrapped in a towel, when she arrived equally bare to take advantage of the same facility. 'Thrills on top of thrills, wife,' he teased, catching her straight into his arms.

'I'm all hot and sweaty,' she lamented.

'I'm not that choosy after so many days without you,' he admitted thickly.

Claire hardened her heart against the onslaught of smouldering caramel eyes of gold. 'Well, I *am*. You have to wait for me to feel clean.'

And Raif laughed, utterly charmed by her as always. Her frank nature enchanted him. There was nothing hidden, no secret tripwires, no manipulation. Following an exhausting afternoon, delicately treading round the government officials besetting him with demands, hopes and persuasions on matters on which he needed to remain neutral, her open natural response to him was as precious as water in the desert to him.

'I will wait,' he murmured softly, nudging her hair back from her neck to plunge his long fingers into the thick golden strands and claim a single scorching kiss that lit her up in a starburst of sensation from the top of her head to the soles of her feet.

Still tingling, Claire laughed and stepped straight into the shower, happiness humming through her in a sensual wave. Forty minutes later, they sat down together at the new dining table. 'Where on earth did you get it from? I've been eating off trays and at my desk,' Raif confided.

'I couldn't have done it without Nahla, and I don't know where she got the set from. I didn't ask.' For a moment, Claire looked comically guilty. 'Oh, my goodness, I hope some other couple aren't sitting with trays now just because we get first dibs on stuff as King and Queen!'

Raif, however, didn't laugh, indeed didn't even look amused. 'Nahla?' he queried, his brows pleating in confusion. 'Nahla who?'

'You know her!' Claire quipped. 'Your uncle's ward. He was so pushy about me giving her a job.'

'I've dealt with that. You don't need to worry about hiring her,' Raif informed her stiffly. 'Umar can be too demanding.'

'Well, that doesn't matter,' Claire assured him hastily, worried that she had offended him by being too outspoken about the uncle she knew he was fond of. 'Nahla was worried that he had been rude, and she called up here to apologise and explain that she wasn't expecting to work for me.'

'That's good.' The tense set of Raif's broad shoulders relaxed a little as the first course arrived at the table and then his speech became constrained again. 'Working as your assistant would be viewed as a plum job in the palace hierarchy. It is wiser that such a position does not go to my royal uncle's ward. It could look like nepotism.'

Claire grimaced. 'Oh, dear,' she breathed in consternation. 'I hired her on the spot—'

'You did...*what*?' Raif demanded in a tone she had never heard from him before. It was both angry and disbelieving and his dark golden eyes had flared like metallic storm warnings.

'I'm sorry, Raif...if you don't approve,' Claire tacked on uncomfortably, taken aback by his annoyance. 'I should've consulted you first. I can see that now but at the time I just liked her and she does seem to be a genuinely nice person.'

Raif's lean, darkly handsome features were rigid. 'I have never heard a bad word spoken of her and she is, certainly, having a difficult time at the moment. My uncle filled me in on her late husband's bankruptcy and all the rest of it. Many of my uncle's friends lost money when the business collapsed, and it is difficult for them to have Nahla and her children in their home at present.'

'But that's not *her* fault!' Claire exclaimed.

'Of course not,' he agreed, relieving her of her fear that he had no compassion for Nahla's plight. 'And that bad feeling and embarrassment will ebb eventually, but Umar is not a patient man, and he is well aware that working at the palace would restore Nahla's reputation.'

'Will it?' Claire grinned at that assurance. 'Well, thank goodness I picked her, then. I *really* like her, Raif.'

Raif gritted his even white teeth behind a resolute smile. 'Yes, I am getting that message.'

'So, it's okay, then? Even if some people say that her getting the job is royal nepotism at work?'

'It will have to be,' Raif conceded, long brown fingers flexing round his knife and fork as he finally lifted them to begin eating. 'You can hardly go back on your word.'

'She felt like a best friend, and I miss Lottie, so it was lovely feeling as though I have a friend here where everything is different,' Claire framed in a rush.

'When we have settled in, when we no longer have to borrow or steal a dining table…' His tension ebbing because he could recognise a *fait accompli* when it happened and accept the inevitable, he continued, 'You'll be able to invite your friend, Lottie, and her family to visit once we have a few more rooms available for use here.'

The speed and brightness of Claire's happy smile at that news was his reward. Claire liked Nahla, Raif conceded ruefully. At this point, it seemed wiser to retain his secret than to tell the unfortunate truth, bearing in mind that Claire had strictly warned him *never* to tell her the name of the woman he loved. And perhaps it would be good for him, he reflected ruefully. Perhaps he could finally put those feelings behind him where they belonged, now that the woman he had once obsessed over and rarely seen would be around him occasionally. In all honesty, he didn't *want* to tell Claire that secret, he acknowledged, not if it might hurt or upset her. He felt quite sick at the idea of Claire being hurt in any way…and especially over anything for which he was responsible.

'I explored this whole bit of the palace this afternoon and I've had some ideas.'

Claire wanted a small kitchen installed for her own use and Raif almost laughed when she asked if that would be achievable. 'Anything you want is possible,' he assured her levelly. 'This place must feel like your home as well for you to be content here.'

'And I picked a room for the baby, just across the corridor from what will ultimately be our bedroom,' she warned him. 'I'll want to choose the decoration myself.'

Raif grinned, amused that she could think such simple normal requests could be out of order. 'I want to contribute my ideas too—'

'Well, I don't want it all blue just because he's a boy. That's kind of a dated approach.'

'My father was truly full of joy when I told him we were having a boy,' Raif informed her in a tight undertone. 'In spite of all our differences, I wanted him to have that comfort and consolation in his last hours. Knowing that the succession to the throne was secured meant more to him than anything else. That was the only reason I told him that you were pregnant.'

Claire was thoroughly disconcerted by that sudden unexpected confession and she went very still, watching the unguarded emotions of regret and sorrow flit through Raif's expressive dark eyes. 'You managed to speak to him, then, *before*—'

'Yes, and I learned some things that made me unhappy,' he admitted in a driven admission of regret.

'Hashir was forced into a divorce because of his lack of a male heir. His ex-wife and daughters had already moved out of the palace before his death. I have asked her to visit us once she is established in her new home in Kazan. I am keen to get to know my nieces.'

'What happened to Waleed's widow?' Claire asked uneasily.

'She has returned to her family as well. I gather it wasn't a very happy marriage, but in his case my father did not want them to divorce because he was still hoping Waleed might provide Hashir with a male heir,' Raif explained wryly. 'But listening to my father trying to teach me how to follow in his royal footsteps taught me a hard lesson. I assumed that my brothers had had an easier time with him than I. Now I realise that I was undoubtedly lucky to be forgotten about and freely live my life all these years without his destructive interference.'

That admission struck a familiar note in Claire's thoughts. She had learned to live with her father and stepmother's lack of attachment to her, but only now could she really comprehend what had lain behind their attitude. Her mother had inflicted a world of hurt on them both and then run away, leaving her child to ultimately reap the consequences. What Claire now knew would make it easier for her to hold out an understanding hand to her stepmother. Nothing, she had discovered, was as black and white as she had once assumed.

'My father did, however, admit that he regretted divorcing my mother and the fact that he made little effort to get to know me. He explained that he felt very guilty over causing my mother such distress and that it was easier for him just to evade any further contact with us. He then urged me to make a go of *our* marriage and not to be distracted by a pretty face when I reached middle age. I gather that, in a nutshell, is what happened to my parents' marriage. He was attracted to another woman and divorced my mother so that he could marry her,' he explained heavily. 'But that second marriage barely lasted two years before he divorced her as well.'

'Well, at least he worked out where and why he went wrong, and, if he had lived longer, he probably would have tried to make amends to you,' Claire pointed out gently.

'We spoke for several hours. It was an exhausting meeting, but I do now understand my own background better.'

Before her very eyes, she was watching Raif relax and slowly shake free of the day's stress and strain. She studied him with silent, appreciative intensity, scanning his lean, sculpted bone structure, the perfect moulding of his brows and cheekbones and wide sensual mouth. Secret, delicious heat curled in her pelvis as she collided with the flare of his stunning dark golden gaze.

'I want you,' he admitted with unashamed hunger.

Claire rose from her seat, and he was just meeting her at the end of the table as the coffee arrived. He laughed and said something in his own language to Shahbaz, and linked his hand freely with hers to walk her down the corridor to their room, leaving the coffee behind untouched. Her face was red as fire.

'What must he think of us?' she muttered.

'That we are a normal couple behind the scenes,' Raif parried with quiet amusement, leaning back against the bedroom door and pulling her close to kiss her with passionate urgency. 'And this is that very special moment that I've been waiting for all day when it is finally just you and I alone together.'

Her skin tightened over her bones and warmth flooded her. Nobody had ever wanted her the way *he* wanted her, and it gave her a high that she could be that important to him. All her life she had longed to be important to someone and she had found that briefly and unforgettably with her mother, but never with anyone else she loved. That Raif, who had so many more important tasks to concentrate on, could still find time to miss her and need her, gave her a powerful sense of well-being and security.

She tipped his jacket off his shoulders and allowed it to fall. He wrenched off his tie and paused in the midst of doing so to crush her lips urgently beneath his, the flick of his tongue inside her mouth making her tremble with anticipation.

He turned her round to unzip her dress, skimmed it off her slim shoulders, pausing to run his lips across the soft smooth skin there before she stepped out of it, her knees weak, her body heating of its own accord. Lifting her onto the bed, he paused to rest his palm against the almost imperceptible but still firm swell of her no longer flat stomach. 'Our son is beginning to make his presence known,' he noted with satisfaction. 'It's incredibly sexy.'

'Sexy?' she repeated in astonishment. 'How can it be sexy?'

In the act of removing his shirt, Raif studied her from below his black lashes, visibly surprised by the question. 'That's our baby inside you and that can only make me feel amazingly proud.'

He spoke with such sincerity that she could not doubt him and she went from pointlessly striving to suck her tummy in to smiling and kicking off her shoes. He stripped off where he stood, unveiling lithe bronzed flesh rippling with lean muscle. For a split second he paused to take in the vision of her in her lacy, highly feminine lingerie and he marvelled that he had found her, that she asked and expected so little from him and yet freely gave him so much.

Excitement lit Claire up inside when he came down to her, fluid and graceful as a jungle cat. She loved the boneless way he moved. She loved the look of him, the scent of his skin, the very touch of him. He eased her gently free of her bra and knickers, knowing that her swollen breasts and distended nipples were tender with pregnancy. He bent his dark head and used the tip of his tongue on the sensitive peaks, until a muffled moan escaped her and her spine arched in response.

'Too much?' he asked.

Claire let her greedy fingers spear through his cropped black hair. 'Not enough,' she told him truthfully, pulling him down to her again with unhidden impatience.

Her entire being was fizzing with energy, her heart racing, her skin buzzing with the kind of need she had not even known existed until she met him. A scorching kiss sealed them close, their bodies straining into connection for the satisfaction they craved. She was ready for him, downright eager as he explored her quivering length. He grazed the tight aching buds of her nipples, delved into the tingling folds between her thighs and, that fast, that unstoppably, her body exploded into a climax. She convulsed and cried out, all tension dredged from her in a wild surge.

'And I have barely started, *aziz*,' Raif groaned.

'Is that a complaint?' she whispered shakily.

'Hell, no. Thanks to you, I'm now on an even bigger high,' he confided huskily, pressing his mouth to hers in light acknowledgement before turning her over and raising her up on her knees.

Her breath caught in her throat as he penetrated her in one fluid stroke. As her sensitive flesh stretched to accommodate him, her heart thundered and the liquid heat in her pelvis increased with an intense burst of exhilarating excitement. Every thrust of his body into hers pushed that excitement higher until she was gasping for breath, overpowered by the raw pleasure engulfing her. The muscles in her lower body pulled tighter and tighter as the tension built until his completion suddenly triggered hers. Heavens, she felt as though her body went flying off into the sun and she burned up in a wave of ecstasy, so powerful that she flopped down on the bed and promised herself that she would never willingly move again.

Raif flung himself down beside her on the tumbled sheets with an extravagant groan. 'You are amazing,' he murmured softly, trailing idle fingers through her tousled hair. 'You're very quiet. What are you thinking about?'

'What you said about seeing your father in a different light after your final meeting with him.' She sighed. 'I think it was because you're an adult now and you saw him and the past through clearer eyes. I've been going through the same process with my mother, my stepmother and my father.'

Leaning up, Raif frowned down at her. 'How?'

'Mum told me how she first met my father. She lost her parents suddenly in a car accident and she joined the church because she felt that she needed a support system. My father became that support system, advising her on everything relating to her parents' estate and, in the process, he fell in love with her,' she explained ruefully. 'But until I met Mum, I didn't know that my stepmother, Sarah, was already on the scene, a leading light in the congregation and in love with my father even then. Then Sarah had to stand by and watch him fall for my mother, which must have hurt her a great deal.'

'You're saying that your mother came between them.'

'Yes, I think he would have married Sarah if my mother hadn't appeared and that when he finally did marry her, she must have felt like second best, however untrue that was. Being forced to bring up her rival's daughter probably didn't help. And I'm not sure I've ever been fair to her. She was never unkind to me, never spiteful. She just never showed me affection the way she did with her own child.'

'You're saying she did her best but couldn't or wouldn't fake an affection she didn't feel for you. Think about something more uplifting.'

'You never ever mention your mother,' she remarked. 'Why is that?'

'I just don't like to talk about her. It feels…disloyal.' Raif turned his head away from her, his profile taut.

An awkward little silence stretched and grated on Claire's nerves, but she was hurt by his unwillingness to confide in her and it made her wonder what it was he was hiding.

'How am I going to buy maternity wear when the palace is in mourning? Shopping will be sure to be seen as frivolous at such a time.' Claire sighed, keen to change the subject to one that would hopefully remove the tension from his lean, strong face. 'And can I buy salt and vinegar crisps anywhere? If my little kitchen was up and running, I could make my own salty snacks.'

'The salespeople will come to you. I will organise it,' Raif told her soothingly. 'And Shahbaz will find you crisps.'

'I was making a mountain out of a molehill,' Claire gathered, and she grinned. 'I do that sometimes.'

* * *

Two and a half months later, Claire beamed at the brilliance of Raif's smile as he posed on the massive yellow excavator for the cameras aimed at him.

Ground was finally being broken at Rabalissa, the very first step in the creation of the new port to be built on the Arabian Sea. It was a newsworthy event, and the watching crowd was filled with politicians, tribal leaders and the media. Claire was dressed for public viewing but also for practicality and cool in loose trousers and a flowing white tunic top that only hinted at the burgeoning swell of her pregnancy. Nothing dressier would have made sense when she had to trek across the equivalent of a building site.

Once the official period of mourning was over at the palace, their lives had steadily changed. Raif was now out and about most days, meeting and greeting people. Quristan was only just getting used to the idea of a young king on the throne. His father had ruled for a very long time and had only ever been seen in public on holy days and at special ceremonies. Raif was much more low-key and accessible, which went down well with the younger generation. Here in Rabalissa, the wild desolate region his mother had once ruled before her marriage to the late King, Raif was in his element overseeing the first steps in the vast development project he had instigated.

It was hot…really, *really* hot…and her tunic was sticking to her damp skin. For that reason, it was a relief when Raif returned to her side and guided her

back across the rough ground into the delicious cool of
the large air-conditioned temporary building where a
reception was being held for the dignitaries. Raif was
quickly drawn from her side to expound on the big
model town set on a table in the centre of the room.
Mohsin brought her ice-cold water and stuck by her
side as interpreter as she made polite conversation with
the people who drifted her way. Nahla was unable to
travel with her because of her young children.

Raif had tried to dissuade Claire from accompanying
him, but she had checked with the palace doctor that
travel was fine and she had stayed by Raif's side, reluctant to let him leave her for more than forty-eight hours.
It was true that the journey had been exhausting, and
that she was tired and hot, but she enjoyed the rhythm
of her life with Raif and knew she was likely to see a
lot less of him if she used her pregnancy as an excuse
and bowed out of official duties. In addition, people
were as curious about her as they were about her husband, and she found it easier to be seen out and about
rather than feel as if she was hiding from that interest.

At the palace, now that all the building work on their
section of the palace was complete, their daily sched-
ule had fallen into a regular pattern. First thing in the
morning they shared the gym, although she was considerably less active than Raif was on the equipment.
She made their lunch every day in her pristine new
kitchen and, wherever Raif was and whatever he was
doing, he tried to join her for that meal. Dinner, breakfast and snacks were provided by the palace chef and

when she was bushed, she was grateful for the meals that arrived without any personal effort on her part. Raif agreed to only occasional evening events.

Lottie and her husband, Rob, and three children had come to stay for the weekend the month before and Claire had thoroughly enjoyed their visit, particularly when Raif had taken them all out on a sightseeing visit. Her best friend had raved about Raif and the way he treated Claire.

'He's crazy about you,' Lottie had insisted. 'He would move a mountain with his bare hands if he thought it would please you!'

And Claire had smiled politely and said nothing. No matter what Raif felt deep down inside, he would be very kind and considerate because that was the sort of man he was. He hid his innermost feelings. She might wonder how often he thought about the unavailable woman he had long loved in silence, but it was probably for the best that she had no idea. What she didn't know couldn't hurt her, she consoled herself frequently.

She had emailed her stepmother, Sarah, and invited her and her brother, Tom, out for a visit. Sarah, however, had explained that she was currently caring for her elderly mother and couldn't leave her, while Tom had a vacation job that he couldn't abandon. Her half-brother had, however, promised to fly out for a weekend during termtime. Claire had promised to call the next time she was in London, but she didn't know when that would be because the more pregnant she became, the less keen she was on travelling, particularly if it meant being without Raif.

* * *

Raif surveyed his wife from a distance and a dozen bright memories assailed him. Claire with headphones, bopping in time to music in her kitchen while she whipped up some flavoursome concoction for him to eat. Claire, remaining admirably serious when a pompous speaker at a museum event tripped over his own feet. Claire, convulsed with laughter, when he tickled her until the laughter had led into the most incredible session in their bedroom. Claire smiling, when someone enquired after Circe, the palace cat, who now rejoiced in a starring role in a newspaper cartoon. Claire chuckling at one of Mohsin's jokes, lugubrious, serious Mohsin, who had never once cracked a joke with Raif. The one talent that Claire had in spades was charm, an ability to relax people and make them feel welcome. She was so unspoilt, he sometimes marvelled that he had found a woman so perfect for him.

'Time for us to depart,' Raif whispered in her ear as he banded an arm round Claire's narrow spine. 'You're pale and you look very tired.'

'I am tired. I'm going for a nap as soon as we arrive at your mother's old home.'

'You'll like it. It's not fancy but it's comfortable. I lived there for weeks when I was working on this project. It made the perfect base.'

It was an old stone castle on a promontory high above the shoreline, overlooking the sea and a long stretch of white sand. 'Does it belong to you?' she asked as the SUV came to a halt outside the entrance.

'Technically, yes. I inherited it from my mother and she from her father, but when Rabalissa was united with Quristan, everything here supposedly went to the throne of Quristan. My father, however, didn't use it and my mother never once visited it after their marriage. Even when she was a child, she hated the location because it was so inaccessible. That will change, of course, with the motorway that is finally being built.'

They entered the castle and moved into a hall that was filled with the cosy clutter of yesteryear, fishing rods, baskets and parasols collected in a stand, worn photos in shell frames still adorning the walls. 'Do you know who all these people are?'

'Some, but only Umar would know them all. This was his childhood home too,' he reminded her.

'Show me your mother,' she urged.

He pointed to a dark-eyed little girl in a very fussy dress.

'She was very pretty.'

'The firstborn, the future Queen of Rabalissa.' He sighed. 'Let me show you upstairs and you can lie down.'

On the wall in the graciously furnished bedroom there was a faded colour photo of a gorgeous brunette in a very glamorous outfit. 'Is that her? Your mother?' Claire asked curiously, removing her shoes and settling down on the mercifully modern divan bed awaiting her. 'She was pretty spectacular in her heyday, wasn't she?'

As Claire began to remove her clothing, Raif tensed. 'Why are you so curious about her?' he demanded.

'Because you don't talk about her,' she pointed out, folding her trousers and top. '*Why?* Of course, I wonder why. I'm only human.'

Raif strode over to the window overlooking the sea, lean back and shoulders rigid. 'Because my mother is a source of both shame and embarrassment to me,' he admitted in a terse, driven voice. 'Talking about her is difficult for me.'

As Claire dug into her suitcase for something light to wear, her brow furrowed into a frown. 'But why is that?'

'Her behaviour as my father's ex-wife in London and abroad caused many scandals and destroyed her reputation. In polite company she will not be mentioned for that reason. She became an alcoholic but also very promiscuous,' he framed curtly. 'She slept with every man available, married or otherwise. My brothers refused to be associated with her and they stopped visiting her early on. I was twelve years old when my father sent word through my siblings that I could come back to live in Quristan at the palace with him.'

Claire was very shocked by what he was finally revealing, and she quite understood his previous silence on the subject. 'My goodness,' she whispered unevenly.

'I don't think my father ever forgave me for refusing to leave her. He took that as a personal rejection but how *could* I leave her?' Raif swung back, his lean dark features pained, and he made an almost clumsy movement with his hands to accentuate the impossibility of his having made such a cruel choice. 'She only had me left. How could I abandon her as well? I was shielded from many of her affairs by boarding school. Even so, I saw much that I shouldn't have seen as an adolescent. But I loved her. I *loved* her to the bitter end when her liver failed from the alcohol.'

Claire shook her head slowly in sadness at what he had described, and her heart went out to him for the pain he was no longer attempting to conceal.

'Don't judge her from what I have told you,' Raif asked in a strained appeal. 'She was very unhappy. She had wealth and beauty but nothing she truly valued. Her depression led to her alcohol addiction and then to the men.'

'I'm so sorry, Raif,' Claire muttered heavily. 'But thank you for telling me. I think I understand you a little better now. Is that why you were still a virgin when we met?'

In silence he nodded. 'For me, sex has to be something more...*not* merely a physical thing...and the association with my mother's lifestyle repelled me.'

'I hope we're something more,' she almost whispered.

'How can you doubt it?' Raif quipped as he sank down on the bed with her and began to help her to slip out of her pretty scraps of lingerie. He dropped the nightdress over her head as though she were a child to be dressed.

He gripped her hand. 'Sleep now,' he urged. 'I'll wake you in time for dinner.'

Claire slumped into the comfortable mattress. As the door closed, she remembered what she had wanted to discuss with him and groaned. It wouldn't have been the right moment to open the topic. Raking up his mother's past had upset Raif. She would wait for a more promising opportunity to ask him if it would be possible for Nahla to move into one of the palace apartments. Raif could be rather standoffish with her assistant. Admittedly their paths rarely crossed but he had an easy manner with his own staff. With Nahla, however, he was reserved and distant. She had begun to wonder if he simply didn't like Nahla for some reason. Why didn't he just say so?

'What was he like back then?' Claire had asked Nahla fondly, some weeks earlier.

'He was quiet and serious. He always had his head in a book. He was also several years younger, so we didn't spend much time together,' Nahla had admitted, and she had giggled. 'By then, I was already falling in love with my Yousuf. I wasn't much interested in teenage boys, even though he was a royal and rather handsome prince.'

The following day, after a tour of the new resort site just along the coast and a late lunch, Claire and Raif travelled back to the palace in separate vehicles, the accident that had led to the death of both of Raif's brothers having confirmed the security risk in official circles. Until Claire had given birth to the heir to the throne, the couple had agreed to exercise caution. Unfortunately, that entailed a very long, boring and lonely drive and Claire dozed most of the way.

It was early evening when Claire reached the palace.

Circe greeted her first. Shorn of her cast and her restrictive collar, the palace cat was her sleek, confident self, only now she rejoiced in a jewelled collar and a name tag, worthy of her newly acquired status as the star of a cartoon based on political satire.

The first thing Claire wanted on her return was a lengthy shower. Clad in a yellow sundress, she waited until dinner was over and they had had coffee served in the sitting room before saying, 'There's something I've been meaning to ask you, but I wasn't quite sure how to open the subject.'

'There should be nothing that you feel you cannot say to me,' Raif countered with a frown of surprise.

'Well…' Claire hesitated and sighed. 'I've noticed that you're a little uncomfortable around Nahla.'

The faintest edge of colour accentuated the slant of his hard cheekbones. 'I hardly know her,' he pointed out. 'But I have every respect for her and am grateful that you find her so useful.'

'Then, can we offer her the chance to move out of your uncle's house and move into the palace with her children?' Claire pressed in a rush.

'No,' Raif countered with finality.

Claire went pink. 'Just…*no*?'

'Yes, just no,' Raif confirmed, compressing his lips in a hard line.

'But why not?' Claire queried in bewilderment.

'The staff quarters here at the palace require renovation and until that work is complete, we can't put anyone else in substandard housing. I am, however, willing to offer her staff accommodation in Kazan, where I have bought property for that purpose,' he countered curtly. 'I would also add that I think it would be inappropriate for you to develop any closer friendship with Nahla.'

Claire reddened in surprise. 'And why would you say that? Am I suddenly supposed to turn into some sort of snob and only rub shoulders in a friendly way with VIPs?'

'Don't be ridiculous!' Raif told her curtly, pushing aside his coffee untouched and springing upright with unconcealed impatience. 'That is not what I'm saying. You must learn to respect the boundaries that we should observe. That is our life now.'

'You don't like her. That's what this is about,' Claire decided, standing up in turn, annoyed by his intransigence.

'That is untrue. I have a high opinion of Nahla… how could I not? She has been very helpful to you and she does not put herself forward.'

Claire straightened, shaken to discover that they were on the very edge of a row and wondering how that had blown up so quickly. 'Then what's your problem with her?'

Raif's brilliant dark eyes hardened. 'There is no problem.'

'Sounds like it!' Claire scoffed.

'Don't be so stubborn,' Raif urged her impatiently. 'Occasionally I will give you advice that is not to your taste and, unfortunately, this is one of those occasions.'

'That's not good enough,' Claire told him irritably. 'I want an answer. I want to know *why* you don't really like Nahla being around.'

Raif stared back at her, scanning her vivid face and the brightness of the blue eyes that had captured him at first glance. He breathed in deep and slow, wishing he could tell her the truth, wishing he could get that off his conscience but convinced that that truth would distress her and cause trouble he would struggle to handle. 'I can't tell you,' he declared with sudden harshness.

'And is this the same guy who told me that there should be nothing I can't tell *you*?' Claire responded. 'What a shame it doesn't work both ways!'

Raif swore under his breath. 'To tell you would entail breaking a promise I made you before our marriage,' he replied grimly. 'I don't know what to do for best. You tell me.'

Claire had no idea what he was referring to. She blinked, drew in a sharp breath and tried to clear her head. 'Raif…' she began quietly.

'Nahla is the woman I believed I was in love with for years,' he stated in a clipped undertone, his strain in making that admission etched in the tension clenching his lean, darkly handsome features.

CHAPTER TEN

For about ten seconds, Claire gazed back at him, her lips parting but not a breath of sound emerging. Shock was flooding her in a tidal wave. She went white. She felt sick. She also felt unbelievably stupid.

How on earth had she been so blind? How on earth had she forgotten that promise she had asked for prior to their marriage? She had warned him never ever to tell her the identity of the woman he loved and, being Raif, he had tried to stick to that agreement until she made it impossible for him by continuing to demand answers. Without another word, she left the room, her steps merely quickening when Raif called her name after her to try and halt her flight.

She raced down the stairs into the hall. And where was she going to run? And what would running avail her? There was no running away, no escaping such an unlovely truth. Once that confession was out, there was no avoiding it, no denying it either. But what could she possibly have said to him in response to that explanation?

She had brought Nahla into Raif's radius again. *She* had fought to employ Nahla, whom she had taken an immediate liking to, a liking that had not wavered once in the weeks since she had met the other woman. Nahla was quiet, discreet, efficient and obliging. She was also strikingly beautiful in that ethereal, delicate, soulful-eyed way. Raif had attempted to dissuade her from hiring Nahla and she had ignored him, much as she had ignored his unease around the other woman, she recalled sickly. It had never occurred to her to suspect that something truly important lay behind his reluctance to employ Nahla.

From the hall, she went out through the French windows into their private courtyard. Stately palm trees of several varieties made it a highly ornamental space surrounding a beautiful mosaic-tiled fountain where water fanned down softly into a pond. Tropical flowers flourished and bloomed in every corner, tumbling in abundance from urns. She hovered by the fountain, watching the water fall and spread a pattern of ripples across the surface while she struggled to get a grip on herself. Circe sidled out from beneath the foliage to brush against her legs, and she distractedly bent to stroke her elegant cat.

Before she'd married Raif, she had told herself that she would not get wound up about the fact that he loved another woman. And yet what was she doing right now? That question was unanswerable. She swallowed hard. Nahla had no idea of Raif's feelings, had evidently never once looked at Raif in a romantic light because he was younger than her and she had already been falling in love with the man she had married...

and *lost*. Belatedly, it dawned on Claire that Nahla was a widow now and available, only Raif hadn't known that crucial fact until he'd returned to Quristan and by then he had already been married to Claire.

Had he railed at the cruel fate that had set him up with such bad timing that he'd lost out on a possible relationship with the woman he loved? Her tummy lurched at that acknowledgement. But nothing could be changed, she thought heavily. She was pregnant, the mother of the future Crown Prince. Raif was stuck with her as a wife whether he wanted to be or not. At this moment, neither of them had the freedom to make other choices and she had to woman up and face the emotional fallout of such a confession.

Certainly, she would not be blaming Raif for seeking out Nahla's company, she thought humourlessly. Raif had avoided the other woman to the best of his ability. No, Raif would not cheat on her. Raif was too honest and scrupulous for such behaviour. She reckoned that both of them were, never mind the fact that Nahla was still grieving for the husband she had loved.

'Claire…' Raif murmured quietly.

The woman I believed I was in love with for years.

His explanation sounded like a crack of doom in her memory and it wounded her like the short sharp shock of a lightning strike, knocking her right out of her happy place of security. And that was the terrible irony, she acknowledged unhappily. Raif *was* her happy place. From the day of their marriage, he had made her happy, so happy she could sometimes barely credit it, and yet right from the outset she had been fully aware that another woman had his heart. How naïve had she been not to appreciate that that horrible truth would eventually come back to haunt her?

'Claire...' Raif repeated, striding down the winding wrought-iron steps that led down from the sitting room into the courtyard. 'Much as I would prefer to avoid ever mentioning that name again, we have to talk about this.'

Claire avoided looking at him and studied his shadow instead. 'I can't think of much to say. That was what you might describe as a conversation killer,' she reasoned in a strained undertone.

'Did you even *listen* to what I actually said?' Raif chided. 'I said the woman that I *believed* I loved. It wasn't love, Claire. It was a teenage crush, which I assumed was love. And that assumption made me feel much more normal mixing with my peers. I may not have been chasing girls with my friends, but I was not sexless.'

Claire wasn't listening as well as she should have been. 'She's very beautiful,' she remarked stiffly. 'And she's warm and kind. As a teenager, you had surprisingly good taste.'

'But unhappily for me, I decided I was in love before I even understood what love was. I was a romantic, an idealist,' he breathed ruefully. 'A young woman who was out of reach...being almost a family member... was a safe focus for those feelings. She was in love with someone else and soon to be married. There was never the smallest prospect of anything of a romantic nature developing between us.'

Claire emerged from her reverie of unhappy thoughts and her brow furrowed as she turned back to him. 'You're saying it wasn't *real* love.'

'It felt real to me because I had no other woman to focus on and, let us be frank, the way I lived before I met you, that was enough for me to feel at the time. My mother's lifestyle had sickened me. Loving cleanly from afar suited me and gave me yet another reason to reject casual sex and relationships,' he proffered. 'Hell, Claire…have you any idea how foolish I feel trying to explain this all to you now?'

Claire lifted her head, her blue eyes wary. 'Why would you feel foolish?'

'Because I was the idiot who thought an innocent crush was everlasting love!' Raif bit out with scorn. 'Even though I never lusted after her, even though I never made any attempt to see more of her, I still didn't understand my own feelings enough to realise that it was nothing more than an innocent boy's infatuation! But I should have seen the difference.'

'Let's go back upstairs,' Claire urged, fearful of them being overheard, already having espied a maid in the hall doorway, the woman clearly wondering if she should offer to serve them refreshments.

Claire started up the staircase in the wake of Circe, struggling to grasp what Raif was telling her. That he didn't love Nahla, after all? Was that what he was saying? Or was she only hearing what she wanted to hear?

Mistakenly interpreting his words to mean what she wanted them to mean? Her brain was whirling with disconnected thoughts and her emotions were running on high. She simply couldn't think clearly.

At the top of the stairs, she moved into the sitting room, where Circe jumped on an armchair and curled up in graceful cat relaxation. 'I'm sorry I took off like that.'

'You're still not listening,' Raif censured, poised and deadly serious.

'You're saying it wasn't love,' she responded, disconcerting him with that quiet analysis. 'When did you decide that?'

'About the same time that I finally realised that I was in love with my wife. That was my true wake-up call. But, unluckily, I'd already shot myself in the foot by telling you that I was in love with someone else.' Raif sighed.

Claire blinked rapidly, not quite believing what she had heard, and she stared at him. 'What on earth are you talking about? We're talking in circles and you're confusing me.'

A groan of frustration fell from Raif's lips. 'You don't believe me, which is why I didn't try to tell you sooner. I went about this all the wrong way.'

He had realised that he was in love with his wife? But that was *her*! Claire gazed back at him, captured by stunning dark golden eyes and the increasing tension in his stance. He couldn't mean that, he couldn't possibly mean that!

'When did you realise that? That you thought you might…love me?' she queried unevenly.

'It was many weeks ago, but I should have recognised my feelings sooner. From the moment I met you, I could think of nothing *but* you! From that day, I was consumed by my thoughts and my memories of you. Doesn't it occur to you that my behaviour with you when we met was wildly out of character? I should have been the least likely man in the world to have a random one-night stand,' he pointed out. 'But you broke through my defences, and it was as though you cast a spell over me because, after you, nothing else mattered.'

'You walked away, afterwards,' Claire objected, because that still rankled and stung.

'And I pined for weeks on the yacht like a blasted schoolboy!' Raif complained. 'But I didn't think I had anything more to offer you because I still believed that I loved Nahla and I didn't want to drag you into some grubby affair that had nowhere to go.'

'You *pined*?' Claire pressed in disbelief.

'I pined. I wouldn't let myself phone or text you and I told myself that a clean break was the best I could offer you.'

'Oh, thanks for that,' Claire quipped, tongue in cheek.

'You deserved more from me, and I knew it,' Raif told her squarely.

'And then you discovered that I was on your yacht,' Claire continued.

Yet the whole time they were talking, her mind was racing ahead. He had said that he loved her. Raif had said that he loved her. She wanted to jump up and down, throw champagne, toss balloons and entire flocks of doves into the blue sky. The man she loved *loved* her right back and that was more than she had ever hoped to have.

'That was a shock. All those weeks I had been thinking about you, you were within reach…but yet *not* because I could not have renewed our relationship while you worked for me,' he asserted tautly. 'Yet I would have wanted to, so I'm grateful that we weren't faced with that temptation.'

'I spent almost half the trip worrying that I was pregnant.'

'I deeply regret that you went through those weeks of anxiety without my support.' His dark golden eyes were glittering like polished ingots in the sunshine flooding through the windows. 'But, let me say this only once… our son is a gift and a blessing. We are very fortunate.'

And Raif truly meant those sentiments, Claire registered with her eyes stinging a little from over-emotional tears. When it came to her pregnancy, Raif daily demonstrated his commitment to them both and he studied every ultrasound image with fascination and pleasure. He had not missed out on a single one of her health check-ups either. Her medical care was incredibly good, with the obstetrician coming to the palace to see her every week.

'You've got no resentment about our baby and the timing at all?'

'The most important thing our son achieved was to bring you back to me,' Raif asserted with a brilliant smile. 'You've turned my whole life around.'

'Well...' Claire murmured, crossing the floor to slide her hand meaningfully into his. 'You gave me a palace to live in, a state-of-the-art kitchen and a great deal of happiness.'

Claire urged him gently in the direction of their bedroom, leaving Shahbaz to work out for himself that there was no point offering them coffee.

'I like watching you dance in the kitchen,' he confided.

Claire flushed and turned to close the door behind them. 'I didn't know you'd seen that.'

'Sometimes I spy on you. I didn't mention it because I don't ever want you to stop dancing,' Raif confessed. 'So you believe me about Nahla?'

Claire wrinkled her nose. 'I'm not sure I understand why you're uncomfortable when she's around—'

'Which of us enjoy being reminded of our teenage misapprehensions?' Raif traded wryly. 'But I'll get over it. Some day I'll look back on that piece of stupidity and laugh, but I cannot laugh at anything that threatens to divide us. I would have been wiser never to mention her at all than to make such a production out of it.'

'No. I appreciated your honesty at the time and I appreciate it now...more than you know,' Claire told him gently as she unknotted his tie and cast it aside. 'But the truth is that I love you to death and even if you *still* thought you loved her, I'd still love you to death because you're a very special man.'

'You love me? Even though I spoiled our marriage from the outset with that stupid confession of mine about Nahla?' Raif questioned incredulously. 'I wanted to tell you weeks ago that I loved you, but I felt that I couldn't because, after what I'd told you about Nahla, you'd never have believed me.'

'I'm believing you now,' Claire pointed out, embarking on his shirt buttons. 'Love shows in so many things you've done for me. If I'd had stronger self-esteem, I would have worked out that you loved me a long time ago, but I was never going to tell you that I loved you when I thought you loved someone else.'

'I take it the Nahla business is behind us now.' Able to take a hint, Raif doffed his jacket and shed his shirt. 'I can't credit that you fell in love with me too. When did that start?'

'That very first night,' Claire admitted, rather misty-eyed.

'I like that,' Raif admitted as he swept her dress up over her head. 'I suppose that's when I started developing feelings too. I didn't want to leave you and I wanted to turn time back and have that night over again. I love you so much. I had no idea that it was even possible to love anyone as much as I love you.'

Claire peeled off her remaining garments and lay back on the bed to watch him strip. 'I still get a kick out of watching you strip,' she confessed.

'Any time…' Raif promised, making a production out of getting down to his bare skin.

Claire laughed as he came down to her on the bed, lean, muscular and golden in the sunshine lighting up the room.

'I will never stop wanting you,' he told her urgently as he claimed a passionate kiss and the silence crept in around them slowly, punctuated only with the occasional moan or sigh. They made love with the urgency of two people who both felt as if they might have missed out on each other. Even so, they had made it through all the misunderstandings and their mutual happiness was so strong they sat up talking and loving half the night. There were no more secrets, no more doubts or insecurities between them.

'Go to sleep,' Raif urged her tenderly around dawn. 'I love you so much.'

'I love you too,' she whispered drowsily. 'But I don't want jungle animals in the nursery, just elephants because some animals are scary.'

'One little tiger hiding in the undergrowth of a jungle wall mural? It's the art of compromise,' Raif bargained, folding her into his arms and drifting off to sleep.

EPILOGUE

Ten years later

CLAIRE TUCKED IN the littlest and latest occupant of the royal nursery. Zakar was six months old, a cheerful baby with an untidy shock of black hair, who slept like a dream. The jungle wall in the nursery, painted by a Quristani artist, still featured a tiger cub below a tree, although Circe and her Siamese partner, Ninja, had acquired a spot as well, posed with regal cool nearby, with kittens round their feet, seemingly unperturbed by the elephants bathing in the river below them.

Claire smiled ruefully, thinking about her eldest, Rohaan, who had regularly disturbed her nights. He was now a lively, highly intelligent nine-year-old, and he still required less sleep than their other children. Her second pregnancy had been a twin one, and her little girls, Salima and Madiya, had arrived a few weeks early and demanded enough attention to ensure that two nannies were added to the staff. Zakar would be their last child, because Claire felt that four children was a nice round number, particularly now that they had two boys and two girls. She knew, though, that

Raif, who adored babies, would probably eventually try to change her mind.

In the years that had passed since their marriage, Claire had gained poise. She had grown into her royal role and had learned that just being herself covered most occasions. She had picked up the language year on year and no longer needed an interpreter at her elbow. Nahla had fallen madly in love with one of Kashif's friends in the diplomatic corps and, having remarried, was now based in London. Claire missed the brunette, but Stella had become a close friend after Kashif was moved back to Quristan and settled into a more senior position in Kazan. As they now had three children, the two couples socialised a lot together.

Her brother, Tom, was a regular visitor and she always saw him when they stopped over in London. Sarah, her stepmother, had, sadly, passed away from an undetected heart condition, which was why she and Tom made an extra effort to spend time together because they were all that remained of their original family.

Circe, still famous from her glory days as a cartoon cat, had a chain of descendants now from her alliance with Ninja, the pedigreed Siamese given to Claire by Raif on the occasion of their first anniversary. They had kept two of their kittens, Ra and Bastet, who were very attached to the children.

Right now, as Claire tucked in her youngest son, Raif joined her, pausing only to smooth a light hand over his son's untidy head. 'All set?' he checked.

'I feel so guilty leaving the kids behind,' Claire admitted ruefully.

'They'll have a whale of a time with Kashif and Stella. Our kids get loads of holidays,' Raif reminded her. 'This is a special anniversary. Ten years since the first day we met.'

It was true that their children enjoyed plentiful away time from the royal household, Claire conceded. There were bucket-and-spade holidays in the old castle at Rabalissa, Mediterranean trips on the yacht and sometimes visits to their villa in the Alpujarra.

And that evening as they walked up the path from the cove to the little cottage where they had spent their very first night together, both of them were awash with fond memories.

'I should make you do a strip in the cove first,' Claire teased him.

'Only after dark and with company,' Raif declared with a wicked grin. 'But I'm not planning to let you outdoors any time soon, *aziz*.'

Claire laughed. Unlike most women, she got to celebrate two anniversaries every year, the anniversary of their first meeting and the anniversary of their marriage. It was so strange to walk into the little house where she had spent all those months with her late mother. Raif had bought it as a surprise for her the previous Christmas and had it renovated, so, although there was a haunting familiarity to the rooms, there was also a much greater level of comfort.

Raif leant up against the bedroom door and then

straightened to remove his jacket very slowly. 'Do you still think I'm beautiful?' he asked her teasingly.

'Yes, and I'm a hopelessly shallow woman who worships you for your body alone,' she teased back.

He captured her face between his big hands and kissed her with passionate fervour. 'I love you so much, Claire. I love you more with every passing year.'

'I love you too,' she whispered with the same adoring intensity, the strength of their love deepened by all that they had shared.

They didn't make it down to the cove until after midnight and Mohsin kept the security team at a safe distance. Owing to Raif's conviction that they had to do everything the same way as they had that first night, Claire conceived a fifth and final time and their youngest son, little Raza, was born nine months later.

* * * * *

BOUND BY THE ITALIAN'S 'I DO'

MICHELLE SMART

MILLS & BOON

This book is for the fabulous and talented
Pippa Roscoe.

Pippa, thank you for making our collaboration
such a joy. xxx

CHAPTER ONE

THE MESSAGE THAT pinged on Issy Seymore's phone was the notification that her taxi had been dispatched.

She met her sister's apprehensive dark eyes. This was it. Everything they'd worked towards this last decade about to come to fruition. All the late-night planning. All the scheming.

She'd imagined she'd reach this moment and be buzzing at this spring into action. She hadn't expected to feel such a weight in the belly she'd spent years working desperately hard to keep flat and toned. Gianni Rossi favoured a specific type of woman. Short brunettes that leaned towards plumpness were not in that favoured league.

'We are doing the right thing aren't we?' she whispered.

Amelia swallowed hard and nodded. 'But if you've got cold feet and want to back out then...'

'No,' she cut her off with a fortifying shake of her head. 'It's not cold feet. Just nerves, I guess.'

Amelia rubbed her arms and gave a rueful smile of understanding. If anyone understood about nerves, it was her sister. The faint bruising under her eyes was testament to the lack of sleep that had gripped them both since they'd realised five weeks ago that the stars had finally aligned and it was time to put the plan they'd spent so long finessing into action.

Amelia had taken all the risks to get them to this point, had spent two years in the enemy's camp, every minute of her working life spent with a cold knot of fear of being found out. As the Seymore sisters knew to their personal cost, the Rossi cousins were men without conscience. Without humanity. They'd ruined their lives and now it was the sisters' turn to repay the favour. Let them get a taste of what it felt to have your whole life destroyed. Because it could only be a taste. It was impossible to replicate the scale of the damage the Italian men had wrought on their family.

While Amelia had put herself on the line every working day for two years, Issy had worked safely behind the scenes, immersed in the online world. Now it was time for her to step up, step out, and play her part in the real world.

Straightening her spine, Issy stood as tall as her five-foot-one body would stretch.

Amelia's smile at this contained the first hint of humour either of them had been able to muster that day. 'Remember to keep your shoes on around him—you don't want him knowing you're short one end before you get him on the yacht.'

A splutter of laughter left Issy's lips, and she threw her arms around her big sister and hugged her tightly.

'You'll let me know as soon as you land?' Amelia asked into her hair, embracing her with equal intensity.

'I promise.'

'You've packed your charm repellent?'

She snorted and hugged her even tighter. 'You know I don't need it.'

Amelia disentangled her arms and cupped Issy's cheeks. 'Promise you'll be careful. Don't take any silly risks.'

'I won't. You be careful too.'

A shadow fell over her sister's face but she smiled. 'I'm always careful.'

Issy's phone pinged. Her driver had arrived.

One last embrace and a kiss to her sister's cheek and it was time to leave.

Time to fly to the Caribbean and put the plan they'd spent ten years strategizing into fruition.

Ten days earlier

Gianni Rossi knew when a woman was interested in him and the beautiful blonde with the fabulous legs at the bar of this ultra-exclusive, members-only club was definitely interested. She'd wafted through the swing doors with a feline grace and as she passed his table, her eyes had glanced at his. When she reached the bar, she'd turned her head to look back at him and this time the lock of her stare had not been fleeting. Now she sat sucking a cocktail through a straw with a gleam in her eye that suggested she would like to be sucking something else.

Never a man to turn down a beautiful woman blatantly showing her interest, Gianni excused himself from the company he was in. He indicated the stool beside her. 'May I?'

Wide, eminently kissable lips twitched. Dark blue eyes gleamed. 'Be my guest.'

He rested his backside on it and beckoned the barman over.

'Drink?' he asked her.

The gleam deepened. 'Sure.'

'A large bourbon for me and a…?' He raised a brow in question at her.

Dimples appeared on the beautiful face. 'Mojito. Please.'

'Mojito for the lady.'

While the barman fixed their drinks, Gianni ran his expert eye over her. Glossy shoulder length honey-blonde hair only several shades lighter than her perfectly plucked eyebrows. Beautiful elfin features. A short, silver sequinned dress with spaghetti straps that came from no high street store. A slim watch on her slim wrist from a brand also unavailable on the high street. The cut of her diamond earrings too showed that this was a woman with a discerning eye and access to an undiscerning bank account. He wondered how their paths had never crossed before.

He extended a hand. 'Gianni.'

Slim fingers wrapped around his. Her expensive, exotic perfume drifted into his space like a fragrant cloud. 'Issy.'

'I haven't seen you here before… Issy.' A name that rhymed with dizzy did not suit this sleek, confident woman with the melodious voice who pronounced her words with the same exactness as the English socialites who flocked to his parties whenever he was in London.

Gently extracting her hand from his, she flashed pretty white teeth. 'It's my first time.'

His lips curved. 'Is that a fact?'

She wiggled one of her perfect eyebrows knowingly and, enchanting blue eyes not leaving his face, closed her lips over the straw to suck the last of her original drink. The eroticism behind it sent a thrill racing through his bloodstream. Damn, this woman was *hot*.

Placing his elbow on the bar, he rested his chin on his closed hand. 'Waiting for someone?'

'My girlfriend. We're meeting here before we go to Amber's. She's running late.'

'Girlfriend?'

Amusement sparkled. 'A friend who's a girl. Why? What did you think I meant?'

He smiled slowly. 'I think you know very well what I meant.'

Another knowing, amused wiggle.

'Do you have a significant other?' he asked, cutting to the chase.

She shook her head slowly. 'Life's too short for significant others.'

A woman after his own heart. 'I couldn't agree more.'

'You're single too?'

'Always.'

'Now that is something I will gladly drink to.' Placing an elbow on the bar close to his, she mimicked him by resting her chin on her closed hand. 'So...' She tilted a little closer. 'Gianni... You're Italian?'

'*Si.*'

She grinned. 'An Italian stallion?'

How he loved a woman who knew how to use a good double entendre. 'So I've been told.'

She looked him up and down without an ounce of shame. 'I'll bet.'

Their drinks were placed before them. Gianni raised his. 'To being single.'

She clinked her cocktail to his glass, dark blue eyes bold on his. 'To having fun.' Then she pinched the straw between her thumb and forefinger and slowly inserted it between her lips. It could not be interpreted as anything but suggestive and the thrills racing through his veins ramped up.

Her phone buzzed.

'Excuse me,' she said, swiping to read the message. She replied quickly then fixed him with a rueful smile. 'That, I'm afraid, is my cue to leave.'

'Already?'

'I didn't expect to leave so soon but it's Camilla's birthday. She was going to meet me here but as she's running so late, she's got her driver to drop her at Amber's and sent him on to collect me. He'll be here in a few minutes.' She gave him an openly provocative stare, and added, 'I'm sure she won't mind if you join us.'

Gianni had been to Amber's, a tiny nightclub with a clientele comprised almost exclusively of British high society, a number of times. With regret, he waved a hand in the direction of the three men he'd not long ago abandoned. 'I'm on a poker night promise, but I can join you later…if you like?'

She finished her mojito and as she pulled the straw from her mouth, her bottom lip pulled down seductively with it. 'I do like,' she murmured, 'but I'm afraid it has to be an early night for me, midnight at the latest or I risk the danger of turning into a pumpkin.'

He rested his fingers on the hand with the immaculately manicured and painted nails that had incrementally moved closer to him and bored his gaze into hers. There was nothing he loved more than a sexy, confident woman who knew exactly what she wanted and wasn't afraid to show it, and this woman had all of that. She was sexy. Beautiful. Blonde. Long-legged. And she was unashamedly making it clear that she wanted him. The perfect temporary bedwarmer. 'I could do with an early night too.'

Her eyes gleamed and her pretty teeth grazed her bottom lip. 'As tempting as your unspoken offer is, regretfully I must decline. I'm flying to Barbados in the morning and need my beauty sleep.'

'Barbados?'

She nodded and got to her feet. 'I keep my yacht at a

marina in Bridgetown. I always spend a couple of months each summer sailing.'

'Now that is a coincidence... I'm flying to the Caribbean myself in a couple of weeks.'

Her eyes widened in surprise and delight. 'Really?'

He nodded. 'We can meet up... If you like?'

She didn't even pretend to think about it. She leaned closer to whisper into his ear, close enough that her silky hair brushed against his neck. 'I would like that *very* much.' Then, smiling widely, she stepped back and pressed her phone. 'What's your number?'

He recited it to her. She entered it into her phone, then held the phone up. 'My chariot is here.'

'Then it is best you go so you don't turn into a pumpkin.'

Eyes shining, she laughed softly. 'Great to meet you, Gianni.' Then she blew him a kiss and strolled away in her fabulously high stilettos with the same ramrod-straight sexy confidence she'd entered the bar, gently curved hips swaying.

Gianni watched her leave, shaking his head and trying to stifle a laugh at what had just occurred in a few short minutes.

Ordering himself another bourbon, he re-joined his friends debating whether to throw the evening's game so he could get himself to Amber's before Cinderella turned into a pumpkin.

A moment later a message pinged into his phone.

The ball's in your court. Hopefully meet you for some fun in the Caribbean soon. Issy x

He messaged her back.

Looking forward to it. I'll be in touch. G x

* * *

Issy hailed the first black cab that passed and jumped in the back. 'Nelson Street, Brockley,' she said to the driver.

Not until the club was a blur in the distance was she able to breathe with any semblance of normality.

She'd done it.

While she kicked off the awful shoes that made her feel like her feet were clamped in vices, she fired a quick message to her sister. Amelia, she knew, would be unable to breathe properly herself until she heard from her.

It worked! Hook, line and sinker. On way home. xx

That done, she rested her head back and closed her eyes.

She felt sick. And exhilarated. And unsettled. So many emotions, all sloshing in her mostly empty stomach.

The closer the time to acting out their plans had come, the more unsettled she'd become at going through with it. When Amelia had started work at Rossi Industries, she'd vowed to find concrete proof of corruption against the cousins. They'd both needed to know that what they were doing wasn't just revenge but a good thing, that they were saving other victims from the fate their family had suffered. When Amelia had told her five weeks ago that their time had come, all Issy had been able to think was they still needed that proof. Amelia had finally found it three days ago, exultantly messaging her with the news.

The mojitos Issy had drunk suddenly rose up her throat. Pressing her hand there, she squeezed her eyes even tighter and willed the nausea to pass.

She willed even harder to banish the image of Gianni Rossi looking at her like he would gladly eat her whole.

And willed even harder than that to forget the thrills that had run through her veins to see it.

Rob Weller, one of Gianni's favourite architects and a good friend though an infuriating timekeeper, arrived at the same time the barman brought Gianni's fresh bourbon to the table.

'Man, I have just seen the hottest woman leave this place,' he enthused as he slid his short frame onto the seat across from Gianni.

'Bet that's the woman Gianni just hooked up with,' Stefan said with a knowing grin.

'We didn't hook up,' Gianni felt obliged to point out.

'I saw you give her your number.'

Gianni smiled but kept his mouth shut. While he dated widely and enthusiastically, one thing he never did was kiss and tell. Not that there had been any kissing to tell about. Just one short, incredibly flirtatious conversation…and the potential for more than flirtatious conversation.

For fifty weeks of the year, he worked his backside off. For sure, he partied hard too, but work came first. It always had. It was the same for Alessandro, his cousin and business partner. Practically raised as brothers, the Rossi cousins had been twelve when they'd determined to carve their own path in life, paths that sped them away from their monstrous fathers, and they had worked their fingers to the bone and overcome huge setbacks to make their property development company the multi-billion-euro, internationally renowned enterprise it was today. Where Gianni and Alessandro differed was on the partying side of life. Andro lived and breathed Rossi Industries. He rarely took time off. He never dated. He liked his own company so much that Gianni had long ago taken to calling him The Monk. But for all his cousin's single-minded drive and monkish ways, he understood Gianni needed to occasionally blow off steam and recharge his batteries and so had never begrudged the two weeks Gianni spent in the Caribbean each summer. That fortnight was sacrosanct, highlighted in the diary of every one of the hundred thousand Rossi Industries employees. The company would have to be burning down before Andro bothered him during it or let anyone else do so.

'Leggy blonde, wearing a skimpy silver dress?' Rob asked.

'That's the one,' Stefan agreed.

'Man…' Rob shook his head. 'I almost threw myself into the cab she hailed so she could argue with me for it.'

'Bit creepy,' Gianni pointed out.

'How else can I get a woman like that to look at me without flashing my bank account at them?' Rob defended himself. 'It's all right for you. Women don't care about the size of your wallet. You only have to look at a woman for her to want to…'

'Did you say she hailed a cab?' Gianni interrupted before his friend could say anything that might prompt a passing woman to throw a drink over his head.

'Yes.'

'There wasn't a car waiting for her?'

'No. She definitely hailed a black cab. Why?'

He shrugged and raised his glass to his mouth. 'No reason.'

Intriguing. Issy had told him her friend's driver was collecting her, which did not imply the beauty hailing a black cab.

Why the lie?

He tipped the rest of his bourbon down his throat and

smiled. The only thing he loved more than a sexually confident woman was a sexually confident enigma begging to be solved.

His annual trip to the Caribbean couldn't come soon enough. If nothing else, it certainly promised to be fun.

Once Issy's stomach had settled a little, she took a deep breath and made the call.

'David?' she said when it was answered. 'It's Isabelle Seymore.'

'Issy!' he cried. She could hear music pounding in the background and guessed he was at a party somewhere. 'What can I do for you, my darling?'

'It's time.'

'Time? For what?'

'You know what. A yacht.'

There was a long pause. 'When do you need it for?'

'Next Friday.'

'That soon?'

'I did warn you that when the time came, I would need it to happen quickly.'

He sighed. 'You still need it for two weeks?'

'Yes.'

'With a full crew?'

She pinched the bridge of her nose. 'Yes. And a minimum of forty feet. As we agreed when I spent six months working for you for free.'

David liked to call himself a broker but really, he was a fixer to the rich. Want the use of a private jet for a weekend? Then David is your man. Need to throw a last-minute party on an obscure island with exquisite catering and hedonistic entertainment? Give David a call. In the mood for charter-ing a fully crewed superyacht? That's right—call David.

Issy had taken a six-month sabbatical from her job as an auxiliary nurse to work as David's girl Friday two years ago, when Amelia had first got the job at Rossi Industries. Six months of free labour at roughly one hundred hours a week, and all for this moment. If she hadn't once been best friends with David's little sister he'd have made her work a full year.

No one could accuse the Seymore sisters of slacking in their preparation. Or their research.

The cab pulled up outside the run-down block of flats she and Amelia called home.

Wedging her swollen feet back into the vices, she walked as gingerly as she could up the stairwell to her flat—the lift was, as always, broken—and Issy's mind drifted back to the day she'd learned monsters really did exist. She remembered it so clearly.

It had been a Sunday. Her mother had cooked a tradi-tional English roast. Issy had been in charge of prepping the vegetables, Amelia in charge of making the batter for the Yorkshire puddings and the cheese sauce. During the meal, their parents had allowed thirteen-year-old Issy and fifteen-year-old Amelia to have a small glass of red wine each. Their parents had argued whether or not to take the girls out of school a week early so they could enjoy their Tuscan home a little longer than planned. None of them had known that in a matter of weeks the girls would be pulled out of their school permanently because the wealth that paid the fees would be gone.

When the doorbell rang, none of them had suspected what was about to happen.

Brenda, their housekeeper, was on her day off so the girls' mother, a vivid, beautiful woman with such *presence*, had answered the door. She'd returned shortly, anxiety on her face, and whispered to their father, who'd then excused himself.

Issy had just put a roast potato in her mouth when raised voices echoed from their father's study into the dining room. Without a word, the Seymore sisters and their mother slipped from the table and hovered outside it.

Male voices, heavily accented but with a precise pronunciation that meant the three of them heard every scornful, abusive word sounded through the crack in the study door.

'You're finished, old man. The sooner you accept that the better—for your sake.'

'What was yours is now ours, you washed-up, sorry excuse of a man. Accept it.'

'*Everything* is ours.'

'Everything. Say goodbye to your company...and hello to Lucifer. He's been waiting for you.'

Footsteps had neared the door. Issy and Amelia had held each other tightly as the door swung open and two tall, dark-haired men in impeccably tailored suits sauntered out of their father's study with all the swagger of a pair of gangsters in the films she was forbidden to watch. They failed to see the wife and daughters of the man they'd just ripped to shreds cowering behind the door. But the daughters had seen them.

Time had frozen. When their father finally appeared in the study doorway he'd aged two decades. The next morning, the frightened adolescent girls, who'd shared a bed that night, had woken from a fitful sleep to find his thinning dark hair had turned white overnight. A year later he was dead. A decade on, their mother was nothing but an empty shell of the vibrant woman she'd once been, distraught to wake each day, reliant on stimulants to get her out of bed.

Issy and Amelia had never been particularly close before that awful day. Close in age, yes, but nothing else. They'd have sooner scratched each other's eyes out than pay the other a compliment. That day, though, had pulled them together in a way the Rossi cousins could never have dreamed if they'd even bothered to consider the two innocent girls caught up in the collateral damage of their heinous actions. It had drawn them into a solid unit with only one purpose—revenge.

For the first time in a decade, Issy had the faint hint of what that revenge would taste like on her tongue.

CHAPTER TWO

THE *PALAZZO DELLE FESTE* gleamed under the dazzling Caribbean sun. It would have dazzled Issy even if it had been raining.

Blinking back her disbelief, she looked at David's deadpan face. 'How on earth did you manage to get this for me?'

He waved an airy hand. 'Just call me a magician.'

She turned her stare back to the humungous vessel docked before her. 'A magician? David, this is way beyond anything I asked for.' Their agreement had been six months free labour in exchange for the use of a sleek, modern yacht of at least forty feet, something a young, independently wealthy or trust-funded woman would reasonably own. This yacht had to be three times that size!

Heart sinking, she shook her head. 'It's amazing but it's too much.' It was too conspicuous. How could she blend in if things went wrong and she needed to escape? Plus something this size would give the impression she was in the league of billionaires. She knew how to pull off rich—after all, her family had once been rich—but this was a whole different league. This was Silicon Valley and oligarch territory. 'I need something much smaller.'

'Sorry, darling, but no can do. We're hitting the summer season. Everything's either booked or the owners are wanting them for themselves.'

'But this isn't what we agreed.'

'Darling, I've managed to acquire one of the finest superyachts in the whole of the Caribbean for your exclusive use, and you're complaining about it? Look at her! She's a masterpiece! She's got a helipad, two swimming pools, a library, an entertainment room, a games room, a movie room, a casino, a beauty parlour, a spa, *and* she has an inflatable slide that you can swish down straight into the sea. And if all that doesn't tempt you, she has her own speedboat, Jet Skis and a load of other water sports goodies tucked away for your personal use.'

No wonder it was named the Party Palace. This was a vessel equipped and dedicated to its owner having a good time.

'Does the owner know you're giving her away for a fortnight at no charge?' Chartering something of this size and opulence complete with full crew would generally set someone back around the hundred thousand mark. Per week. In English pounds. She would have had to work for David for free for ten years to pay for this.

'Ask me no questions and I will tell you no lies.'

She fixed him with a stare that, instead of making him quail, made him laugh and throw his arms around her. 'Oh, Isabelle, Isabelle. Why so serious? You're in the Caribbean. You have a superyacht with a crew of twenty at your disposal. *Enjoy it*, my darling. Everything is taken care of. Anything you could possibly want will be provided. If you're anchored at sea and want a Methuselah of Moët flown in or a hundred white roses, ask and it shall be delivered.'

'Have you really not got anything smaller I can use?'

'Do you know what the definition of stupid is? Asking the same question again and again hoping for a different answer.'

* * *

From the other side of the harbour, standing at the balustrade of his hotel room's balcony, Gianni watched the exchange between Issy and the broker through his binoculars. His beautiful hustler did not look pleased at the broker's offering. He didn't need to be a lip-reader to know she was arguing about it. He smiled when her shoulders sagged and she finally appeared to concede defeat. He was proved right a moment later when they climbed the steps onto the *Palazzo delle Feste*. The captain joined them. She shook his hand then followed the two men inside and out of Gianni's view.

Well played, David, he thought. There was nothing in the broker's demeanour to suggest anything was amiss. The promise of a further quarter million if the con woman accepted the yacht was too big a temptation for him to want to screw this up. That money was on top of the hundred thousand Gianni had already paid him. Information came with a price, and Gianni was happy to pay it.

He sent her a message.

Just landed. Can't wait to see you. G x

How did he know she was a hustler? His gut. It was never wrong. The one time he'd ignored it, the consequences had been disastrous. The evidence was pretty damn convincing too. Beautiful woman entering a club renowned as a haven for the rich and powerful, on the lookout for a man to reel in. She'd played her part beautifully. Those come-to-bed eyes. The seductive smile. The *pièce de résistance*— her enthusiasm for the single life. Unspoken had been the promise of a no-strings-attached fling that any man would salivate for while cleverly and subtly establishing that she *was* rich by mentioning her yacht. Putting herself on an equal financial footing to quell any doubts her victim might have. She'd been *magnificent*. If Rob hadn't seen her get into a cab and establish that she'd told at least one lie, Gianni wouldn't have doubted her at all. That's how good she'd been. And if he hadn't doubted her he wouldn't have got a close associate in Barbados to ask around at all the marinas in Bridgetown about a beautiful blonde called Issy who kept her yacht moored there. No one had heard of this woman… but all the digging around did reveal one delicious nugget. The slippery English broker David Reynolds was trying to pull in a favour and borrow—not charter—a modest yacht of no less than forty feet. What made this nugget so delicious was that the notoriously greedy David lived on his own yacht so was unlikely to need it for himself. Oh, and the date he needed it for was, coincidentally, the day Gianni flew out to the Caribbean.

On a hunch, Gianni got his associate to have a little chat with David Reynolds. After handing over considerable cold hard cash, he hit pay dirt. The yacht was needed for the exclusive use of a woman called Isabelle Clements.

It could have been a coincidence. Except Gianni didn't believe in coincidence. Only one way to find out, and that was to offer up his brand-new yacht, the *Palazzo delle Feste*, to the mysterious Isabelle Clements.

His gut and hunches had all been proved right. The beautiful Issy was indeed Isabelle Clements.

The beautiful Issy was indeed a hustler. A con woman.

His phone buzzed. The hustler had responded.

What a coincidence! Just docked! Still up for meeting at Freddo's later? x

They'd exchanged dozens of messages and numerous phone calls since their contrived meeting. It had been great fun stringing her along, asking her questions about what she was up to, wondering what outrageous lie she'd come up with next. 'Oh, I've spent the day snorkelling,' or, 'I spent the day with friends in St Lucia. Have you been? Oh, you must, it's to die for!' It was the phone calls he'd enjoyed the most, and not just because he could imagine her squirming over the lies he was forcing her to fabricate on the hoof. He kept capturing hints of genuine humour in her beautiful voice that only added to the anticipation. A hookup with a beautiful hustler with a sense of humour? What man could resist?

He fired a quick reply.

Wouldn't miss it for the world. 5 p.m.? G x

Her response flashed moments later.

Perfect. x

He read their most recent exchange a second time and grinned.

Let the games commence.

Issy was trying very hard not to panic. She needed to entice Gianni onto 'her' yacht by tomorrow at the latest. She knew that wouldn't be a problem, but what *would* be a problem was how she'd be able to act the role of superyacht owner when she didn't know her way around said superyacht.

She could have cheerfully kicked David in the ankle for screwing this up. She'd been specific about her requirements. Six months spent as his unpaid dogsbody meant she'd earned the right to be specific about them. Issy and Amelia had spent hours debating the best kind of yacht for Issy to have, and in all honesty, a battered old fishing boat would be better than this floating palace.

Still, David had assured her the crew would lie to any guest she brought on board and say she was the owner, and all that time spent as David's dogsbody meant she knew yacht crews were meticulously trained and would cater to her every need without her having to actually open her mouth and order them about. She'd never been any good at ordering people about, mainly because she hated being bossed about herself and so cringed to hear commands come out of her own mouth.

Knowing Amelia would be worrying, she took a picture of her opulent bedroom and sent it to her. She didn't dare tell her sister about David's cock-up, but a nice internal picture that didn't give anything away would do fine. Amelia needed to focus on her own task of pushing through her recommendation of a specific company for the Rossi Industries project she was managing. In reality, that specific company was nothing like Amelia had made it appear on paper. Going with that company would be an unmitigated disaster for Rossi Industries. The knock-on effects would destroy their entire enterprise. And destroy them. Perfect.

The sisters had known for a long time that the only way to topple the Rossi cousins would be by separating them. Together, they were as solid as rock, the cousins perfectly complementing each other so that nothing ever slipped past them. It would be impossible for Amelia to succeed if both cousins had to sign the project off and with it, sign off her recommendation. One cousin might miss or overlook something but the other would always pick it up.

Divide and conquer. It was the only way for the Seymore sisters to win, and it was with that thought at the forefront of her mind that Issy forced her feet into a pair of impossibly high wedged sandals—stilettos were forbidden on this yacht—and inspected her appearance one last time. Seeing as Gianni believed she'd been in the Caribbean for ten days already, fake tan had been a necessity, and she paid special attention to her exposed flesh to ensure her skin was streak-free. Satisfied she looked as good as she could for the money she'd paid, Issy made her way out of the floating palace to meet her handsome nemesis.

Here she came, striding gracefully towards the beachside restaurant, blonde hair blowing gently in the breeze, large designer shades covering much of her beautiful face, lithe body showcased to perfection in a pale green shirt dress that skimmed her deeply golden thighs and was complemented by a large, brightly coloured beaded necklace.

He rose from his chair to greet her.

Pretty white teeth flashing in delight, she strode straight to him and rested a hand on his shoulder so they could exchange kisses to each other's cheeks. A cloud of her exotic perfume enveloped him. He inhaled it as greedily as he relished the brush of her lips against his skin.

His memories hadn't played him false. She was every inch as stunning as he remembered.

'Well, here we are,' she said brightly once she'd settled herself in the seat across from him, lifting her shades to rest on top of her head.

He smiled slowly, noting the shirt dress was unbuttoned

enough to expose a glimpse of black lace bra, a deliberate tactic he was sure, and one he wholeheartedly approved of. If this was a taster of Isabelle Clements tactics for hustling money out of him then he was in for one hell of a ride. 'Here we are. I hope you don't mind but I've taken the liberty of ordering you a mojito.'

Those deep blue eyes he remembered so vividly sparkled. 'You have an impressive memory and no, I don't mind at all.'

For the longest time nothing was said as they gazed at each other, both feigning disbelief that they had actually made this happen, that they were sat across a table from each other in a restaurant located thousands of miles and numerous time zones from where they'd met.

Books had been written and films made about people like Issy Clements. Gianni cared not at all that he was the man her net had been thrown at. On the contrary. Anticipation as to how far she was prepared to go in her hustle thrummed heavily in him.

It had been a long, long time since he'd experienced excitement on a level like this. It wasn't that his life was boring—far from it—but Gianni and Alessandro had achieved such success with their business and after such torrid beginnings that there was no challenge left to it now. Nothing to strive for other than success on top of success. He would never be so immodest as to deny that Mother Nature hadn't blessed him with looks that most women found attractive but since his bank balance had sprung into the stratosphere, women had ceased to be a challenge too. Sometimes he would go to a party and have so many feminine eyes openly seduce him that he felt like a kid in a sweetshop who'd already gorged on all the chocolate. He could take his pick. And he did.

Like the cars he drove, Gianni liked his women fast, sleek and glossy; preferably tall and blonde. He also preferred them to have money, not from any form of snobbery—after all, he and his cousin came from nothing—but because he'd tired of reading about his 'sexploits' in the press. As he didn't date any woman long enough to learn if she was trustworthy or not, it made sense to shrink his dating pool to those he knew from the off didn't need to sell stories about him.

'So...' he said, breaking the silence with a seductive gleam. 'Do you come here often?'

Was it possible for the man to have a cheesier chat-up line? Issy wondered, mentally rolling her eyes. He was just so sure of himself, so keenly aware of the power of his sexuality and the effect it had on women that she supposed he didn't feel the need to bother using his wit. And he had wit. A great deal of it. She knew. She'd researched the man for years, night after night spent searching his name, learning the minutest detail about him. Of course, Amelia had got to know him quite well in a professional capacity and she'd grudgingly admitted he was as good-humoured in real life as he came across in interviews and the snippets of conversation attributed to him. Most of the time, in any case. It never boded well on anyone who dared cross him...but the Seymore sisters already knew that. They'd lived it.

His rampant sexuality had no effect on her. Gianni's handsome face, with its square jaw and the firm lips considered by many, many women to be *kissable* repulsed her. How many hours had she sat at her laptop staring into those light blue eyes with her stomach churning violently? Too many. There was not a millimetre of his face she was unfamiliar with, from the slight cleft in the tip of his broken nose—she would one day learn who broke it and shake their hand—to the way his left eyebrow sat a fraction higher than the right. She knew the dark hair currently exposed at the top of his unbuttoned black shirt whirled over defined pectoral muscles and down over a flat washboard stomach. She knew he was exactly six foot three. She knew he had his thick dark hair trimmed every fortnight. She knew that by the end of his two weeks in the Caribbean the currently stubbled square jaw would be covered in a thick black beard that would then be shaved before he returned to the world of business. She knew that if it was possible to think of Gianni dispassionately, she'd agree he was a walking shot of testosterone and that his muscular frame contained a potent sexuality that would make any other woman weak at the knees.

But not her. Issy was immune to any sexuality he exuded. The burn that had ignited in her veins in the London bar was the deep anticipation of impending revenge. The haunting of his gorgeous face in her thoughts was nothing new. He'd haunted her for years. What made the haunting bearable was imagining it crumpling the day he realised she'd taken everything he held dear from him.

Still, she'd thought better of him than cheesy chat-up lines.

Returning the gleam, she answered, 'Barbados is great, but I prefer to be out on the open sea. You?'

'Depends on my mood. When I'm on land all I require is great food, great beer and an excellent view.'

She let her gaze bore into his. 'The view from where I'm currently sitting is pretty something.'

He returned the heated stare. 'Really?'

She smiled suggestively and took great pleasure in watching his light blue eyes darken. Two years spent starving herself to create the feminine stick insect look he desired was paying off.

Her mojito and a fresh lager for Gianni was brought to their table. He held his bottle aloft. 'To the start of a beautiful new friendship.'

Smiling, Issy clinked her glass to it and took a flirtatious sip of her cocktail through the straw.

'I have to say, your command of the English language is seriously impressive,' she said, stroking his ego. 'If it wasn't for the hint of an accent, you could believe it was your first language.' A decade ago, his accent had been strong. 'Were you raised bilingual?'

'I'm self-taught.'

'Even more impressive. What spurred you on?'

'My business is based in England. I run it with my cousin.'

'What kind of business?'

'Property. What business are you in?'

'I'm not—I'm a trust fund baby.'

'Rich mummy and daddy?'

Ignoring the faint mocking tone of his voice, she nodded and had another drink.

'And what do Mummy and Daddy do?'

She told him the first real truth of their acquaintance. 'Daddy died quite a few years ago and Mummy's in rehab.'

Gianni made a suitably sympathetic face. So *this* was how the hustle was going to work. Personally, he would have put his money on her letting slip about a seriously ill close family member—a small niece or nephew would be ideal—whose life was hanging in the balance but who could be saved if only they could afford the excruciating amount of money needed for a proven but experimental treatment that poor Issy would love to pay herself if not for a temporary cash-flow problem. Mummy being in rehab was less heart-rending but, on reflection, a safer bet. No medical jargon to remember.

He mentally applauded her for sowing the seed so early, and made another private bet to himself that by the end of the evening she would have mentioned the excruciating costs of the rehab facility.

'That must be tough for you.'

'What doesn't kill you makes you stronger,' the clever hustler dismissed airily.

He raised his beer. 'I will drink to that.'

Clinking bottle to glass again, they finished their drinks. While they waited for fresh ones to be brought over, Issy scoured the menu searching for the meal that contained the least amount of calories.

When this was all over, she was going to hit her favourite fast-food restaurant and bury her face in all the burgers and chips and ice cream she'd spent the last two years denying herself.

She ordered a low-fat Caesar salad and made sure not to sound like she was ordering her personal equivalent of dog food.

'What does a trust fund baby do all day?' he asked once their order had been taken.

She fluttered her eyelashes. 'Why, has fun of course.'

'And where do you like to have your fun?'

Smiling suggestively, she wrapped a lock of hair around her finger in the same way she'd noted a couple of his old lovers had done. 'That all depends.'

'On?'

'My mood… And the company.'

Eyes gleaming, he laughed. 'Has anyone told you you're beautiful?'

I should ruddy hope I look beautiful, Cheesy Chat-Up Man. It cost a ruddy fortune to achieve this look.

Until exactly two weeks ago, when Amelia found the proof they'd been seeking and they'd realised the stars had finally aligned for them, Issy had rarely worn make-up, never bothered with fake tan and her hair had been a lank dark chestnut normally shoved back in a ponytail or plait.

'Has anyone told you you're an incredibly sexy man?'

He leaned forwards, wafting his cologne with him. 'Not in the last ten days.'

Been slacking, have you? Or too busy with the Aurora project that's about to come to fruition for Rossi Industries and is worth billions to you? Or so you think.

'Have you been hiding in a cave?'

He grinned. 'Not quite. Work has been all consuming. Believe me, I've earned this break.'

You certainly have. Earned it off the grave of my father when you forced a hostile takeover of his company.

'A week to unwind and recharge your batteries?'

'Two weeks.'

'Two?' She raised one of the eyebrows she'd plucked into submission, as if she didn't know exactly when he was due to return to what would be left of his business. 'How much fun can one man have in two weeks?'

'That all depends.'

'On?'

'If there's someone for me to play with.'

She held his gaze and smiled. 'Oh, I imagine a man like you would have no shortage of playmates.'

'It's never been a problem for me before.'

Such modesty. It was so becoming. Not.

'You know, my yacht has many toys on board.'

The sexy gleam shimmered. 'Really?'

'Uh-huh.' Emulating his gleam, she mimicked him further by leaning forwards, deliberately allowing him a good peek of her cleavage. 'I even have a slide.'

'Who doesn't love a good slide on a yacht?'

She grazed her teeth over her bottom lips and dropped her voice to a seductive purr. 'My thoughts exactly. If you haven't got anything planned, how would you like to join me on it tomorrow? We can take it to sea…try the slide out.'

'I can think of nothing I'd rather do.'

She raised her glass and flashed her first genuine smile. 'It's a date.'

He practically stripped her naked with his eyes. 'I'm already looking forward to it.'

CHAPTER THREE

ISSY EXAMINED EVERY inch of her bikini-clad body. The last time she'd worn a swimsuit she'd been twelve and forbidden from wearing anything but a full-piece swimsuit by her protective parents. She had a feeling if either of them could see the teeny-weeny white bikini she was wearing now, they would spontaneously combust.

She was scared she might spontaneously combust too, in embarrassment.

But this was the kind of bikini Gianni Rossi's lovers wore. She couldn't afford to disappoint him until they were far out at sea and she'd managed to throw his phone overboard.

But, heavens, it was revealing. Luckily it covered her bottom half quite well apart from where it tied together at the side of her hips, but about the only thing it covered up top was her nipples.

Feeling the panic that often tried to grab her throat rise, Issy breathed deeply and wrapped a sheer blue sarong around her to give herself the illusion of modesty. It was too late to back out now.

She only had to lead him on until she got rid of his phone, and then she could dress herself in a sack if she so pleased.

The problem was she could taste danger. It had been there on her tongue since she woke that morning. She had no idea where it was coming from, but her Spidey senses were warning her of *something*.

Warning her of Gianni? And if so, why?

Was she playing with fire?

Gianni was a playboy, but he was not a man to force a woman. None of his legion of lovers had a bad word to say about him and there was no way Amelia would have gone along with this if she'd thought Issy would be putting herself in any kind of physical danger with him. As she'd grudgingly put it, he was gentleman playboy.

Issy's gut had aligned with Amelia's description of him during their first meet in London. Her gut told her he posed no physical danger to her. So why did she feel so threatened? Was it even threatened that she was feeling?

Too late now. Today was the day Amelia made her bogus recommendation to Alessandro Rossi and the rest of the team. Issy needed to get Gianni out to sea and keep him there, without communication, until she had word that the contracts were signed and the deal that would destroy the Rossi cousins was done. That should take around three days but could be longer. She would have to flirt. Lead him on. Maybe allow him a kiss or two…and trust her sister and her own gut that he wouldn't force those simple kisses or two into anything more.

Heaven help her, she'd never led a man on before.

Truth was, she'd barely been kissed either. Her one barely kiss had occurred when she'd been David's dogsbody, by one of his caterers. Unfortunately said caterer had been handling fish and the smell oozing from him had put her off so much that she'd spent the rest of her dogsbody career avoiding him. There had been no one else. Between her real day job in the children's ward and her night job of learning everything there was to know about Gianni, there had been no time for anyone else. Besides, it was a bit hard to look at men in a romantic way when your thoughts were consumed by someone else, even if that was someone you despised with a passion, and she hated that she'd relaxed into his company over their meal and that the hours had passed so quickly. He'd regaled her with tales of his friends' exploits that had genuinely amused her. If she didn't know who he was, she would be in danger of actually liking him.

But that was the power of the man. Beneath the handsome, easygoing exterior, Gianni was the devil in disguise.

Straightening her spine, she left her bedroom and made her way to the deck Gianni would enter 'her' yacht from. After their meal, she'd spent a couple of intense hours familiarising herself with the main areas of the yacht and felt a lot more confident about passing it off as her own than she had when David had shocked her with it.

Two crew members were already on deck, ready to greet her guest.

Issy was about to take a seat in the shaded section when a tall figure emerged dockside in the distance.

Her heart and belly did a simultaneous flip.

The closer he strolled, the harder her heart pumped.

Even though he wore shades as large as her own, he still turned heads from both sexes. Maybe it was the black polo shirt he wore, which fit snugly across his broad chest and showcased his spectacular physique. Or maybe it was the canvas khaki shorts that she knew without having to check showcased his tight butt cheeks.

He stopped a few feet from the yacht, looking as if he were reading its name to make sure he'd reached the right one, then caught sight of her. A devastating smile stretched across his face and he bounded up the right-hand steps to board.

Her heart pumped even harder and faster.

'*Bella*, your yacht is as dazzling as you are,' he said as he closed in on her and laid a hand on her hip. He kissed both her cheeks before taking her hand and bringing it to his mouth. He grazed his lips over her knuckles. 'A stunning vessel for a stunning lady.'

To her absolute horror, Issy felt a burn crawl over her cheeks and knew she was blushing. Or was that flushing? Because she didn't know if it was the heat of his breath on her skin causing it or the seductive appreciation in his stare.

'I enjoy my time on it,' she murmured, hoping her own huge shades covered enough of her face to disguise the flush.

'I can imagine. Her name tells me you're a lady who lives to party.'

She bestowed him with a knowing smile and slowly extracted her manically tingling fingers from his hold. 'Today, the party is just you and me. Drink?'

He checked his thick watch and raised a neat black eyebrow. 'Too early for champagne?'

'It's never too early for champagne.' She nodded at one of the hovering crew, who bowed his head in answer and disappeared to sort the drinks for them, then turned to the other one. 'Tell the captain we're ready to set sail.'

Subtly bracing herself first, Issy tucked her hand into the crook of Gianni's muscular arm. 'That's if you're happy for us to set sail?'

Removing his shades, he practically stripped her naked with his hungry stare. 'I am at the mercy of your every whim.'

The sensation of being under threat hit her so hard that she had to grind her toes into her impossibly high wedged sandals to stop her feet running and throwing herself overboard. The flesh of Gianni's arm was warm beneath her hand. Smooth. A texture completely different to her own. The tingling in her fingers seeped through her skin and into her bloodstream, making her already frantic beating heart increase in tempo. There was nothing fake about the breathlessness of her voice when she managed to tease, 'Oh, I do love it when a man's at my mercy.'

Eyes alight with sensuality, he wolfishly, playfully, snapped his teeth together. The tingles in her blood seeped even lower. Deeper. Her legs had become distinctly wobbly.

They'd barely stepped inside when Danny, who'd worked for Gianni for six years, carried their champagne over, holding the tray out and not betraying by so much as a flicker that he knew him.

'Thank you,' the con woman said. 'Please tell Chef we will want lunch on the pool deck in an hour.'

Gianni didn't try to stop the swelling laughter. His head chef, whose name she'd clearly not learned, was called Christophe and had worked for him for even longer than Danny. This was all just too delicious.

Seeing Issy's curious stare, he merely held his glass out so they could make yet another clink, tipped half the champagne he himself had paid for down his throat, then took hold of her free hand and leaned his face close to her ear. She was wearing that wonderful perfume again and, having twisted her blonde hair into a chic knot, he could smell the underlying sweetness of her skin layered in it. For perhaps the hundredth time, he allowed his imagination to run riot as to how far Isabelle Clements was prepared to go in her hustle. He could only hope she would go far enough that he got to inhale more of her scent than the delicate arch of her neck. 'Show me around your party palace.'

The quiver of her skin was so subtle he could easily have missed it. But he didn't miss it. He saw it. He felt it.

He smiled.

This just got better and better. His hustler genuinely desired him. Since realising she was a con woman, he'd wondered if she'd targeted him deliberately—Gianni was well-known in the media and the club she'd turned up at was one he was known to frequent—or if any man there that night who'd caught her eye would have done. He didn't suppose it mattered. But it did make the game a lot more fun to suspect a genuine desire on her part.

As Gianni had yet to spend any real time in his new yacht, it was quite surreal to be given a tour of it by the great pretender. Everything had been designed with his input. The fact all the entertainment, from the casino to the movie room, was confined to the main deck was deliberate, and when they reached the games room with the full-size snooker table he couldn't resist raising a querying eyebrow. He suspected that when those heels were removed, Issy would reveal herself to be much shorter than she carried herself. Snooker was by no means a man's game but it helped to be able to see over the table. 'You're a snooker player?'

'Some of my guests like to play,' she neatly deflected. 'I'm not known as the hostess with the mostest for nothing.'

He grinned. She might be a con woman but beneath the high-society persona she was playing for all its worth he thought might lurk a woman who was genuinely fun. 'Want to play?'

'And miss out on the sunshine? We can play when the sun goes down.'

'You're not going to return me to shore before you turn into a pumpkin?'

Her dimples appeared—a sign he was starting to recognise meant she was genuinely amused. 'Want to swim?'

'Does that mean I get to go on your slide?'

Stepping closer to him, she picked a speck of flint off his polo shirt and huskily said, 'That all depends.'

He rested a hand on her hip. The gap between them was so small he could feel the heat of her hot body. 'Depends on what?'

Her teeth grazed her bottom lip and her eyes gleamed. 'On where we anchor, of course.' A smile lit her face and she tugged at his hand. 'Come on, I want to swim before we eat.'

Issy discreetly checked her watch as she removed it. The meeting in London would be well under way. Casually, she placed the watch with her phone on the table and made sure not to react when Gianni placed his own watch and phone next to them, then added his wallet to the pile.

She just needed to keep him off that phone until the moment to get rid of it presented itself...

Pondering on how to dispose of it dissolved when Gianni pulled off his polo shirt.

Suddenly she was overcome with the need to fan herself. Dear God in heaven, that body...

That thought dissolved too when his hands went to the button of his canvas shorts.

Her mouth ran dry.

It hadn't occurred to her until that precise moment that Gianni hadn't brought anything with him other than what was laid on the table.

The zip went down. Eyes locked on her face, his hands went to his hips and he tugged the shorts down.

Issy caught a glimpse of thickened hair at the base of his abdomen...at his groin...before the shorts fell to the floor and, with the hint of a wink, he casually pulled up the swim shorts he was wearing beneath them to a more modest level.

'Do you have sun cream?' he asked.

'Sorry?' she croaked.

'Sun cream. You know, the stuff you cover your skin with to stop you burning and hopefully prevent you from getting a melanoma?'

Pull yourself together! she shouted at herself. *You've seen his body before, many, many times.*

But, dear God in heaven, it was one thing to see that body on a laptop screen and quite another to see it in the flesh.

No picture, however talented the photographer, could do that body justice. Or that face.

'Yes.' That was better. More normal. She pulled a smile to her face and took out the expensive sun cream from the bag that had cost her two weeks' wages, and handed it to him. She was struck, not for the first time, by the size and strength of his hands, and fresh tingles zipped through her skin and veins to imagine those hands...

To imagine those hands *what*? Touching her?

Had she already had too much sun? Because she was fast starting to think her brain had become addled. There was no reason on earth for her to imagine that, just like there'd been no reason on earth for the heat that had pulsed through her when she'd picked at the imaginary fleck on his polo shirt a while ago, or for that heat to deepen in her most intimate part when his hand had rested on her hip and only the sheerness of her sarong had been a barrier between their flesh. No reason for that moment when anticipation had thrummed through her at the thought of his firm lips closing on hers.

Issy had a job to do. This man was her enemy. If her body was developing signs that could be mistaken for attraction then she had to rise above them. No way it was attraction. No way Jose.

'Would you do my back for me?' he asked once he'd finished slathering every inch of his limbs and torso.

Absolutely not!

'My pleasure,' she purred, taking the bottle from him and resisting squirting it in his eyes.

Standing behind him, she controlled the urge to squirt it cold straight onto his naked skin and dolloped a load into her hand.

Holding her breath, she put her hands to his back.

The muscles bunched.

Her heart clenched with her lungs.

She rubbed the lotion into the smooth skin. Her heart unclenched and began to pound.

Up to his neck her hands worked, over the shoulder blades, down the spine, around the sides. By the time she reached the waistband of his swim shorts her lack of breath was no longer deliberate and her lips were tingling as she fought their yearning to press a kiss right into the centre of this sculpted masterpiece.

She had to physically force herself to step back, and when he turned and caught her eye, every organ in her body made a double flip.

'My turn,' he said, a slow, sensual smile forming.

'I...' The urge to lie and say she'd already screened her back was almost stronger than any future potential melanoma threat.

The sense of danger was stronger than ever.

She turned around.

Saying a prayer for luck, she forced air into her lungs and untied her sarong. It floated to her feet.

She heard him take a sharp intake of breath.

Her refilled lungs expelled in a whoosh the moment his fingers made contact with her skin.

Sensation shivered through her, deepening as his fingers slowly caressed the lotion over her back. When they dipped under the thin string holding her excuse of a bikini together, a wild fantasy sprang into her mind of him untying the knot and cupping her aching breasts...

She didn't even know breasts *could* ache. She didn't have to look down to know her nipples had puckered. She couldn't look down even if she wanted. It was taking everything she had to keep her gaze fixed ahead and to stop her legs from collapsing beneath her.

His fingers skimmed the top of her bikini bottoms. This time she could do nothing to stop the betraying quiver of her body.

Too much sun.

But this was okay! The thought punched through. This was okay. Better than okay. Wasn't she supposed to be leading Gianni on? Holding his interest in the only way a woman could because all he cared about when it came to women was the superficiality of their appearance and what he could get out of them in the bedroom.

She just had to keep hold of herself and not let her sun-addled brain trick her needy virgin body into believing it could possibly be attracted to one of the men directly responsible for the loss of everything she'd ever held dear. Her body was so starved it would likely react in the same way to any man!

His hands clasped her biceps. He was going to press himself against her.

Without warning to either him or herself, Issy stepped out of his hold, kicked her sandals off and, only just remembering to throw a cheeky grin over her shoulder, ran to the pool and jumped into the cool water.

Gianni didn't hesitate to follow her.

Dio, there was something about Issy's skin he reacted to, from her touch on him to his touch on her, infecting the whole of him, soaking him in erotic awareness.

By the time he dived into the pool, she'd swum to the far end, treading water as she faced him.

Half a dozen long strokes and he reached her.

Although she met his stare with that fantastic insouciance, she was trembling.

He closed the gap, gripping the walls of the pool on either side of her slender body, trapping her, and drank in her beauty.

She was ravishing. The most beautiful con woman to roam the earth. And the sexiest.

Thrums of desire beat heavily in him.

From the darkness in her pulsing eyes and the unsteadiness of her breaths, Issy was feeling it too.

It was time to up the ante.

Let the pleasure commence.

He sank his mouth into the softness of her lips in a full-bodied charged kiss of attrition. *Dio*, she tasted of champagne with added heat, a taste that roused his already electrified body, and he wrapped his arms around her and pulled her tight against him.

Her surrender was immediate. Her lips parted and in an instant her hands clasped the back of his head, fingers scratching through his hair and into his skull, and she was devouring him with the same hunger infusing him. With her small, high breasts crushed against his chest and her legs wrapped around his waist, her tongue duelling with his, Gianni's arousal was as thick and heavy as he had ever known it, jutting hard against her inner thigh.

Kissing Issy was like tasting honey from heaven and his excitement somehow managed to thicken and tighten even more to wonder if the rest of her tasted as if she'd been gift-wrapped by the king of the gods, Jupiter himself.

He would have to discover that another time because the moment he broke the kiss to drag his mouth over her cheek and to her neck, her fingers gripped his hair tightly and pulled his head back.

Her eyes were drugged with desire. He knew his eyes reflected the same.

She swallowed, then sucked in a breath. And then she released her grip on his hair, placed her hands to his chest and, with a giggle, pushed him back. 'Not so fast, big boy.'

He snapped his teeth at her. 'I can do slow.' Then he licked the lobe of her delicate ear and huskily added, 'I can do whatever you like.'

Hands laid lightly on his shoulders, she stretched her neck and, with a smile, gazed up at the clear azure sky. 'We have all the time in the world.'

Cupping her chin, he pressed a feather-kiss to her lips. 'All the time we need,' he whispered.

The drugged daze came back into her eyes but she blinked it away, then looked over his shoulder at something that had caught her eye and brightly said. 'Looks like lunch is ready. Come on, let's eat.'

Gianni stepped aside to release her. 'Give me a minute and I'll join you.'

Her pretty eyebrows drew in.

He grinned ruefully and dropped his stare to below the waterline. 'I need to cool off for a minute. I don't want to frighten the crew.'

She followed his gaze. A bright stain of colour crawled over her cheeks as understanding sank in, and it took her longer than normal to compose herself. 'Okay, probably best you stay here a while. Cold beer?'

'That would be great.'

She hauled herself out of the pool.

He didn't think he was imagining the slight stagger in her walk back to the lounging area.

Dio, her body…

No more focusing on that hot body, he scolded himself even as he internally sighed with disappointment when she wrapped a towel around it. Not while arousal still had its tentacles in him.

Maybe he should get Issy to bring the cold beer over and pour it down his swim shorts.

The staff were busy setting out plates and glasses on the deck's dining table. Issy had just finished retying her hair when she suddenly snatched her phone up and read whatever had just pinged into it. She was still reading when one of the crew approached her. She put her phone back on the table, nodded at whatever the crewman said, then indicated she would be two minutes to Gianni, and disappeared inside.

Gianni had never swum so fast in his life. He streaked through the water, hauled himself out and strode quickly to the table their stuff was on. Pressing his hand onto a towel a crew member had left for him, he grabbed Issy's phone.

'Tell me when she's on her way back,' he ordered the nearest crew member as he removed his own phone and top-of-the-range cloning device from the back pocket of the canvas shorts he'd left slung over a chair. In moments, he'd copied all the data from her phone onto his.

Carefully placing Issy's phone back where he'd found it, he dried himself off, removed his swim shorts, wrapped a dry towel around his waist, took a seat at the dining table and drank thirstily from the bottle of cold beer placed before him. Then, with a huge grin of satisfaction that came from knowing he'd upped the stakes in this game of chance in his favour, he swiped the screen of his phone for the first look at his bounty. Issy's screen saver appeared.

The grin died as his heart thumped then nose-dived in recognition.

He blinked, then blinked again, certain he must be seeing things.

The image of two young women, faces pressed together, smiling for the camera, remained.

The pulse at the side of his jaw throbbing, head pounding as he tried to make sense of something that absolutely did not make sense, he went into her messages.

The last of his euphoria died at the exact same moment his screen faded into nothing. Cloning Issy's phone had drained his battery.

But he'd seen enough.

This was no hustle.

This was a deliberate, targeted attack.

CHAPTER FOUR

Issy TOUCHED UP her lip gloss with a shaking hand. She needed to touch up her eyeliner but was too scared of stabbing herself in the eye to dare.

The lip gloss dropped from her hand and clattered in the sink. She clutched her flushed cheeks and gazed at her reflection. Her eyes had a fevered brightness to them. It was nothing to what was going on inside her.

Her heart was a pulsating mess, her limbs weak, her stomach as tight a knot as she'd ever known it. Between her legs...

She squeezed her eyes shut and tried to fill her lungs.

Okay, so she wasn't immune to Gianni's animal magnetism. No point in denying it. The main thing to remember was that she'd come to her senses before the situation had got even close to getting out of hand.

The situation that entailed Gianni turning her into flames. What did flames do? They burned the object into ashes. She'd kept control of the situation. She'd dealt with it.

But, heaven help her, her body still felt scorched in all the places they'd bound themselves so tightly together.

She could still feel his mouth devouring hers.

As part of all her preparation for this, she should have found some men to practice kissing with. Maybe then she'd have developed some immunity to the act and wouldn't have turned into a molten flame for him.

A careful swipe of bronzer against her cheeks and a fresh sarong around her, and she was ready to face him again. As ready as she'd ever be.

She found Gianni at the dining table, leaned back in his seat, casually drinking lager from a bottle so cold rivulets of condensation dripped down it. Not until he rose to his feet did she realise he had a towel wrapped around his waist. A quick dart of her eyes to where they'd been sitting found his swim shorts drying on the back of a chair. His canvas shorts were where he'd left them earlier.

A pulse throbbed between her legs. Beneath that towel, Gianni was naked.

'Everything okay?' he asked.

She nodded and smiled brightly. 'Just needed to freshen up. I hope you're hungry—Chef's made us a feast.'

His gaze held hers then drifted slowly down her bikini-clad body. 'I'm ravenous.'

Their first course was a fire roasted tomato soup Issy had loved since she was a little girl but had never been able to re-create for herself. The French chef must have sought an authentic Italian recipe for it because it was even better than she'd tasted as a child.

'Don't you eat bread?' Gianni asked, nodding at the freshly made bread roll she'd left on her side plate.

She shook her head and offered it to him, then tried not to salivate when he ripped it in two and slathered each piece with butter.

Not long, she consoled herself. Not long until she could bury her face in an ocean of carbs and not care that they all landed straight on her hips. She could heap a spoonful of sugar into her coffee *and* a dollop of cream if she wanted. She could buy herself a huge bar of hazelnut chocolate and eat it all in one sitting.

She'd been hungry for two whole years. She could wait a few days more. She would celebrate Gianni and his equally abhorrent cousin's destruction by indulging herself in all the delicious foods and treats she'd had to deny herself to maintain the stick insect look.

For their second course she'd selected fresh tuna, pan-fried in Japanese spices and served on a bed of couscous with roasted peppers. Fresh tuna was an expensive treat she could never normally afford under the strict budget Issy and Amelia imposed on themselves, and as it was healthy and her portion small, she ate the lot, then made sure to drink a whole glass of water to fill her up.

Dessert was freshly made strawberry ice cream on a chocolate crumb base but, as divine as it tasted, she allowed herself only a couple of small spoonsful before pushing the bowl to one side.

'Are there no foods you enjoy so much that you allow yourself to gorge?' Gianni asked, watching her closely. Issy's return to deck meant he'd had to compose himself quickly. Years of being able to adopt a poker face in stressful moments, dating back to a time when he didn't even know what a poker face was, just knew he didn't want to give his father the satisfaction of seeing fear in his eyes, meant his outward composure was no effort at all.

What was occurring beneath his skin was a whole different matter.

He felt like he'd been sucker-punched.

The lying, conniving temptress shook her head in answer. *Mio Dio*, even Issy's slender frame was a lie.

Her screen saver kept playing in his mind's eye. He'd recognised the other woman before he'd recognised Issy. Well, what person wouldn't struggle to recognise the slender blonde picking at her food before him with the plump dark-chestnut-haired woman in the photo? The chestnut-haired woman, her face pressed against the other woman's, had gripped tightly to a huge ice cream sundae, as if afraid someone would snatch it away from her if she let go of it even for a photograph. Only the dark blue eyes had revealed her to be the lying, conniving temptress before him.

The broker must have lied to him about her name because the woman nibbling on a piece of lettuce was not Isabelle Clements. She was Isabelle Seymore. Daughter of the bastard who'd ripped off the Rossi cousins by selling them land it was impossible to build on and bribing the very people whose due diligence should have picked up that fact. Their first business deal still left a bitter taste on Gianni's tongue that even the revenge they'd taken on the man once they'd rebuilt themselves and conducted a hostile takeover of his company hadn't lessened.

Like father like daughter. Or, as he should say, like daughters. Plural. Because there were two Seymore sisters. And the other sister, the woman he'd instantly recognised in Issy's screen saver, was in a far more dangerous position to inflict lasting harm on the Rossi cousins.

Amelia Seymore. *Dio*, how long had she worked for them? Had to be two years. She was a good, diligent worker, the type who always arrived early, got her head down and got on with the job. No fuss. The kind of worker Gianni often wished others would be more like.

It had never crossed his mind that she was the daughter of the corrupt bastard who'd taken advantage of them in their first business deal. Not even her surname had given him pause for thought. Seymore was a reasonably common surname, and besides, who would be so blatant as to set up camp in the enemy's quarters under her real name?

Amelia Seymore, that's who.

Damn his phone for dying on him. He needed to warn Alessandro. He'd managed to get one of the crew to take it inside and charge it for him before Issy came back on deck, and it was taking all his willpower to keep his backside rooted to his chair and not storm inside to use it. To not unleash the full force of his fury on the conniving hussy actively seeking to destroy him.

He needed to keep his head. Give nothing away. Keep playing the game.

He took another drink of his second beer and contemplated Issy some more. There were many things he needed to do to shore up his defences, and warning his cousin was only one of them. From what he'd gleaned skimming her messages, the sisters were conducting a two-pronged attack, Amelia targeting the company, Issy tasked with keeping Gianni distracted until her sister's mission was complete. That mission revolved around the Aurora project for which she was the project manager.

Rossi Industries were on the cusp of making a creative partnership deal that would shake the property development world and send the cousins' already incredible wealth into the stratosphere. Today's leadership team meeting would be the decider on which company they partnered with. Gianni had already vetted it. He'd gone through every document with a fine-tooth comb. Nothing had jumped out at him. No warning flags about either of the final two short-listed companies. Nothing. He'd flown to the Caribbean content to leave the final decision on this to Alessandro knowing he would nip any trouble in the bud if it came to it. Whichever company they went with, they would be onto a guaranteed winner. Or so he'd believed.

What had he missed? He must have missed something. *Dammit!*

He drained his bottle and reminded himself that whatever the outcome of the meeting, nothing would be signed today. He had time in that regard.

Issy didn't know he'd discovered her true identity. He would make sure to keep it that way until they reached St Lovells, which was two days' sailing away from Barbados. Once on St Lovells, Issy would be powerless. St Lovells would be her kryptonite.

He needed to get rid of her phone. If he'd known when he cloned it the power it held, he'd have thrown it overboard or accidentally dropped it in the pool. It was seeing the two messages between Issy and her sister that had stopped his brain functioning as it should. The realisation that this was no mere hustle.

It was the message Amelia had sent to her sister two weeks ago that really churned his stomach.

They're corrupt. I have proof.

Churned it far more than the one written minutes after their meeting in London.

It worked! Hook, line and sinker.

What proof of corruption? Gianni and Alessandro were united in their demand their business be run straight down the line. They did not bribe. They did not lie. They did not cut corners. Their bastard fathers were the role models they used to work against and ensure everything they did was the opposite of how they would do it. Thomas Seymore's corrupt actions had only reinforced that ethos. Never mind the destructive fall-out such an accusation would bring, they'd been on the receiving end of malpractice and would never put anyone else through the same.

Any interrogation had to wait until they docked at St Lovells. Until then, he would take a leaf out of Issy's book and unleash the full force of his magnetism on her. Because that was the one big advantage he had—he knew damn well that for all her heinous plotting, Isabelle Seymore wanted him. He would play on that desire without mercy.

She didn't deserve his mercy.

He cast his gaze on her melting bowl of ice cream. 'May I?'

She lifted the bowl to him. 'Be my guest.'

'*Grazie.*'

'*Prego.*'

'You speak my language?'

There was a slight hesitation. 'Some.'

'I should have guessed seeing as you've given this beautiful vessel an Italian name.' Dipping his spoon into the ice cream, he lifted it to his mouth and added in Italian, 'I always think the best place to serve ice cream is on the naked body...and the best way to eat it is with my tongue.'

The dark stain of colour that flushed over her told him she'd understood him perfectly. The way she adjusted herself in her seat told him the image he'd evoked in her mind had infused into her body.

Smiling, he popped the spoon into his mouth.

Issy had to cross her legs tightly to stop herself from overtly squirming. But the bastard knew. She could see it in his eyes. He knew she'd understood his seductively delivered words and the effect they were having on her.

His command of the English language was so good it was easy to forget when speaking to him that Gianni was

Italian. Hearing that deep, sensuous voice in his mother tongue though…

It landed like a caress that penetrated deep into her core. His words had only added to the effect, and scrambled her brain to stop any quip forming.

Quite honestly, she needed to throw herself back into the pool to cool down.

God, she hoped the meeting in London was going to plan. Hoped the signing of the contracts was sped up and that it would all be wrapped up in a matter of days as Amelia expected and didn't drag on, because sitting there with Gianni's divinely masculine torso and heaven-sent face in her eye-line, the aftermath of the crush of their bodies still zinging through her skin and the mark of his mouth still on her lips…

This was hell.

Somehow she had to find a way to keep him distracted without compromising herself any further because she couldn't do this. It was too dangerous. Her awareness of Gianni was going through the roof. It was torture to even look him in the eye.

But look him in the eye she must, and she put her elbow on the table and rested her chin on her hand to murmur, 'We seem to be in a quiet stretch of water. How about I get the captain to anchor and we can get the slide out or take the Jet Skis for a spin?'

His eyes gave the sensuous glitter that melted her pelvis. '*Bella*, I've been fantasising about your slide since you first mentioned it.'

Issy contemplated the slide the crew had just finished inflating. Attached to the top sun deck and sweeping straight into the sea, it reminded her of a taller, narrow version of an airplane's safety slide. It wasn't just the slide that had been inflated. Next to where it jutted into the sea bobbed a giant square inflatable that could easily fit ten people on it. That too had been attached to the yacht.

She contemplated it because she wasn't the strongest of swimmers. She'd spent her childhood summers in and out of their Italian holiday home's swimming pool, but that had been a long time ago and, until that day, she hadn't been in a pool since. Even back then she'd never been interested in swimming itself, more interested in splashing around and trying to get a rise out of her sister by hurling beach balls at her head. Also, that had been a pool, with a definable bottom. She didn't dare ask the captain how deep the passage of water they'd anchored in was.

'Ready?' Gianni asked with that devilish grin of his.

Reminding herself that she was supposed to be a fearless society party girl, Issy grinned back. 'Race you to the top.'

She was off before she'd finished making her challenge, already darting up the steps to the next deck before Gianni realised what she was doing.

One good thing about working so hard on sculpting her body in recent years was that it had made her fit. Hungry, yes, but definitely fit. Also, it had made her quick on her feet, and she'd skipped up the first set of steps before Gianni even reached them. Laughing over her shoulder, she raced up the second set to the next deck, easily maintaining her lead, maintaining it too as she whipped up the third and final set... But no sooner had she put her foot on the top deck than a strong arm wrapped around her waist and lifted her in the air.

Legs flailing, she screamed, half in laughter and half in fright. For such a big man, she hadn't heard him closing in on her. He must have been holding himself back.

Dear God, she'd known Gianni was strong but he carried her near the top of the slide as if she weighed nothing, and when he put her down and twisted her round to face him, the size difference between them, even more prominent as she was barefoot, hit her starkly for the first time.

This man could break her in two with no effort whatsoever.

The sense of danger crept its way back through her but even as she tried to decipher it, she knew it was nothing to do with his size, that he would never use his physicality to hurt her.

He gazed down at her, blinked and shook his head. 'You're tiny.'

Uh-oh, she could feel a burn spread across her face. Gianni liked his women tall and leggy. In all her research she'd never learned of a lover who stood under five foot seven.

He placed his fingers under her chin and bowed his head. 'You carry yourself so tall but you're *tiny*.'

Impulsively, she pressed a finger to his lips. 'Don't tell anyone,' she said in a mock whisper. 'It's a secret.'

He stared at her for another beat and then burst into a roar of laughter. Issy couldn't help it. The sound was so infectious that laughter escaped her own lips, and when he put his hands to her sides and lifted her into the air so her face rose above his and her hair, which she'd set free, hung down like a waterfall, the compulsion to kiss him was so strong that it took everything she had to resist.

But resist she must. Even if her body did feel like it was on fire. 'Can you put me down please?'

His shoulders rose slowly before he acquiesced. But there was no time for her to make a break for distance. No sooner did her feet touch the deck than he pressed a hand into the small of her back and wiped a strand of hair off her face. 'You're beautiful.'

'Even though I'm short one end?' she quipped, a quip she was thankful and proud of making because those two words made her feel all fuzzy…but not as fuzzy as the look in his eyes did.

Heaven help her, everything about this man made her feel fuzzy.

Did she fancy him?

His gleaming sensuality burned through her. 'Small but perfectly formed.'

A sharp pang sliced through her chest and she had to work doubly hard not to show it.

It shouldn't even bother her! After all, wasn't this proof that all the money she and Amelia had scrimped and saved for over the years so Issy could pull off Gianni's version of perfection had worked? She should be glad they hadn't needed to invest in a stretching machine for her, not have her heart twist at the knowledge that he wouldn't look twice at the real Issy and certainly wouldn't consider her perfect.

Who *cared* what he thought? Not her. Once the deal in London was signed, sealed and delivered, she would disappear from his life and never see him again.

For the first time, Gianni saw the brightness Issy had maintained all this time in her eyes dim. In seconds she'd blinked it back to brightness, but he'd seen it and he wondered what had caused it, and then wondered why the hell he cared for the cause.

Aware of arousal strengthening in him, he reluctantly slipped his arm away from her, took a step back and indicated the slide. 'Ladies first.'

She smiled sweetly. 'Age before beauty.'

He sniggered. She might be a lying, conniving temptress

set on his destruction but she amused him. It had been a long time since he'd enjoyed a woman's company—anyone's company, come to that—so much, and when he cupped her cheeks and planted a hard, passionate kiss to her mouth, it was sheer impulse driving him with nothing calculated behind it.

Dio, she tasted so good.

'Seeing as I am here at your whim, ready to comply with your every wish, I will do the honours.' And with that, he climbed the three steps to the top of the slide, sat himself down and then let himself fall.

Issy peered over the balustrade and watched the enormous splash made when he landed. A knot of anxiety formed when he didn't immediately surface but it barely had time to root when his dark head suddenly appeared and, after wiping water from his eyes, his grinning face tilted up to hers.

Okay. Now it was her turn.

She could do this. To back out would only make him suspicious, and she couldn't afford that.

She remembered a time when a day at a splash park had been the height of fun, and charging down water slides of all shapes and sizes the biggest thrill of her life.

But those slides all landed in pools of water with a definable bottom and a host of lifeguards overlooking.

Stop being a wimp!

Resolved not to think about what she was about to do, she skipped up the three steps, waved at Gianni treading water a safe distance from the landing zone, plonked her bottom down and let go.

It felt exactly like what she imagined it would feel to free-fall. It was also much quicker than she'd anticipated, the water pouring down the slide as a lubricant hurtling her to the upward curving base so quickly she had no time to prepare or brace herself for the landing. Into the air she flew before slamming into the sea with a scream. Salt water shot up her nose and into her open mouth as she submerged into the depths.

CHAPTER FIVE

GIANNI'S AMUSEMENT AT the spectacularly ungraceful way Issy flipped in the air before crashing into the water vanished when she resurfaced in a panic of flailing arms. He didn't hesitate to streak through the water to her.

The moment he hooked an arm around her waist to stabilise her, she flung her arms around his neck and clung like a limpet to him.

'Hey, take it easy,' he chided when there was a danger she would drag him under. 'I've got you. Relax.'

Blonde hair splattered all over her face, dark blue eyes fixed onto his. She loosened her hold the tiniest fraction.

'Okay?' he asked.

Her lips pulled in before she nodded.

'Good.' Treading water for them both, he kissed her lightly. 'Can you swim to the inflatable?'

Still holding tightly to him, she turned her head to gauge the distance. It was only ten metres or so from where they were but he guessed from the look in her eyes that it could be ten miles as far as she was concerned.

'Hold on to my back,' he said. 'I'll swim us to it.'

Without losing her touch on his body, she twisted around him until she was gripping on to his back like a baby orangutan clinging to its mother.

'As great as it feels to have your legs wrapped around me

like this, you need to loosen up a bit if I'm going to be able to swim,' he told her drily. 'Trust the water's buoyancy and trust me. I've got you.'

Issy's definition of loosening up differed greatly to Gianni's, but at least she relaxed her hold enough for him to move his arms semi-freely.

Life took the strangest of turns he thought as he made his way steadily to the inflatable. Issy Seymore was here to destroy him and now she was holding on to him as if he were her personal life raft. If this had occurred two hours ago when he'd first learned her real identity, he'd have been tempted to let her suffer and flail her own way there. He almost grunted aloud to know this thought was a lie. He planned to make Issy Seymore suffer for the hell she intended to unleash on him but that didn't extend to physical harm.

Once they reached the giant inflatable, he helped her crawl onto it then hauled himself up beside her.

She'd laid herself on her back, her gaze fixed to the sky, breathing heavily.

Stretching himself out on his side beside her, he traced a finger along a high cheekbone. 'Better now?'

Her eyes closed before she turned onto her side to face him and locked on to his stare. 'Thank you for rescuing me.'

'My pleasure,' he murmured.

'Your pleasure? I almost drowned you.'

'*Bella*, you're half my size. You couldn't have drowned me if you'd tried.' Except maybe with her eyes. Gazing into them was like gazing into a deep, hypnotising pool. *Dio*, even half drowned, and with most of her make-up washed away apart from where her mascara had smeared beneath her eyes, she was ravishing. Desire stirred within him and he inched his face closer to hers and splayed a hand on her hip. Her drying skin felt impossibly smooth and soft to his touch.

But he could have drowned her, Issy realised, shivering at the thought even as tendrils of awareness unfurled inside her at his touch and the closeness of their bodies. It would have taken no effort on Gianni's part at all. He could have simply watched her splash around until exhaustion got the better of her. If he knew who she really was he'd probably have helped her drown.

Oh, what a plonker she'd made of herself, and it made her cheeks burn to think of how she'd banged on about 'her' yacht's slide, and then how, at the first go on it, she'd panicked at the speed she'd hurtled down it and flailed like a madwoman when she landed.

The burn deepened to recall how her fear had left her the moment Gianni had taken hold of her. She hadn't clung so tightly to him out of fear of drowning but because her body had instinctively equated Gianni, the man who'd destroyed her life, with safety. The irony was enough to make her splutter a laugh even as an ache deep inside her grew at the wish to wind her arms around him again.

'What's so funny?' he asked, nudging close enough for the tips of their noses to touch.

She plucked a plausible answer out of her scrambling brain; scrambling because it wasn't just their noses touching. The tips of her breasts had brushed against his chest and in an instant, the tendrils of awareness had turned into flames. She cleared her throat. 'I'm just thinking how undignified I must have looked when I landed in the water.'

Amusement played on the lips that had given her so much heady pleasure. 'It was one of those moments where you wish for a video camera.'

Her splutter turned into a giggle. As much as she despised

him, there was a dry wit about Gianni that tickled her, and she hated him even more for it. She loathed everything about him. Most especially loathed that he was the sexiest man to roam the earth and that she was practically melting with anticipation for his hand to move from her hip and explore the contours of her body properly.

God help her, she was aching for his touch.

God help her, she *did* fancy him. There was no other explanation for it. She desired the devil.

'I can't believe I panicked like that,' she bluffed, scrambling even more valiantly for clarity in her thoughts. She couldn't let her body's treacherous responses get the better of her, not when so much was at stake. Having sold herself as a party girl and water sports lover, she couldn't have Gianni think she'd panicked because she hated being out of her depth in water. That would contradict everything she'd purported to be.

His smile was lazy and totally belied the heat pulsing from his eyes. 'These things happen. No harm done.'

But she feared harm had been done. To her. Because the warmth of his breath brushing over her mouth and his thumb gently making circles on her hip was filling her with even more of those thrilling flames. An ache had formed deep inside her, the urge to press her pelvis forwards so that her groin locked with his almost unbearable in its intensity.

'Have you saved many hapless women's lives before?' she asked, striving for a form of nonchalant brightness in her tone but succeeding only in sounding breathless.

'You're the only one I've succeeded with,' Gianni replied, and as his fingers tightened their grip on Issy's delectable hip, his thoughts strayed to his mother. He'd wanted to save her and his aunt from their bastard husbands. Alessandro had too. When their fathers' mother, the matriarch of their family, died, the buffer to their cruelty had gone. Neither Gianni nor his cousin had appreciated how much their *nonna*'s presence at their farmhouse had kept a curb on her sons' malice. Her death unleashed it to a terrifying degree. How he'd longed to have superhero powers—he'd believed back then, when he was eight, that it needed a superhero to stop his father using his fists against himself and his mother—and the money to whisk them off somewhere safe. Turned out his mama didn't need saving. She'd saved herself. When Gianni was nine years old, he'd woken one morning to find her gone. He'd never seen her again.

Naturally, it had been a distressing time for a young boy, but he'd got over it. By the time he was twelve, Gianni and Alessandro had dreamed up their plan to leave. A cast-iron dream left little room for the adolescent Gianni to think about his mother or deal with the churn of anguish as to how she could have left him.

Strangely, he hadn't allowed himself to remember that long-ago anguish for so long that to suddenly think about it now was disconcerting. Emotional pain was something he'd never allowed himself to feel again. In this whole world he loved and trusted Alessandro, and that was it. This beautiful conniving woman gazing at him with eyes ablaze with desire was poison. If she had her way, she could destroy him as effectively as his mother had once done. But not emotionally. When it came to his heart, she couldn't touch him. No one could.

Issy was poison…but she was a hot poison. Her poisonous intentions couldn't quell the attraction smouldering thickly between them. Her poisonous intentions only added piquancy to it. Gianni wanted to taste her venomous lips again and, when her fingers finally closed around his hips and the tips dug through the material of his shorts, his desire ran free to imagine losing himself in all her beautiful toxicity.

'We'll have to get you a pair of red lifeguard shorts and one of those banana board things,' she murmured, her mouth so close to his that the scent of her sweetly toxic breath filled his senses.

There was venom in her breath for sure, a potent drug designed to bewitch and enthral and thicken the desire already rampaging through him. What she didn't know was that her poison could only work on a base level with him. He didn't deny that on a base level it was stronger than any other desire he'd experienced, infecting him right through to his pores, coming close to making him tremble with its strength. Dragging his hand around her back, he clasped her bottom and pulled her flush against him, letting her feel the strength of his excitement. 'Banana board things?'

She hitched a breath before answering. Her eyes had become glazed and when she spoke, there was a breathless quality to her voice. 'You know, those things lifeguards carry under their arms when they're running to save someone from drowning.'

He brushed his mouth against her toxically sweet lips. 'Do you mean a float?'

Her beautiful face flush with colour, she made a noise through her nose he supposed was meant to be a laugh and pressed her breasts tighter against his chest. 'Probably. I'll send you one for your birthday.'

He squeezed her bottom and ground himself harder against her, loving the barely perceptible shock that quivered through her and the pressure of her fingers on his hips. 'What if I need to save your life again before my birthday?'

Her eyes were now so dark and drugged with desire he could see the fight she was waging to keep control of herself.

There was barely any coherence in her voice, but somehow she managed to keep the banter going. 'You'll just have to use your superhero powers again.'

'I'm no superhero, *bella*. Just a man.' A man with a deep hunger for another taste of Issy's poisonous lips. Finally fusing his mouth to hers, Gianni rolled on top of her and sank into the heady pleasure of her mouth.

Oh, God, didn't she know how much of a man he was? Issy thought wildly as red-hot lava pumped through her veins. The feelings Gianni elicited in her were so out of this world, a craven need that his touch and ravenous mouth only fed, that she gave no thought to resisting. With his weight on her, covering her, subsuming her, the essence of herself slipped out of her grasp and she stepped into the flames of desire.

His kisses were hard and demanding, a devouring of mouths and tongues, a sensory whirl that had her press her screaming, sensitised skin tightly against every inch of him that she could. Dragging her fingers over Gianni's smooth, muscular back, she revelled in the groans he made at her touch and kissed him even harder, only breaking her mouth from his to gasp at the shock that thrilled through her when the weight and length of his excitement jutted through his swim shorts and jabbed against the scrap of material covering her most intimate parts. It was a thrill that burned deep in the heart of her and instinctively, she wrapped her legs tight around his waist and raised her hips.

She didn't know if the rocking motion was all them or if the swell of the water beneath the inflatable they were locked in each other's arms on was the cause and she didn't care. A burning coil had wound itself tightly in her core and was throbbing with a desperate need for relief, and she clung even tighter, kissing him even harder as the length of his thick hardness thrust against her swollen nub and...

The coil sprang free without warning. One minute she was rocking against him, caught up in the most heavenly thrills she'd ever experienced in her life; the next she shattered, and even as the unexpected explosions of her very first climax throbbed and raged through her, still she clung to Gianni, burying her face in his neck, desperate to keep the connection between them and draw out this most incredible moment of her life.

It was only when the spasms subsided and Issy realised Gianni had stilled that she came back to earth with a sharp bump. In an instant, the crest of the most glorious experience she'd ever ridden was over and sanity crashed into her like a bucket of ice being tipped over her head.

Oh, God, what had just happened?

She squeezed her eyes shut and wished for a hole to open in the inflatable and to sink beneath the surface and never come back up again.

This was terrible. Horrendous.

She tried to breathe. Tried to think. Then she tried not to think because even as the last thrills limped through her, her head was swimming with the fact that she'd just come completely undone and behaved in the most shocking, wanton, shameful fashion. And for *him*.

And all in her bikini. He hadn't even needed to touch her there.

The weight crushing her slowly lifted, but only the physical weight. She could feel Gianni staring at her. What must he think of her? She shouldn't care what he thought of her. She *didn't* care. She didn't.

She needed to bluff her way out of this, and as she realised this, the path of least humiliation opened to her. She just had to get back into character. It was beyond belief that any of his previous lovers had cared two hoots about seeming wanton to him. Wanton was what Gianni wanted!

As humiliating as her responses to him were, she needed to think of them in a positive light. Most importantly though, she must take more care than ever not to let desire for him overtake her sanity again. Use this as a warning to keep her internal guard up.

Gianni, struggling to find his breath, studied Issy's flushed face intently. His head was reeling from what had just occurred between them. Their kiss in the pool had blown his mind. This had come close to blowing his head off his shoulders. And hardly anything had happened. He was still to taste anything but her mouth.

But never had he experienced such unbridled hunger before. *Dio*, the ache in his loins was like nothing he'd felt before. Her passion…

His loins were on fire. He ached so badly to smother her mouth again and continue what they'd started. The fusion of their mouths had sent an inferno raging through them, from simmer to scorching in an instant. When he'd sensed what was happening to her… It hadn't seemed possible.

But it had been real. Issy had climaxed. He guessed from the ragged sharpness of her breathing and the way her eyes were still screwed so tightly together that it had been as big a shock to her as it was to him.

Just as shocking was how close to the edge he'd come too.

What the hell was happening to him? He was thirty-two years old. He'd learned to control his bodily responses to beautiful women before the end of his adolescence. He took *pride* in his control so to know that a few beats longer with their groins locked together would have tipped him over the edge too was beyond his comprehension. Issy was beautiful and sexy but so were plenty of other women. He'd never come close to losing control like that before.

Finally, Issy's eyes opened. After a moment's hesitation, they locked on to his. Gianni's heart slammed hard against his ribs.

After another beat, a lazy smile formed on her beautiful face. 'I need a drink. Let's go back.'

Disbelief almost made him mute. 'That's all you have to say?'

'I'm thirsty.' Laughing, she pushed at his chest and rolled out from beneath him.

His mouth opened and he shook his head. This woman was unbelievable, and he shook his head again as he watched her grip one of the handles around the inflatable's edge and slip into the water.

'Are you coming?' she asked with a tilt of her head and a knowing smile.

He laughed through the pain in his loins. 'I wish.'

She gave the faintest of winks. 'I guess you'll just have to wish harder.'

Before he could think of an answer, she'd pushed herself away from the inflatable and swum the metre distance to the steps the crew had earlier lowered for them.

Warm though the sea was, Gianni's body was on such a high simmer that when he followed Issy's lead, it was like sinking into a cold bath. He welcomed it. God help him, he was as horny as a sex-mad teenager, and as he watched her step onto the deck, all he could think of was untying those scraps of material covering her most feminine parts and screwing her until neither of them could stand.

Issy had no idea how she kept her back straight and stopped her legs from collapsing, and when she looked over her shoulder as she padded over the deck and saw Gianni's head appear by the railing, the swelling in her heart was so painful and the weakness in her legs so strong that the truth that she was in over her head slapped her like a wet fish.

She needed to message Amelia and beg her to at least try and fast-track the signing of the contracts. Get them signed immediately. She couldn't play this game for much longer. She needed to get as far away from Gianni as she could. He was just too much. All the research in the world couldn't have prepared her for the reality of seducing a man into distraction when the man in question brought out feelings in her that had never existed before. *She* was the one being seduced here, by the devil himself.

Upping her pace, mentally composing the message she would send to her sister, she reached the table she'd left her stuff on and in seconds found herself close to tears. Her phone had gone.

CHAPTER SIX

'SOMETHING WRONG?' GIANNI asked casually as he reached for his towel. He could not fathom why Issy's obvious anxiety should make his heart twinge.

She shook her sarong out. 'I can't find my phone.'

Of course she couldn't. He'd instructed the crew to hide it in his cabin, the only space in the yacht kept locked and off-limits to Issy. She could have it back when this was all over.

'It can't have gone far,' he assured her. 'Where did you last have it?'

'Right here. I left it on this table.'

He looked at his watch. It was coming up to ten p.m. in London. The meeting on the Aurora project would have finished hours ago. He could not let what had happened between him and Issy distract him from what needed to be done. He'd got rid of her phone so she was unable to contact her sister. His priority now was to warn Alessandro.

'Ask your crew,' he said. 'Maybe one of them took it inside for you when they took mine in to charge or when they finished clearing lunch.'

She bit her lip and nodded. 'Good idea.'

'If they haven't got it, it might be worth checking your cabin in case one of the crew put it in there for you and forgot to tell you.'

She nodded again, and hurried inside, forgetting to sway

her hips seductively in her distraction. For some reason, this too made his heart twinge.

Pushing away the strange feelings threading through him—he needed to work fast and concentrate—he indicated to Mara, the head of his crew, to bring his phone to him.

He switched it on and immediately called his cousin.

Alessandro's voice sounded down the crackly line. 'Gianni, how—?'

'Andro, listen, I don't have much time.'

'Okay, but what's the—?'

'Amelia Seymore,' he interrupted. 'She's Thomas Seymore's daughter.'

'*What?* I can't hear you properly.'

'Listen to me, Amelia Seymore is a traitor. She's been a spy this whole time. She's working with her sister to destroy us.'

'Amelia Seymore?' Alessandro's incredulity was clear.

'Yes! Seymore! The Aurora project is compromised. And listen, she claims to have found some kind of proof of corruption against us.'

'Did you say corruption? What corruption?'

'I don't know, but according to the messages I read, Amelia Seymore has found evidence of corruption by us. I'm in the Caribbean with her sister. I'll keep her out of the way here and stop her communicating with anyone and causing any more damage. Can you deal with Amelia? This needs to be nipped in the bud and damage limitation undertaken immediately.'

'Consider it done,' Alessandro said, his voice now low and dangerous.

Despite the bad reception, the message had got through, and a fraction of the tightness in Gianni's chest loosened. 'I may be out of reach for a while,' he said, 'but I'll try and get a message to you when I know what's going on.'

'Likewise. Speak soon, cousin.'

Gianni disconnected the call and took a deep breath of relief. His cousin was like a human missile when it came to taking down targets. Amelia Seymore stood no chance now she was in his sights. Whatever she and her sister had planned against them would fail.

But that still left Issy to deal with. She was an unknown quantity. The messages he'd read suggested her only job was to distract him while Amelia did the dirty work, but who knew what plans they'd concocted in the privacy of their home that had left no digital trace.

By the time she came back out on deck, now wearing a black vest with spaghetti straps over a black bikini and a pair of tiny denim shorts, her large shades once again covering much of her face, he knew the only safe thing to do was proceed with his own plan and get her to St Lovells. On the open sea at this time of year, there were too many other yachts about, too many ways for her to escape the *Palazzo delle Feste* and reach safety and communication with another vessel. There would be no escape for her from St Lovells. Not without his explicit agreement.

'Did you find your phone?' he asked as she approached him.

She shook her head. 'I have no idea what's happened to it.'

'It will turn up,' he assured her.

Flopping onto the sofa across from his, she tucked her legs under her bottom. 'I hope so.'

Unable to resist, he held his phone out. 'You can always use mine if you need it. It's fully charged.'

'Thank you but I don't know any of my contacts' numbers.' Her shoulders rose. 'I suppose it's the curse of the age we live in that we don't need to commit people's phone numbers to memory.'

'You mean you want to use your phone to make an actual phone call?' he asked in pretend horror, and was rewarded with a definite loosening of her taut frame and a snuffle of laughter.

'I know. Who'd have thought it, 'eh? Using a phone to call people on. Whatever next?'

'People using televisions to watch TV?'

'Now you're going too far.' The amusement on her face dimmed a little. She raised her face to the sky and sighed. 'When I was a little girl, my mum had one of those old-fashioned address books, you know the ones where you could write someone's name in it along with their address and phone number?'

'I am familiar with old-fashioned address books,' he said drily. His *nonna* had had one that had been crammed full of names, and random pieces of paper with scribbled numbers that used to fly onto the floor whenever the book was opened. 'Some people still use them.'

'Do you reckon? I used to laugh at Mum for keeping one and thought it hilarious that she could still recite her childhood phone number from memory. It just seemed so old-fashioned and unnecessary to me when everything could be stored on your phone. I know my phone will turn up and if it doesn't, I'll be able to buy another one and retrieve all my data, but I can just imagine my mum—as she was back then—laughing at me now for relying on technology when the old-fashioned way would have made it more likely I had it stored in my brain.'

'You say as she was back then... You mentioned before something about her being in rehab. If you don't mind me asking, what is she in rehab for?' He leaned back, managing to resist the temptation to fold his arms across his chest and stare at her like a headmaster waiting for a rule-breaking student to come up with a wild non-convincing lie to get them off the hook.

Slowly, Issy lowered her face and met Gianni's stare through the darkness of their respective shades. While she'd made her fruitless search for her phone and showered the sea salt off her skin, the space away from Gianni had been the space she needed to talk sense back into herself. She and Amelia had spent ten years working towards this point. She could not throw it away just because of a major case of hormone problems for the bastard she was so desperate to bring down. And one of those reasons she so desperately wanted to bring him down was because of her mother. Because one of the many consequences of Gianni destroying her life had been the loss of the mother who'd once cherished and adored her two daughters. Jane Seymore was alive only in the sense that her heart still pumped blood through her body. 'She has many issues. Drugs is the biggest one.'

'Your mother is a drug addict?'

Yes, you bastard. Because of you.

'She's not a junkie in the traditional sense that people think of drug addicts. She doesn't inject herself thank God but that's only because she has a needle phobia. It's mostly strong prescription stuff delivered to the comfort of her home—dealers nowadays have diversified into home delivery. Basically, she takes whatever she can get her hands on that stops her having to think or feel.' Anything that stopped her remembering all that she'd lost.

There was a flicker in his eyes and she suddenly had the sense that he was weighing up whether or not to believe her. 'How long has she been like this?'

'If you don't mind, I'd rather not spoil this beautiful day by talking about it.' Not with him, the cause of it all. Not when she was unlikely to be able to get through a conver-

sation about it without breaking character and screaming
and hurling anything she could get her hands on at him. It
was hard enough maintaining the high-society character
as things stood, what with all the awful, awful, *wonderful*
feelings he'd let loose in her body. She'd deliberately seated
herself on a separate sofa to him but the tempest happening inside her was as acute as if she'd curled herself on his
lap. God help her, he didn't need to actually touch her for
her to want him. All he had to do was look at her, and for
the first time, she felt a pang of sympathy for all the women
who'd fallen under his spell before her. She'd assumed for
years that all they wanted of him was his money and the
glamour of his lifestyle but as she was learning, there was
far more to him than that. What chance had those women
had? No wonder Gianni had a litany of broken hearts strewn
in his wake.

After a long beat, he said, 'I respect that, but if you're
worried about her not being able to contact you then we can
get in touch with the rehab facility and give them my number to reach you on.'

Issy hated the pang that ripped through her chest and
belly at this sincerely delivered offer. Her mother was in
rehab because of him! She shook her head. 'It's fine. They
can call my sister if there's a problem. It's Amelia I'm more
concerned about not being able to reach me—I can't remember her phone number or email address off the top of
my head.'

'Amelia is your sister?'

'Yes.' Mentally kicking herself for mentioning Amelia
by name, Issy shifted in her seat and quickly changed the
subject, moving the conversation along to the next phase of
keeping Gianni distracted and preferably uncommunicable
while Amelia made the final moves in the Seymore sisters'

destruction of the Rossi cousins, casually saying, 'As we're too far from the nearest island to dock before night falls, I thought we could anchor at sea tonight.'

His eyes flickered at the change of subject before a slow smile spread across his far too gorgeous face. 'Is that an invitation for me to spend the night with you?'

'It's an invitation for you to spend the night on the yacht. Not necessarily with me.' Never, never, never. No matter how badly she burned for him.

A gleam formed. 'Playing hard to get?'

'Nothing good ever comes easy,' she riposted sweetly, thinking she didn't need to just play hard to get but needed to build a fortress of concrete to make herself immune to him.

He raised the short crystal glass filled with an amber liquid that she hadn't noticed him holding, probably because she was too mesmerised by his face. 'That's a truth I will gladly drink to.'

'So what do you say?' Issy asked after he'd taken a sip. She wished she had a drink. It was easier to play seductress with a prop in her hand.

'About me staying the night here?'

She nodded. If he said no then she'd move to plan B and order the captain to fake engine problems. 'All the cabins are made up.'

'As you just said we're too far from anywhere to dock tonight, that suggests I don't actually have a choice about staying on board,' he pointed out.

'You can always swim.'

His strong throat extended as he laughed. How she hated the way the sound of it rang like balm in her ears and hated the way it enlivened his face, amplifying his heartbreaking handsomeness. 'I'm a strong swimmer but as we've already determined, I'm no superhero.'

'You could steal one of the Jet Skis.' That would work. If she was lucky, he might fall off. But even as she thought that a nibble of panic chewed at her heart at the prospect of him falling into open waters without even a life jacket for safety, and she quickly scrubbed it from her mind.

He pretended to mull this over. 'Hmm… Escaping on a Jet Ski or spending the night with the most beautiful woman in the Caribbean… That's a hard choice.'

'Spending the night on board a *yacht* with, not necessarily in *bed* with,' she reiterated.

He sighed mockingly. 'It's the hope that always kills, but even so, that's hope enough for me.'

'You'll stay?'

The gleam in his eyes turned up a notch and lasered straight into her pelvis. 'Trust me, *bella*. I'm not going anywhere.'

'Nice cabin,' Gianni commented as he stepped through the door Issy had opened for him on the sleeping deck. He'd wondered which cabin she would put him in. He'd bet she'd been tempted to put him in the smallest. Not that any of the cabins were small by any reasonable judgement. Gianni loved to party and took his duties as host seriously. The last thing he wanted was for any of his guests to feel slighted by being given inferior accommodation. The irony that his first night on his new yacht would be spent in the third-best cabin—the master suite was locked and Issy had claimed the second-best for her own—did not escape him. Still, it was spacious and had a perfectly respectable king-size bed. Gianni usually slept in an emperor bed, but this would do for one night. He turned his gaze from the cabin to the woman hovering at the foot of the doorway.

'The en suite is filled with toiletries and there's robes in the wardrobe you can use,' she said. For once, she seemed to be avoiding his eye. She'd dodged the elevator that would have taken them to the deck, skipping up the stairs ahead of him and then heading straight to the cabin. He knew perfectly well Issy was doing her best to stay out of arm's reach of him and knew perfectly well why. When she'd set off on her mission to destroy him she hadn't factored that she would actually want him, that she wouldn't have to fake desire for him. It must be killing her. Great. Let her suffer, trapped in the web of her own making.

He had to give her kudos though for the slick way she'd engineered for him to spend the night and admire how she'd made promises that weren't promises at all. The promise of what could come...but only maybe.

Did she really think she could hold out against the scorching chemistry between them for the duration of however long she intended to entrap him for?

'I'm going to get ready for dinner,' she added. 'I'll see you in an hour.'

Before she could run away, he pulled his polo shirt off and dropped it on the floor. She hesitated, her gaze fluttering over his chest before rising to meet his stare.

Poor Issy. She had no idea how expressive her eyes were, how her desire rang out from them. If she knew, she'd wear her shades permanently.

He stepped over to her. Linking his fingers through hers, he gently pulled her hands above her head and trapped her against the wall. Her breathing shortened. That delicious colour he was coming to get such a thrill at provoking stained her cheeks.

'Want to take a shower with me before you go?' he murmured.

Her throat moved and her chest rose before she managed

to make her lips curve and huskily say, 'A generous offer but judging by the size of you, you'll hog all the water.'

'Oh, I can be generous, *bella*.' Dipping his mouth down to her neck, he traced his tongue over the delicate, toxically sweet skin, revelling at the quiver of her body in response. 'Before our time here is done, I'll prove just how generous a man I can be.'

'Your self-confidence is staggering,' she said, only the hitches in her voice betraying her nonchalance as a facade.

Dropping her hands, he dragged his fingers through her hair and down her neck until, for the very first time, he palmed a small, pert breast. A shock of electricity zinged through them both, so tangible he could swear he heard it crackle.

'*Dio*, you're sexy,' he muttered into her mouth before kissing her. His arousal, a semi-permanent state since their first kiss in the swimming pool, sprung back to full length at the first flicker of her tongue against his and when she cupped his head and her fingers dug through his hair to scrape against his skull, his intention of merely teasing her was completely forgotten as the heat she evoked in him unleashed in all its power, a surge of energy that burned from his loins to every crevice in his body.

The way Issy Seymore made him feel was more than a mere game. He'd never wanted anyone like he wanted her.

This time, though, Issy was the one to keep her head, suddenly pulling her mouth from his and pushing him away from her.

'I can't do this,' she croaked, breathing heavily.

'Do what?'

'This. Gianni…' Clearly flustered, she pressed a hand tightly against her heaving chest. 'I…'

'You what?' he encouraged. Would this be the moment

Isabelle Seymore confessed? Or did the little minx have something else up her sleeve?

Her dark blue eyes gazed into his with something akin to desperation. 'I'm saving myself for marriage.'

As soon as the words left her mouth, Issy wished she could take them back. She had no idea where they had come from. Of course she wasn't saving herself for marriage— she wasn't a Victorian!

But she *was* frightened. Terrified. Terrified at how easily her body overrode her sanity when it came to Gianni. Terrified at how deeply she was coming to crave him. So while her words of marriage had dredged themselves from nowhere, there was a slight calming in the wild thumps of her heart to know they were the words to make the commitment-phobic Gianni Rossi back off.

Gazing into his shocked eyes, she determined that when this was all over, she was going to find herself a boyfriend. She'd make Amelia get out there and find a boyfriend too. The Rossi cousins had stopped them living for long enough.

This craving for Gianni was all his fault. If Gianni and his hateful cousin hadn't ruined their lives then they would have continued developing like other teenage girls, getting boyfriends and partying, not trying desperately to save their father from himself and then trying to save their mother, and all the while working and working to reach this point where they could bring down the men who'd turned their lives into rubble. Gianni's actions all those years ago had stopped her forming the emotional and sexual attachments other twenty-three-year-old women took for granted. Something else to hate and blame him for.

Her loathing ratcheted up when his shock slowly dissipated and that hateful gleam flashed in his devil eyes. 'You're saving yourself for marriage, *bella*?'

Grinding her toes into her sandals, she jutted her chin. 'Yes. I'm sorry if that disappoints you.'

He shrugged with the nonchalance she kept aiming for, and, leaning his face closer to hers, folded his arms across his naked chest. How her fingers itched to swirl through the dark hair covering it. The bastard had probably taken his polo shirt off deliberately. She wished he'd put it back on.

'Why would I be disappointed? There are other ways to share pleasure.'

Oh, God, did he have to say *pleasure* so ruddy seductively? 'I just thought you might have expectations…expectations that I've admittedly fed…' There was no getting around that. She'd practically promised herself to him. Feeling more confident, she continued. 'I am very much attracted to you, Gianni…' She managed to flash a grin. '…as you've probably noticed.'

'I'm pretty damned hot for you too.'

'And I know I've led you on but it's only because I fancied you from the moment I met you and I thought you could be the one I dropped my morals for, but they're too strong. I can't give myself to you without a ring on my finger. I'm sorry.'

His mouth curved and his forehead creased in understanding. 'No need to apologise. If you have morals then you must stick by then.'

'I'm so glad you understand.'

'I understand perfectly. You'll only have sex with me if I marry you?'

'Yes.'

'Then I accept.'

'Accept what?'

'Your proposal.'

'I beg your pardon?'

'Your proposal of marriage.' He stepped forwards and pressed her back against the wall, bringing his face so close to hers that she could practically feel the glitter burning from his eyes in her retinas. 'I accept.'

CHAPTER SEVEN

THE MIXTURE OF emotions that flittered over Issy's beautiful face filled Gianni with amusement. He'd caught her out. Anticipation for what she would do now filled him.

'You cannot be serious,' she said incredulously. 'You want to marry me just so you can sleep with me?'

'Why not? We're having fun, just as you promised, aren't we? What could be more fun than getting married?' He cupped her breast. *Dio*, it felt so good against the palm of his hand. He'd be tempted to marry her for real just to feel it naked against him. 'Come on, Issy,' he goaded, moving his hand from her breast to thread his fingers through her hair and clasp the back of her head, 'what is life for but taking risks, and we're both risk takers. Let's get married and spend the rest of our time on the Caribbean having wild sex.'

He was playing her, Issy knew, even as a thrill of need pulsed low in her pelvis at the unbidden thought of locking herself away with Gianni and acting out every depraved need that had exploded for him. This was nothing but a Gianni tactic to get her into bed. Pretend to want to marry her so that she'd drop her bikini bottoms for him. The man must be a bigger sex-mad cad than she'd supposed.

Knowing this was all just a game made it easier to deal with. She didn't even have to fake her laughter at the absurdity of the swerve to their conversation. 'I'd be up for that but I'm afraid I'd need a ring on my finger before having the wild sex you promise, so unless you can think of a way for us to get hitched before our time here comes to an end...' She let her words trail off and raised a shoulder in pretend disappointment.

'The captain,' he said with a gleam.

'What about him?'

'Some ship captains have the power to conduct weddings. If yours has the requisite powers, he can marry us. Does he?'

'I don't know.'

'Let's ask him.' Unthreading his fingers from her hair, Gianni ran them down her slender, golden arms. 'I assume you have your passport on board?'

'It's right here in my cabin... What a shame you don't have yours,' Issy added with fresh pretend disappointment.

'Oh, but I do,' he said triumphantly, patting his back pocket. 'I always carry it with me.'

So he wanted to drag this absurd game out did he? 'Then let me get mine.'

Issy retrieved her passport from the handbag she kept it in, lifted the receiver of the cabin's phone, which connected to all the different parts of the yacht, and smiled beatifically at Gianni. 'Shall I call the captain then?'

Thoroughly enjoying himself, Gianni nodded. 'Tell him to meet us in the lounge.'

Gianni watched her press the captain's number, certain she'd slam the receiver down before the call connected and put a halt to this charade. It was ludicrous to think they could marry. Almost as ludicrous as Issy's declaration that she was waiting for marriage. Still, she'd upped the ante of their game superbly. He'd twisted and she'd matched. He couldn't wait to watch her fold.

But she didn't fold. Instead she politely asked the captain

to meet them in the lounge to discuss a personal issue. That was one thing he did like about her; that she spoke to the crew respectfully. Many yacht owners and charterers treated their crew like dirt; as if they were their personal slaves.

Call over, her lips curved. 'He'll meet us in the lounge now.'

He held his hand out to her. She laced her fingers through his and let him lead her down to the entertainment deck.

Captain James Caville entered the lounge at the same time as them. Not by word or gesture did he give away the fact he'd worked for Gianni for the last four years. Gianni was proud of his loyal crew. They'd transferred seamlessly to his new vessel and, when told that their boss—him—was being targeted by a hustler and to play along with the hustler's game, had risen to the challenge. It wouldn't even cross Issy's mind that Gianni and the good captain had spent more than a few evenings drinking their way through bottles of Scotch and playing Three Card Brag, or, on the occasions they were joined by other crew members, hunkered down at the poker table playing Texas Hold 'Em.

As a result of their friendship, Gianni thought he knew the captain pretty well and so was almost dumbstruck when, asked if he was allowed to officiate marriages, James nodded. 'The *Palazzo delle Feste* is registered in Bermuda and I have a Bermuda licence, so if you want me to marry you then I can. I'll just need to contact the ministry to go through the necessary requirements…' There was a beat of hesitation. 'Do you want me to do that?'

Gianni had to pull himself together quickly. He'd expected James to laugh at the request, had envisaged turning to Issy and teasing her about researching an island they could marry on and then winding her up into believing they would sail there. It had never crossed his mind that James would actually be allowed to marry them; he'd thought stories of ships captains marrying couples was an urban myth. He'd only chosen Bermuda to register the *Palazzo delle Feste* because that's where his last yacht had been registered.

Surely now was the time Issy would think this was getting out of hand and fold her cards. But instead of finding doubt or panic on her face, she simply gazed at him with challenge in her stare. She was waiting for Gianni to fold.

He'd never folded in his life.

Challenge accepted.

'Do it,' he said decisively.

James' only physical reaction to this was the slight raising of an eyebrow. 'And when will you want the ceremony?'

Gianni winked at Issy. 'Right now would be great but I appreciate that's unreasonable so as soon as possible. If anything can be fast-tracked then do it—money is no object if palms need to be greased.'

James pulled his phone out of his pocket. 'I'll get onto it now.'

'A drink while we wait?' Gianni suggested to Issy.

The beatific smile returned. 'Champagne would be fitting.'

The honours done, eyes locked together, they toasted each other and each drank half their glass.

Come on, Issy, fold, he mentally urged her. *You know neither of us will go through with this charade.*

How much longer until Gianni roared with laughter and admitted this was all just a wind-up, Issy wondered. She almost felt sorry for the captain working so hard to make a fallacy happen, but it was only when he covered the speaker on his phone and asked for their passports that the first twinge of doubt hit her.

She sipped on her second glass of champagne telling herself not to be silly. It didn't matter how much money Gianni had to grease palms, marriage was not something that could be fast-tracked. Any minute now and the captain would regretfully tell them it couldn't be done before Gianni flew back to the UK, and then they would both pretend to be disappointed and Gianni would have no choice but to back off from her physically for the rest of their time together. She would just have to think harder for ways to entertain him. The yacht was a veritable party palace—even its name denoted that—so in theory it would be easy.

Theory though, as she'd come to learn since arriving in the Caribbean, was no guarantee of success when put into practice.

A member of the crew came in with a sheaf of freshly printed-off papers in her hand, which she gave to the captain. Still talking on the phone, he riffled through them, then beckoned Gianni over. Their voices were too low for her to hear but when Gianni's gaze directed itself to her, there was a calculation in it that stiffened her resolve not to be the one to throw her hands in the air and say this had gone too far.

Stifling laughter, she drank more of her champagne and watched him do something on his phone that she suspected involved transferring money. Excellent.

A stronger pang of doubt hit a short while later though when the captain started laughing to whoever he was now talking to on the phone. The laugh and the tone his voice had now adopted reminded Issy of her father's the time she'd been playing on the floor of his study while he'd been conducting a business deal. He'd taken that same lighter tone and laughed in the same manner right before he'd ended the call. He'd been so happy with the deal he'd concluded that he'd scooped Issy up and spun her in the air.

She caught Gianni's eye. He'd topped them both up with

the last of the champagne then seated himself across from her, an ankle resting on a thigh, an arm strewn across the back of the sofa, the very epitome of nonchalance.

The devil raised his glass to her.

She raised hers right back.

'We're all set,' James said a minute later, rising from the table he'd set himself up on. 'We just need a couple of witnesses—I've sent a message to my officers—and we're good to go.'

The vaguely smug look that had been on Gianni's face while they'd waited, like that of a chess player waiting for their opponent to realise they were heading for a loss, flickered. He straightened. 'You can marry us now?'

The captain shrugged. 'It's cost you a lot of money, but I have the authorisation.'

Gianni somehow kept his features straight as he swore loudly to himself. This had gone too far. Issy *had* to fold now. He looked back at her. 'Ready to marry me?'

Eyes not leaving his face, she drained her champagne. 'Why not? Like you said, it'll be fun... Unless you have cold feet?'

'No cold feet from me.' He would *not* be the one to fold.

Two men in navy shorts and pale blue polo shirts with the same emblem as the crew had on their uniforms came into the lounge.

Gianni got to his feet. 'We need a ring.'

'Two rings.'

Issy got to her feet and realised she was a bit wobbly. Half a bottle of champagne on an empty stomach was probably not her best idea, but seeing as she was still sharp enough to recognise that, she wouldn't worry about it. This actually had become fun, and she giggled at the absurdity of it all, and giggled too, to think of Gianni wasting oodles of his money on a marriage that wouldn't take place. 'Any spare paper?' she asked the captain.

When he gave her a sheet, she knelt at a coffee cable and quickly ripped two strips off it. Each strip she rolled lengthways between her fingers until it resembled a long wriggly worm, then tied each one into a circle, which she held out to Gianni with a flourish. 'There,' she said, flashing a grin at him. 'Two makeshift wedding rings.'

'You're ready to do this?' he reiterated.

He wanted her to back out. He *expected* her to back out. She could see it in his eyes. And it was that expectation which filled her with serene defiance. Gianni had started this game of chess and it was up to him to put an end to it.

It was only when he clasped her hand and together they faced the captain that she realised neither of them was prepared to back down.

They'd reached stalemate.

Gianni had the strangest feeling of leaving his body and floating above and looking down on himself and Issy, hands clasped and reciting vows before the captain and growing number of crew come to see for themselves if the boss really was marrying the hustler. He watched himself sign the certificate where the captain told him to and watched Issy sign her name—her real name, Isabelle Christine Seymore—and the two witnesses sign theirs. Then he watched himself slide the paper ring over her finger and Issy slide the one she'd made for him over his finger, and continued watching with the same detachment while they kissed to seal their vows.

And then he re-inhabited his body as a flurry of handshakes and embraces were shared, the heavy beats of his heart rippling through him at the knowledge that the game of bluff he'd just played with Issy had backfired.

* * *

Issy popped two painkillers into her mouth with a shaking hand and washed them down with cold water. The after-effects of the champagne she'd drunk just a short while ago were making themselves known in the form of a headache. Or maybe the cause of it was the sudden loss of the adrenaline that had pumped through her in that mad hour that had ended with her married.

The amusement that had been carried with the adrenaline had gone too, reality as cold as the water she'd just drunk pouring over and through her.

She'd just married her nemesis. She hadn't merely exchanged fake vows but signed legal documents. Signed them in her real name. The only saving grace was Gianni had failed to notice anything about her surname.

But what on earth had possessed her? What had possessed *him*?

Amelia was going to kill her...

Oh, hell, she hadn't thought of her sister in hours, had completely forgotten about her lost phone and that her sister would be waiting anxiously with her own phone in hand for an update. She *had* to find her phone.

Closing her eyes, Issy took some deep breaths to force a modicum of calm into herself. It was the middle of the night in London. Amelia wouldn't be worrying; that was Issy projecting. Amelia would only worry if Issy went the whole of the next day without communicating. If her phone stayed missing, she would borrow one off the crew, search the main number for Rossi Industries and call Amelia through it. Her priority, she realised with a flash, was to tell the captain to destroy the marriage papers. If they weren't lodged, they wouldn't be properly registered, ergo, the 'marriage' would never be legalised.

These things decided in her mind, she expelled a more settled breath and called the captain. Told by one of his officers that he was currently unavailable but would call her back soon, she said, 'Don't worry, I'll speak to him first thing in the morning.' They were in the middle of the Caribbean Sea. Nothing would be done with the papers before morning and Gianni was due soon to escort her to dinner. She needed to work out how she was going to play things.

It was a thought that set her heart thumping again.

How was she supposed to brazen this out? Marriage.

Not marriage, she told herself stubbornly. Just a joke, a game, whatever, that had gone a step too far. So long as the papers weren't lodged, there would be no real marriage. She was safe.

Her head sorted and the painkillers kicking in, she decided the best thing to do was continue the joke and play up the marriage, so selected a slinky white fitted dress with spaghetti straps that came just below the knee and had a slit cut into its skirt that ran almost to the top of her thigh. For her feet she chose a pair of white spaghetti strap sandals to match. With her hair blow-dried into the illusion of thickness and her eyes painted a smoky grey, she finished the look off with a smear of red lipstick.

As prepared as she thought she was though, she still needed a moment to collect herself before answering the knock on her cabin door.

Gianni stood there, wearing the same polo shirt and canvas shorts that had been draped over his too magnificent body at various times throughout the day and with that devilish smile her brain hated but which her body adored on his too gorgeous face. 'Ready for dinner, Signora Rossi?'

The longing that ran through her came close to making

her legs collapse, and right in that moment Issy knew this had to end.

She couldn't handle Gianni or her feelings for him. She wasn't just in over her head, she was close to *losing* her head. She'd married him for heaven's sake! There was no way she could spend a whole week with him without losing her mind and probably the last of her self-respect. She had to trust that Amelia had done her part in the meeting that day and that their operation to destroy the Rossi cousins had reached the point of no return.

Because much more time spent with Gianni was going to push Issy to the point of no return.

She had to end this. She *would* end this.

A modicum of peace settled in her wildly fluctuating heart.

She would get their marriage papers destroyed and this horror story would end as soon as they docked on whichever the closest island was. She would insist they go off and explore and then she'd give Gianni the slip and escape without him, even if it meant abandoning the yacht.

All she needed to do was brazen things out and hold him off sexually for a few more hours.

'*Si, signor,*' she murmured, giving him a look of adoration that scarily needed no effort whatsoever.

He held his elbow out to her.

She didn't hesitate to slip her hand through it.

His eyes gleamed. 'I don't know about you but I'm already looking forward to dessert.'

The crew had transformed the dining room into a silver and gold extravaganza. It never ceased to amaze Gianni how ingeniously creative they could be in catering to his whims, and also the whims he hadn't even expressed. How they'd got hold of balloons, glitter and confetti and decorated the room accordingly would remain a mystery. He wouldn't ask. Sometimes the mystery was enough.

The dining table, which could comfortably seat twenty people, had been laid in an L at one end, with Gianni at the head and Issy to his right. Romantic candles had been lit, the reflection of their flames dancing off the crystal chandelier above. The huge windows lining the left of the dining room added to the romantic ambience, the setting sun on the horizon turning the sky a burnished orange that made it appear to be on fire. It perfectly matched the fire taking place inside him.

Gianni raised his glass of champagne to his bride and, for at least the dozenth time since he'd turned up at her cabin, marvelled at how ravishing she looked. He could hardly believe the beautiful creature beside him was the same woman in the screenshot he'd cloned. Alone in his cabin, he'd found himself staring intently at that picture with the strangest mixture of emotions playing through him. He strongly suspected the screenshot was Issy in her natural state and this blonde vision of perfection was a carefully curated image in which to ensnare him. What he couldn't understand was why the plainer, unpolished, plumper version on the screen made his chest tighten so much.

He'd shoved the strange emotions aside while showering for dinner, shaking off, too, the strange flux that had taken him out of himself during their 'wedding ceremony.' The papers they'd signed would never see the light of day. More than an annulment, their 'marriage' would never have happened. He was confident Issy shared the same thoughts on the matter but that, like him, she'd decided to play it out. How long did she think she could do that for?

Come the morning, they would dock at St Lovells and this charade would be over.

For tonight, he would enjoy his time with this dazzling woman and see what tricks she had planned to back out of consummating the marriage that would never be.

CHAPTER EIGHT

To Issy's surprise and relief, the dinner was actually fun. As course after course of the most exquisite food was brought out to them—the chef really had pulled out all the stops to create a feast for them—they slipped into light, impersonal conversation. Neither of them even bothered faking conversation about their future together. They both knew it wouldn't happen. It didn't need to be spelt out. The subjects they did touch on, though, gave her a greater insight into the man she'd believed she knew so well before meeting him, minor things no amount of research on Gianni could have dredged up.

'You don't read?' she asked in astonishment when they moved from music they liked onto books, and he couldn't name a single one he'd enjoyed.

'Not since I left school. The books they forced us to read were too boring and worthy for me to get any enjoyment from.'

'Didn't your parents encourage you?' She thought of how both her parents had helped and encouraged her to read, sparking a love of literature in her that she'd carried all her life.

His features tightened at this. 'My father is a homophobic and misogynistic bully. If he'd seen me reading a book for pleasure he'd have probably assumed I was gay and beat me.'

Shock at this brutal admission came close to making her choke on the raspberry she'd just popped in her mouth.

From the way he grimaced and the deep breath he took, she sensed this was an admission he hadn't intended to make. Swirling the wine in his glass, he tipped it down his throat. 'Sorry,' he said as he refilled both their glasses. 'I didn't mean to lower the mood.'

'That's okay… Did you mean it?'

His gaze was steady. 'I would never lie about something like that. My father is a monster.' The beginnings of a smile formed. 'But I don't want to talk about him on my wedding night so why don't you tell me about the books you enjoy.'

Issy had no idea why the thought of Gianni's father being a monster hurt her chest so much or why she felt something much like a yearning that he'd shut the subject down. It didn't make sense. She knew the bones of his childhood— the whole world did—so why the sudden craving to know more, to have flesh put onto those bones? She knew his mother had left his father when Gianni was a child and that she lived in Milan. She knew his father ran the same family vineyard in Umbria with his brother that the Rossi cousins had been raised in and that Gianni and his cousin were both estranged from their fathers, going so far as to change their surnames when they were eighteen. It was all part of their legend as self-made men who'd risen from nothing to the stratosphere. What more did she need to know?

It frightened her that she *wanted* to know more.

For the first time since they'd entered the dining room, she had to force a smile to her face. 'There's no point in me telling you if you haven't read any of them.'

Gianni stared at her for a beat. There had been a moment when he'd been certain she was going to press him for more information about his father. Instead, she'd chosen to respect his wish to end the subject. He never spoke about his father. He wasn't worth the wasted breath. He rarely thought about him either. He wasn't worth the headspace.

To find himself thinking about both his parents in one day and to actually mention his father, to confide a snippet of his life to Isabelle Seymore of all people, was perplexing, and he rubbed his hand over the thickening stubble of his jawline. What the hell was it about her that made the past feel so much closer than it had in over a decade?

'You've read a lot of books?'

She nodded.

'Don't tell me a party girl like you is a secret bookworm?' he teased.

She put a finger to her lips. 'Secret being the operative word.'

Unable to resist, he snatched at the finger and brought it to his own lips. 'Something tells me you're full of secrets, Signora Rossi.'

Her eyes glittered, and she stroked the finger pressed against his lips across his cheek, whispering, 'And something tells me it won't be long before you discover all of them.'

He captured her hand again and pressed a kiss into the palm. 'I look forward to it.'

The glitter darkened. 'So do I.'

An undercurrent had built, a tension laced with more than the sexual chemistry that kept drawing them so close together. Gianni could almost taste the deception swirling between them, nearing the surface, straining for the moment when their masks—already slipping—could be ripped away and nothing but the truth would be enough to satisfy them.

'What do you say to a game of snooker?' he asked.

'Only if you promise not to thrash me.'

He leaned his face close to hers. 'I never make promises I can't keep.'

Issy chalked her cue, watching as Gianni folded his huge frame to make the break. There was nothing gentle in his stroke. He hit the white ball with an accurate determination that rolled it forcefully along the table and smashed it into the red triangle of balls.

She smiled to herself. He'd played the shot like that for her benefit. Separating the red balls from their triangular cluster made it easier to pot them, not something a serious player—and she could tell from the way he played his shot that he was a serious player—would do if they didn't think their opponent would be easy pickings.

Deciding on and playing her shot quickly, she chided herself when the red ball she'd shot at missed the pocket.

Gianni didn't miss. He potted a red, then followed it by potting the pink, then potted another red. He missed the green by millimetres, switching the game back to Issy.

This time, she took her time, angled the cue carefully and made her shot. The white glanced the red, sending it into a pocket. She followed this with four successful shots, red, green, red, brown, but then, seeing there was no way she could pocket another red from where the white ball was placed, she hit the white softly, so it only brushed against the red, then gently rolled to slip behind the pink. She'd snookered him.

The look he gave her made her feel ten foot tall. Total confounded admiration.

'I thought you didn't play?' he accused, leaning over the table to reach the white.

'I don't remember saying that,' she refuted innocently.

His chin now lined against the cue, he raised an eyebrow at her. 'You implied it.'

Smirking, she shrugged. 'I haven't played for ten years.'

He took his shot. He managed to hit the red but didn't pot it. 'How old are you?'

'You should know that seeing as you're my husband,' she teased. 'I'm twenty-three. My dad had a snooker table. I always wanted to play but I couldn't reach the table so he bought me a child-size one for my seventh birthday and taught me. I upgraded to the full-size one when I was ten.'

'How were you able to see over the top of it?' he teased back.

'I used a stool. Being so small meant the distances looked longer to me but I think that improved my game.'

'Have you actually grown at all since then?'

'Very funny.' The red she was aiming for went straight into the pocket.

'Give me a chance,' he mock-pleaded. 'Go on, make it harder to see over the table. Take your shoes off.'

'They're sandals, you philistine.'

'A philistine?' His expression suddenly changed to serious and he lost the English accent he'd clearly worked so hard to make faultless. 'I do not think it means what you think it means.'

'Inconceivable.'

Their eyes met, identical amazed gazes at the recognition that they were with a fellow *Princess Bride* buff formed, and then they both started laughing. Issy laughed so hard she completely missed her next ball.

Grinning widely, Gianni took his shot and pocketed it, but missed his next one.

'Maybe I *should* take my sandals off if it gives you more of a chance,' she taunted.

His eyes drifted down her body. 'I don't know...' His voice dropped to a murmur as his gaze drifted back up to capture her eyes. 'Those sandals are very sexy.'

And just like that, the heat of awareness Issy had been vaguely dampening by sheer willpower flamed back to life, sending her heart into a pulsing mess at the strength of longing rampaging through her. If Gianni hadn't been standing on the other side of the snooker table her legs might just have propelled themselves to him.

She picked up her glass and took a long drink of her mojito, fully aware the skin on her face blazed with the same intensity as what was happening beneath it, fully aware too that Gianni knew exactly the effect those five little words had had on her.

But he didn't say anything, simply stood there waiting for her to take her turn, his cue in hand, that sensuous, knowing, *sexy* look...damn him...playing on his face.

Damn him!

Damn him too that, in order to stretch across the table and reach the white ball, she had to hitch the skirt of her tight dress up, something she'd done numerous times during their game already but which she'd done automatically, barely even thinking about it. This time, she was painfully aware of the suggestiveness that could be interpreted with the gathering of the silk, painfully aware too of how sensitive her thighs had become as the material rode up them.

Trying her hardest to control her breathing and concentrate, Issy draped herself over the table and aimed the cue.

'The rest of you is pretty damn sexy too,' he said at the exact moment she took her shot. 'Your backside is delectable.'

She misaimed the cue. The white ball scuttled off in the wrong direction, limping to a stop without hitting anything.

That pulled her together sharpish, and she glared at him. 'You said that on purpose to distract me.'

He raised a hefty shoulder. 'And?'

'And?'

He took his position at the table and winked at her. 'And what are you going to do about it?'

God how she hated how much she wanted him. Almost as much as she hated how greatly she was coming to enjoy their time together and how she could veer from amusement to full-blown desire from nothing but a tone in his voice or the raising of an eyebrow.

'I could sing to you,' she suggested, managing to sound reasonably normal in the process. 'People have offered money to stop me doing that before.'

He grinned. 'You can come up with something better than that.' He potted the last of the reds and fixed his stare straight back on her. 'I guarantee if you were to strip that dress off, I'd be unable to take another shot.'

She squeezed her eyes to counter the image that zinged straight into her mind of holding Gianni's gaze and peeling her dress off for his delectation. She had to force her eyes to open again and force her voice to sound blasé. 'I prefer the singing option.'

Chin on cue now lined up for the next shot, he smirked. 'I don't.' The yellow ball potted straight into the pocket.

Knowing she needed to steer them onto safer conversational territory, she asked, 'How come you're so good at this? At snooker,' she hurried to clarify before he could deliberately misinterpret her question and give a suggestive answer.

He took another shot. 'I have a snooker table in my London penthouse and my home in Tuscany. I like to play.'

'That fits in with your playboy image so well.' That's what she needed to remind herself of, she realised. When the force of Gianni's magnetism and personality was strong enough to blur the damage he'd wrought on her family; made it seem distant and faded, she needed to remember the chain of broken hearts he'd left littered around the world.

'I don't have a playboy image.'

'You do! I've looked you up.' About a gazillion times. 'You have your own hashtag. HotRossi.'

'Not started by me.'

'Started by your adoring groupies. You're a playboy who loves to party.'

'It's not a crime for a single man to party and date women.'

'I'm just saying your image doesn't fit a man who must have spent hours at a snooker table to get as good as you at it.'

'Snooker helps my brain relax. It's a good way to unwind in the evenings...' His lips curved in a lopsided smirk and he wiggled his eyebrows. 'When there's no hot woman available to help me relax, of course.'

This time she was able to maintain her composure, serenely saying, 'You're trying to needle me.'

'Am I succeeding?'

'No.'

His knowing grin showed he didn't believe her. 'It would be impossible for me to have such a successful business if I partied every night. I've reached the age where I get hangovers.'

'Oh, no. You poor thing.'

'Thank you for your sympathy.'

'You're welcome.'

'You do realise I've won?'

She looked at the snooker table. While they'd been bantering, Gianni had cleared the table so only the black ball remained. She couldn't beat his score with the value of it.

'Do I get my prize?'

'What prize? You cheated,' she accused.

'No, I didn't.' He placed his cue on the table and stalked to her. 'I was observing. Your bottom really is delectable.'

Heart thumping again, she sidestepped away from him and pulled the triangle for the red balls out of the slot. 'You distracted me. Play again without cheating.'

'You call that a distraction? *Bella*, that is *nothing* on what I could have done.'

Her pelvis practically contracted at the meaning, but she kept her focus. 'I call it cheating, and you're going to play fairly this time. I'll make the break.'

Completely blurring him from her vision, Issy ordered fresh drinks over the intercom then set the table. After chalking her cue, she folded herself to take the first shot but before she could hit the cue, she forgot to keep blurring Gianni and he appeared in her line of sight. He'd removed his polo shirt. His glorious chest was naked.

His eyes gleamed as he noticed that she'd noticed. Raising his drink to her, he said in an innocent tone, 'I was getting hot.'

'Then turn the air-conditioning up.'

'And waste power unnecessarily?' He tutted in disappointment. 'Feel free to remove your own clothes if you find it hot too.'

'Shut up.' Issy gritted her teeth to concentrate and hit the white ball with just enough force for it to reach the triangle of reds without breaking them up.

Gianni stepped to the table, hardly glanced at the balls as he took his shot and smashed them. Two reds dropped into the pockets.

Within ten minutes he'd cleared the table. Other than making the opening break, Issy didn't get a single shot. It was a masterclass in snooker, as good as anything she'd watched on TV as a child.

But she'd hardly paid attention to the shots. Throughout, Gianni kept his focus entirely on the table, not looking at her once. There had been nothing for her to fight against, no sensuous glances, no velvet-delivered innuendoes...

She'd fallen into a trance, mesmerised by the raw grace of the man and the beauty of his masculinity as he'd demolished the table.

By the time he potted the black ball for the last time and, finally, lifted his eyes to her, she couldn't have torn her gaze from him if she'd tried.

A smile slowly ghosted his face. Casually placing his cue on the table, he drained his Scotch and, with the gait and expression of a lion approaching its prey, stalked to her.

His eyes were intent, deadly, his words husky. 'I think that has earned me my prize.'

Her heart filled her chest with thick, heavy beats.

Fight or flight. That's what prey experienced when their senses registered the big cat emerging from the flora. Those semi-seconds of intuition and experience before adrenaline kicked in was the entire difference between life and death. Fight a lethal predator bigger than you and die. Take flight a moment too late and die.

There came a point when every captured prey gave up the fight and welcomed death to release them from the pain.

Gianni had captured her that night in London. She'd arrived at the club having badly underestimated the power of his sexuality and spent every waking moment since battling her own reactions to it.

She couldn't run any more. The will to fight had deserted her.

Submitting didn't mean death. Gianni wouldn't inflict pain on her, only pleasure, and for this one night, she wanted to explore where that pleasure could take them because she knew, with a marrow-deep certainty, that she could live a hundred lives and never feel what she felt for Gianni with anyone else.

Feeling a strange combination of shyness and boldness, Issy took a step towards him. 'What prize?' she whispered.

Gianni's chest swelled before he splayed a hand against her back to draw her flush to him. Her eyes were wide and filled with the desire he caught so often in them, but they were filled with something else too that he'd never seen before, an openness, as if she'd ripped an invisibility cloak away.

He dipped his face to hers. 'You.'

As their mouths fused together, Gianni had the strangest sensation that this was Issy kissing him. Issy, the young woman in the screenshot with the ice cream sundae, not Issy the polished seductress. Whichever Issy it was, he hungered for her with a power that was coming close to taking possession of him, and as her lips and tongue danced against his, the electricity that had flickered and crackled between them the entire day magnified and fired huge jolts through his veins and deep into his loins.

Dragging his fingers down her back, he clasped the bottom he'd spent most of the day fantasising about and gathered the silk of her dress until it was high enough for him to lift her onto the snooker table.

When she opened her eyes the strange sensation hit him

again, and with it the belief that he was looking into the eyes of the real Isabelle for the first time. There was nothing calculated in it. No guile. Just her. Just Issy and her desire for him.

He cupped her cheeks and kissed her so passionately she moaned into his mouth and scraped her fingers over his back. A zipper ran the length of her dress to her bottom and he pinched it and drew it down. Not breaking the lock of their mouths, she shrugged the spaghetti straps off her shoulders so they slipped down her arms and the dress fell to her waist, allowing her naked breasts to crush against his bare skin for the first time. *Dio*, he'd never known bare skin against bare skin could feel so incredible.

Breathing heavily, Gianni broke the kiss so he could gaze into her desire-drugged eyes again and drink in the heightened colour staining her cheeks.

He placed a hand to her chest and gently pressed her back. And then he brushed his hand over a breast that fitted into the palm as if it had been specially made for him. Pressing her back even further, he dipped his head and captured a dusky pink nipple in his mouth.

Issy jolted and gasped at the unexpected shock of pleasure that coursed through her. But it didn't end there, not with Gianni kissing and biting and sucking the overly sensitised skin, moving from breast to breast, flickering his tongue down lower still to nip at her navel, his hands roaming the contours of her body, fingers sliding over silk and flesh, leaving her skin flamed in their wake.

The flames deepened when his mouth found hers again and his hand slid beneath the bunched hem of her dress and grasped the band of her knickers. Thrilling at the hunger of his kisses, greedily devouring him with the same intensity, she gripped Gianni's shoulders and raised her bottom. He yanked the knickers down her thighs. A couple of flicks of her legs and they slipped down her calves to her feet, from where she kicked them off.

His desire when he pulled back to soak up her semi-nakedness, etched in every line of his hooded, heavy stare, overrode any of Issy's shyness at being displayed like this. There was a pained reverence in the look, as if she were the first woman he'd ever seen like this.

Could he see through her skin to the wildly beating heart? Could he see the flames licking her veins and bones?

One pop of a button and tug at a zip and his shorts fell down.

Issy roamed her gaze over him in the same way he'd soaked her up. She could hardly breathe. All her life, she'd thought the female body the more pleasing of the sexes. Gianni Rossi was the only man whose body had ever drawn her eye but for years she'd told herself it was because of her intensive research on him, that the reason she kept going back to pictures of him half-naked holidaying on his yacht was for whichever companion he happened to be with so she could study them in her pursuit of copying their look.

It had always been him. The devil disguised as Apollo. The sexiest man to roam the earth.

But she'd never seen a picture of him fully naked. Just as the pictures of him had never done him justice, seeing him naked was a revelation in itself. Magnificent was too lame a word to describe him. Every part of the devil was beautiful.

'Kiss me,' she whispered. There was something about his kisses that fed her hunger and made her greedy for more. Much more. Greedy for everything.

In a flash their mouths locked back together. Hands dragged heavily over skin, a need to discover and taste pulsing through them both, pulses that turned into throbs when Gianni cupped her sex and pressed his thumb against her swollen nub. Dear heavens, she'd thought it had felt good earlier... That was nothing...nothing.

She rubbed against him, moaning her pleasure into the deepening tangle of tongues.

Gianni could hardly believe how hot and wet Issy was for him. If the cells of the human body could make sound, hers would be crying out their need. He could feel it, taste it, smell it, and, keeping the pressure on the source of her pleasure, slipped a finger inside the sticky heat, his senses thrumming as her moans deepened and she clung even tighter to him.

Panting, she broke the fusion of their mouths and, still rocking into him, almost bit his cheek as she gasped, 'Condoms?'

He could hardly speak. 'In my pocket.'

'Get...' But her words died. Her eyes glazed, her pants shortened and suddenly her neck arched and her mouth opened. No sound came out. It didn't need to. Issy's silent climax shuddered through her, its ripples practically visible, and suddenly the need to take possession and lose himself inside her peaked to the point of desperation.

Only when he was certain that she'd passed her own peak did he gently remove his hand and kiss her. 'Let me get the condom.'

'Do it,' she whispered.

In a flash, he pulled a condom out of his back pocket, ripped the packet with his teeth and sheathed himself. Her hands were reaching for him, and when he stepped between her legs, she clasped the back of his neck.

He guided his erection to her damp opening.

Still breathing heavily, she swallowed and huskily said, 'Be gentle, okay?'

He jerked a nod, gripped a hip and, with anticipation almost too heavy to bear, was about to press himself inside her sticky heat when it flashed in his mind: the question *why* she would ask him to be gentle. 'Is this your first time?' He had to drag the words out.

Her grip tightened on his neck and she pushed back, encouraging him to take possession. His arousal throbbed so hard it burned through every part of him. 'Yes,' she breathed.

How desperately he wanted to thrust himself inside her. It was a desperation he'd never felt before. Not like this.

She was a virgin.

'It's okay,' she said raggedly, bringing her mouth to his and scraping the pads of her fingers over the bristles on the back of his neck. 'You won't hurt me.'

Her simple declaration landed like a punch to his solar plexus.

His confession came from nowhere. 'I know who you are.'

CHAPTER NINE

ISSY WAS SO consumed with the incredible feelings building on the tendrils of her climax and heightened anticipation for Gianni to take that final step and take possession of her that his words simply bounced like music through her head.

She wanted to experience everything, feel everything, lose herself in the hedonism of Gianni's touch…

But he was no longer moving. The fusion that would take her to heaven had stopped before it had properly started.

'Is something wrong?' she whispered, brushing her lips over his, trying to discern why his eyes were squeezed so tightly shut and his jaw clenched.

He breathed heavily through his nose before his eyes opened. His throat moved before he hoarsely repeated, 'I know who you are.'

Understanding seeped slowly into her dazed brain, and she had to blink a number of times to help clear it. 'You know…?'

'I know you're Thomas Seymore's daughter.'

But still her brain refused to fully comprehend. His words made no sense… Not until ice began to creep its way up her spine and through her chest, and the breaths she'd struggled to find in the throes of passion became lodged in her throat and lungs.

The dazedness in her head melted and swam, white lights

flickering, the ice in her body spreading until comprehension hit her fully and the breath exploded out of her. Slamming her fists against his chest, Issy pulled her thighs up and together, then twisted to one side and dropped off the table. Her feet slammed onto the floor, but she'd forgotten she was still wearing the stupidly high sandals and her ankle buckled at the impact, making her fall.

In an instant he was at her side, concern written all over his face.

Frantically trying to cover her modesty with the dress that until moments ago had been bunched around her waist, she huddled into herself. 'Get away from me.'

'Issy...'

She wanted to spit in his face. 'I said get away from me. Get out. Get out now.'

'Issy, please...'

'Get out!' she screamed, losing all control of herself. 'Get out, get out, get *out*!'

His broad shoulders rose and his chin lifted. Tension lined his face and made his body appear carved from stone.

She couldn't bear to look at him a moment longer and buried her face in her knees. She thought she might be sick.

As much as she tried to tune him out, she was acutely aware of movement around her and stiffened when a breeze feathered over her bowed head and the slightest pressure brushed against her hair.

She sensed rather than heard Gianni leave the games room. The emptiness he left in his wake confirmed he'd gone.

Gianni splashed cold water on his face and tried to regulate his breathing. Guilt pulsed strongly inside him.

Gripping tightly to the sink, he dragged air into his lungs

and tried to banish the image of Issy, humiliated and vulnerable, huddled on the floor.

The game they'd been playing had come to its conclusion but he'd been incapable of playing the final round.

He knew he'd done nothing wrong. *He* was the innocent party in all this. Issy had been playing him long before their first encounter, a meeting *she'd* engineered. Everything that had followed had been by her design. Everything. She'd played herself off as a socialite party girl and seduced him with her eyes and words. She'd even blagged his own yacht as a prop for her game. All he'd done was play along. Even when he'd learned her true identity and discovered she'd set all this up as part of a plan to destroy him and his cousin, the worst he'd done was hide her phone.

Yes. He was the innocent party in all this so why he should have had that awful paralysis of guilt when they were finally acting on the desire that had sparked at their very first meeting was inexplicable. And why he should still feel that guilt lying so heavily inside him was doubly so.

Issy peeked out of her cabin's curtains. The sun was rising, the last remaining stars twinkling before daylight extinguished them. The *Palazzo delle Feste* was already cutting its way through the Caribbean Sea.

She took a deep breath and put an internal call—the only calls her cabin phone could make—through to the captain.

By the time the call ended, despair had her in its grip.

The marriage papers were already lodged with the ministry.

Gianni showered and dressed. He'd spent the night in his own cabin. He'd been looking forward to spending his first night in it—sleeping in an opulent room with all the amenities a man could need, knowing how hard he'd worked for it and that no one could take it from him was a thrill that never grew old—but he'd been unable to settle. Sleep had been elusive. Every time he closed his eyes, it was Issy he saw, huddled on the floor, humiliated and vulnerable.

He'd put the order through to set sail for St Lovells before the sun had even risen and asked for the marriage papers to be destroyed. The captain had been able to comply with the first request. It was the second that was a problem. Believing the happy couple wanted the papers lodged as soon as possible, the captain had paid—well, Gianni had paid—for a member of the ministry to take a speedboat to the *Palazzo delle Feste* and collect the documents. Working back through the time line, Gianni estimated the official had arrived when he and Issy had been in the games room. All the crew had been under his strict instructions not to enter or disturb them unless specifically asked. Worse still, the bribed official had already lodged the papers. To disentangle them from their joke of marriage would now take an annulment.

That would teach him to give someone else power to spend his own money without limits, he thought wearily.

The marriage disentanglement was something that could wait. For now, it was Issy at the forefront of his mind. He knew he shouldn't care about her state of mind but that didn't stop his chest sharpening every time her image flashed in his head. Seeing as that was every other second, his chest felt like it had an ice pick jammed in it.

He found her on the sundeck, dressed in a long-sleeved sheer white kaftan eating her breakfast. She looked different, her hair tied in a loose ponytail, not a scrap of make-up on her face. She looked younger.

Breathing deeply to quell the tempest raging in his stomach, Gianni put his phone on the table and took the seat across from her. She didn't look at him, concentrating on the plate of eggs on toast with sides of bacon and mushrooms she was steadily making her way through, pausing only to pour herself more coffee from the cafetière. She added cream from the jug then a heaped spoonful of sugar, stirred vigorously, took a sip and then picked her cutlery back up and continued to eat.

Helping himself to coffee and a selection of the fruit, yogurt and pastries also laid out on the table but untouched by Issy, he had to force the food down his throat and into his stomach. He had no appetite.

'How long are you going to ignore me for?' he asked when her plate was empty and he could no longer tolerate the silence.

She responded by helping herself to a chocolate croissant and pretending not to hear him.

'I appreciate you are angry with me but you only have yourself to blame. You hustled me, Issy. You brought me here to distract me so your sister could set a bomb off in my company.'

That made her still. For a moment he thought she would speak but the moment passed when she took another bite of her croissant.

'I know this will disappoint you but your plans have been thwarted. I warned my cousin as soon as I discovered what the two of you were up to.'

There was the slightest flicker on the face that still refused to look at him.

'I knew in London that you were a hustler,' he continued conversationally. 'So I cloned your phone. Once I realised what you and your sister were up to, I had your phone locked away in my cabin. I will return it to you when this is all over and there is no longer danger in allowing you to communicate with Amelia.'

She pushed her chair back from the table and got to her feet. Still not even acknowledging his presence, she plucked an apple from the fruit platter and stepped away.

A flash of anger scalded him. 'I suppose I shouldn't be surprised at your silence. Your father had little to say for himself either when Alessandro and I confronted him with his corruption.'

For the beat of a moment her foot hovered in mid-air before she spun around and, ponytail swishing, stormed back to the table and grabbed hold of Gianni's phone. Moving too quickly for him to react, she raced to the railing and hurled it overboard.

Open-mouthed, hardly able to credit what she'd just done, Gianni watched Issy stroll back inside without once turning back to look at him.

Fury like she'd never known raged through Issy as she stormed over to the first member of the crew she came across. Realising her anger must make her look like a harpy, she took a deep breath before saying, 'Excuse me, but can I borrow your phone please? I still can't find mine.'

Leanne, probably even younger than Issy, bit her lip and dropped her stare.

Confused at her reaction, Issy put a hand to Leanne's arm. 'Are you okay? I'll pay for any roaming fees.'

Leanne shook her head. 'I can't. It's more than my job's worth.'

'What, lending me your phone? What do you mean?'

'We've all been ordered not to lend you our phones if you ask,' she mumbled.

'Ordered by who?' But she knew. Who else could it be?

'Mr Rossi.'

Issy gritted her teeth and filled her lungs to stop herself biting poor Leanne's head off. 'Look, Leanne, it doesn't matter what orders Gianni has given you. This is *my* charter. Please, let me use your phone, just for five minutes. Please.'

But the young woman only shook her head. 'This is your charter, but he's my boss.'

That swimming feeling in her head she'd experienced in the games room when she'd finally comprehended that Gianni knew exactly who she was started up again. She was almost afraid to say, 'Your boss? How?'

Eyes laden with sympathy met hers. 'Because this is his yacht.'

Issy's cabin phone rang. She glared at it. She'd spent the last hour locked away in here glaring at it, hating it for its refusal to dial out of the yacht. It was taking everything she had to maintain her fury because she knew the minute it started leaching out of her, terror for her sister was going to grab her.

Scrambling across the bed she'd been glaring at the phone from, she lifted the receiver and snapped, 'Yes?'

'Miss Seymore?'

Recognising the captain's voice, she closed her eyes and strove for a gentler tone. Much as she wanted to scream and shout at him, the captain had only been obeying orders from his real boss. 'Yes, Captain Caville. What can I do for you?'

'I thought you should know we'll be docking in twenty minutes.'

'Where?'

'St Lovells.'

'Is that an island?'

'Yes.'

'I've never heard of it…but thank you for letting me know.'

'You're welcome.' He hesitated before adding, 'My apologies again for the confusion about the wedding papers.'

But no apology for leading her on and letting her believe she'd chartered the *Palazzo delle Feste* for real when all the time he was working under Gianni's orders.

The entire crew worked for Gianni. The yacht belonged to Gianni. He'd played her like a puppet-master with sole control of the strings.

Oh, why hadn't she listened to her gut when David had shown her the *Palazzo delle Feste*? On some basic level that went beyond fear of not being able to pull off Silicon Valley or oligarch rich, she'd known the yacht was too much for what she needed. She'd known the charter was worth far too much for David to hand it over for free.

Desperation had made her ignore her gut. The window for her and Amelia to enact their revenge would only stay open for a strictly limited time and, once closed, the opportunity would likely never come again.

She'd ruined everything.

Putting the receiver back in its cradle, Issy covered her face. She mustn't cry. Not yet. Just as she wouldn't allow herself to think of how deeply wounded…broken… Gianni had left her last night. The tears would have to wait. The only thing she could allow herself to focus on was escaping Gianni. Once she'd accomplished that, she'd find a way to contact Amelia, not to warn her—she knew in her heart it was too late for that—but to make sure she was okay. That she was safe.

Both Rossi cousins were ruthless but it was Alessandro Issy found the most frightening. Unlike his cousin who the press adored, Alessandro stayed firmly out of the spotlight and so there were very few pictures of him online. Those there were showed a handsome but darkly menacing-looking man, the kind you crossed at your peril. His face perfectly matched the image Issy had conjured for him all those years ago when he and Gianni had walked out of their family home with all the swagger of a couple of gangsters who'd put a bullet in their mortal enemy. As far as Issy was concerned, they might as well have done. At least it would have spared her father a year of torment.

When she'd first seen a picture of Gianni, it had taken her a while to compute that the handsome man smiling so gregariously at the camera could be the same man who'd done and said such cruel things to her father. She'd had no such issue with Alessandro.

For all that, she'd thought Amelia was safe working for the Rossi cousins. Rossi Industries employed a hundred thousand people. Of course, only a fraction of them worked at The Ruby, the moniker given due to the pink tinge of the magnificent skyscraper the Rossi cousins had created in the heart of London as their head office, but there was safety in numbers.

Issy's negligence had put her sister in danger. She must have been negligent and overlooked something, or how could Gianni have got the measure of her so quickly?

Peering out of her cabin window, her spirits lifted the tiniest of fractions to see the small island they were sailing to. Very small. Too small for an airport but if it was big enough to dock a yacht of this size then that had to be a good thing. Her spirits lifted a fraction more to catch glimpses of pretty dwellings amongst the thick palms and verdant topography. Human life. Hopefully there would be an airfield with small charter planes. If not, there would be boats. She had emergency cash for this exact purpose. She'd known from the start that when her job was done, she'd need to make a quick escape.

It killed her to know the job would never be done. She'd blown it.

She waited until the yacht docked before slipping her feet into her rose-pink flips-flops—she would never wear heels again—and unlocked her cabin door. Satisfied the corridor was empty, she wheeled her suitcase down it. If she could make it to the metal stairs that would be unfolded for them onto the jetty without bumping into Gianni, there was a good chance she'd be able to reach safety without any further interaction with him.

The sun was high when she stepped out onto the deck, a warm breeze immediately blowing her hair around her face. She wished she'd kept her hair tied back in the ponytail, wished too that hadn't chucked her shades in her suitcase. She didn't want to waste time searching for them, not when escape was so close.

Members of the crew stood at the top of the stairs. Part of her wanted to snarl at them like a wounded cat, but she knew that impulse was unfair. Not only was Gianni their boss but his magnetism was such that even she'd come close to falling under his spell, so she fixed a smile to her face and thanked them for taking such good care of her.

About to take the first step on the stairs, a shift in the atmosphere made her hesitate. Despite the promise she'd made to herself to just leave and not look back, she turned her head before she could stop herself.

Gianni had appeared.

The punch to her heart was even stronger than the punch that had come close to flooring her when he'd joined her for breakfast.

In three long strides he was at her side and enveloping

her in a fresh cloud of his gorgeous cologne. 'Let me take that for you,' he said. Before she had time to react he'd lifted the suitcase from her hand and set off down the steps and onto the jetty.

Knowing that to open her mouth and speak would unleash the hellfire burning inside her, Issy had no choice but to follow him.

He walked purposefully, not looking back. The length and speed of his stride meant she had no chance of keeping up, so she set off at her own pace after him. If he refused to give the suitcase back then so be it. She had a bum-bag around her waist with her passport, bank cards and all her cash in it.

As she walked the long jetty, she tried to take in her surroundings. The harbour was small, only a handful of gleaming yachts moored. There were a few impossibly glamorous people in teeny bikinis and swim shorts milling around, all admiring the superyacht and no doubt trying to work out who the disembarking passengers were.

Issy tried so hard to take everything in but her eyes kept betraying her, seeking Gianni instead of seeking possible routes off this beautiful and clearly exclusive island.

He'd changed out of the familiar polo shirt and canvas shorts into a short-sleeved black shirt untucked over smart tan shorts that landed mid-thigh and a pair of brown deck shoes. He might have worn them at breakfast but she couldn't remember. She'd been too intent on comfort eating and keeping herself together to even dare look at him. Then, as now, she couldn't decipher the mountain of emotions thrashing through her. Too many. Too frightening to contemplate.

Seeing the fresh clothes he wore only heaped more humiliation on her. Gianni had embarked the *Palazzo delle Feste* with nothing but the clothes on his back and the items contained in his shorts' deep pockets. He must have had a stash of clothes locked away in the master cabin she'd been forbidden, by the owner, from entering. Forbidden by Gianni.

How she wished her heart didn't make such ripples to see the muscles of his calves tighten as he walked and the bunching of the muscles across his back.

And, when Gianni reached the end of the jetty and turned his gaze on her as he waited for her to join him, how she wished the burning ache he'd ignited inside her would douse itself to ash.

For the first time since she'd huddled on the floor of the games room, she was helpless to stop herself from meeting his eye. What she found in his glittering stare only compounded the ripples in her heart, a mirror of the tortured emotions racking her. For one mad moment, a longing ripped through her, for Gianni to cup her face in his hands and press his firm lips to hers and...

It all happened so quickly that there was no time for her to react. A man she hadn't noticed hovering beside Gianni grabbed hold of her suitcase at the exact same moment Gianni swept her into his arms and deposited her in the back of a black four-by-four car she'd also failed to notice. He quickly folded himself in beside her. The door closed.

'What are you doing?' Issy squealed, scurrying to the other door and immediately tugging on the handle. Panic gripped her harder when she found it locked. 'Let me out!'

'Soon.' He tapped on the dark window dividing them from the front of the car.

'Let me out, *now*!' The car started moving. Throwing herself forwards, Issy banged on the dividing window. 'Stop the car!'

'They won't stop.'

She banged again, harder. The glass must be reinforced otherwise her fist would probably have smashed through it.

'We're going to my complex. We'll be there in a few minutes.'

She glared at him and snarled, 'I'm not going anywhere with you.'

He sighed as if already weary of her anger and rubbed his hand over his ever-thickening stubble. 'The travel of this car says differently.'

'If you don't stop this car and let me out this minute I'll report you for kidnap.'

'Any report will have to wait until you leave St Lovells. I'm afraid you will stay here with me until I have word from my cousin that any damage you and your sister have caused our business has been contained and mitigated.'

'You can't do that!'

'I can and I will. It's not for ever, and I give you my word no harm will come to you.'

'As if I'd believe a single word that came out of your mouth,' she spat.

'That, I believe, is a classic example of a pot calling a kettle black.'

The look Issy gave him reminded Gianni of a wildcat that once made the mistake of hanging around his child-hood farmhouse. This was before his mother left so he'd been nine at the most, but he remembered trying to befriend it and having a set of claws swipe his face in response. His bleeding face hadn't stopped him screaming and begging his father not to drown it. His father had proceeded to drop the cat in the well and then smack Gianni so hard around the back of his head that he'd actually seen the stars beloved of cartoon characters.

'You *can't* keep me here against my will. There are laws, you know.'

He almost felt sorry for her. '*Bella*, I *can* keep you here. I can keep you here because this island belongs to me and there is no way for you to leave without my permission.'

CHAPTER TEN

GIANNI HAD EXPOSED Issy for the conniving charlatan hell-bent on his destruction that she was, so why the emotions that passed like a reel over her face made his stomach clench made no sense. The tenderness that kept slamming into him, the longing to gather her tightly and swear on all that was holy that he would never let harm come to her...it could only be caused by sleep deprivation. He should never have spent those insomniac hours looking through the data he'd cloned from her phone. So few contacts. So few photos. So few signs that this young woman had any form of a life that could be called sociable.

He'd read the messages between her and her sister hoping to learn more about their plans but there had been little more to be gleaned, and in any case it was the photos he kept coming back to. Every woman Gianni had dated catalogued every aspect of her life with selfies. He'd got so used to it that he barely even noticed their phones being permanently turned towards themselves. Issy had thirty-three photos stored on her phone. The ice cream sundae screenshot was the oldest. A handful of others were of her sister, who looked no different to the woman he'd last seen at The Ruby barely a week ago.

The first signs of Issy's weight loss began around the time Amelia started work at Rossi Industries, bookmarked in a series of photos of her smiling brightly with various equally smiley children. Her hair was that beautiful deep chestnut in every picture so he guessed she must have dyed it for their first meeting. So intent had he been on studying Issy and gauging from the timestamps that it had taken her four months to reach the size she still maintained that it was a while before he noticed all the photos were taken in a hospital and that many of the children captured had little or no hair.

'You own this island?' she whispered in horror, backing herself against the door on her side.

'Don't worry, your research skills didn't let you down.' Why he should want to reassure her on this aspect was anyone's guess. 'I brought St Lovells two years ago. I got all involved in the sale to sign a non-disclosure agreement to keep my name secret from the press—I know I can't keep it secret for ever, but I hope to enjoy it for a short while in peace. Your research skills didn't let you down with the *Palazzo delle Feste* either. The company I employed to build it also signed an NDA for the same reasons. It doesn't matter if they discover it's mine now—I've had anti-paparazzi technology embedded into it.'

'Since when has being in the press bothered you?'

He shrugged. 'The press are like the hangovers I've been getting since I turned thirty—wearisome.'

'Maybe you shouldn't court them then,' she suggested tartly.

'I don't court them, I engage with them, and always for business reasons. Believe me, I have never invited the paparazzi to send a drone over my yacht to take photos of me.'

'No, that would be your girlfriends.'

'My lovers,' he corrected. 'Girlfriend implies a form of permanence.'

Something spasmed across her face at his mention of the word lover. 'Don't worry, no woman would ever be stupid enough to date you thinking it could lead to for ever.'

But Issy knew more than a few of his lovers—hateful, hateful word—would have entered a relationship with him with their eyes wide open only to be dazzled and then blinded by the light he exuded. She'd had years to prepare and protect herself against his sexual magnetism but the reality of Gianni in the flesh had penetrated the thick stone wall she'd built.

'I should hope not,' he murmured, then looked outside the window. 'This island is the perfect sanctuary. There's tourist development on one side but it's limited. I've taken the south side for my personal use. There is no docking without permission. Any journalist stupid enough to send a drone over the island can expect to have it shot down.'

'And any kidnap victim can expect to receive zero help.'

'You will have half the island to explore and do as you wish in.'

'Great, does that mean I can swim to the nearest island?'

He pulled a face. 'If you like but I wouldn't rate your chances. Even the strongest long-distance swimmer would find it a challenge swimming forty kilometres without support.'

'You can't do this, Gianni. You know you can't.'

'How many times do I have to tell you that I can? And, please, stop with the outrage. What the hell did you think would happen if I found out what you were up to? You're a clever woman—you must have imagined the scenario.'

Feeling her temper rising, Issy closed her eyes and took a deep breath. 'Where's my sister?'

'In Italy with Alessandro.'

'Voluntarily?'

'I have no idea.'

'It can't be voluntary. She'd never go anywhere alone with that beast.'

His gaze swiftly darkened. 'Do not speak of my cousin in that way.'

'Or what? You'll hit me?'

He blinked as if surprised she would even suggest such a thing. 'Never.'

'Then what? Your cousin is a monster and you are too, and I want proof my sister is safe.'

'I would give you proof if you hadn't thrown my phone into the sea.'

'Give me my phone back then so I can call her.'

'No.'

'*Please*, Gianni. Please. Keep me locked in a dark basement with spiders if you must but please, let me call my sister. *Please.*'

It was the distress on her face that made Gianni come within a whisker of granting her request. When a solitary teardrop rolled down her cheek he had to clench his fist to stop from reaching into his back pocket for her phone.

'*Bella*, listen to me,' he said gently. 'Your sister is safe, I swear it. Alessandro is not the monster you believe him to be. He would never harm a hair on her head.'

Chin wobbling, her teeth grazed her bottom lip. 'You expect me to believe you?'

He brushed a finger across her cheek and gave a rueful smile. 'I expect nothing, but on this I want you to put your trust in me and believe me when I say Amelia is safe and no harm will come to her.'

He could not fathom why, after staring intently into his

eyes for so long it felt as if she'd delved into a lifetime of his memories, her soft nod and the loosening of her taut frame as she whispered, 'Okay,' should make his chest fill so strongly.

She must be mad. Issy knew that, gazing out of the window but with her thoughts too full to see. Trusting *him*? Trusting the devil? And it wasn't because she had no choice in the matter, it was a trust that came from her heart, a relief that spread through her and eased the tightness in her lungs. It was a trust she felt guilty for having, almost as guilty as she felt when she remembered how close she'd come to giving her virginity to the devil. If Gianni hadn't confessed to knowing who she was, she would have let him make love to her, and gladly. That he'd obviously had a fit of guilt himself to make such a confession at such a time should not mean anything. He'd led her on to that point. Every word he'd said had been a lie.

But every word you've said has been a lie too…

That's different, she argued with herself. Gianni was a corrupt…she almost called him a monster but for some stupid reason her brain recoiled from allowing her to think it. But he was definitely corrupt! He was the corrupt bastard who'd stolen her father's business and destroyed her life. He deserved everything she and Amelia had been planning for him.

Are you sure about that…?

Shut up! she shouted to her stupid brain. Of course she was sure! Amelia had discovered proof of their corruption and her sister wouldn't lie.

But why did you refuse to go ahead with the plan without proof?

Because I needed to be certain we were doing the right thing! They both had been! They had agreed from the off that they wouldn't go ahead without proof that it wasn't only their father the Rossi cousins had destroyed!

Why was she having this argument with herself again? Before meeting Gianni, as Amelia's side of the plan had been gaining speed, Issy had put her fresh insistence that Amelia find proof of corruption down to cold feet. Secret doubts had gathered, and she'd become increasingly needful of something concrete and physical to throw at the Rossi cousins if it ever came to it, a certainty that this wasn't just the vengeance of two adolescent girls who'd probably been blind to their father's faults.

It was working at the hospital, she was sure, that had put those doubts about her father in her head, and she hated herself for them, would never admit to Amelia that they even existed.

Working on the children's ward meant Issy spent a lot of time with parents whose precious children hovered between life and death. Those parents were fallible. Human. But the children never saw them like that. Their children trusted them implicitly. If Mummy or Daddy said they were going to get better then they unfailingly believed them, even if that assurance was a lie. Not one parent lied out of callousness but because they couldn't bear to deal with the consequences of the truth, both to their child and to themselves.

'We're here.'

Issy blinked herself out of her reverie and looked at her watch. Only ten minutes had passed since Gianni had kidnapped her into the back of his car and she hadn't paid any attention to her surroundings.

They'd stopped at an electric gate with a guarded security box built into a high stone wall that ran as far as the eye

could see either side. The narrow road they'd taken continued on the other side of the of gate, surrounded by thick,
tropical foliage. As they travelled it she tried not to mar-
vel at the beauty surrounding them but when they emerged
through it and the stunning vista revealed itself, she was
unable to stop the gasp that escaped her lips.

A huge cove with the clearest turquoise water she'd ever
seen lapped onto the cleanest, whitest sand she'd ever seen.
The rays from the sun high above them made the water and
sand sparkle like a billion tiny jewels had been scattered
over it. Virtually hidden amongst the palm trees lining the
beach was a handful of thatched roofed chalets. The central
one, set back from the other four and easily the size of them
all combined, rose like a Tibetan monastery.

It was the most stunning sight she'd seen in her life,
beautiful enough to make her heart twist and then pump
with a sigh.

The driver parked in a sheltered garage hidden from the
naked eye.

'Let me show you around,' Gianni said quietly.

Issy closed her eyes before following him out of the car.

Close-up, the complex was even more stunning than it
had been from a distance.

'This is the first time I've come here since the work was
completed,' he told her as they neared the chalets, each
larger and set further apart from the others than she'd originally thought. Reaching the first, she realised each chalet
was set in its own private landscape.

'My original intention for this holiday was to spend a
week sailing on the *Palazzo delle Feste* and the second week
here,' he added when she made no response.

'You've spent an enormous amount of money on something you'll only use for two weeks of the year,' she ob-

served as he guided her past a swimming pool that looked as if it were naturally created. Palms offered natural shade on one side of it, the other a sunbather's paradise.

'I'm planning for the future.'

'Oh?'

They'd reached the grounds of the second chalet. Leading her up the path to reach it, he explained, 'I work an average of eighty-hour weeks. I've worked those kind of hours since I was a kid. At some point in the future I will want to take my foot off the brake.'

'My heart's bleeding. Still, it's your money. You can spend it how you want.'

'You're too kind.'

'I know... Although I do wonder how you can be so free with it knowing everything you have came from stealing from my father.'

'We didn't steal from your father,' he bit back.

'Yes, you did.' She wanted to glare at him but her face wouldn't cooperate, the swell of emotions rising through her made her chin wobble and her voice tremble. 'I was there, Gianni. You invited yourself into our home and took everything we had from us. You ripped the business my father had spent his life building away from him and belittled and humiliated him. You didn't just steal his business—*you destroyed everything.*'

The darkness of his stare almost made her quail. When he finally spoke, there was an ice in his tone she'd never heard before. 'Your father stole from *us*. He sold us land unfit for development and bribed surveyors and officials to cover it up. It was our first business deal and we'd worked our backsides off from the age of twelve to pay for it *and* took a loan to make up the shortfall. Thanks to your father, we were left with crippling repayment charges for land that was worthless. It took us years of working every hour God sent to make those repayments and build a nest with which to start again, and the day we took control of your father's business and kicked him into the long grass remains the best day of my life. He deserved everything, had had it coming for years, not just for how he treated us but all the other businesses and individuals he'd ripped off over the years.' He threw the chalet door open. 'This is for your personal use. Do as you please.'

And with that, he strode back down the path, tension practically vibrating from his taut gait.

Gianni was too angry to appreciate anything about the sprawling lodge he one day intended to spend half of each year living in. He toured it fighting to stop himself from snarling at the housekeeper, who must have spent hours making everything shine so brightly and kept giving him anxious looks as if afraid he was about to explode.

It took a lot to make him lose his temper. His father was a squat bundle of aggression who used his fists as weapons and his tongue as a whip. Gianni had lived with him for eighteen years, but that aggression had neither been inherited nor rubbed off on him. If it had, he would have fought it with every fibre of his being. That didn't mean he disliked or avoided confrontation, just that the anger that could make a person's face go red and voice rise and words—often regretted after—splutter from his mouth rarely worked its way through him.

Issy's accusation that he'd stolen her father's business had slashed open a wound that had been sealed a decade ago when he and Alessandro had ousted him. It had taken every ounce of control to stop his voice from rising and to stop himself leaning right into Issy's face to shout his home truths and rip the blinkers from her eyes.

There had been no stealing. If Thomas Seymore had run his business legitimately they would never have been able to take it from him. They would never have needed to.

It had been the contempt in her stare while she'd thrown the accusation at him that had bit more than her words. Contempt laced with pain. Biting more than that had been the absolute certainty that she believed it. That Isabelle Seymore believed him a thief, that she believed him *capable* of being a thief. And corrupt. Mustn't forget that. He hoped like hell Alessandro had got to the bottom of the slanderous proof of corruption Amelia had messaged Issy about.

Alone in his master suite, he sat on the bed and rubbed his temples.

It shouldn't matter what Issy thought of him. It shouldn't matter that she hated him. He had no business feeling sick to the pit of his stomach that taking the business from Thomas Seymore had affected his youngest daughter so greatly. That was on Seymore. He was the father. It had been his duty to protect his children.

Gianni grunted a morose laugh and fell back. Spreading his arms out over the mattress, he gazed up at the ceiling. Fathers were supposed to protect their children. Mothers were too. The only person Gianni and his mother had needed protecting from was his father, and then his mother had run away and left him to take the blows and bullying alone.

Issy was refusing to leave her cabin. She'd asked the staff to provide her with food she could cook for herself and then locked the door. All this had been reported to Gianni, who was glad of it. In the short space of time that he'd known Isabelle Seymore she'd managed to get under his skin and dredge up memories of a past he preferred not to remember in any detail.

The tourist part of St Lovells was an exclusive resort he'd had built when he bought the island. Already it had gained a reputation as the ultimate luxury retreat for wealthy young things looking for a good time. Gianni was on his one full holiday of the year, the break he took annually to recharge his batteries and he was damned if he was going to let Issy's sulking prevent him from enjoying himself, not when it was her connivance that had stopped him making the usual plans in the Caribbean. On a normal holiday, he would hook up with a group of friends who spent their summers bumming around the Caribbean, invite along his latest lover to join them and generally have a great time doing nothing but enjoy himself for fourteen days.

He'd had a good night's sleep and now he was ready to enjoy himself and party. Issy could stay in her cabin and sulk for the duration of their stay here if she so wished but he was not going to let it stop him having fun.

The number of visitors was kept strictly limited, not as a means of keeping people out but as a means of preserving the island's natural beauty. One thing he'd learned in his career as a property developer was that there was always a trade-off when making a development between what humans needed and what the planet's other inhabitants needed. He much preferred developing on sites that had already been in use or on land that was ecologically worthless. The land they'd bought off Thomas Seymore was in the latter category, although just how worthless had been kept hidden from them until it was too late to do anything about it. The land Gianni's father and uncle owned containing the vineyards Gianni and his cousin had been forced to toil on throughout their childhood was heading the same way. Their fathers were ravaging the land, literally running their business into the ground.

When Gianni bought St Lovells he'd had a clear idea of how it would be developed: minimally. The work on both the tourist part and his private complex had been completed with ninety-five percent of the island left untouched. It was a tropical paradise alive with noisy, colourful wildlife, and as he took a golf buggy—his four-by-four was the only full-size motor vehicle allowed on the island—to the tourist part on his second day there, the darkness of his mood lifted.

One day, he would force his cousin to visit. Alessandro never took time off. The man was a machine. It still amazed him how two boys who were born only months apart, shared so much of the same DNA and had been raised like brothers could be so different and yet remain so close. Gianni would take a bullet for his cousin and he knew Alessandro would do the same for him.

He suspected Issy's relationship with her sister was similar. He didn't know Amelia well but knew she was a different kind of personality to her sister, more focused and analytical, more introverted. Issy had tried to hide her real self beneath the fake, polished exterior she'd projected to entrap him and portray herself as someone completely different to who she was, but he'd caught enough glimpses of the real Issy and studied enough of her photos and messages to know she was a smiley, kind, good person.

He stopped the buggy and rested his head back. Closing his eyes, he took a long breath. Issy had dedicated many years of her life to working against him, building a plan to ensnare him into a distraction so her sister could bring down his company. Good, kind people did not behave in that way. Just because she was a nurse who worked with sick children did not make her an angel.

Snapping his eyes back open, he continued his drive to the tourist resort.

The main resort pool was edged with beautiful people sunbathing and drinking cocktails. He rubbed his growing beard, fixed a grin to his face, and set off to join them.

The beach party went on until the early hours. Having had too much to drink to safely drive, Gianni got one of the resort staff to drive him back to his complex. Needing air to clear his head, he walked from the security gate and reflected on what a great day it had been. As he'd expected, he was already acquainted with a number of the vacationers: a supermodel whose best friend he'd once had a fling with and her latest beau, a genius app creator who frequented many of the same clubs and bars as him in London. They'd greeted him like an old friend and quickly introduced him to the rest of the party they were vacationing with, bright shiny, rich and beautiful twenty-somethings. One of them had been an American television actress he'd vaguely recognised, a tall, slender blonde with come-to-bed eyes she'd kept firmly fixed on him. She was exactly Gianni's type and he'd flirted with her for hours before realising his heart wasn't in it and that she didn't do anything for him. When she'd whispered in his ear on the beach about slipping away to her chalet, he'd graciously turned her down and called it a night.

He was still mulling over what it was about the actress he'd failed to respond to considering she ticked every box he wanted in a lover when he reached Issy's cabin. One of the lights was on. His heart turned over then rose up his throat, and he had to tread his feet firmly to stop them taking the path to her door.

CHAPTER ELEVEN

THE KITCHEN IN Issy's chalet was, in comparison with the rest of the place, tiny. Compared to the kitchen she shared with Amelia, it was humungous. Obviously installed with no expectation the occupier would ever use it—the staff had been astounded that she wanted to cook for herself, and had kept reiterating that there were world-class chefs on site who could whip up anything she desired—it nonetheless contained everything she needed.

Issy loved cooking. There were certain aromas, like freshly baked cakes and bread, that never failed to transport her back to a time when her family had been whole and happy. So far that day, she'd baked a lemon drizzle cake and made herself an Italian sausage pasta dish laden with parmesan. Comfort food. Instead of soothing her though, the aromas twisted her stomach to the extent that her plan to demolish the lot was foiled. It had been the same the day before, when she'd made profiteroles laden with whipped cream and chocolate and only managed to eat two of them.

If she was to believe Gianni's twisted accusation against her father then that meant the happy memories she relied on to lift her spirits and make her believe that good times could once again come for her and Amelia and maybe even their mother were built on a lie. She couldn't believe her father had been corrupt. She just couldn't. Until the day the Rossi cousins had barged into their home and destroyed their lives, her father had been a kind and loving man who'd lavished all the love and time he could spare on his family. Would a corrupt man cut short a business meeting so he could watch his six-year-old daughter perform the challenging role of a snowflake in a ballet recital? Would a corrupt man make every effort to be home by his daughters' bedtimes each night so he could read to them?

And would her mother, a once fun-loving, sweet, kind, joyful woman marry a corrupt man? Absolutely not.

Gianni was lying to her. He had to be. Probably because he didn't want to have to confront the damage *his* thievery and corruption had caused, and the more she thought this, the greater her outrage grew. How dare he twist things to make her father the bad guy?

There was a knock on her cabin's front door.

Crossing the airy living area adorned with the most exquisite furniture to the door, she guardedly asked, 'Who is it?'

'Me.'

She pressed a hand to her chest to stop her suddenly thrashing heart from bursting out. 'Are you here to set me free?'

'You are free, *bella*. You can go wherever you like in the complex.'

'Am I free to leave the complex?'

'No.'

'Then go away.'

'You can't spend all your time in here. It's not good for you.'

'If I was to leave this chalet I guarantee it wouldn't be good for you.'

His laughter rumbled through the door and made her

want to cover her ears. 'That's a risk I'm prepared to take. Come on, Issy, we could be here for a few more days. You can't spend it locked away. Come out and explore with me. We can talk.'

'In case you hadn't noticed, I don't want to talk to you, and I don't need to leave this cabin. You're a great host and there is plenty here to keep me occupied, so do me a favour and leave me alone. I'm not going anywhere until you let me go home.'

'You'll be free to go home as soon as I get word from Alessandro, but we will need to talk at some point.'

'We have nothing to say to each other.'

'We have a marriage to dissolve.'

'Then get dissolving it and leave me alone.'

Realising she was close to tears, Issy hurried back through the living area and out into her stunning private garden.

Gianni stared at Issy's chalet door. Still locked. Still no sighting of her. He regretted now making sure each chalet had all the privacy the occupants could wish for. These were the chalets for his close friends to use and for Alessandro, who he fully intended to one day drag here.

He knocked on the door. No answer came so he knocked again.

Her voice was even more guarded than it had been the day before. 'Yes?'

'It's me.'

She didn't respond at all.

'You can't avoid me for ever,' he said, and as he said it, he smiled ruefully to imagine her thinking, *Just you ruddy watch me.*

'Okay, you don't have to let me in,' he said after she'd ignored him for another twenty seconds, 'and I can't force you to talk to me. But I can sit here and talk to you and hope that you'll listen.'

Although the windows of the chalet were tinted to ensure complete privacy and her shutters closed so he couldn't see in, he sensed she was still at the door and hadn't rushed into the garden to escape his voice as she'd done the day before.

Lowering himself onto the front door step, he took a drink of the water he'd brought with him, made himself as comfortable as he could and rested his head back against the door.

'My father is a monster,' he said. 'A true monster. His brother—Alessandro's father—is the same. I don't know how they came to be that way, maybe their own father who I never met was the same, but their mother, our *nonna*, was a great lady. She lived with us and her presence tempered the worst of them. She died when I was eight.'

Gianni swallowed the acrid taste that had built in his mouth.

'Before she died, I was used to being hit. It was normal. Alessandro suffered the same. After she died the monsters came out. You know we were raised in Umbria?'

There was no answer but something told him she was listening.

He gave a morose laugh through his nose. 'I assume you know. I assume you know too that our fathers' business is wine. That's public knowledge for anyone who searches for it and I think you have searched my name and discovered everything the internet can tell you about me. If I were in your shoes and believed my father to be innocent then I would have done the same with the same intent, and I think that speaks of how different our childhoods were. If you were to tell me my father was innocent of something I would laugh in your face.'

Issy had tried to walk away from the door and out of the living area when Gianni had identified himself as her visitor but her feet had refused to obey. She'd tried to cover her ears when he'd started talking but her hands had refused to obey.

With a choked sigh of defeat, she slid her back down the door until her bottom reached the bamboo floor, then pulled her knees to her chest and hugged herself tightly.

'The wine they produce used to be great but when their mother died, they started cutting corners wherever they could. When Alessandro and I left, they cut even more corners. I give them two more years before the vineyard stops producing. At the most.' He laughed. Issy imagined his throat extending. 'Now, they're too lazy to even fertilise their land properly and since we left, too mean to pay anyone else to do it for them. Add all the other corners they cut and it's no surprise their Sangiovese tastes like battery acid.'

A long silence followed before he continued, still speaking in the same even tone as if relating a story he'd heard many times. But this wasn't *a* story. This was *his* story. All the things she'd longed to know even though it had had no relevance to her quest. Issy had wanted to know for her own sake because as much as Gianni had repelled her, deep down in the place she'd never dared acknowledge to herself lived an aching fascination for him.

'We were their little slaves,' he said. 'I remember crushing grapes with my feet until midnight and going to school the next day with purple feet and ankles. We were forced to work from sunrise until they said stop. If we complained, we were hit. Once Nonna died, we didn't have to complain to be hit. Her death unleashed them. They were our true slave masters and we their punching bags. Our mothers too. They never needed an excuse to beat them.'

Issy covered her mouth to stop a moan of distress escaping. She thought of the bump in Gianni's nose and how she'd wanted to shake the hand of the person who'd done it. That person must have been his own father.

'My mother ran away a year after Nonna died.' For the first time she heard an inflection of emotion in his voice. 'I haven't seen her since. She lives in Milan. I pay money into her account each month, but I never see her. She abandoned me to that bastard. It took months before I accepted that she wasn't coming back for me.' The tinge of sadness that laced his next laugh made her insides contract. 'My mother left me to my fate. Andro and I made a pact when we were twelve that as soon as we'd both turned eighteen we would leave and build new lives for ourselves. We worked even harder, taking jobs outside the vineyard wherever we could and saving every cent our fathers didn't demand we hand over to them. My father never knew, but I left school at sixteen and got a full-time job at a pizzeria—he'd have only taken my wages from me. The first thing we did when we finally left the vineyard was change our surnames.'

Vizzini, she remembered. That had been his original surname. It had taken her ages to dig that up. She remembered thinking Rossi suited him better and then had chided herself for thinking such a thing. Who cared whether his name suited him?

'We chose our *nonna*'s surname,' he said quietly, and though she had no way of knowing, Issy was certain he knew she was sat on the other side of the door to him. 'We sorted all the legal side out and then we made an offer on Tuscan land we'd huge plans for. We hadn't saved enough money to purchase it outright but we were able to borrow the shortfall.'

Dread crept its way up from the pit of her stomach.

'Only after the land was paid for and transferred into our

names did we learn it was unstable. There was no possibility of building a housing development on it. We'd been conned. The seller had seen two fresh-faced eighteen-year-olds and took advantage of our naivety. He bribed the surveyor and everyone else involved in the transaction and left us staring at bankruptcy.'

The seller. The man he claimed was her father.

'He underestimated us,' he said simply. 'We'd worked too hard and overcome too much to accept defeat. We started again. We worked like Trojans to repay the loan and build a new nest. As soon as we had the money we bought our first property and flipped it; gave it a makeover and sold it for a profit. We brought our second property and then our third and then we set our sights further taking on bigger and bigger projects with proportionate profits until we had the money to force the takeover of the business of the man who'd ripped us off. It took us four years. I don't think either of us slept more than four hours a night in those days. I do not regret what we did to that man. It didn't take much detective work to discover we weren't his only victims. I cannot abide corruption, Issy, and I hope that one day soon you will tell me of this proof of corruption Amelia spoke of because I swear on Alessandro's life that we are not corrupt. Everything we have we've built with our own toil using our own blood and sweat.'

Gianni's backside had become numb. Issy hadn't made a single sound but he was certain she'd heard every word. He rolled his neck and got to his feet. 'I'm going for a swim. Dinner will be served in the open dining room of my lodge at seven. All you need do is follow the path facing the beach and it will lead you to it. There is no pressure but know I would be glad to see you. I don't like to think of you alone with your thoughts…' He exhaled slowly before admitting,

'I want to get to know the real Isabelle Seymore because I already miss the Issy I spent that ride wild on the *Palazzo delle Feste* with. I know she's not the real you, but something tells me the things I like the most about her *are* real.'

Issy tried desperately hard to concentrate on the game of solitaire she was playing but her eyes kept being drawn to her watch. Gianni would be in his dining room, but he wouldn't be waiting for her. She'd left word for him declining his invitation when she'd requested dinner be brought to her cabin.

She couldn't face her stomach turning over at the aromas of her own cooking and she couldn't face him. It was too dangerous. She'd listened to Gianni relay the story of his life and wanted so much to open the door, crawl onto his lap and hold him tight. She'd long suspected his estrangement from his father was rooted in something bad—children rarely cut themselves off from their parents without good reason—but to imagine the suffering he must have gone through...

As hard as she tried to keep her emotions contained, the stone wall she'd built was breaking down, the contents of her heart bleeding out of it.

But there were three villains to his story. His father, his uncle and her father.

She couldn't accept it. Her bleeding heart wouldn't accept it. Her father would never treat two young men the way Gianni had described. He just wouldn't.

Are you sure...?

She slammed a card down then grabbed a chip. They were the most delicious chips she'd ever eaten in her life and she wished she wasn't feeling so down while eating them. She should be savouring their deliciousness.

Gianni must have been mistaken about her father. Because that was the crux of the problem—she believed him. Believed that he believed it.

And what about her sister? Because if Gianni was speaking the truth then it meant Amelia, the anchor that had kept Issy afloat all these years, had lied to her.

Mid-morning the next day, Gianni knocked on Issy's door again.

This time there was more hesitancy than guardedness in her voice. 'Yes?'

'It's me.'

Silence.

'I missed you last night.'

A long beat passed. 'Did you get my message?'

'I did.' He hadn't expected her to come. He'd hoped but his gut had told him not to hope too hard. He couldn't understand why her message, when it had come, had still landed like a blow.

There were many things about his reactions to Issy that Gianni didn't understand. Reactions and feelings he'd never felt before. They were growing stronger. The need to seek her out even if only to hear her voice gaining strength.

'Ready to come out yet?' he asked.

There was a slight hesitation before she said, 'No. Not yet.'

Not yet? That was a huge improvement and his chest lightened to hear it. 'That's a shame. It's a beautiful day.'

'I know. I've been in the garden.'

'Swimming?'

He swore he heard her laugh. 'No. I don't think it's safe for me to swim without a lifeguard close to hand.'

'That's one less thing for me to worry about,' he joked

back. He resisted offering to be her lifeguard. One step at a time. After days of silence and her cold shoulder, her voice sounded markedly warmer. Softer. 'Have you always been a lousy swimmer?'

'No... I... It's just been a long time. That's all. And I was never that strong a swimmer.'

He sat down in the same spot as he'd taken the day before. 'Tell me about it.'

'About what?'

'Swimming. Your life. Anything you want to tell me.'

'What do you want to know?' she asked doubtfully.

'Everything.'

When she next spoke her voice sounded so close to his ear that he knew she'd sat down too and that her back was likely pressed against the door the same as his, like two bookends. 'Be more specific.'

He wondered if her head touched the door too. She was so much shorter than him that it would rest lower than his. He wondered, too, why he'd always been inclined towards tall women before Issy. 'Tell me about your job. You're a nurse?'

'I'm an auxiliary nurse, not a medical nurse.'

'Is there a difference?'

'About four years of education.' Another quip? Things really were improving. He heard the smile in her voice as she explained, 'My job is basically to make sure the patients are comfortable and to help them with anything they can't do for themselves.'

'You work with children?'

'Yes. I'm on the children's ward.'

'You enjoy it?'

'I love it.'

'Is it not hard dealing with sick children?'

'It can be. You have to stay professional but it's hard not to build attachments. Especially with the really sick ones.'

'The ones you know will die?'

Her next, 'Yes,' was barely audible through the barrier of the door.

Her voice lifted a little. 'But they're incredible. All of them. Children are so brave, much braver than adults.'

'Do you really think that?'

'That's just from my observations over the last four years.'

'I know very little about children,' he mused. 'I've never been in a social setting with a child.'

'Never?'

'Never,' he confirmed. 'I've never held a baby either.'

'You've missed out.'

'How?'

He imagined the shrug she gave at this. 'Holding a baby is the most contenting thing in the world.'

'You want children of your own?'

'Definitely.' She paused before adding, 'You?'

'I've never thought about it until this minute, but I think I would like children. With the right woman.' The image of a small, plump, chestnut-haired Issy holding an ice cream sundae flashed in his mind. Immediately disconcerted, he blinked the image away and moved the subject away from children. 'Did you never want to be a real nurse?'

'Nursing was founded on caring for the sick and that's what I do, but originally I wanted to be a medical nurse.'

'What stopped you?'

There was another long beat before she softly answered, 'You.'

He closed his eyes and filled his lungs with air. 'Tell me, *bella*. Tell me everything.'

She took so long to speak he became convinced that she'd

slipped away. 'When our father lost the business it had a domino effect on the rest of our lives. Looking back, it feels like it happened overnight, but I must have been sleepwalking through it. One minute I was the luckiest girl alive, living in a big, beautiful house in London and spending my summers in our home in Italy. I went to a school I loved, I had great friends, a loving family… The next minute it was all gone. We lost our home. Amelia and I were forced to leave our school—our parents couldn't afford the fees—and start again at a new one where the other students hated us. Most of our friends abandoned us and our parents' friends abandoned them too. Dad always liked a drink, but I don't remember ever seeing him drunk before, but from that day I don't have a single memory of him sober. A year later he was dead. He literally drank himself to death.'

Gianni rubbed his temples. He remembered hearing on the grapevine about Thomas Seymore's death. The grapevine had whispered about alcohol. For once it seemed the grapevine had been correct.

'After his death, Mum was forced to file for bankruptcy and we were forced to move again—we'd become so poor the council had to provide us with accommodation. I think, though I don't know for certain, that that's when her drug dependency started. Amelia clocked on to it before I did—she's always been more observant than me—and protected me from it as much as she could but she couldn't protect me for ever. I just know that when I lost my dad, the last of the mother that lived in the woman that is Jane Seymore died with him.'

'She really is addicted to drugs?'

'Yes. We looked after her as best we could, but we were kids. As soon as Lia got the job with you, we could afford to send her to rehab in South America. Lia found it. Mum likes it there…as much as she likes being anywhere on this earth.'

A long passage of silence passed before she said, 'Everything we went through pulled me and Amelia together. Her strength was amazing and, in a way, inspired me to be strong too. She kept me sane. We took care of Mum and each other, and we vowed revenge on the men we believed killed our father and drove our mother into addiction. We wanted to hit you where it hurt and that meant your business. Every single thing we've done since Amelia went to university to get the qualifications that would make her the ideal candidate for your company has been with that end goal.'

'You've played the support act?'

'No. I was the backroom worker in the project but we've supported each other. Every decision we made together. All the money we earned went into the same pot.'

'But you wanted to be a medical nurse.'

'I needed to be earning money. Believe me, we both made sacrifices but neither of us saw it as that, and it worked out for the best. I love my job and being so hands on with the kids. It's the most rewarding job in the world and I wouldn't change it for anything.'

The ache that formed in Gianni's chest at this was so acute that he had to exhale slowly to relieve it. 'A few times just then when you were speaking of your revenge, you spoke in the past tense…' He was, absurdly, almost afraid to ask. 'Does that mean you believe me?'

CHAPTER TWELVE

Issy bowed her head and breathed deeply before leaning back against the door and dragging her hair off her face. 'I don't… Gianni, please…' She pinched the bridge of her nose and fought back the hot swell of tears. 'I've… I've had some doubts.'

'What kind of doubts?' he asked gently.

Bitter-tasting guilt rose up her throat at what she was about to admit. 'We took everything he said in blind faith.'

'I know it hurts, *bella*, but admitting that he was a bastard in business does not have to taint your memories of who he was as your father.'

'But I feel disloyal for even questioning it to myself,' she whispered.

'A child is programmed to trust their parents,' he said in that same gentle tone. 'When my mother ran away without me… It came close to breaking me. My own mother abandoned me and I've never been able to trust anyone but Alessandro since.'

Not wanting to inadvertently offend him, Issy hesitated before asking, 'Is that why you've never had a long-term relationship?'

He gave a low laugh. 'I never think about it but that's very likely. My social life is great fun and I have many friends, but no one I would consider close. That includes my past lovers. I've never had a conversation like this with anyone before or shared the confidences I did with you yesterday.'

'It's the same for me,' she admitted. 'I've always had Amelia to talk to and we confide absolutely everything in each other, but I think that's because we *had* to pull together. If she hadn't been there I think I would have grown to hate my parents for sinking into dependency, you know, for not being enough to keep them sober. I always make myself remember how it was before the business was taken and how happy we were as a family and how secure I felt—I *have* to hold on to that. When I FaceTime my mum, I sometimes catch glimpses of the mum I remember and I cherish those moments, and when I think of my dad I remember the man who read to me and led all the standing ovations at my ballet recitals, and it kills me to think that wasn't who he really was.'

'That *is* who he was, *cara*. The family man and the businessman were separate parts of him.'

'But if he sold you that land fraudulently and bribed officials to make it happen then his protestations of innocence after you forced the takeover were lies, and if you're right that there were other victims then that means my entire childhood is tainted.'

'Only if you let it be tainted.'

'But it means everything we had, all the privileges Amelia and I enjoyed, were built on fraud and lies.'

'But the father he was to you wasn't a lie. He loved you and Amelia and it seems to me that he destroyed himself in alcohol because he couldn't live with the repercussions of what his business decisions had done to his family.'

'I can't believe you're sticking up for him.' Not after everything. How could Gianni give her reassurance after what she'd tried to do to him?

'He must have had some good in him to produce a daughter like you.'

'What, a vengeful liar who was hell-bent on destroying you?'

'No, a fiercely loyal, kind-hearted, beautiful woman who couldn't go through with her vengeance without additional evidence. Don't forget, I have read the messages between you and your sister. When she messaged you that she'd found proof of corruption against us, your reply said, Thank God for that. That same day you took a photo of yourself with a patient and your hair was still chestnut. In the few days between that message and photo being taken to when we met in the club, you'd dyed your hair. You had doubts, *cara*, I know you did, and your sister knew it too and told you what you needed to hear to get you to actually act on your plans.'

The tears Issy had been holding back fell down her cheeks. How could a man she'd known for such a short time have the power to decipher her own thoughts and feelings better than she was able to?

'Bella?'

Breathing deeply, she wiped her eyes on her knees. 'I can't believe I'm admitting this but you're right, I've had doubts about his version of what happened between you and him.' Doubts that had grown the deeper she'd delved into Gianni's life and found nothing remotely untoward about his business conduct, doubts compounded with every gushing interview and profile published about him. No one had a bad word to say about him, not even his broken-hearted lovers. 'But, Gianni, I don't have any doubts about Amelia. None at all. She's my rock and guardian angel rolled into one. I can't bear to think of what would have happened to me without her. Why would she lie to me? *Why?*'

Now he was the one to take his time to answer, saying

slowly, 'I can't answer that but you need to think on this—why did she message such important news to you instead of calling you? Your whole plan hinged on Amelia finding proof that we were corrupt to push you into action. Consider if it is possible she messaged instead of calling because she was afraid you'd hear the lie in her voice.'

Issy sat on the edge of her private swimming pool with her legs submerged in the warm water up to mid-calf. Soon, the sun would make its descent and fill the sky with the orange haze that had captured her attention every night she'd stayed on this island. It had been her only respite from thinking of Gianni.

She was still thinking of him.

Gianni Rossi had occupied much of her thoughts in the years since she and Amelia had first hatched their plan. At the start of it all, it had been a tiny flightless fledgling plan but over the years it had grown in substance. Grown wings. As the plan had developed and she'd begun her research on him, slowly but surely Gianni had begun to occupy more headspace. By the time she'd started her job at the hospital he was the first thing she thought of when she woke and the last image she saw before she fell asleep.

She would never know the truth of what happened between Gianni, Alessandro and her father but she accepted that whatever Gianni had done, he truly believed her father had fleeced him. She did believe that. Gianni was not the monster she'd believed for so long; a belief she'd had to keep feeding to herself over the years to stop from faltering in her quest.

Amelia had sensed Issy's doubts. She was certain of it.

She closed her eyes and pressed her hand to her belly to ride the spasm of guilt that came from her own doubts. She couldn't think of Amelia right now, couldn't bear to let her mind take her where it so desperately didn't want to go.

Her eyes snapped back open. What she wanted was Gianni. To feel the light that always filled her when his gaze captured hers. To go to him as Isabelle Seymore, the auxiliary nurse who liked ballet, books and junk food more than was good for her, both of them stripped back to just their essences, all pretence and deception between them gone.

And she wanted to know the real Gianni, the man who'd opened up to her and without an ounce of self-pity told her his story.

She had a strong feeling that all the things she'd been helpless to stop herself from liking about him were the real Gianni.

No more thinking about the past.

Gianni sat at the end of the twenty-foot dining table laid for two, as it had been on board his yacht that night, and had a large drink of cold white wine.

Would she come?

He hadn't felt this nervous since his first date all those years ago.

He'd invited Issy to share dinner with him. Again. She hadn't given him an answer. Again. But her silence had been different this time. Allowed a sliver of hope to settle in him.

She hadn't left a polite message declining. Yet. He looked at his watch and popped a large green olive in his mouth. There was still time for her to back out…not that she'd actually said yes.

Hope was dangerous, he rued, now reaching for a breadstick and forcing his gaze on the spectacular sunset unfolding before him rather than keeping it fixed on the path she would join him from. If she came.

How had this happened? Going from a potential fling to a seductive game with a hustler, to learning the truth about her, to this? All along this was supposed to have been nothing but fun, the same as all his other flings but with added bite.

He'd never imagined he would feel like this, that he *could* feel like this. Like he was losing his head.

The hairs on the back of his neck rose. His heart thumped.

He whipped his head to the left before his brain caught up with what his senses were telling him.

Emerging from the darkening shadows of the foliage-lined path, her eyes locked on his face, was Issy.

The closer she moved towards him the harder his heart pumped. Dressed in a pretty pale yellow sundress with the spaghetti straps she favoured but which caressed her body with a swing around the knees rather than constricted it, barely a scrap of make-up graced her face. It had no need of it. Her silky blonde hair hung loose, sweeping over her shoulders, the first real hint of chestnut that had so captivated him in her photos emerging at the roots, the two colours blending together to create something uniquely beautiful.

Unable to tear her gaze from Gianni's face, Issy climbed the three steps onto the podium that served as his outside dining room. In the periphery of her vision silver fairy lights twinkled the perimeter of the wooden roof, a row of nightlights flickering on the table. With the sound of the sea lapping on the beach behind her, the whole scene was so dreamily romantic her whole being felt consumed by it.

But it was the man in the crisp white open-necked shirt and smart dark grey shorts who'd risen to his feet and taken slow steps towards her who consumed her the most. To see the way his chest was rising and falling as if it had a weight in it and the expression in the eyes as rooted to hers as hers were to his, an expression that was more, much more, than hunger...

Standing before him, she raised her arm and palmed his cheek. The thick stubble from four days ago had grown into a fully fledged beard. The pads of her fingers tingled madly in reaction to the sharp yet soft texture and her longing for him intensified.

His nostrils flared. His strong throat moved.

The tiny gap between them closed. His hands skimmed her waist then tightened around it.

Without a single word being uttered, he lifted her into air. Her face hovering above his, her hair brushing against his face, he continued to stare at her as if she were a miracle come to life before lowering her gently and then sweeping her into his arms so she was cradled against his chest.

Nestling her cheek against his beating heart, Issy breathed him in. The freshness of his cologne mingled with his clean skin enveloped her open senses. Open because she would no longer close any of herself off to him.

Gianni carried Issy up the stairs to his bedroom. She fit perfectly in his arms.

Gently, he sat her at the foot of the bed. Her eyes were open. Trusting. She reached a hand out to him. Capturing it, he kissed her pretty fingers, then stepped back to strip his clothes. First came the shirt which he shrugged over his head and let drop wherever it landed. Next came his shorts. He unbuttoned them and tugged the zip down, then, pinching his snug boxers with them, pulled them down his hips and thighs until gravity took care of the rest. Stepping out of them, he kicked his deck shoes off and had to force air into his lungs at the expression on Issy's face as she drank him in… Because that's how it felt. As if she were drinking in every part of him.

For the first time in his entire life, Gianni felt stripped to his marrow.

He took a step to close the small gap between them but she shook her head softly to stop him and got to her feet.

His heart had swollen so hard it came close to choking him. He watched as she pulled the dress up her beautiful body and over her head. Just as he'd done, she gave no care to where it landed.

Her hands went around her back. A moment later her pretty white silk bra fell the same way as her dress and all that was left were the matching panties. Clasping them with the tips of her fingers, she pinched the sides and pulled them down until she was able to step out of them. And then she straightened, cheeks flush, barely breathing, and it was his turn to drink *her* in.

During their time on the *Palazzo delle Feste*, Gianni had feasted his eyes on her for hours and hours. It felt like he was looking at her anew. Slowly, he soaked in every inch of her, from the tiny brown mole on the side of her neck to the small, pert breasts with their beautiful dusky pink nipples to the neat triangle of dark brown hair between her legs all the way down to her painted toes.

Head tilted back, eyes wide on his, she took the step to him. His arousal jutted into the base of her belly. Her lips parted, a small breath pulled in. Her eyes darkened and pulsed.

Slowly, he ran his hands down her bare arms. *'Tu sei bella…'* he whispered hoarsely.

Her chest rose, her voice barely audible as she whispered back, *'Anche tu.'*

So are you…

He lifted her back into his arms. Her arms locked around

his neck. Carrying her around the bed, he laid her down so her head rested on a pillow. Her hair spilled around her like a fan.

He didn't know what ached the most, his heart or his arousal.

He had never felt like this. Never felt such need for someone that his whole body trembled at the strength of it.

Issy felt like she'd been transported into the fairy lights that had barely penetrated her consciousness before Gianni swept her into his arms, a magical dreamlike reality filled entirely with him. When he laid himself on top of her, resting his weight on his elbows either side of her head so as not to crush her, the tips of her breasts pressed against the hardness of his chest, she would swear she felt the strength of his heartbeat as clearly as she felt her own.

The wonder in his stare as he lowered his face to hers made her heart beat even faster, and when his lips finally captured hers, flames ignited in it, pumping fire through her veins and melting the last of her thoughts.

Closing her eyes, she sank into the wonder that was Gianni and the tenderness underlying the passion of his kisses.

His mouth and hands explored her with a reverence that left her molten. Barely an inch of her flesh went untouched, unkissed, unloved. When he trailed his tongue up her inner thigh and pressed it against her swollen nub, every nerve ending in her body responded and she was helpless to do anything but cry his name and ride the thrills of the climax he slowly brought her to.

Dazed, drugged on bliss, she pulled herself up as Gianni raised his head. This time she was the one to kiss him. This time she was the one to lay him down and worship every inch of the body of the man who had captivated her for so long.

With the taste of Issy's climax still on his tongue, Gianni submitted to an assault of his senses that would have lost him his mind if it wasn't already gone. Every touch and mark of her mouth and tongue scorched him. Never had he been on the receiving end of such pleasure, but it was much more than that, more than a bodily experience, this transcended *everything*...

He groaned and had to grit his teeth when she took hold of his erection, then grit them even harder when she took him in her mouth.

Mio Dio...

He looked down and her gaze lifted to his. His heart punched through him to see the desire-laden wonder in her stare.

Closing his eyes, he gathered her hair lightly and let her take the lead, throwing his head back as her movements, tentative at first, became emboldened. The fist she'd made around the base tightened and she took him deeper into her mouth, moaning her own pleasure at the pleasure she was giving him.

If heaven existed he'd just found it.

Mio Dio, this was like nothing...*nothing*...

The tell-tale tug of his orgasm began to pull at him, and with an exhale of air, he gently pulled away from her.

Her gaze lifted to him again, a tiny knot of confusion on her brow.

Throat too constricted to speak, he cupped her cheeks and kissed her deeply, pushing her onto her back and sliding himself between her legs with the motion.

The tip of his erection brushed against her opening, the urge to just bury himself inside her with one long thrust so strong he had to clamp his jaw and squeeze his eyes shut to stop his basest instincts from taking him over.

Issy was a virgin. They needed protection.

The burning desire to say to hell with the consequence of no protection...

Keeping himself positioned between her legs, he stretched his arm out. No sooner had he tugged open the drawer of his bedside table than Issy lifted her head and began open-mouth kissing his neck while dragging a hand down his chest and abdomen to take hold of his erection.

Dear God in heaven...

He groped and fumbled for a condom; fumbled because she was masturbating him and deepening the French kisses on his neck.

The foil open, he removed the condom and took the hand Issy was giving him such glorious pleasure with. Her mouth moved up to his jaw until she found his lips, and, somehow, tongues fused and their hands clasped together, they rolled the condom on. Barely a second passed before she was flat on her back again, short, jagged breaths coming from her mouth, her eyes boring into his, his erection jutting and straining against her heat.

Issy felt possessed, that there was every chance she would go insane if Gianni didn't take possession of her. She had never wanted anything as badly as she wanted this. Every inch of her body was alight with the flames he'd ignited, her senses consumed with him. His beautiful face was all she could see, his ragged breaths all she could hear, his musky skin all she could smell and all she could taste, the smooth-ness of his skin all she could feel.

His lips grazed hers lightly and then he began to press his way inside her.

There was no pain, no discomfort, just a slow-building sensation of being deliciously filled and stretched until their groins locked together and they were as one.

Gianni thought he'd found heaven when Issy had taken

him into her mouth. If that was heaven then this was paradise, a miracle of the flesh and soul.

They could just stay like this, he thought dimly. Fused together. As one.

Never had the need for release burned so deeply but the urgency had gone. Now all he wanted was to savour this moment, savour Issy…

Issy had thought she'd already experienced all the sensual pleasure there was to feel but when Gianni began to move inside her, a whole new feeling grew, the burn in her core deepening and then uncoiling like tendrils through her very being.

Hooking a hand to his neck, she kissed him and closed her eyes.

Slowly, slowly, his thrusts lengthened and deepened. Slowly, slowly, the incredible pleasure increased until she was nothing but a mass of nerve endings and the burning pressure deep inside of her exploded.

With a long cry, she buried her mouth into his neck and held tight as rolling waves of bliss flooded her. Somewhere in the recess of her mind, she heard Gianni groan loudly, and then there was one last furious thrust that locked their groins together for one final time.

Buried as deep inside Issy as he'd ever dreamed it was possible to be, Gianni's climax roared through him. And still he tried to bury deeper, still she tried to pull him deeper, both of them desperately drawing out the pleasure for as long as they could until there was nothing left but stunned silence.

CHAPTER THIRTEEN

GIANNI STARED AT the sleeping face turned to his and smiled to see the light smattering of freckles highlighted on Issy's nose and cheeks by the early morning sunlight streaming in.

The temptation to wake her was strong but his conscience would not allow him. She must be exhausted. Three days and four nights of almost constant lovemaking had left her with faint bruises under her eyes. As for him... Despite the lack of sleep, Gianni felt the best he'd felt in so long that he couldn't remember when he'd ever felt this good. This alive.

Carefully rolling onto his back, he stretched an arm above his head.

'Morning.'

He turned his head. Issy's eyes had opened, a sleepy smile playing on her lips.

He leaned his face to hers and brushed a kiss to her lips. Her smile widened.

'It's early,' he said quietly. 'Go back to sleep.'

She nudged herself closer to him and placed a hand on his chest. 'I don't want to sleep.'

Taking her hand, he took a long breath knowing exactly what she meant. The four days they'd spent as lovers had passed almost like a dream. It had been just them. Gianni's room covered the whole second floor, a sprawling open-plan space with his hand-crafted emperor bed, a small dining table, a large corner sofa with accompanying entertainment centre, a bar, a walk-in wardrobe and en suite. They'd eaten in this room food brought to them by staff who left it at the door, drank from his bar which was topped up the few times they'd escaped to his private pool. It was as if they were the only two people in the whole world.

He raised his head at the sound of rustling and saw a note being pushed under the door.

Kissing Issy first, he climbed out of bed for it. As he opened it, he looked at her. She'd thrown the bedsheets off and struck such a provocative pose that he almost threw the note away unread. Almost.

The message was from Alessandro, four words: The business is safe.

That was it. No other information.

He read it again and waited to feel something lift in him. Something didn't come.

Why wasn't he ecstatic? For sure, he'd known Alessandro would fix things. He'd never doubted that. But he'd expected to at least feel relief, not an immediate plummet of dread in his stomach.

'What's wrong?' she asked softly.

He met her stare. For a long moment he debated whether or not to tell her. 'Alessandro has sorted everything.'

'With the business?'

'Yes.'

'Oh.'

He had to swallow to make his throat move but before he could speak, she said, 'I'm glad.'

'You are?'

To his horror, tears filled her eyes. She nodded. 'I'm sorry for what we tried to do to you. Really sorry.'

His lungs compressed. 'I know you are.'

'Please forgive me.'

Sitting on the bed, he brushed away the tear that rolled down her cheek. 'It's already forgiven.'

Issy tried desperately hard to stop any more tears from leaking. She didn't want to cry in front of him but reality had just inserted itself into the dream of their life. She'd refused to think of anything but Gianni since they'd become lovers. It had been the same for him too, she was certain. It had been the two of them in a private, dreamy bubble. When not making love they'd spoken about so many things, had long, laughter-filled discussions about their lives and interests, getting to know each other as who they really were, but by unspoken agreement there had been no mention of his cousin or business—other than generically—or her sister or parents. What they'd found together was too special, too *magical*, to allow the things that meant it had to come to an end spoil it for the time they had.

He wiped another tear. 'You are free to go home now.'

But that only made her want to cry harder. 'Do you want me to go?'

He shook his head with vehemence. 'No.'

'Good,' she said in a whisper. 'Because I don't want to go either.'

He closed his eyes as if in relief, his shoulders rising before he locked them back on hers. 'Your phone is in my dressing room.'

That made her smile. 'I'd forgotten all about it.'

'You can call your sister.'

But there was a reason Issy hadn't allowed herself to think of her sister let alone talk about her. 'You said she was safe.'

'She is.'

'Then I don't need to call her. Not yet.'

From the way Gianni's eyes were searching hers, she had the feeling he knew exactly how torn she was about Amelia.

Wrapping her arms around his neck, she pulled him down for a heady, passion-filled kiss.

The man who made her feel so, so much didn't have to return to his real life for another four of five days…oh, hell, she was losing track of time…and she would extract every ounce of the pleasure and joy being with him brought her until their time ran out.

Reality could wait a while longer.

The sea was much warmer than Issy anticipated, and she didn't even flinch when it reached the top of her legs. When it reached her bellybutton, she stopped. 'This is as far as I go,' she declared.

'Wimp,' Gianni teased with that smile that never failed to make her heart go all squidgy.

'I am not a wimp!'

He threw the beach ball at her. 'Yes, you are.'

She caught it and threw it back. 'No, I'm not.'

His grin widened. 'How am I supposed to pull you under if you won't go any further than your stomach?'

'You want me to drown?' she asked in mock outrage.

'No.' He lobbed the ball hard at her. 'I want to save you from drowning so I can give you the kiss of life.'

'You need one of those banana float things if you're going to act as lifeguard again,' she reminded him.

'I can't wait to unwrap it on my birthday.'

'I'll need to use a whole tree's worth of wrapping paper,' she said, and used all her strength to chuck the ball at him and laughed with glee when her aim finally came good and the ball bounced off his head.

'You did that on purpose!' he accused, scooping the ball up and tucking it under his arm.

'I don't know what you're talking about.'

He strode through the water towards her. 'You have an evil streak in you.'

Giggling, she waded backwards, trying to escape him. 'Only when it comes to beach balls.'

He held the ball above his head, eyes gleaming as he loomed down on her. Having such long legs and only being thigh-high in the water meant he'd closed the gap far quicker than she'd been able to flee. But instead of dropping the ball on her head, he threw it aside and then, with a speed and grace that had no place on a man of his size, lifted her by the waist and threw her in the air.

She landed backside first with a squeal, kicking feet and flailing arms submerging at the same time as her face went under. Rising back to the surface, trying her hardest not to laugh, a task made harder by the throaty, uproarious sounds coming out of Gianni's mouth, she half crawled to him and grabbed his calves.

'You think you can knock me over?' he mocked, and in a flash he had her by the waist again and for the second time in less than two minutes, Issy was flying in the air and landing with a splash. When she resurfaced, the ball was in reach. Grabbing it, she threw it at him and got him on the forehead.

'Oh, that does it,' he said with a shake of his head, now wading towards her like a panther on the prowl.

By now breast height in the water, Issy, cackling with laughter, tried to swim away from him. She'd barely managed three strokes when he captured an ankle and pulled her under. She came up for air with a splutter, only to be bodily lifted from the sea by a single arm wrapped around her waist and carried to the beach.

Laughing too hard to scream or pretend any form of protest, the most she could do was slap feebly at his shoulders when he laid her down on the sand.

'I just saved your life!' he admonished sternly, which only made the absurdity of it all funnier. 'Now stop laughing so I can give you the kiss of life.'

Clamping her lips together so stop any more giggles coming out, Issy immediately played dead.

The expected kiss took much longer to press against her expectant lips than she'd anticipated. She peered through one eye to see what the hold-up was and found Gianni gazing down at her with an expression in his eyes that made her heart clench. Breaking character, she pressed a hand to his cheek and rubbed her palm against his beard. He captured the hand and kissed it reverently. 'You're beautiful, did you know that?'

Her chest filled with an emotion she didn't understand but which was thick enough to cramp her lungs. 'You make me feel beautiful,' she whispered.

'You are beautiful, Isabelle, and I want you to promise me you will never starve yourself again.'

She thought of the meals they'd shared these last six days, how happiness and wonderful sex had increased her appetite, how her bikinis—literally the only clothing she'd worn since they'd become lovers—were already feeling tight at the hips. The emotions filling her swelled even more. 'I starved myself to entrap you.'

He kissed her hand again. 'I'd already guessed that. And I can guess why you felt you needed to do that and to dye your beautiful hair.' He shook his head tightly. 'None of those women were real to me, Issy.'

'What do you mean?'

Gianni took a breath and tried to collate his thoughts. 'They were status symbols, like my penthouses, the watches I wear, the cars I drive or have driven for me. A way for me to flaunt the man I'd become to my father.'

She just stared at him.

'I've not seen him since we left Umbria,' he explained quietly. 'I never want to see him again.'

She threaded her fingers into his and squeezed.

'We knew, Alessandro and I, that changing our surname from theirs would hit them where it hurt the hardest.'

'Their egos?' she guessed.

He smiled at her astuteness. 'I know it must kill my father to see my success and know his place in my history has been severed. I wanted him to see me with the best of everything the world has to offer and not even be able to take credit for my name.'

'And the best of everything included women?'

'Yes,' he agreed unflinchingly. It was only now, speaking it aloud, that Gianni understood how shallow and, yes, misogynistic his attitude to the women in his personal life had been. 'If I had passed you as you were two years ago in a street I would never have looked twice at you. I wanted what I believed was the male dream; the killer supermodel on my arm and in my bed.'

He deserved the hurt and distaste curling Issy's mouth, and gently tightened his hold on her hand to stop her pulling it away.

'I need to be honest with you,' he said. 'I have to be. After the way we started and all the lies, I don't ever want deception of any kind to come between us.'

Her eyes flickered.

'I wouldn't have looked twice at you because I'd trained

myself only to see tall, blonde, obviously rich women,' he continued. 'I didn't need to see anything more than that because I wasn't looking for more. I had no interest in anything real.' He managed a smile and kissed her clasped hand. 'It's all this time with you, Issy, the way you make me feel... I didn't stand a chance. And being with you, the uniqueness of how we came to be; it has brought the past back to me in a way it hasn't been in a long, long time. I think of my mother now, alone in her Milanese flat and for the first time in over two decades, I don't hate her for not coming back to me.'

'Maybe she couldn't,' Issy suggested quietly. There was something about Gianni's tone and the way he was looking at her that made her heart thump. For the first time in what felt like for ever, there was dread in the beats.

He grimaced and shook his head. 'She could. The first place she fled to was a woman's shelter. I know this because my aunt told me. The people there would have helped her but she chose not to tell them about me.'

A whimper crawled out of her throat.

The grimace turned into a smile. 'Don't be sad for me, *cara*. It is thanks to you that I can now confront my past in a way I never let myself before—I *have* to confront it. I don't want it to have power over me any more. My mother left me because she didn't love me enough to take me with her. That is the crux of it.'

'I don't believe that,' she whispered vehemently. How could any woman on this earth fail to love Gianni, let alone the woman who'd given birth to him?

He brushed a finger against her cheek. 'I think my father beat the love out of her. She has never remarried or taken a lover. She doesn't even have friends. That used to make me happy but now...' His chest rose then fell with flump.

'*Bella*, your mother abandoned you too in her own way, but you don't hold any anger or bitterness towards her. Instead, you try to understand and help her. You forgive her. And that is what I must do. Forgive my mother for the hand life dealt her and trust that her abandonment was not my fault.' His eyes held hers. 'And trust that it doesn't have to affect the rest of my life.'

The dread that had been building in the thumps of Issy's heart were now so loud they almost deafened her. Instinct was screaming at her to change the subject now, right now, another, stronger part yearning to wrap her arms around him and hold him tight and swear that he could put his trust in her, that she would never let him down, that she would always be there for him. That she would never leave him.

But those words would be a lie. There was no future for them to place his trust in her, not in the way she sensed he'd been driving this conversation towards. In a few days they would go their separate ways. They would leave each other. That's how it had to be, and she stared at him, pleading with her eyes for him to understand, silently begging him not to say the words that would force her to hurt him, hurt them both.

Just two weeks ago Issy would never have believed she or any woman would have the power to hurt Gianni Rossi. But then, two weeks ago, she'd never believed he would have the power to hurt her. She'd thought herself immune to him. She'd been too stupid to see that she was already half in love with him.

His lips parted.

No! She wanted to scream. *Please, don't.*

'I love you, Issy,' he said quietly. Sincerely. Breaking her heart. 'I love you. I know our marriage was a game of bluff we both told ourselves we'd lost but…'

She scrambled up and onto her bottom and shook her head frantically. 'Please, Gio, don't.'

He blinked as if something had flown into his eye.

'Don't say it,' she begged. 'It can never be. You must know that.'

He stared at her for the longest time, fingers still tight around hers, a contortion of emotions flickering on his face. 'Tell me you don't love me.'

'Don't do this.'

'Tell me you don't love me.'

'Please.'

'Tell me you don't love me and I will end this conversation and seek an annulment as soon as we return to the mainland. All you have to do is say the words.'

'I don't l...' But her tongue refused to cooperate. Refused to tell the lie. Finally snatching her hand free from his she buried her face in her knees and cried, 'I *can't.*'

Gianni made himself breathe through the sharpness in his chest. Issy's inability to refute her love didn't ease the tension tightening throughout him. 'You do love me, *bella,*' he said steadily. 'What we have found together is something we had no choice over. I couldn't stop myself falling in love with you and you couldn't stop it either. That spark was there from the very first moment. Our wedding was a farce but our marriage doesn't have to be. I have no idea how we will make it work but I know we can because what we have is too special to throw away. I never in a million years expected to feel like this about anyone and yet here we are. Give us a chance. Please, don't turn your back on something we could both search for another million years and never find.'

When she lifted her face to him, tears were streaming down her face. That was the moment Gianni knew he'd lost.

Chin wobbling manically, she shook her head and choked, 'I *can't*. You must understand that.'

He had no idea how he was able to keep his voice even. 'I understand that we love each other.'

'Stop saying that, it only makes it harder. We can never be. I can't betray Amelia. You have to go back to your own life and let me go back to mine.'

'Amelia betrayed *you*.'

She shook her head violently. 'No. Never.'

'She lied to you. You know it in your heart.'

'No! She wouldn't! And even if she did, she would have had her reasons. Oh… You don't understand!'

'Then make me. Tell me. Tell why you are so ready to throw us away.'

'I don't want to throw us away! I want to be with you but it's impossible.'

'Explain it to me. You owe me that much.'

'Gianni… You said I don't hold bitterness and anger towards my mother, and that I learned to understand and forgive her and help her…none of that came easy. There were times I *hated* my mum for what she was doing to herself but I never let myself fall into despair because through it all, I had my sister. I have looked up to her my entire life, even when I was a brat to her in the days when I believed everything was perfect. Amelia's the one who held what was left of our family together and held me together. She's the one who helped Mum, not me; I only helped Amelia help her. She's the one who protected me from the bullies at the horrid school we were sent to after Dad…' She cut herself off and took a long breath before looking him squarely in the eye. 'I know dad ripped you off. I believe you. If you say he ripped off other companies and people too then I believe you. And if you say Amelia lied to me about finding proof of corruption against you then I believe that too.'

Oh, but it *hurt* to finally admit that, and Issy had to wipe away more tears before adding, 'I believe you, Gianni. She lied to me.'

God help her, she was taking Gianni's word over her own sister's. But she knew it. From the moment he'd denied it, she'd known in her heart, just as he'd said, that he was telling the truth. It was a truth she'd locked away from herself in the beautiful days they'd just shared, burying it because she'd fallen madly in love and had selfishly wanted to have this time with him, because he was right about that too—what she felt for him would never be replicated.

All along though, she'd known it would have to end. What she hadn't known was how much it would hurt.

'You believe me?' He grabbed the back of his neck and sucked air in.

'It doesn't change anything. She hates you and your cousin too much. Her lie must have been born out of desperation, there's no other explanation for it. You should have seen her in the days leading up to my leaving for the Caribbean; she was so tense at the thought our time was finally coming that I thought she would snap. That we've failed will be destroying her. I can't add to that. I just can't. I can't betray her.'

'You already have,' he stated flatly.

'I know.' God, she was going to cry again. 'But this… here…what we've shared…soon it will be just a memory. For me to leave her and make a life with you… It would devastate her. She would never forgive me.'

'Do you not think it is the same for me?'

Taken aback at the tightness in his voice, Issy met his stare. The coldness shining from his eyes made her quail.

'Do you not think Alessandro will think I have betrayed him? Me, the one person in this world he trusts, falling in love with one of the women who set out to destroy us?' The more he spoke, the more the ice-like fury that had been building in Gianni while Issy had been making all her excuses spread. 'Me, falling in love with Thomas Seymore's daughter and wanting to build a life with her? Do you not think that will land like a kick in the teeth to him? And do not forget, Alessandro is as much of a victim in this whole charade as I am. More so. While you and I have been having fun here in the Caribbean, he's been fighting for the very existence of our company. Don't you think I know what the consequences could be? Exactly the same as what you fear. The difference is I love you enough that I'm willing to lose everything to be with you. I would walk on hot coals for you, but you…' He laced his voice with all the contempt he could inject into it. 'You're a coward. You won't even try, and you're using your sister as an excuse.'

She looked like he'd slapped her. 'How can you say that? You know what we've been through and what we mean to each other.'

'That's my whole point,' he spat. 'If your sister loves you as much as you love her then she will want the best for you. She will want you to be happy. If you wanted it enough, you would convince her. I don't deny she will be angry and betrayed but in time she would come round. Maybe she would never accept me as a brother-in-law but she sure as hell wouldn't want to lose you, but we will never know, will we? And I will never know if Alessandro would forgive me because you're so scared that I'll end up abandoning you as your parents did through their addictions that you'd rather cling to your sister's skirt and use her as an excuse than take the leap of faith with me.'

'I'm not scared,' she whispered.

'Liar.' Rising to his feet, he dusted the sand from his hands. 'And so much for trusting me.'

Unable to bear looking at her stricken, cowardly face a moment longer, Gianni turned on his heel and walked away from her.

'Where are you going?' Issy scrambled to her feet, panic suddenly clawing at her.

'To call Captain Caville. The *Palazzo delle Feste*'s moored on an island fifty kilometres away. It will not take long to reach us. I suggest you start packing.'

She had to practically run to catch him. 'What, we're leaving?'

'I have no wish to stay here another minute longer than necessary.'

'But we're not expected back in London for a couple more days.'

'Our time here is over.'

'Please, Gianni, don't let it end like this.'

He came to an abrupt halt and spun around to face her. 'What the hell do you expect? A few more days of *fun* together? No, you have made your decision and I have made mine. We will sail to the nearest island with an airport that flies to the UK and I will buy you a ticket for the first flight home.'

'And what about you?' she asked, almost numb with shock at his implacable coldness.

'That, *bella*—' he virtually spat the endearment '—is none of your business. My lawyer will be in touch over the dissolution of our *marriage*...' There was even more venom in his voice. 'Do not expect anything from me. This marriage meant nothing. *We* meant nothing. Enjoy your life.'

When his long legs set stride again, Issy let him go.

CHAPTER FOURTEEN

ISSY SAT ON the balcony of her cabin on the *Palazzo delle Feste* gazing up at the stars. There were so many of them twinkling down on her from the moonless sky. She wished they injected warmth as far as Earth. Despite the balminess of the night she was huddled under the wrap she'd packed for the unpredictable weather when she returned to London. She'd felt chilled to the bone since Gianni had so coldly and ruthlessly severed her from his life.

And it had been a severing. A member of staff had collected her suitcase from her chalet and walked her to the yacht. Since embarking, she hadn't caught a glimpse or heard a whisper from Gianni. She'd wandered aimlessly through the familiar rooms, half hoping and half dreading bumping into him. She'd even knocked on his cabin door and still didn't know if she'd been relieved or devastated that it went unanswered. She'd tried the handle but it had been locked. Probably for the best. She didn't know what she'd have said to him.

He must have had a change of heart and stayed behind on St Lovells.

Maybe it was better this way. A clean break. It would have happened in a few days anyway. It was just in the few times she'd envisaged it—only brief visions, because nausea had roiled strongly inside her at the images in her mind's eye—they had parted with tender words. She'd imagined a life spent weaning herself off her internet addiction to him.

She pulled the wrap tighter around her shoulders and wished she could call Amelia, tell her she knew what she'd done but that it didn't matter because whatever reason had propelled her sister to act so out of character and lie to her must have been important. The more she thought about it, the more it hurt her heart that Amelia hadn't felt able to confide that reason in her.

But she couldn't call her. In the days of bliss when she'd been blocking the world from her head, she'd left her phone in Gianni's dressing room. To take it back would have let the world intrude and she'd been desperate to avoid that. And then everything had crumbled between them and she'd hidden in her chalet until the call to leave had come. She'd been too numb to think about anything.

She wished she was still numb. Now, she felt sick to the pit of her stomach and it hurt even more to know that even if she had remembered her phone, she'd not be able to confide any of the pain she was feeling to her sister.

Or would she?

Gianni's cold voice kept echoing like a taunt in her ear. *Coward.*

How was she being a coward? And as for his ridiculous assertion that she had abandonment issues?

A spark of fury suddenly fired in her. If she did have abandonment issues—which she didn't—hadn't his behaviour proved her right to have them? And just like that, the coldness left her. Jumping to her feet, Issy paced her balcony, wishing Gianni was on board so she could confront him with the home truths she wished she'd thought of earlier. That it was grossly unfair to call her a coward just because she put her sister's feelings above her own. That if he thought she had abandonment issues, at least she didn't cut the abandoner from her life even if they did deserve it, which Gianni's mother undoubtedly did. That...that...that...

The stars began to blur. And then they began to spin.

Dazed, Issy staggered back to her seat and breathed deeply, waiting for the dizziness to pass.

But it didn't pass, just built up and up more and more as the truth rose in her stomach and chest and up her throat and she had to cover her mouth to stop the agony escaping.

She *was* a coward. Of *course* Amelia would forgive her. Maybe not overnight but in time she would, just as Issy would forgive her anything, even lying to her about something so dangerous as the Rossi cousins.

Gianni wasn't dangerous. Not in the way she'd once believed. He was dangerous in the way he could sever a relationship without batting an eyelid. Issy had obsessed over him and witnessed from afar his litter of broken hearts for so many years that taking that final leap—what had he called it? A leap of faith?—had been too terrifying to contemplate. Because her parents' addictions *had* felt like abandonment, like she wasn't enough to keep them sober and on this earth with her. Not even enough to keep her mother in the country with her. Yes, she'd long ago accepted it and forgiven them both for it but it had done something to her she hadn't even realised and so when the chance had come to give herself properly, heart, body and soul to Gianni, she'd cowered in fright because deep down she was so goddam scared he would leave her too. And so she had pushed him away before he could push her and now the truth was demanding she confront it, and she realised he never would have. Gianni would never have left her. It wasn't that she had tamed the lothario or anything clichéd like that, but a magical alchemy of chemistry and passionate desire sprinkled with a meeting of minds and humour had captured them and woven their hearts together. They belonged together.

And she'd thrown it away. Been too frightened to take what he was so gladly offering.

No wonder he'd been so cold and furious. For the first time since his mother had abandoned him, Gianni had handed his heart over on a plate and Issy had rejected it.

In the distance the dark shadow of approaching land appeared and it was the knowledge that on that island sat the airport from which she would take the flight that would fly her away from him that finally broke her.

Sliding off the chair, Issy fell onto her knees with a thump, opened her lungs and howled.

Gianni had been sat on his balcony for over two hours hardly daring to breathe in case Issy heard him. He'd cursed to hear her step out on her balcony, cursed himself too for not putting her in a cabin far from his.

He wanted nothing to do with her, not even a glimpse of her, and when she'd knocked on his door he'd taken great pleasure in ignoring her. What the hell did she even want with him?

And now he was trapped on his balcony waiting for her to do the decent thing and go back inside so he could wallow in the bottle of Jack he'd brought out here for company.

Movement came. Great! She must be going inside.

No, she was stomping around, which was unusual as she had such a light, graceful tread to her step.

Dammit, all he wanted was to wallow until he reached the bottom of the bottle and be drunk enough not to notice when the yacht docked and Issy disembarked for the final time from his life. He was going to sail on to Barbados and take his jet back to London from there. It was safer that way. No risk of accidentally bumping into her.

She stopped stomping. Excellent.

He folded his arms across his chest and waited impatiently for her to finally disappear inside. Except there was no obliging sound of a door being slid open or closed.

A loud thud made him jump to his feet.

What the hell...?

But the thought had barely formed when an animalistic howl of agony rent the air.

'Issy?' he shouted, rushing to the barrier separating their balconies. Dammit, why the hell had he insisted the barrier be high enough for complete privacy? He called her name again but the only sound from her balcony was heart-wrenching sobs. 'Stay where you are,' he ordered, trying not to let the panic that she'd seriously injured herself consume him. 'I'm coming.'

Racing through his cabin, he yanked his door open and ran straight to Issy's door, praying she hadn't locked it. God answered that one, and he pushed it open before racing to her balcony door and sliding that open too.

What he found stopped him in his tracks.

Issy was curled on the floor in the foetal position, great sobs racking her entire body.

In an instant he was beside her and hauling her into his arms so she was cradled on his lap.

'Where are you hurt?' he asked urgently. 'Please, *mia amore*, tell me where you're hurt.'

Slowly it dawned on Issy that she wasn't dreaming. Hallucinating Gianni's voice had been more than she could endure and she'd covered her ears like a child against the cruelty of it, crying so hard her ribs felt bruised.

She hadn't hallucinated it. She hadn't hallucinated him.

Tentatively, still afraid he would disappear in a blink, she touched his cheek. It was as warm and solid as it always was but still she whispered, 'Gianni?'

'Tell me where it hurts,' he repeated in the same urgent tone that had finally cut through her despair.

'Hurts?' she echoed.

'You have hurt yourself. You are in pain.' His Italian accent was stronger than she had ever heard it. 'Please, you must tell me where it hurts.'

More tears streamed down her face as her hand fluttered to her chest and pressed against her left breast. Against her heart. 'Here.'

'What have you done?'

'Pushed you away.'

He didn't understand.

'Oh, but I'm the biggest fool in the world.' Trembling, she cupped both his cheeks tightly. 'Please forgive me. Please give me another chance. Please don't give up on me and cut me from your life. I couldn't bear it. I *can't* bear it. I love you, Gianni, and I want to build a life with you.'

He hardly dared believe what her lips were saying and her eyes were pleading.

'It's not even been ten hours since you walked away from me and they've been the longest ten hours of my life. What we have found together…you're right. I could walk this earth for a million years and never find it again.'

'And your sister?'

'She loves me. She'll forgive me in her own time, but right now it's you I need forgiveness from.'

'Mia amore…' A bubble of hope was starting to build inside him. 'There is nothing for me to forgive. I didn't react as well as I should and lashed out at you and for that, I am sorry too.' He took a deep breath before admitting, 'I think I have a problem with rejection.'

Her chin wobbled but she managed a smile. 'A small one, maybe.'

He raised an eyebrow which made her smile widen and a small laugh escape her lips, and then before he even knew it was happening, her arms were wrapped around his neck, his hold around her had tightened and they were kissing with such passion and love that the bubble of hope exploded in a blaze of joy so strong that the last of Gianni's fears abandoned him.

'Your reaction was understandable,' she murmured when they came up for air. 'We both have abandonment issues.'

'Had,' he corrected, kissing her again. 'But not any more. You love me and you'll never let me go.'

'And you love me and will never let *me* go.'

'Never.'

'Never.'

And they never did.

Issy stretched luxuriously within the silk sheets of Gianni's bed...*her* bed...and yawned widely. She loved this room. This bed. This penthouse. She'd only spent two nights in it but already she felt at home. Gianni had made it feel like home for her.

The only thing that stopped Issy feeling like she could spring to the clouds in a single leap was dread about what was to come when Amelia finally arrived back home. Gianni had given her phone back to her and when she'd checked it, there hadn't been a single message or voice mail from her sister. Just a wall of silence. In a way, that had made it easier for her to maintain her own silence too, especially when Gianni's contacts had quickly confirmed she was still abroad with Alessandro.

When the bedroom door opened, she sat up, a smile already on her face at the joy that fizzed through her at the mere anticipation of seeing her husband—it was taking some getting used to, actually thinking of him as her husband—after being separated from him for fifteen whole minutes while he made them eggs for breakfast. One look at his face and empty hands wiped the smile away.

'What's happened?' she asked.

He shook his head and sat next to her to stroke her hair. 'Alessandro has sent me a message.'

Issy's heart thumped. Like her, Gianni had been waiting for his cousin's return to London before telling him about their marriage. 'He knows about us?'

'I'm not sure but that isn't why he messaged me. He's asked me to bring you to the airfield.'

'Why?'

Sympathy lined his face. 'Amelia's flying back to the UK. Alessandro says…he says she needs you.'

It was like ice had been injected into her veins. As sisters, they'd pulled together and always been there for one another emotionally, but Amelia had never *needed* her.

Gazing into the steadfast eyes of the man she still couldn't quite get her head around was her husband, bone-deep certainty grew that her sister was in great distress.

'You'll come with me?' she whispered.

Strong arms wrapped around her and held her close. '*Mia amore*, I would follow you to the ends of the earth.' He kissed her gently. 'I'll call our driver. We can leave in ten minutes.'

Our driver. *We*. Simple words but words infused with meaning.

It was the two of them. Together. For always.

EPILOGUE

GIANNI CLOSED HIS eyes contentedly as he swayed gently on the hammock under the rising early sun. Snuggled on him, his chubby cheek pressed against his chest, his youngest son, Matteo, slept. At only eighteen months, the little ratbag—an affectionate term Gianni's beautiful wife called him—had recently mastered the art of escaping his cot. That morning he had toddled into his parents' bedroom and woken Gianni by prodding his nose. With the rest of his family sleeping, Gianni had taken him outside to watch the sunrise.

He tried not to sigh to think that soon they would have to return to Europe. Mia, their eldest child, was a couple of weeks away from starting school. They'd debated whether to employ a tutor so they could continue spending six months of each year in their Caribbean hideaway but decided that would be selfish of them. As far as they were both concerned, children needed playmates. St Lovells would be there for all the school holidays and then, when their brood had all flown the nest, they would make it their permanent home. At least, that was the plan. How long it would take for that to happen was anyone's guess, a thought reinforced when a sound made him peer through one eye and spot his heavily pregnant wife sneaking towards him, carrying a huge, elaborately wrapped box, Mia bringing up the rear with carefully balanced, much smaller boxes in her own tiny hands.

His family. God, he loved them. Sometimes he would look at his children's happy faces and his heart would squeeze so tightly it left a bruise. Sometimes he would look at his wife and take in her flowing dark chestnut hair and curvy body and those beautiful blue eyes that always shone with such love, and thank every deity he could think of for bringing them together. Six years of marriage and their devotion to each other had only grown. She was his entire world. Their children were their universe.

'Happy birthday, Daddy!' Mia suddenly yelled.

He opened his eyes fully and feigned surprise.

Matteo lifted his head and grinned at him. ''Ap Birfday.'

Pressing his son's button nose, Gianni then held him tightly and swung himself off the hammock. Issy was beaming at him. The box was practically as tall as she was.

'Happy birthday, you gorgeous man. Bet you can't guess what your present is...*don't* tell him, Mia!'

Watching his daughter carefully place the other boxes on the table, he pretended to ponder. 'Hmm. Whatever can it be?'

Issy's beam grew.

Somehow they managed to exchange Matteo for the box, and then Gianni ripped the wrapping, already grinning, imagining what she'd come up with this time.

It was a banana float. At least, that's what Gianni and Issy called it. Every year she brought him the same thing for his birthday. He was growing quite the collection. But each was decorated in its own unique way and he burst out laughing when he pulled it out of the box and found it had been cleverly painted with caricatures of his wife and two children's faces squashed together.

Placing it against the tree the hammock was tied to, he wrapped his arms around her as much as Matteo in her arms would allow, and kissed her deeply. 'Thank you,' he murmured.

'My pleasure,' she murmured back, before dropping her voice to a whisper. 'You can have the rest of your present when the children go to bed.'

He snapped his teeth with a mock growl and squeezed her delectable bottom. 'I look forward to it.'

'Stop being soppy and open our presents!' Mia demanded, spoiling the moment in the best possible way.

Laughing even harder, he scooped his daughter up and planted an enormous kiss to her cheek.

Not a day went by when Gianni didn't consider himself the luckiest man alive.

* * * * *

COMING SOON!

We really hope you enjoyed reading this book. If you're looking for more romance be sure to head to the shops when new books are available on

Thursday 1st April

To see which titles are coming soon, please visit
millsandboon.co.uk/nextmonth

MILLS & BOON®

Coming next month

THE ITALIAN'S INNOCENT CINDERELLA
Cathy Williams

"Explain," Maude whispered, already predicting what he was about to say and dreading confirmation of her suspicions. "What…what was in the paper, Mateo?"

"I debated bringing it, but in the end, I thought better of it."

"Why?"

"Because we're engaged."

Maude's mouth fell open and she stared at him in utter shock.

"Sorry?"

"It would seem that I found the love of my life with you and we're engaged."

"No. No, no, no, no…no…"

Continue reading
THE ITALIAN'S INNOCENT CINDERELLA
Cathy Williams

Available next month
www.millsandboon.co.uk

LET'S TALK

Romance

For exclusive extracts, competitions
and special offers, find us online:

For all the latest titles coming soon, visit
millsandboon.co.uk/nextmonth

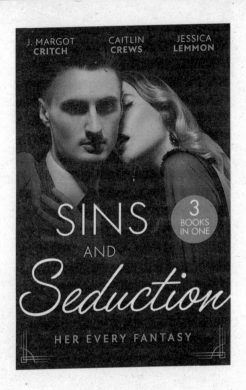

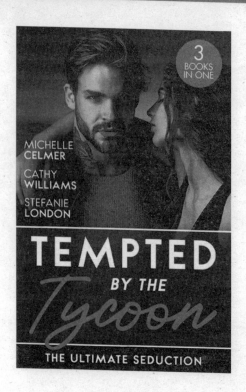

MILLS & BOON

THE HEART OF ROMANCE

A ROMANCE FOR EVERY READER

MODERN

Prepare to be swept off your feet by sophisticated, sexy and seductive heroes, in some of the world's most glamourous and rom locations, where power and passion collide.

HISTORICAL

Escape with historical heroes from time gone by. Whether your pas is for wicked Regency Rakes, muscled Vikings or rugged Highland awaken the romance of the past.

MEDICAL

Set your pulse racing with dedicated, delectable doctors in the high-pressure world of medicine, where emotions run high and pa comfort and love are the best medicine.

True Love

Celebrate true love with tender stories of heartfelt romance, from rush of falling in love to the joy a new baby can bring, and a focus emotional heart of a relationship.

Desire

Indulge in secrets and scandal, intense drama and plenty of sizzlin action with powerful and passionate heroes who have it all: wealth, good looks…everything but the right woman.

HEROES

Experience all the excitement of a gripping thriller, with an intens romance at its heart. Resourceful, true-to-life women and strong, f men face danger and desire - a killer combination!